Scribe Publications
THE FEW

Nadia Dalbuono has spent the last fifteen years working as a documentary director and consultant for Channel 4, ITV, Discovery, and *National Geographic* in various countries. *The Few* is her first novel.

the few

NADIA DALBUONO

SCRIBE

Melbourne • London

Scribe Publications
18–20 Edward St, Brunswick, Victoria 3056, Australia
2 John St, Clerkenwell, London, WC1N 2ES, United Kingdom

First published by Scribe 2014

Typeset in Dante MT by the publishers
Printed and bound in England by CPI Group (UK) Ltd.

National Library of Australia
Cataloguing-in-Publication data

Dalbuono, Nadia, author.

The Few / Nadia Dalbuono.

9781925106121 (Australian edition)
9781922247674 (UK edition)
9781925113303 (e-book)

1. Detective and mystery stories. 2. Criminal investigation–Italy–Fiction.
3. Political corruption–Italy–Fiction. 4. Politicians–Italy–Fiction.
5. Organized crime–Italy–Fiction.

A823.4

scribepublications.com.au
scribepublications.co.uk

For my family

Part I

Prologue

From his window on the fourth floor of Palazzo Chigi, he watches the skyline blacken, and feels the same stirrings of anxiety he'd experienced as a boy when he'd sensed a storm blowing in across the Aeonian sea. It is time to make the call, but he lingers at the window and tracks the shifting scents moving up from the garden below. The charged air runs across his skin, stirs his hair. In the garden the blossom is newly out, but he sees it hours from now, broken and battered by the rains, smashed into a thousand pieces against the stone. He closes his eyes and tastes the earth as it releases its ripeness, hears the pounding torrents as they tear the pavements, feels the Tiber on his lips, in his nose, as it breaks its banks and engulfs the city — all the filth of Rome momentarily washed away.

He crosses his office to the oak desk at its centre. Three telephones face him, but he pulls a mobile from his pocket followed by a scrap of paper. He carefully punches in the number, arthritic fingers struggling with the tiny keys. It has been a long time.

It rings just twice. 'Garramone.' It is a hard voice. Thirty years later, and the boy is now a man, tired and beaten by a life of work.

'It's Pino.'

'Don't know a Pino.'

A pause: 'Think back, to Gela.'

Silence, then a whisper: 'Pino? That Pino?' He takes a moment. 'Why?'

'Can we meet? I need your help.'

Hesitation and something else, maybe fear: 'I work for the police now.'

'I know.'

1

He laughs, tightly and awkwardly. 'But don't you have a whole army? Secret Service, whoever you want?'

'I want you, Garramone.'

Silence again, then a fragile breath: 'When?'

1

THE RAIN HAD turned the streets to chaos. Roadside repairs had been abandoned, broken concrete lost to sludge. Frustrated pedestrians wound their way between rows of illegally parked cars, desperately seeking out a gap that would allow them access to the pavement. Up ahead by Piazza Repubblica, the traffic had come to a halt, red necklaces of brake lights morphing through the windscreen.

Scamarcio slammed his hand against the dash, then did it again because it brought some muted sense of something that wasn't quite relief. How he hated this city: it was impossible, uninhabitable, corrupt, overpriced. Eight in the evening on a Friday was not the time to call a meeting in Via Nazionale, but he couldn't say no to Garramone. Last month's hand smash had knocked one of the chief's framed certificates irreverently off-balance and had left a hole that needed repair. There had been the usual trite jokes about southern blood, but he knew that Garramone was watching him now. It was common knowledge that Garramone had been uncomfortable about Scamarcio's appointment from the start, but had gradually grown to trust him as a man he could count on. Then had come the foul-up of last month and the unequivocal sense that the relationship had been pushed back to another, uncomfortable start, regardless of any previous victories. He wondered idly why he found it so hard to control his rage — whether it came from the maternal or paternal side, whether he should invest in some anger-management courses, whether he was beyond help.

The traffic was starting to shift up ahead, the furious horns of the drivers backed up behind him dying away as they sensed the change. The miserable column of cars edged slowly around the curve of the piazza, and the fountain came into view, bleached grey and cold. The rain had stripped it of its splendour, and the usual cluster of threadbare pigeons had fled. He swung a right into Nazionale. Garramone had said Number 42. Why here and not HQ? Was the chief on the take? He had him down as clean.

He found the building, and swung the car onto the kerb. There were no normal spaces, so parking in front of a goods entrance was the only option. Garramone had said to ring the bell for Bevilacqua. He did so, and the chief's baritone crackled out over the intercom.

'Fourth floor, first on the left. Make sure nobody sees you.'

Scamarcio made a quick scan of the street and then pushed the door. He took the stairs because he needed the exercise. The chief was waiting for him in the doorway, his gaze shifting nervously. He looked like he had just been roused from a deep sleep: there were darker rings than usual beneath his eyes, and his greying hair stood up in greasy tufts.

'Get inside.' He placed a hand on Scamarcio's back and almost pushed him into the narrow hallway.

The flat was pokey and barely furnished. There was a door off to the left, and then ahead of him down the hallway a small room with a window facing the street. He saw a plastic desk to the right of the window with several cheap-looking chairs on either side. The floors were tiled and dirty.

'Whose place is this?'

'No idea,' said the chief.

He thought about making a joke, asking whether the chief was planning to seduce him, but decided against it. 'What's going on?'

He ignored the question and reached for the chair nearest the window, beckoning for Scamarcio to do the same. From a briefcase, he pulled out a thin cardboard file and slid it across the desk. He offered no explanation, and just nodded.

Scamarcio opened the file. It seemed to consist of a series of grainy photographs, blown up to A4. A fit-looking man was in various stages of undress. He was surrounded by two muscular men in their underwear, both of them raising champagne glasses, with several spent bottles resting on a side table next to overflowing ashtrays. The furnishings were expensive; the lighting, low. They were smiling, toasting each other — it looked like the end of a good night. Then the photos suddenly became a whole lot more graphic. Scamarcio looked away for a moment, trying to catch his breath, and in the same instant he realised two things. The first was that one of these men looked young, perhaps slightly too young — there was a fullness in the cheeks, a brightness in the eyes, that gave it away. The second was that the man in the midst of it all was the foreign secretary, Giorgio Ganza. It hadn't been clear at first because he'd been photographed in profile, but the final images left no room for doubt. The date stamp indicated that they had been taken three months ago.

Scamarcio looked up at the chief. There was no smile, no sense of them sharing an amusing secret. He struggled to keep his face sombre, to match the mood.

'Who took these?'

'No idea. But the photos were handed to two of your colleagues four weeks ago.'

'My colleagues?'

'Two officers from Salaria precinct. Some guy they had never seen before gave them an envelope, and then disappeared.'

'So why are we only hearing about this now?'

'They've been blackmailing Ganza, and it's only just been brought to my attention.'

Scamarcio wasn't completely surprised. It wasn't unheard of for colleagues to try to supplement their meagre 1,200 euros-a-month salary. But something wasn't making sense.

'How did you hear about this?'

'From the prime minister.'

'What?'

The chief barred his arms across his chest, saying nothing.

'How?'

'He called me.'

Scamarcio had no idea that Chief Garramone was on speaking terms with the prime minister. He didn't quite know how to feel about this, and wasn't sure how it reflected on the chief.

'Anyway,' said Garramone, 'I don't want to get into the whys and wherefores. We don't have time. The PM learned about this because someone tried to sell the photographs to one of his magazines.'

The prime minister presided over a sizeable media empire that included magazines, newspapers, publishing houses, bookshops, and several TV channels. He had begun his career as a business consultant, and had then set up a successful IT company that had allowed him to purchase a football team. The media empire had followed on from there. It seemed that everything the man touched had turned to gold — until, that is, he became prime minister. As Scamarcio saw it, Italy had not turned to gold under his stewardship; it had turned to shit. Some people wondered whether the problems were insoluble: if a dynamic businessman like the PM couldn't do it, who could? Then there were others, like Scamarcio, who questioned whether he had the will — whether running the country was nothing more than an amusing personal project, the ultimate power trip at the expense of the millions of unemployed and underpaid.

The chief was eyeing him closely now, as if he was testing a personal theory and observing whether Scamarcio was responding as expected.

'This will be your case, Scamarcio. I am giving it to you as a demonstration of my faith in you.'

Scamarcio shifted in his seat and rubbed his neck. He didn't like the feel of this. He had the sense that he was here because no one else wanted to be, or because the chief needed to keep it under the radar. He knew that Scamarcio was a loner at work and would best be able to do that.

'It goes without saying that this must be kept solely between ourselves. It's not on the books at HQ yet. For now, I am handling it unofficially and have passed it to you in the same capacity.'

Scamarcio nodded. There was a moment of silence, and he heard the slap of tyres wet and slick on the street below. Had he missed something? 'I'm sorry, but what is it exactly that you want me to do?'

The chief picked up a photo, and then laid it down again.

'The story is about to go public. *People* magazine has bought the pictures, and most of the media knows about it. It will probably break tomorrow. Ganza has already packed his bags, and has spent the last forty-eight hours safely installed in a retreat outside Florence where he will enjoy several weeks of rest and reflection.'

'So you want me to pin down our guys — tie them up for blackmail?'

The chief waved a hand away. 'No, that's an internal disciplinary matter — I will deal with it.'

Something wasn't adding up. 'Why are you trying to keep this secret if it's about to break in the media?'

The chief rubbed tiredly under his right eye. His skin held an early tan from several May weekends at the beach at Sperlonga, but right now it looked liverish and sickly in the ebbing light.

'It's not that part of the story I'm worried about. It's the second part I want you to deal with.' He pulled a photo towards him, scanned it, and then turned it to face Scamarcio. His index finger was resting on the man to the right of the foreign secretary.

7

'His name is Arthur.'

He was striking — with dark brows and burnt-amber eyes — but there was something about him that wasn't quite right, that remained perhaps just the wrong side of legal.

'Arthur … as a name, I'm not sure it suits him.'

The chief sighed. 'Doesn't matter now. He was murdered this morning — stabbed to death in his flat in Trastevere.'

2

It saddened him that it had come to this. It was not how he liked to run things. He looked down to the gardens and saw the smashed blossom like blood, cast around in the new eddies of the fountain. He had sensed that these would be cleansing rains, but now he knew that they were just the opposite: With them they would bring a tide of filth, all the sewage of the city pushing up to drown them all.

Trastevere was quiet for a Friday night. The weather must have been keeping people away. He saw a man pushing a trolley full of empty bottles up ahead, the clink of glass echoing down the street as the bottles rattled across the paving stones. A group of young people were huddled in a doorway, a raincoat stretched out above their heads, waiting for the deluge to subside. A girl was struggling to light up under the coat, and Scamarcio decided to trouble her for a cigarette — not because he particularly felt like a smoke, but mainly because she had an interesting face.

He stood with them for a few minutes, trading small talk about the rain, and then he raised his jacket collar against the elements and continued his journey towards Via Cosimato. This was a part of town he liked: cobbled alleyways finishing at nothing; darkened windows with tiny diamond panes pushing out through webs of ivy; wooden shutters barred above mysterious workshops. It was the sense of the medieval that he enjoyed — the chance to escape from that other century outside.

There was a single officer on the doorway of Number 20, just as Garramone had told him there would be. It was still quiet for now, because no one realised the connection. As far as the police were concerned, Arthur was just another rentboy who had met an untimely end.

Scamarcio murmured a greeting to the officer, who turned to push open a huge oak door. He stood back to let him through. 'Upstairs, first on your right.'

Scamarcio thanked him and climbed the stairs. There were patches of damp on the walls where the paint was peeling. The place needed work. They'd have to sort it all out anyway after the murder — if they wanted to entice new tenants, that is.

A light was coming from the entrance to the flat. As he drew closer, he saw that the door was ajar. It had been kicked in, leaving small craters in the wood to the right and tiny shards of paint across the carpet. He eased through the gap, and the first thing he saw was Filippi, on his hands and knees, his gloved hands searching for something on the floor. Scamarcio hadn't seen him for a while, but wasn't altogether surprised to see him here; Trastevere was his beat, after all. Scamarcio surveyed the flat, or what was left of it. Nearly every painting had been smashed and knocked off-balance, photos had been ripped from their frames, and rugs cut to shreds. A plush-looking sofa bore a thick gash through its middle, which had caused foam to spill out in all directions. Oily black paint had been strewn everywhere — on the floors, across the ceiling, coating walls and partitions. He guessed he was standing in the living room, but the general chaos left some room for doubt.

Filippi grimaced as he tried to straighten from his crawling position. A slight man, no more than five foot seven, whose suits always hung badly, he was in his mid-forties, with thinning blond hair and quiet blue eyes. Scamarcio remembered that he was originally from the north, transferred down from Brescia. He held out a hand to help him up and Filippi accepted it, although irritated by the gesture. Once on his feet, he stretched slowly, hands behind his hips. 'I don't suppose you have this problem.'

Scamarcio was a good ten years younger, and known for keeping in good shape. He didn't push it to extremes, though; he didn't want that freakish look.

'What are you doing here? Last time I looked, this was my neck of the woods.' Filippi had to raise his head when he spoke, because of the height difference. Scamarcio could tell that this also troubled him.

'Just taking a look — wondered if it might tie into something else I've got going on.'

'What's that, then?'

Scamarcio smiled and said nothing.

Filippi shook his head, bored, as though he'd seen it all. 'You're welcome to it. I've had more than my fair share of road-kill this week.' He brushed some dirt from the knees of his trousers and gestured through what remained of the living room to a doorway at the back. 'He's still in the bedroom, and it's not a pretty sight. Forensics are on their way, so don't touch anything. I'm going round the corner for a bite — back in five.'

As Scamarcio approached the doorway, the air seemed to thicken. He stopped where the door should have been and looked through, heeding Filippi's warning, not wanting to contaminate the scene. On what remained of the bed he could just about make out a human form. There were two legs, two arms, and a head, but that was as far as it went. The corpse was so deeply bloodied that it was practically a hunk of meat — it was impossible to see whether it was male or female.

The smell was overwhelming. Scamarcio pulled a paper tissue from his pocket and spread it over his mouth. He'd seen shootings, beatings, and knife fights, but never a stabbing like this. He was about to go and find Filippi, share the experience, and laugh it off, when he became aware of a dim light coming from somewhere deep in the room — an alien glow that didn't quite belong. He stepped forward, careful not to cross the threshold. To the left was

11

a bunch of shattered fragments of something wooden — maybe a chest of drawers — and then to its right, in the middle of what remained of a tall cabinet, was a small shelf with a mirror, its glass strangely white in all the blackness. A high-end camera lay open in front of it, its lens and body smashed, but the green light still pulsing.

3

He remembers the day they were on the hill, the whole city spread out beneath them, the glassy expanse of the sea giving back the light of the sun. The Moltisanti were crushing ants beneath their fingers, holding their broken bodies to the light, sucking the residue from their palms. He turned away, disgusted. The older brother saw and said, 'I'm bored with this, let's find a dog.' The younger brother was silent, and turned to follow, dragging a stick through the dust. He wanted to go home, to spare himself what was to come, but he couldn't. He knew that if he stayed he might be able to stop this thing — maybe save the poor animal, and take it home.

Scamarcio decided to stick around for Forensics, hoping to hear if they'd be able to read anything off the camera. He stepped over to the window that overlooked the street. There were a few more people around now, braving the rain for a respectable meal in one of the tavernas. He cast his thoughts out into the darkness. Who was this Arthur, and what had he got himself involved in? Marital infidelity was not uncommon among middle-aged politicians, and Italians didn't get their knickers in a twist about it like they did in some of those northern countries. Usually, it wasn't even worth resigning for. But the gay element racked the whole thing up a notch, and the underage question pushed it into another league, especially as Ganza was seen to be such a family man. Scamarcio remembered the photo spreads: Ganza on his yacht with his beautiful wife, three blonde kids in tow; Ganza in the garden with his dog; Ganza at church with the family at Christmas. It was possible, of course, that Arthur's involvement with the foreign secretary was not connected to his death — possible, but unlikely. Scamarcio had never believed in coincidences. And if his death wasn't a coincidence, it meant that Scamarcio was dealing with a political case; and if this was a political case, it would spell trouble. He didn't need a political thing — he, of all people. He wondered anew just why the chief had chosen him. After all, it made little sense if you were looking at it in PR terms. He was damaged goods; his hands weren't clean, some might say. Under his breath he cursed Garramone, but his violent thoughts were interrupted by a flurry of footfalls moving up the stairs from below. Although he knew who was coming, he felt oddly anxious.

A trio of CSIs bustled into the room. Two, he knew; the third looked like a new guy.

'Didn't know this was your beat,' said Antonio Manetti, the most senior of the team. He extended a hand, and his two colleagues surveyed the blackened walls, the new guy whistling softly.

'Technically it isn't, but it might have a bearing on something else.'

'Right you are.' Manetti gestured to the bedroom, seemingly uninterested. 'The body is in there, I take it.'

'Yes, not pretty.'

'Thanks for the warning.' Although his tone was cold, Manetti was known for being quite sensitive at times. He made no attempt to hide his emotions when cases got to him, although most of the time he saw his way through by using the biting black humour they all employed.

He picked up his silver cases and headed for the bedroom, his team trailing behind. They all crowded on the threshold for a moment, and the new guy whistled again. He would have to stop that, thought Scamarcio. He couldn't be whistling forever.

'I'm going to leave you guys to do your thing, but before I go,

I need to draw your attention to that camera on the shelf over there.'

All three heads turned. There was a moment of silence.

'That's a strange one,' said Peletti, the second of the CSIs. 'Just left there like that.'

'Do you think all the pictures would have been lost? Could there be anything left on an internal memory?'

'I'm presuming the card has been removed,' said Manetti. 'We'll take it to the IT guys — see what they make of it. If there's an internal drive, they'll probably try data recovery — it sometimes works miracles on real wrecks; sometimes not. I don't know whether this one is too far-gone. Judging from the general state of the place, it doesn't look good.'

'When do you think they could give me an answer?'

'What am I, a fortune-teller?'

Scamarcio smiled, playing along. 'What if I call you tomorrow to see how it looks?'

'Sure.' Manetti turned his gaze from the room to the detective. 'What's the deal then? What are you working on?'

'Can't say.'

Manetti rolled his eyes. 'Yeah, yeah, whatever ...' He looked back to the camera.

'Why leave that thing? It looks like it's been picked up and put back. Why not just take it with you?'

'My thoughts, exactly,' said Scamarcio. He gave Manetti a gentle back slap and waved to his team. 'Filippi's already here. He'll be back through in a minute.'

They were already putting on their protective suits, and didn't seem to hear.

The chief had called him back to the apartment on Via Nazionale. It was 11.00 pm, and Scamarcio wondered at the late hour. Garramone's old friend must be putting the pressure on.

He told him about the camera.

'But that makes no sense. Why not just take it with you?'

'I guess it depends on which way you look at it.'

Garramone scowled, and scratched at an unruly eyebrow.

'We're thinking about it in terms of someone other than Arthur putting it there. But what if his killer didn't know about the camera? What if he just stabbed him and left? It was Arthur, knowing he was going to die, who placed it there — left it as some kind of sign that it contained material pertinent to his death, material he wanted to preserve.'

The chief nodded slowly. 'Maybe, but if he had the strength to do that, didn't he have the strength to escape or call for help?'

'Perhaps he already knew it was over, that he wouldn't make it.'

They both fell silent, imaging the horror of his final minutes.

'And what are the chances that we'll be able to lift anything off the memory — off one of those card things?'

'I don't know. We're presuming the card's been lifted, and we're not sure it has a drive. I have to talk to Forensics tomorrow.'

The chief looked down for a moment, his gaze losing focus. After a little while, he rubbed his fingers across his forehead and raised his eyes to Scamarcio. There was something almost apologetic in the way he looked at him. 'This thing is sensitive.'

Scamarcio said nothing. He didn't need a sensitive case, not after the media frenzy of the last 12 months. At the back of his mind was the suspicion that he was here because he was expendable, because if it all went to the wall he could leave without a fuss — it would be a departure that everyone understood. Now he wanted that doubt assuaged, but he held himself together, kept it down. After everything, he needed the chief to believe in him; still needed to prove himself.

He could see that Garramone was watching him carefully, observing how he was responding to whatever experiment he still had in play. 'The good news is that it looks like the media have been persuaded to keep a lid on it for now.'

'How so?'

'They've been told that if they go with it, they will be denied access to certain people, certain stories further down the line. They took a long-term view about whether the story was worth the risk.'

'And they decided it wasn't?'

'Seems that way. It's good for us — means things stay calmer for longer.'

'So now …'

The chief rose from his seat and walked to the window. Passing brake lights etched a ghostly course through his tired skin.

'Now you need to find out all you can about this Arthur, his relationship with the foreign secretary, other people in his circle. We need to know who killed him and why.'

'And then?'

'And then we think about the implications.'

'But what about Filippi and the Trastevere squad? Won't they make the connection for themselves, start digging?'

'I've been assured that, as far as they are concerned, he's just another dead hooker.'

'Who's assured you? How does that work?'

Garramone raised a hand to silence him. 'Scamarcio, stop asking the wrong questions and start asking the right ones.' He paused. 'I don't want you in the office — you can work from home. Call me if you need access to any files; I'll get you what you need.'

A knot of anxiety tightened in Scamarcio's chest. Something felt wrong here, and yet again he'd been placed right in the middle of it.

4

There was no trace of Arthur anywhere on the internet. From the information the chief had been able to gather, it seemed that, surprisingly, he was possibly already 20, but unlikely much older, and had gone by the name of José Maraquez during an early life spent in La Quiaca in the north of Argentina where it bordered Bolivia. Google images showed La Quiaca to be a depressed slum town — its muddy alleyways straddled with drooping electric cable, barefoot children, chickens, and rangy dogs playing together in the filth. It seemed that as soon as they were old enough, many of these children would leave for Cordoba or Buenos Aires, where there was at least some small chance of finding work.

According to Garramone, their two blackmailing colleagues had been handed the photos by a man unknown to them. So if Scamarcio was to get any real background on Arthur, he would need to talk to his friends and acquaintances. The problem was that Forensics had found no trace of a mobile. Any address books or letters had been impossible to come by, and the jury was still out on the camera. That meant that, right now, they only had two people who knew the victim: One was the foreign secretary, now safely ensconced in his retreat; the other was the second young man in the photo, whose identity remained a mystery. He would need to call someone in Vice — probably Carleone. Their paths had crossed once or twice, but he would need to tread carefully.

'Carleone.' It was the voice of an unhappy man, clearly put out to be troubled on a Saturday.

'It's Leone Scamarcio. Sorry to disturb you at the weekend.'

'Weekend? I haven't seen a weekend in a long time.'

'You got a case on?'

'Got a bust coming — hours of overtime. Seems like we'll never see the back of it.'

'Been there, got the T-shirt. Listen, I was wondering if you could help me out.'

'As long as it's quick.'

'It's a hookers' thing: I was wondering about the gay scene. The rentboys. If you were looking for one — good looking, youngish, not the rough trade at Termini — where would you try? Do they have a street where they hang out?'

Carleone laughed: a dirty, dry little laugh. 'It's come to that, has it? Want me to draw you a map?'

'Yeah, yeah, whatever. I just need a way in.'

Carleone's tone grew marginally more serious. 'This for work?'

'Yeah, but I can't go into it.'

He yawned down the line, registering his lack of interest. 'I know a couple of people who'll see you right. Hang on.'

Scamarcio heard typing, the whirr of a fan, some distant laughter in the background.

Carleone came back on. 'The first is quite something — Maria, formerly known as Raffaele. She's interesting because if you didn't know the truth, I don't think you'd be able to guess.' He paused for a moment, maybe remembering the first time he'd seen her: 'It's quite a thing to behold.' Scamarcio wondered whether Carleone had ever blurred the lines between his professional and private life.

'You'll find her down in Testaccio, along with a few girlfriends. Next to the McDonalds by the bridge is the main pick-up point, and they're there most nights. I've got a number for her, if you want.' Scamarcio took it and hung up.

Testaccio had none of the charm of Trastevere. If anything, it looked like a grim Naples suburb, a malignant growth hidden within the sumptuous folds of the eternal city. The girls were on the corner by McDonalds, all decked out in knee high-boots, zips, and PVC, just as Scamarcio had expected.

'Hey, gorgeous, you look cold.'

'Want someone to snuggle up to?'

Carleone was right. One of them was stunning, and there was nothing to suggest that she could be anything other than female. The other three were slightly tougher to digest.

Scamarcio pulled out his badge, which triggered a group sigh of exasperation. The beautiful one, who he presumed was Maria, took a step forward and grabbed him by the wrist. It was a strong grip.

'Listen, we got all this straight with Carleone. We been through it hundreds of times.'

Scamarcio raised a palm to calm her. 'I'm not here for that. I was hoping you could help me with an inquiry. No trouble for any of you — no repercussions.'

'How do we know you're straight?'

'Check with Carleone.'

Maria flipped open a mobile, pressed a number on speed-dial, and distanced herself from the group. He reckoned that she was almost his height. Her hair was long, lustrous, and dark, and left to hang loose. It framed almond eyes of a startling blue, a shade so intense that he felt sure it was artificial — the result of coloured contact lenses, or some such trick.

She finished the call and flipped shut the phone, pulling a cigarette from a pocket as she did so. She rooted around for a lighter and lit up, shielding her face from the wind and the damp.

'Carleone says you're clean. What is it you want?'

Scamarcio pulled the photos from his shoulder bag, and passed them around the huddle.

'Do you know these boys?'

Maria rejoined them now, and leaned in to get a better look.

He could smell her scent. It was familiar to him, and a memory stirred: a summer evening by the sea in Gallipoli, and a girl from Salento — a girl he had cared for.

They had cut the foreign secretary out of the picture, and had made singles of the two young men.

'That one.' Maria tapped a red fingernail against the photo of Arthur. 'I think that's Max — I knew him once.' She scanned the faces of her friends for confirmation. One of them, an older, too-tall blonde, nodded. 'Yes, it's him, but he's changed a bit. Looks like he could have had some work done. As for the other one, no idea.'

Scamarcio tried to read her, to make sure she wasn't playing him. 'You sure it's Max, because we know him as Arthur?'

'It's definitely Max. Maybe he changed his name — it happens. Perhaps it's his new working name.'

'When did you see him last?'

The two women exchanged glances. 'It's been a long time — maybe a year, maybe more. He used to hang with us here.'

'Then what happened?'

Maria shook her head. 'No idea. He just stopped turning up for work, and then he didn't return our calls. We thought he'd gone on to bigger and better things.'

'Bigger and better?'

Maria glanced at her colleague again, and he thought he saw something strange pass between them. 'It's just an expression. I have no idea what happened to him.'

'And you?' Scamarcio turned to the other prostitute.

'Ditto. It happens. Girls and boys get lucky and are able to take themselves off the street, or they get unlucky and fate decides for them.'

'So you would never call in a missing colleague?'

Maria laughed 'Back then, no. Now things have settled, maybe. But it's not like you guys would care. A dead hooker is low down

21

enough on the list. But a foreigner? I don't think we'd get five minutes, do you?'

He pushed on, unwilling to be drawn in. 'What did you know about Max when you did work with him?'

Maria shrugged. 'Not a lot. He wasn't here for long. I think he said he was from Argentina, that he came here some years before. He'd wanted to be a dancer in clubs, but that hadn't worked out, so he'd ended up on the street. He was a looker, Max, as you can see. He got a lot of attention.'

'Was he underage?'

'No idea. I don't think so. He was a wise soul.'

That meant nothing, thought Scamarcio. 'Any family back home?'

The two women traded glances again, conferring, waiting for the other to speak.

The older prostitute went first: 'He never mentioned anyone. I got the feeling that he'd left on bad terms — traditional family, couldn't accept what he'd become. The usual story.'

'Did he seem happy?'

Maria took a long drag on her cigarette. It trailed an amber wake in the darkness, and melted into the sodium of the street-lamps. 'Hell, who's happy? But he was making enough to eat and pay the rent. And, yeah, he was always cheerful — upbeat, if that's what you mean. He had what you'd call a sunny disposition.' There was a bitterness in the way she said the words.

'Were there any particular punters who liked him — regulars, returning customers?'

'I'm sure there were, but I couldn't tell you who. It was far too long ago.'

'No one among your current clients?'

'Of course not.' She seemed almost put out. 'We were completely different types. Obviously.' Scamarcio wasn't sure he agreed. If you took away the long hair, the Latin look was the same, and the doe eyes quite similar.

'Could you ask around the punters, and see if anyone remembers him?'

The two women shook their heads while others in the group sighed. 'What tree did you fall out of?' said Maria. 'Questions are bad for business.'

Scamarcio sensed his time was up, but knew that Maria was holding out on him — maybe not because she didn't want to talk, but maybe because she didn't want to talk here. He pulled out a few business cards.

'If you remember anything, please give me a call. Any time.'

'Any time?' one of them tittered.

The blonde flipped the card, and frowned. 'What's this about? Has something happened to Max?'

His eyes met theirs as he pulled up his collar against the wind, tightening his scarf about his neck. But he said nothing and just turned, saluting them gently as he left. The huddle fell silent.

5

The dog was completely still now. Marco Moltisanti sat on some rocks, drawing patterns in the sand with the bloodied stick. His little brother was some way away, skimming stones across the water. He could still hear its whimpers, its howls; he could still feel the full force of Marco's punch when he'd tried to stop him. It was the end of September. There was a slight chill in the breeze, a hardness to the sand, a silence in the birds that spelled the close of summer. He knew that this day marked the end of something: something that had been inside him but had left; something that was never coming back.

Scamarcio slept fitfully that night, his dreams troubled by strange creatures: half-man, half-woman, faces distorted to a bloody mess, eyes missing. He had called off his date for Saturday evening. He figured that breaking it up early to go and visit some transgender hookers was probably worse than cancelling. He'd need to make it right, though. He needed a second life to distract him — needed it like air.

He opened the blinds and got back into bed. He observed the milky sunlight soak its way through the brickwork of the building opposite, and watched a couple of pigeons stand in companionable silence on the ledge above, surveying the ant-like activity of human life below. He longed for a joint. If there was still a point in going over to the bookshelf, extracting the tin, flipping the lid, and lighting up, he'd now be enjoying the calm sweep over him: the sweetness, the rest, the emptiness of the moment. But the cupboard was bare: there was nothing in the house — his attempt at some kind of self-preservation. He sank back into the pillows, studying the ceiling and its intricate rings of damp. He wasn't sure how long he could maintain this particular battle of the will — it was tougher than he had anticipated.

He went into the kitchen and made a coffee, and then lifted the newspaper from under the door. *La Repubblica* had a small piece on Ganza on page five. They said he had gone to a secret location for a period of rest and reflection following the recent death of his beloved mother, Alessandra. It was expected that he would return to parliament soon. Not bad being a politician, he thought — not only were they the highest-paid MPs in Europe, but they could just take time off whenever they wanted. He wondered how many workers at Fiat could take a proper break following the death of a relative.

He sat at the kitchen table and sipped the coffee. How long would the PM be able to keep this out of the papers? Was he really that powerful? He found it hard to believe that every editor in the land had been persuaded not to run with this story. He was no journalist, but to him it seemed that a married father of three found with young rentboys was a pretty good tale as it was, and the fact that he just happened to be foreign secretary gave it a nice spin, particularly in the current political climate. Surely *la Repubblica* would have given their back teeth to sock it to the PM and the cabinet? Nothing made sense any more.

His mobile rang and he gave a start, his coffee spilling across the table and soaking the edges of the newspaper. He had a feeling it might be Aurelia complaining about having been stood up the night before, but wasn't sure that was her style. He also didn't know whether he wanted to talk to her or not. He hadn't quite worked out how he felt about her — whether he wanted this one to go the distance, or just stumble on for another few dates.

The bass on the other end of the line told him it wasn't her.

'Scamarcio, Filippi. Got something for you.'

'You working Sundays now?'

'Shitty new rota — two weekends a month. I get Monday and Tuesday off, but that's a fat lot of good when the kids are at school. I never see them.'

'Sorry.'

'I'm angling for a transfer. The wife's breaking my balls.'

Scamarcio heard the scratching of a pen. Filippi took a slurp of something: it came out too loud down the line.

'What you got for me?'

'Yeah, your boytoy …' There was a question, a hint of curiosity, in his tone. Scamarcio smelt danger.

'Seems like your lad was mugged a week before he died — had his rucksack stolen, and with it his mobile phone and house keys.'

'You're kidding me.'

'Wish I were, Scamarcio. Wish I were.'

Scamarcio thought about the memory card. Had it been in the bag? Had it been another reason for the theft? Instead he said, 'How did you hear about it?'

'He visited the precinct. I found out when I put his name into the system, looking for 'Previous'. He'd come in to report the theft. The desk sergeant remembers him. Well, you would, wouldn't you — all that mincing. Says he was very upset; lots of tears.'

'Did he give a description of the mugger?'

'Didn't give us much — it was late at night, near his place. Two of them, apparently, well built, both in balaclavas. Roman accents.'

'Any chance I could have a look at the report?'

'No problem. I'll put it up on the network.'

Scamarcio felt his nerves triggered, like someone had broken the electric current surrounding his defences. 'Can you email it? I'm out the office for the next few days.'

'No worries.' Filippi paused for a beat. 'What's all this about? It seems odd to me you're interested in a dead renter on my patch.

Even odder that he's a dead renter who just happens to have been mugged.'

Scamarcio laughed gently. 'Oh, it's nothing. Just something I said I'd follow up for a friend. He knew the vic, and wanted to know what happened to him.'

'Strange friends you have.'

There was a shout — an indication of sudden movement — from somewhere in the background of Filippi's office. It sounded like something was going down in Sunday-morning Trastevere.

'Scamarcio, I've got to go. One other thing: check out the neighbours, if you want. There's another one of them in the flat above. Came down to find me last time I was there, crying and wailing, but I didn't have the time, so I just put her on the backburner. If you want to talk to her, you'd be doing me a favour getting her off my back. Name was Sanchez, or something like that.'

What did he mean by 'another one of them'? But Filippi had already hung up.

6

WHATEVER HAD BEEN going down in Trastevere was a long way from Arthur's street. The alleyway was quiet. There was a bar on the corner, and Scamarcio caught a warm waft of coffee grounds and fresh baking over the usual undercurrent of decaying sewage pipes and stale alcohol. Through the window he spied a couple of old guys at the counter and an even older guy behind the bar. Sky News was on mute in the background: the PM was dressed down in casual clothes, showing Putin around Portofino — another uncomfortable alliance in Europe.

The door to Arthur's building was locked. He scanned the buzzers and found a Santa, but not Sanchez. He tried it, but there was no response. He tried again, and eventually a voice came on.

'Who is it?'

'I'm from the police, a colleague of Mr Filippi. He sent me to see you. Is it OK if I come up?'

There was a pause.

'I'm sorry, I'm not dressed. I just need five minutes.'

Instinct kicked in. Perhaps she was having second thoughts — maybe she wanted to flee?

'That's OK. I can wait in the sitting room while you get dressed. It's cold down here.'

A sigh: 'Second floor.' The voice was low and gravely, and Scamarcio got it then: Filippi had meant another gay man, this time a trans. The door buzzed open and he pushed his way in. Old cigarette smoke coated the air, and he saw the police tape flicker in the draught from downstairs as he passed Arthur's doorway.

The body was gone now, safely in the morgue waiting for the ME. The ME was next on Scamarcio's list, but he didn't know how to work it — it really would be a breach of protocol as far as Filippi was concerned.

Miss Santa was waiting for him on the second floor, wrapped in a tired-looking kimono, its red and green silk depicting a lizard poised to strike. She extended a hand. Her eyes, ringed and puffy, still bore traces of last night's make-up, and her dark hair was dried out and broken yet greasy at the roots. Scamarcio would have put her at over forty, and would have been in no doubt as to her original gender.

'I'm sorry that you catch me like this. I worked late last night.'

She headed back into the flat, and Scamarcio followed. He caught a blast of perfume, newly applied.

She gestured him to a sofa in the centre of a large room. Exposed beams lined the ceiling, and diamond windows looked out onto the street, just as Arthur's had done. It was a nice apartment, tastefully decorated: he took in line drawings in silver frames, expensive upholstery, silk scatter cushions. The apartment didn't match its owner, somehow, and he wondered how she could afford it. Rents in Trastevere were high. He wondered how someone as young as Arthur had afforded it.

'Please make yourself at home — I won't be a moment.' She retreated into a back bedroom. Again, it had the same layout as Arthur's place.

He noticed some photos on a bookshelf, and walked over to take a closer look: there was a huddle of young people, a family, all from somewhere in Latin America maybe, with palm trees in the background and brightly painted houses. There were also a couple of portraits of a teenage boy, with something familiar in his features — maybe he was a brother or a nephew. He couldn't find Miss Santa in the pictures.

She was back in the room now, her hair scraped back into

a ponytail, her face clean, dressed down in jogging pants and a sweatshirt. She had tied a silk scarf around her neck, but he didn't understand why — it had nothing to do with what she was wearing.

'Can I get you anything to drink?'

'No, I'm fine, thanks — all dosed up on coffee already.'

She smiled tightly and sat down carefully on an armchair facing him, as if she were a guest in her own home. He noticed that her hands were smooth and well manicured. The nail polish was a subtle colour, almost nude, not the garish red he had seen on the girls from the night before.

'Detective Filippi says you came to speak with him when he was in the apartment downstairs.'

She looked to the left, towards the window, as if sensing the presence of a spirit below.

'I was in quite a state. I probably wasn't making much sense, so I can't blame him for not listening. I think he was in a hurry, and needed to leave.'

'He asked me to apologise. He was called away on another case. I want to assure you that we are very interested in whatever you can tell us about Arthur.'

The woman sighed, and smoothed one hand inside the other. Her eyes were still fixed on the window.

'It's such an awful thing. He was so good.'

Good at what, he wondered, or in what way good?

'Had you known him long?'

She turned her head slowly and let her eyes meet his. But he could tell that this was unnatural for her — she was shy, and would have preferred to look away.

'Me and Arthur, or Max, as he used to be known, we go back a bit. We both used to work in a club in Magliana, a kind of cabaret place. I served behind the bar, and Arthur was one of the dancers. It was a grim place, after hours, all-male clientele.'

'How old was he?'

'He never told me, although I asked several times. He just said something about being in his early twenties. He always boasted that he looked good for his age.'

'Did you sense he might be younger?'

She looked down for a moment. 'In the beginning, perhaps. Then I think I kind of forgot about it. He seemed very mature for a teenager, so I figured he was probably telling the truth.' She paused. 'It's very hard to tell peoples' ages sometimes.'

'Do you think they suspected he might be underage at the club?'

She responded with a fragile laugh, almost a sigh: 'I doubt very much they cared.'

Scamarcio smiled. 'How long were you both there?'

'I arrived a while before he did and stayed on after he left, but we kept in touch. We used to look out for each other.' She swept her arms around her. 'It was Arthur who arranged this apartment for me.'

He tried to conceal his surprise. He surveyed the room once more, appreciatively, slowly. 'It seems like a very nice place — it must cost you a fortune.'

She waved the thought away. 'I don't have to worry about the rent. Arthur saw to that.' Her gaze fell to her lap — maybe she was reflecting on her sudden change of circumstance.

He couldn't square it away. How could Arthur afford to pay one rent in Trastevere, let alone two?

'He must have had a good job.'

'He never talked with me about his work. He only stayed at Il Lupo — the cabaret place — two months, and then he said he couldn't make ends meet and needed to find something better. I had a feeling he'd gone on the street. I think he'd got an intro at the bar — customers wanting more, you know? He probably realised it was a way to make more money more quickly, so figured it was worth taking up.' She paused. 'But, like I say, he never discussed it with me. After Il Lupo we stayed friends, saw each other often, and I guess I kind of became like a mother figure to him, being that much older. Also, we're both from Argentina, so it gave us that link to home, you know.' She tailed off, lost in another thought. 'But he never discussed his work with me. Never.'

'Arthur was from La Quiaca, right?'

'That's what he told me. But I don't think he was close to his folks — there was a falling out with his father, and his mother had to take sides, and it was all downhill from there. Arthur left when he was 17, went to Buenos Aires, found work in a bar. Then he fell in love with an Italian, and ended up here.'

'The Italian, you have a name?'

'Only a first name: Fabio, I think. But he didn't talk about him much. It ended just a few months after he arrived — ended quite badly. They were no longer on speaking terms.'

'How old was Fabio?'

'Mid-thirties.'

'Was he happy to be dating someone so much younger?'

Ms Santa arched an eyebrow. 'I imagine so. That's not why they split, if that's what you mean.'

'Well, it's not the usual choice.'

Her gaze was cool. 'Maybe not for you, detective, but it drives some people wild.' The words were neutral and matter-of-fact — there was no outrage. Ms Santa seemed too tired and worn-out for that, as if life had dealt her too many bad hands.

'Why did they split?'

'Fabio cheated on him. Broke his heart.'

Scamarcio let that sink in for a second, wondering if a betrayal like that might push you onto the street.

'Were there any other boyfriends in his life? Anyone you knew of?'

She shook her head. 'He was always working and, when he wasn't, he was sleeping. He never spoke to me about lovers —

32

there never seemed to be anyone special.'

'And you have no idea what line of work he could have been in to afford to pay two rents in Trastevere?'

'He wasn't paying the rents. He owns both apartments.'

Scamarcio lost his breath for a moment. By his reckoning, that was well over a million euros of real estate.

'I don't think you make that much money working the streets,' he said, searching Ms Santa's face for some kind of answer.

'You don't. If you did, I'd be doing it.'

She looked away, losing her gaze to the window once again. He sensed that she knew something more and was deliberating whether to share it.

'His parents weren't wealthy?'

'No, and after the row with his father they wouldn't have given him a cent anyway.'

She fell silent again, her eyes off to one side, like Princess Diana in that famous TV interview.

'So you don't have any idea how you come to be living in a rent-free apartment in Trastevere?'

She sighed and got up from her seat. 'I need a drink. You sure you don't want anything?'

'Quite sure.'

He followed her retreating back as she headed for the kitchen. It lay behind a wide annexe that opened onto an oak table and chairs. He caught a glimpse of stainless-steel cabinets and expensive tiling. He heard the clinking of glasses, liquid being poured, and ice broken, and then she was back again with a tumbler of something clear — maybe water, maybe vodka.

She reclaimed the seat opposite and started taking tentative sips, as if she wasn't quite sure whether she wanted the drink after all. They sat in silence for several moments.

'I think he had a patron,' she said eventually. Scamarcio's thoughts had been elsewhere.

'A patron?' Perhaps her Italian was letting her down. The word didn't quite make sense to him.

'A sponsor — someone who looked after him, gave him money.'

He leaned forward slightly, trying to lock eye contact. 'He or she must have been a very generous sponsor.'

Ms Santa nodded slowly and pulled at the dry tips of her hair scraped into the ponytail. 'He never told me this, you understand. It was just a feeling I had. I got the sense that if I asked too much, it would all be over — that if I wanted to keep this place, I had to accept the way things were, and not pry.' She paused. 'So I never asked, and he never told, and it all ticked over just fine.' She paused again. 'Until now.'

7

He stands on the terrace of the villa near Radda. It is the end of summer, and only the smallest wisp of red still clings to the horizon. As the light bleeds from the sky, he feels the day's heat rise up from the earth, and hears the gentle murmur of the cypresses as they shift in the breeze. He is reluctant to go inside; he would prefer to stand here longer, tasting the air, swimming awhile in the musk of roses, the scent of Mediterranean pine.

From inside, Lucioli shouts: 'I think they're here. There are cars on the drive.'

As if in confirmation, he hears the crunch of tyres on gravel, the slam of doors. He wills himself inside.

Lucioli is standing in the light, drink in hand.

'You sure this makes sense?' he asks him for the third time that day.

'The banks are on our backs, Pino. Of course it makes sense. We need cash; they need a home. It's what they call a symbiotic relationship.'

'But it's afterwards I'm worried about — the repercussions.'

Lucioli sighs, and runs a hand through his hair. 'Without these guys, there is no afterwards.'

The door opens, and two men step into the room. He feels his breath catch, feels it freeze in his lungs.

'I bet you never thought you'd see us again.'

They move towards him, almost in sync, but he just stands motionless, suddenly severed from the world.

Uninvited, they put their arms around him, enfolding him in an iron embrace. 'Pino, our Pino.'

Lucioli says afterwards that he looked like he'd seen a ghost.

'I NEED TO speak to Ganza.'

'That's not possible,' said the chief. He sounded tired and depressed, as though he wanted to escape — to take the car and get the hell out of Italy.

'Why not?'

'Because he's not to be disturbed. Besides, he's in the retreat. We can't just go waltzing in.'

Scamarcio felt a knot of anger burn in his gut. 'You know that's not how these things work!' Was the chief losing it? For now, Ganza was their chief suspect; their only suspect.

'Don't talk to me like that.'

He took a breath, trying to count to five. 'It's just that he's crucial to the whole investigation.' Then, as an afterthought: 'Obviously.'

'But he was in the retreat when Arthur died.'

It was as if Garramone had forgotten his training, and Scamarcio was there to drag him back to rational reality. 'For all we know, he could have hired some guys to take him out.'

'But why would the prime minister call me if that's what he suspected? Surely he'd try to keep that quiet?'

'Maybe he has no idea.'

Both of them fell silent for a moment.

'Where are you phoning from?' The chief sounded alarmed.

'The car.'

'Are you out of your mind?'

'What?'

'Shut up. Meet me in the usual place in an hour.' Garramone hung up, and the empty line echoed back at him. Scamarcio felt suddenly hollow. He was getting tired of this. He couldn't spend his life going up and down to Via Nazionale, couldn't spend his life lying to his colleagues.

The chief was waiting for him in the flat. There was no suit, today being Sunday — just a worn jumper and some dirty mustard

36

cords. Scamarcio wouldn't have thought his wife would allow him to go out like that; on the few occasions he had seen her, she was buttoned down and immaculate. Garramone pushed a package across the table towards him, saying nothing. A quick glance told Scamarcio that it contained a new mobile phone and SIM card.

'I don't want our conversations to be overheard,' said the chief. 'I've been told not to trust the normal lines. I should have given this to you when we started.'

Scamarcio took a seat. There was an overwhelming heaviness in his bones. He didn't like the way this thing was progressing. Worse, he had a feeling that it couldn't end well for either of them.

'Seems like Arthur had a benefactor.'

'How do you mean?'

'I talked to a friend of his who lives upstairs: it appears that someone bought him two apartments in Trastevere. The friend lives in the other flat.'

Garramone pulled out a seat and sank into it. He crossed one leg over the other, and then uncrossed it.

'Did the friend know who?'

'Says he never told.'

'And your money is on Ganza?'

'Well, it's a possibility.'

'It's a possibility but he's out of bounds for now. The PM was insistent — says that he made a marital indiscretion, and that's as far as it goes.'

'So what is the prime minister looking for, exactly? Does he know who's behind this death?' Scamarcio got up and started pacing. 'And if he does, why did he bother to call you?'

The chief sighed, and yawned. The skin around his eyes was tight; it looked bruised. 'He knows nothing — that's why he called. But he clearly doesn't put Ganza in the frame, for various reasons, and not just the retreat.' He paused, leant forward a little, pushed the palms of his hands together.

'Look, just see where you get with these other lines, and then we can think about taking it back to Ganza. But I don't want to do it just yet, not now.'

Scamarcio's mind turned on Garramone's new position. Was what they were doing even legal? Could the PM really get a detective to do his bidding, unbeknownst to the chief of police? Was it even constitutional? He paused. Maybe the chief of police already knew about all this. It would be so much better for the both of them if he did.

Scamarcio used the new mobile to call Forensics on his way home. Lately, everyone seemed to be working at the weekends, so there was a chance that Manetti would pick up.

'What do you want?' He sounded like he hadn't slept since they'd last met, which was always possible.

'Why does everyone seems to work Sundays now?'

'Need the overtime — the basic is so shitty.'

'I hear the same story from everybody.'

'You ask me, we all need to leave, get the hell out. This country has no future: we're broke, we no longer produce anything useful, and we've got a bunch of corrupt cretins in charge.' Manetti paused for breath. 'The wife wants to go to Australia; she says the kids would have better prospects.'

'She could be right.'

'I know but, hell, it's a big step. Got a 90-year-old mother living alone in Ostia — you know how it is.'

They both said nothing for a moment, pondering the options.

'So I guess you're calling about Filippi's dead hooker?' said Manetti, breaking the reverie.

'Just wondered if you'd found anything.'

'Only what you'd expect. The place was obviously trashed to shit, but the perps didn't leave much behind — very careful job, despite the chaos. We got a few fibres, but we're not pinning much hope on them. There are pints of blood in the mattress — but just his, unfortunately. My guess is that he bled out fast. They meant business.'

'Who is the ME?'

'Aurelia D'Amato.'

'Ah, Aurelia.'

Aurelia was young, good looking, and a rising star. Scamarcio had wondered in the past whether she had a soft spot for him, but had dismissed it as improbable — although recent events had made him think again. Were he to justify his last-minute cancellation of their date, she might be persuaded to turn a blind eye if he were to root around in Filippi's case.

'Yeah, "Ah Aurelia" indeed — that woman gets better looking every time I see her, but I guess you're not allowed to say that kind of thing nowadays. It was more fun in the old days, but you wouldn't remember them.'

'Any news about the camera?'

'No card, as we suspected, but there's a drive. I spoke to Gunbach in IT yesterday. He explained all the technical stuff, but left me none the wiser. I reckon you need to speak to him direct.'

'He in?'

'No, but I've got a mobile. Hang on.'

Gunbach in IT had a thick Neapolitan accent. Scamarcio wondered when his relatives had arrived from Germany. Maybe it didn't go that far back — perhaps the father was German and had married an Italian. He wanted to ask, but it didn't feel appropriate.

Gunbach didn't seem at all bothered to be disturbed on a Sunday. Scamarcio had the sense that he was at a loose end, that maybe he was a geek loner and had no one to hang out with. What was it with these IT guys and personal relationships — was it some kind of autism thing? It was one of those clichés that seemed to come good every time.

'We took out the internal drive, and tried to run it to see if there was any data left to find.'

'And?'

'And we've just got a few fragments. Hardly anything — JPEG fragments.'

'Photos?'

'Yes, photos.' There was something strange about the way he said it.

'Can I take a look?'

'Well, like I say, they're just fragments.' Gunbach paused and then coughed, seeming almost embarrassed. He was an odd guy, Scamarcio decided. Maybe it was the blend of Italian and German. Those were two cultures that shouldn't mix.

'And ...'

'Well, to me, detective, it looks bad. But I think you need to judge for yourself.'

8

GUNBACH HAD NOT needed much persuading to open up his lab for the afternoon. He had seemed almost glad of the distraction, if not somewhat uncomfortable about the photos and whatever it was they revealed. Scamarcio was fighting a growing sense of apprehension; he had a feeling that he wasn't going to like what he saw, that it would have adverse implications for a whole lot of things.

Gunbach was fiddling with the mouse, opening files and doing something to the images that Scamarcio couldn't understand. The technician was an unusual-looking guy, in his late twenties, pale, with red hair. There was nothing Italian about him — nothing that would ever lead you to guess he was from the south.

'Just trying to make them clearer,' he explained. 'I think you will get a sense of the overall picture pretty quickly.' He paused, and shuffled from one foot to the other. Then, after a few seconds, he laid down the mouse and said: 'I'll leave you to it. I'm going to get a coffee from the machine. You want one?'

'Please.'

It was like he couldn't leave the room quickly enough.

Scamarcio's eyes remained fixed on the first picture in front of him — the last image that Gunbach had been working on. His brain moved fast to decipher the meaning, to grasp the bigger picture, as Gunbach had predicted. The image was blurry and low res, but slowly it came together and, as it did so, a sickly feeling started forming in his stomach. He clicked on another fragment file at the bottom of the screen, and once again his brain rapidly processed the contours, supplied the missing information. The image now filled the frame, and the sickness began to spread through his abdomen, taking hold of him, making him sweat. He steeled himself for the remaining two images and clicked rapidly, trying not to give himself too much time with them. The last was the worst, because it was the clearest and left the least room for doubt. He could see the fear in the child's eyes.

He got up from the computer and stepped outside Gunbach's office, rooting for a cigarette in his pocket that he knew wasn't there. He'd have to buy a packet tonight — these were extraordinary circumstances. He'd never had to see that kind of stuff before. He knew guys that dealt with it daily, but had never understood how they managed, how they didn't let it ruin them. Someone had told him once that they didn't deal with it — that they were all head-cases under regular care from psych — but he wasn't sure if that was just exaggerated gossip. Now he wished he'd never seen it, and knew it would stay with him forever and would colour other experiences in a way he didn't want. He felt sorry for Gunbach. The poor guy had been asked to fix a camera, and he'd had to look at this. He was coming towards him with the coffees now, anxiety clouding his pale face.

'You okay, Detective?'

'Should be asking you the same. I'm sorry you had to see that— it wasn't what I'd been expecting. I thought I'd be looking at something rather different.'

Gunbach handed him the coffee and leant against the wall across from him.

'No sweat. I know how it is.'

'You tell Manetti about these?'

Gunbach shook his head. 'No. When he called me yesterday, I hadn't seen them. I put it all together before I went home last night.'

'Could you keep this to yourself?'

He looked confused, and seemed to want an explanation. 'Sure, if you need it that way ...'

Scamarcio put out a hand, and leant against the wall. He felt like he needed to catch his breath.

'The thing is, this relates to something else I'm looking into, and I need to keep the two investigations separate for now. Could you just bear with me for a while?' He looked into his eyes, trying to find the real Gunbach.

'Sure, I understand.'

'I'll remember you for this.' The words were both a promise and a threat — an ambiguity not lost on the boy.

Scamarcio returned to the tiny office, and retrieved his jacket from the chair. 'Can you do me print-outs?' Gunbach, who had followed him in, was sweating under the fluorescence.

'No problem.'

He leaned over and clicked the mouse a few times, and the printer whirred into life. They waited in silence, neither sure what to say, the images on the screen killing any conversation. Scamarcio glanced over his shoulder, checking whether there was anyone in the corridor who might pass by and see what they had been looking at. The place was silent, but he swung the door shut nevertheless.

Gunbach handed him the prints. 'You still want me to see if I can retrieve any more fragments?'

'Yes, but be discreet. If Manetti or Filippi come asking, you have nothing.' He knew that there was next to no chance that Filippi would trouble the boy. Manetti was his point of contact for the CSIs — if, that is, he took the trouble to pursue the murder, which so far seemed unlikely.

Scamarcio thanked him and left, avoiding the other offices along the corridor for fear of running into Manetti. He took the fire escape rather than the elevator, and exited onto a side street. His caution paid off: as he joined the main road, he saw the chief

CSI and some colleagues returning from lunch, laughing — over some sick joke, no doubt. He waited until they had entered the building before he stepped out of the shadows. This didn't feel right, all this cloak-and-dagger stuff, hiding from his colleagues. Once again, he had the sense that it could not end well.

9

Luca Moltisanti opens the cabinet, takes out the trophy, handles it in the light, and puts it back. He picks up another and does the same. 'You did good,' he says.

'And so did you.'

'Not like you, Pino. No-one's done good like you.'

His brother is at the window, looking out at the rain-soaked pitch, the scar beneath his left eye livid in the light.

'It's been a long time.'

'Thirteen years.'

'Thirteen years.' He savours the words, as though it's a crowning achievement.

'We've missed you, Pino.'

He laughs tightly, looks away, wants to ring for Security, but knows he can't.

'That why you're here?'

'In a way.' He takes a seat, and straightens a trouser leg. The suit is Armani; the shoes are brogues.

'We think it's time.'

'YOU FOUND WHAT?'

'Child porn, sir.'

The chief fell silent for a moment, and then the tension of the last few days finally broke surface: 'What sick-pig bastards are we dealing with? Why the hell did he bring me into this?

Scamarcio let him run with it for a while, figured he needed to vent. He had two young boys, after all. 'I don't get it, what is he doing with child porn on his camera? You think he was into that? You think he took the photos?'

Scamarcio still knew so little about Arthur, but what he did know had led him to believe that it was unlikely. It didn't feel right; it didn't square with the picture that Ms Santa had painted. He had a sense that the photos served a secondary purpose — possibly financial, but probably not dealing. He didn't like him for a dealer.

'So what's your take on this? Help me out here.'

He watched the thoughts forming, saw them take shape as he spoke. 'He had all this money, right, from this so-called patron he never talked about ...'

'Yes ...'

'Well, what if that money wasn't given over so freely?'

The chief fell silent for a moment, thinking it through. 'Blackmail, you mean?'

'He had photos of someone important doing something appalling, and he made him pay for his silence. When he knew that his time was up, that he had come to find him, he couldn't let him have the last word. That's why he tried to save the camera, and put it back on the shelf. He wanted us to find the photos.'

'These photo fragments — do you see the face of the adult?'

'No, just the kid. Anyway, I think it could be more than one adult. But they're men — definitely men.'

'Ganza?'

'Impossible to tell.'

Garramone drew breath, and swore some more. 'This sick shit ... Who are these people? Do you think we're dealing with politicos, VIPs?' He stopped to let the possibility sink in, to absorb it. 'The connection to Ganza, it's all too close. Chances are that we're talking about government — if that was Arthur's clientele, if he knew people like Ganza. Now I'm really wondering why Pino brought me in.'

It was the first time he had referred to the PM by his first name.

'What's the deal with you two anyway?' Scamarcio knew the question would be unwelcome. But he felt he deserved some kind of explanation, given the turn of events.

Garramone seemed untroubled, his mind elsewhere, turning on all the implications. 'We grew up together in Gela. Schoolfriends from way back when — that's as far it goes.'

Scamarcio had thought the PM was from Como in the north. He knew Gela and what it stood for — knew what it meant if you grew up in Gela and then made it to prime minister.

'But they say he was from Lombardy. No one ever mentions Sicily.'

'He was there for a few years for his father's business. They came down from Lombardy and then went back. Anyway, that's not common knowledge, and I don't want it spread.'

Scamarcio had been too lost in the phone call to realise that, yet again, he was stuck in traffic. The orchestra of horns tuning up for a fight broke his concentration. How could there be traffic on a Sunday afternoon? The Coliseum — the scene of so much suffering, such inhumanity — was on his right now, battered and ominous in the rain. Once, when he'd been inside, he felt sure the smell of fear still lingered there. Two thousand years on, and what had really changed? Maybe the location had just shifted half a mile up the road.

'I think you need to talk to the friend again,' said the chief. 'See if she knows more. And we need to ID that second guy in the photo. Someone must know who he is. Call me when you have something.'

Scamarcio shut the mobile and eased back against the headrest. The rain was running in small rivulets down the window, morphing the world outside into a strange secondary reality, far removed from his own. He reflected on the circularity of it all: two of his colleagues blackmailed Ganza, then Arthur blackmailed him or someone else. Everyone was out for what they could get.

Garramone had said the two police officers had been handed the photos by a man they had never seen before. Who was he, and who stood to gain from his actions? Scamarcio had wanted to speak to the officers; but, according to Garramone, they had fled Rome on news of their suspension, and gone back to their folks. He would need to pay them a visit, see if they'd tell him more than they'd told the chief. His thoughts flipped to Garramone and his position in it all. It seemed so odd that he had selected him, Scamarcio, with all his baggage, for this. There were countless other people he could have called on — people with lower profiles, people who kept their heads down. But again he reminded himself that he was probably the easiest option. He could be sucked up and spat out by this investigation, explained away by his conveniently inconvenient past, comfortably consigned to history as another failed social experiment. And who was to say it wasn't actually better that way?

Scamarcio saw a cluster of Japanese tourists lining up like anxious starlings ready to have their photos taken in front of the Coliseum. This was the arbitrariness of history — these unlikely fragments the past left behind, and how we then chose to interpret them. And it was in this moment of watching that he sensed that he had perhaps misunderstood, that maybe there was a subtler explanation: the chief had chosen him because he was accustomed to the grey areas. He'd grown up with them. He'd never been able to see cases as being just black or white. He hadn't had the luxury of that kind of upbringing, and that was why Garramone knew he was right for this. Scamarcio cursed him again.

10

He stands up from the desk, goes to the cabinet and pours a scotch, then asks them if they want one. 'Of course,' they say. 'Let's drink a toast.'

'There will be no toast.'

'No toast? Why ever not?'

Funny how Luca does all the talking now: he was always so silent as a boy, always in his brother's shadow. He'd heard that Marco had been administered a beating, that it had made him soft in the head. Luca has stepped in, taken the reins, and is running his lieutenants hard.

'I am satisfied with my life. I prefer to keep things as they are.'

'You prefer?' Luca drains his scotch, rocks back in the chair, and laughs. 'Hear that, Marco? He prefers!'

The older brother grunts, and keeps his eyes on the pitch.

'Pino, I think we need to teach you one of our life lessons: there are certain things that you can't avoid, certain things that will always come back to find you, whether you want them to or not.'

SCAMARCIO HAD THOUGHT about calling Aurelia and inviting her over to make up for Saturday night; but when it came down to it, he was way too tired. By nine he was asleep, but that turned out to be a good thing because he woke on Monday ready to face the day, ready to pay her a professional visit.

The mortuary lay just three streets back from Flying Squad Headquarters, shaded by a wall of orange trees. It must have been one of the most attractive locations for such an establishment in the world, although the illusion ended as soon as you stepped inside: the paint was peeling from the walls, and the stained floor tiles probably hadn't been washed since Mussolini addressed Rome from his balcony.

'Aurelia in?'

The guy on the desk looked exhausted. He seemed to have lost even more hair since Scamarcio had last seen him, a month before.

'She's always in. It hasn't stopped for a fortnight. Is there a serial killer on the loose that no one has told us about?'

'Not as far as I'm aware.' The joke made him anxious — a fleeting, paranoid notion that events were escalating silently, unbeknownst to him or the chief, running away from them to a place beyond their control.

The guy on the desk gestured to the autopsy room behind him. 'Back there.'

When he walked in, Aurelia was dragging a body out of a tub, leaking blood and water everywhere, splattering the walls and flooding the floor.

She hadn't seen him enter, and he watched as she manoeuvred the corpse onto the examining table, sliding it into place and spreading out its arms and legs. Luckily for her, the man was small and painfully frail — he probably weighed no more than fifty kilos.

She stopped for a moment and turned, sensing his presence.

'Ah, Scamarcio, you always catch me at my best.'

He retreated towards the door, anxious about the reception she was going to give him. 'Shall I come back later?'

She pushed her goggles up onto her head and used the wrist of her gloved hand to scratch below an eye. She looked tired, and seemed older than the last time he'd seen her — her skin was paler and less taut, and her eyes were lacking their usual shine.

'No. It won't be any different then — probably worse. What's happening in this city? The last few weeks have been crazy.'

'It's the change of season; it has a strange effect on strange minds. Who've you got there?'

'Not sure yet, but it seems like a reprisal.'

'In the bathtub?'

She touched the head, and inclined it towards him. 'There's a tiny entry wound to the right — it must have been done from very close. And, as we all know, the closer you get, the more professional you are.'

'The bathtub's a bit way out there, isn't it? What happened to the trusty drive-by?'

She yawned and almost covered her mouth with a bloody glove, then thought better of it. 'God knows, it's changing all the time. When they lock up the old guys, and the young ones take over, you start to see all sorts of weird shit. Anyway, that's not why you're here, is it? I didn't think this was one of yours.'

He felt relieved. Whatever she thought of him, she wasn't going to hold it against him now. He stepped nearer, but not too close. The smell from the bath guy was overpowering.

'No, I'm here for something else, but it's not mine either.'

She raised a quizzical eyebrow.

'Long story. Wouldn't want to bore you.'

'Don't insult me. Whose case?'

'Filippi's. Filippi's rentboy.'

She laughed, and almost broke into a cough. 'I like that: "Filippi's rentboy." Poor Filippi would never have a rentboy — he's far too henpecked.'

She turned towards the freezer cabinets behind her, searched for the correct door, turned a key, and pulled out the drawer. There was the usual luggage tag on the end of a blackened foot protruding from beneath a sheet.

She threw off the cover, challenging him to take a look. The body was worse now: He could see traces of tissue, and a gelatinous eye among the blood. It was more real this time — more human.

He tried not to seem affected. 'Find anything of note?'

'It was the obvious that killed him — no surprises there. But there was something, yes.'

He could tell that she was amused by him; that she understood he was struggling with the wrecked body right there between them.

'Tell me,' he said. He needed a glass of water, but didn't like to ask.

'He'd been injected with something before he died — morphine, to be precise.'

'Morphine?'

'Not enough to kill him, but enough to knock him out, to stop him from feeling pain.'

'What? That doesn't make any sense.'

She shrugged. 'I can only tell you what I found.'

He thought for a moment and tried to take it in.

'You mean like a mercy killing — like the killer didn't want him to suffer?'

'It would seem that way, yes.'

He breathed slowly. To his right, he saw the bathtub man's rubbery arm now hanging from the exam table, the threadbare thatch of pubic hair, and the emaciated thighs, saw the watery blood slowly dripping onto the tiles below. It wasn't adding up.

'If someone had been injected with this dose of morphine and had been stabbed this many times, would they be capable for a moment of standing up, and retrieving a camera from the floor and placing it on a shelf?' He realised how stupid this sounded as soon as it had left his lips.

Aurelia D'Amato shook her head and threw him a concerned look. 'I suppose it's possible — stabbing victims are capable of energetic actions before they collapse, and his brainstem was untouched. But it seems unlikely. I imagine that he'd have been out cold pretty quickly — although, like I say, the dose wasn't enough to kill him.' She tugged a stray strand of hair behind her ear. 'Is that what happened? You found a camera?'

'Yes — all smashed in. But we've drawn a blank; it hasn't given us anything.'

She frowned. 'Strange. Why not just take it away?'

'I'm asking myself the same thing.' He paused, and locked eyes with her. 'Is Filippi pursuing this one?'

'He's got his hands full like the rest of us, and when was the last time any of you had time for a dead hooker?'

'OK — just wondered.'

She pushed the drawer back into the cabinet. 'The strange case of Filippi's rentboy,' she said, almost as a parting eulogy to see it on its way.

'Filippi's what?'

They both swung round. Filippi was in the doorway, and he didn't look happy.

'First, he's not my rentboy; second, what the fuck are you doing, Scamarcio? Why are you following me around like a fucking shadow?'

Scamarcio raised both palms in a placatory gesture, and took a step towards him. 'Sorry, Oscar, sorry. Fact of the matter is that I wanted to do one last check before finishing this favour for a friend. I didn't want to bother you, as I know you're up to your eyes right now. I was down here on another case, and just thought I'd ask Aurelia about this one while I was in.'

'And what was this last thing you were checking up on?' Filippi sounded sceptical now, like he wasn't going to be a pushover this time.

'Like I say, the vic was a friend of a friend. I can't go into details. He was worried about him for a while — worried he'd got into drugs, and worse. He asked me to find out if there was anything in his system. Aurelia has just confirmed to me that there was, so now I have to break it to him that his worst fears were true. It probably would have been better if he hadn't known, but there you are.'

Filippi blew the air out through his cheeks, like a baby in a pram, Scamarcio thought. 'OK, I get it. But can you leave this alone now? Nothing personal, but I don't like you treading on my toes. We're all watching our backs these days — cuts are in the offing.'

Scamarcio smiled. 'Understood. I'll get out of your hair.'

Filippi waved a hand away. 'Listen, this is not a huge case, and you've always seemed like a decent guy. I just don't need any extra hassle, that's all. Need to keep things sweet.'

Scamarcio took his hand, held it up, and grasped it in the Roman way. 'Got you. You won't see me again, I promise.'

He turned and threw a parting salute to Aurelia, who was now casting him a sideways look. 'I'll call you about the other thing.'

'Make sure you do,' she said.

'By the way', said Filippi. 'You speak to that creature upstairs? Did she give you anything?'

'No. She didn't know of any enemies, didn't know why anyone would want to kill him.'

'I see.' Once again, Filippi seemed unconvinced.

Scamarcio had settled into a café on Piazza d'Aracoeli, in need of some time out after the head-to-head at the morgue. He called Garramone.

'I've got a problem with Filippi.'

'Which is?'

'I was with the ME this morning, talking about Arthur, and he walked in and started throwing a fit about me cramping his style, taking his case.'

'Why does he care? It can't be a major deal, this one.'

'God knows, but he's antsy. Maybe he thinks someone's checking up on him — doesn't trust him to do his job.'

The chief fell silent for a moment. 'Let me think about it, while you stay away from him and follow up the other stuff — the other guy in the photo.'

'And I want to talk to our blackmailing colleagues. Can you get me their details?'

'Yeah, sure. I hope they give you more than they did me.'

'Perhaps they're covering for someone. Maybe they'll say more if it's just me, informal setting and all?'

The chief fell silent again. Scamarcio heard a pen tapping against a desk, a drawer being opened, the gentle beat of the clock on the office wall. He pictured the certificates beneath it, straightened out, all back to normal.

'Now I think of it, I'm not sure it's a good idea you leaving Rome.'

'You just said I needed to get out from under Filippi's feet?'

Garramone sighed, sounding like he was sinking beneath the weight of it all. 'One of the officers is up north now, in Milan; I think the other has gone home to Naples, but I'll check. I'll call you later with the info.'

He hung up, and Scamarcio observed the passers-by making their way across the piazza. This was the diplomatic district: an army truck stood idle at the corner, chugging exhaust fumes onto the pavement, while two soldiers in fatigues chatted inside. Opposite was the Syrian embassy — another one of Pino's friends. He tipped back his espresso, felt the anxiety build, figured the coffee wasn't helping. His mobile buzzed almost in step with his addled brain: it was an unknown number this time.

'Scamarcio.'

'It's Maria, from the other night.' It was a strange voice, affectedly feminine, but too low. 'From McDonalds in Testaccio. You asked me about Max.'

Scamarcio sat up straighter. 'Ah, of course. Sorry, I was somewhere else for a moment.'

'Figured me for an old girlfriend?'

He laughed. 'You know how it is.'

'Sure do.' It was sad the way she said it, as though she didn't.

'I'm glad you called. You remember anything?'

'Maybe. But I'd like to talk to you in person. You know the Riviera café in Trastevere — Via delle Luce? Could you meet me there in an hour?'

Via delle Luce was quiet. She'd chosen a place away from the lunchtime throng. It was shirtsleeves weather, and Scamarcio caught an early promise of summer in the warm currents on the breeze. In a month, the heat would be uncomfortable; in two, the city would no longer be habitable, and they'd all be counting the days until they could flee for the coast or their second homes in Umbria. But that wouldn't be his choice — he preferred to take his leave when no one else was around, when the angry shouts and self-pitying tears of stressed parents and spoiled children had finally left the beaches.

He tracked her approach: well-cut jeans, a diaphanous blouse, designer sunglasses. A young man stopped to look, and others in the café followed suit.

She tried a smile, displaying perfect teeth and a perfect jaw-line — maybe a too-perfect jaw-line?

'Detective.' They kissed on both cheeks in the formal manner, and she threw her bag onto the nearest chair.

He pulled out a seat for her, opposite. She sat carefully, fished out a packet of Camels and a lighter from the bag, lit up, and blew the smoke to her left, careful to avoid the table. He watched her for a while, trying to work something out; he wasn't quite sure what. Maybe how it all hung together, why it all worked — aesthetically, that is.

'So, how's your investigation going? Getting anywhere?'

He ignored the question. 'You want a coffee, something to eat?'

She waved a hand. 'No, I'm fine.' Then, 'Maybe just a mineral water: still.'

'Why did you want to see me?'

'Tell me what all this is about first.' He sensed an uncompromising glare behind the glasses.

'Can't do that.'

'This meeting seems a bit one-sided then.'

'We're worried about Max — that's all.'

She laughed. 'Yeah, right. You guys are always worrying about people like us.'

The sore point again. 'He's dead.'

'What?'

'He was murdered on Friday — stabbed to death in his flat in Trastevere.'

She stared into space for a long time, saying nothing. Then she took a long drag on the cigarette and didn't worry so much about the smoke this time. 'You're saying that someone cut him up.' She paused, letting it all sink in. 'In his place.'

'Looks that way.'

She placed one hand over the other, apparently studying a fingernail.

He willed her to remove the glasses. 'So what did you want to tell me?'

He noticed a slight tremor in her hand now. She was reaching for the Camels again, lining up a second before she'd finished the first.

'Listen, forget I called. It was a mistake.' She suddenly tossed the butt onto the ground, placed the new fag in her mouth, and reached for the bag. She was out of her seat before he had a chance to react. He leaped to his feet and grabbed her by the shoulder, more roughly than he'd intended. 'Given what I've just told you, surely it's even more important that you talk to me.' He felt the tremor in her shoulders, felt it spread out across her back. 'What's with you?'

She sank back into the seat as if all the strength had been sucked out of her. 'I don't know,' she said. 'I don't know.'

He called the waiter over, and ordered a large brandy and a mineral water.

'Listen, I'm not going to reveal your identity to anyone, believe me. That's not how it works.'

They both fell silent for several moments, and then the waiter was back with their drinks. He placed the brandy in front of Scamarcio, and the water by Maria; Scamarcio switched them as soon as he was gone. Maria took a sip, waited for a moment, then took another. She breathed out, leant back in the chair, and seemed to relax slightly. She took a long drag on the cigarette.

'I was made an offer a while ago — an offer to go into a new line of work. The money was good, but I didn't like the smell of it. I turned it down.'

'What kind of work?'

'No different from now, but with a special kind of clientele and in a nicer location. Everything would be managed by a handler; I'd just take my cut, but the cut would be good.'

'Rich clientele?'

'He didn't go into details — just said they'd be important, influential. He made a big deal out of the fact that only the top girls were selected and that confidentiality was essential.'

'Who was this guy? How did you meet him?'

'I'd seen him drive past a couple of times in a Mercedes. He was good looking. I'd taken him for a punter, but he never stopped. I got the feeling that he wanted to, but hadn't got it in him. Maybe he had a wife back home, kids, guilt complex — the usual.' She stopped, and took another sip of the brandy.

'Go on.'

'I was in the McDonalds one night, about a year ago now — that same McDonalds in Testaccio where you saw us on Saturday. I was in the queue, waiting for them to bring me my burger, when this guy jumps in front of me and I'm about to give him hell when he says he's paying for my meal, and would I like anything else. I see that it's the same guy, the guy with the Mercedes. He seems nice enough, so we sit down and start making small talk, and then he comes out with it — asks if I'd be interested in coming to work for this organisation he knows, explaining it the way I told you.'

'Then what?'

'I say, thanks, I'll think about it, I'll call him if I'm interested. But I never call — I don't know why. I guess it was cos I don't like to lose control, I want to be my own boss, and also cos I had a sixth sense that it could be something dodgy and bring me trouble, just when I'd got things straight with you guys.' She paused and took a long drag on the cigarette. 'A couple of months later, I needed money real bad and changed my mind. I decided to call him, but I realised that I'd lost his card — I couldn't find it anywhere. For a while I hoped he'd drive past again, but he didn't. In the end, I figured it was fate deciding for me. I'd lost his card because it wasn't meant to be.'

'And you have no idea who this man was?'

'None. But, like I say, he was a good-looking guy.'

'What kind of accent?'

'Roman, I think. But I'm not good on accents.'

'What did he look like?'

'Medium height, dark hair, blue eyes.'

'And you believe this could have something to do with Arthur, or Max as you knew him then?'

'I have no idea. I guess I just wondered if he'd found him, too, made him the offer and he'd accepted, if that's why he went — gone on to bigger and better things.' She looked to her left, to the street beyond: Trastevere was growing busy as lunchtime approached. A striking woman passed them: blonde, tall, Scandinavian maybe. Maria followed her for a while and then returned her gaze to Scamarcio, flicking her hair behind her shoulder. For a moment, he sensed insecurity there.

As if in response, the sun emerged from behind a cloud and

revealed the imperfections in her skin: there were small lines around the mouth, and the beginnings of worry lines above the nose.

'Max was good looking. He stood out, so I wondered if he'd also caught his eye. When someone makes you an offer like that, you don't tell the others; you keep it for yourself. When you came round the other day, I got to wondering — wondering whether that's what happened, whether he'd left to work for him. But Max wasn't a trans, so maybe there was no offer. Maybe I've got it wrong.'

Scamarcio watched the answers hover in front of him and then evaporate into nothing, dissolve into the May haze.

'And this guy told you no more about the work, about what would be required?'

'No, that was it — just that it was good money, a nice location, top-drawer clients.'

'Can you remember anything from the card? A name, an address even?'

She looked down, rubbed at a nail, chipping away at the varnish where it needed retouching. 'I'm sorry, it was a long time ago. There are so many names and faces, I can't remember them all.'

'Why were you so uptight before?'

She glanced up, and he saw himself reflected in the lenses of her glasses, leaning in, trying to make contact.

'Don't you hear the stories? Some of these rackets: once they get a hold of you, that's it. Maybe Max wanted out, and that's why they killed him. And here I am talking to you, and he's talked to me, and who knows … who knows where it could all end?'

11

SCAMARCIO DIDN'T KNOW what to make of his conversation with Maria. It could be nothing, or it could be everything. He thought of the unknown man who had given her his card, and the unknown man who had handed the photos to the officers. Who were they? Were they one and the same? He walked up Via Marmaggi and crossed into Via Fratte. He wasn't really sure where he was heading — he just enjoyed the coolness of the shadows, the damp smell of moss on stone. He realised that he was just two streets away from Arthur's building now, and he suddenly felt the need to walk past, to see the place again, although he didn't quite know why, didn't know what it would bring. He felt his pulse quicken, and noticed that his heart was beating so loudly that he could hear it: it was almost a pounding vibration in his ears. Finally recognising the throb of his mobile above the rhythm, he scrambled for it in his back pocket, almost dropping it into the road. He felt a stab of panic as Filippi's number flashed up. Was he spying on him? Had he seen him make the turn into Arthur's street?

Best to keep it casual. 'Oscar, listen. I'm sorry about before.'

'Don't sweat it. Thing is, this case is starting to get weird on me, and I need your help.'

'What are you talking about?'

'Where are you now?' Obstinate to the last.

He thought it best to avoid the truth, so decided to put himself a few streets back. 'I've just met a friend for lunch in Via delle Luce — your neck of the woods. Why?'

'Good, get down here to the station. I want to show you something.'

The Trastevere station was cool and half empty, but it still carried the usual male undertones of old sweat and cigarettes and something else — Scamarcio couldn't be sure what —fear perhaps, maybe from the guys, maybe from the perps. Filippi was at a desk by a window that overlooked a courtyard boasting a cluster of healthy palms and an orange tree. It was a nice view, better than Scamarcio's. If Filippi were to turn in his seat for a rest from his paperwork, he could enjoy his coffee looking out at that view. Scamarcio felt envious for a moment.

'OK, so what's all this about?'

Filippi looked up from his paperwork and motioned Scamarcio to the chair opposite.

'Strange thing, given how much you've been sniffing around.'

He opened one of his desk drawers to the right, and pulled out a plastic evidence bag. Scamarcio saw a single piece of paper inside.

'Take a look — it arrived an hour ago.'

Scamarcio took it from him, and turned it in the shaft of sunlight from the window. Only one side had been written on. The words were scratchy and hard to read, and the spelling looked off. 'If you are looking into the murrder of Arthur the rentboy you mite care to look again at the "suecide" of Geppo the bookie.' It ended there, with no date and no name.

'Where's the envelope?'

Filippi pulled out another evidence bag from the drawer with an envelope inside, and handed it over.

It wasn't addressed to anyone in particular — just the Trastevere station. It bore a Rome postmark and had been sent on Saturday, the day after Arthur's death. Scamarcio glanced up. Filippi was leaning back in his chair, a pencil stuffed behind his ear.

He looked like something out of a 1970s cop show. 'So what am I to make of that? You mind telling me what the fuck's going on?'

Scamarcio rearranged himself more comfortably, and tried to stay relaxed. 'Like I told you: I'm doing a favour for a friend, nothing more.'

'Which friend?'

'Can't say.'

'So why am I being told to investigate the suicide of some two-bit bookie?'

'No idea. How should I know?'

Filippi leant forward in his chair, rested his forearms on the desk, and studied him. 'OK, this is how I see it. It seems odd to me, to say the least, that you've been snooping around this thing — a case that's got fuck-all to do with you — and now I get sent this.' He leant back, and crossed his arms behind his head. 'Something doesn't add up, wouldn't you agree?'

Scamarcio rubbed at a knot in his neck, and eased an elbow onto the arm of his chair. 'What can I tell you? I'm as much in the dark as you are.'

He surveyed the untidy piles of paperwork covering Filippi's desk; it seemed like the guy had quite a backlog. 'You know anything about this Geppo, then?'

Filippi sighed, tired of it all already. 'Never heard of him. I need to ask around on the street, consult the low-life. Then, if that draws a blank, I'll be onto Vice, see if he's somewhere else in this cesspit of a city.'

Scamarcio fell silent. Nothing came to mind; it was all just a blank.

'But if you're holding out on me, Scamarcio, I'll make trouble for you. We're colleagues — it shouldn't work like this.'

Scamarcio came to, sensing it was time to cut it short. 'You have my word: I know nothing of any Geppo. But I can ask around, if you like. You want me to ask around?'

Filippi waved a hand, as though he already knew it would come to nothing. 'Ask around — ask that friend of yours. I don't need this extra shit right now.'

'Geppo the bookie? Is he some kind of major player?'

'I don't think so, but we'd need to check with Vice. They haven't heard of him down in Trastevere, anyway.'

'Well, that doesn't mean anything,' said the chief.

'I'm worried about Filippi. This case has his attention now.' Scamarcio was heading towards the centre, his tiredness bone-deep, even though the day was only halfway through.

'I told you I'll deal with it. In the meantime, you head up to Milan, and see what you can get out of Limoni.' He gave him the address for the young officers' parents, and then hung up.

Scamarcio let his head fall against the wheel. Suddenly, he wanted to stay put. The anxiety was growing steadily, like a tumour, taking root in his gut, pushing into his ribs, filling his lungs. Instinctively, he felt that leaving the city would be dangerous, that it would be too big a step into the unknown, would be severing some kind of umbilical attachment that was keeping him safe, for now.

He eased the car into Via Clementina, and found a space up on the curb opposite a goods entrance. He'd flash them his police badge if it got nasty. The doorway to the Palazzo was open, and he stepped into its marble lobby, glad of the cool and the opulence: the fresh lilies on the desk, the pencil drawings of Rome. He took the stairs, and tried to calm himself and steady his breathing, but felt the tension build with every tread.

He reached the first floor and pressed the buzzer. The glass door released almost immediately, and he saw that it was the pretty brunette on reception. 'The doctor's waiting for you — go on through,' she said. He was relieved. Better this, than too much time with the magazines, too much time to polish his story.

Doctor Salvai was at the window, the light catching her hair. She looked well — there was colour in her cheeks, and her blue eyes were alive.

'Detective Scamarcio, good to see you. Please take a seat.'

He slouched down into one of her huge leather armchairs, leant back, and considered the ceiling for a moment. She moved away from the window and came to sit opposite him.

'You look tired. Hard week?'

He moved his eyes from the ceiling and took her in. She was fifteen years his senior, but ever since their first meeting he'd spent many hours imagining them in a whole host of scenarios — none of them professional.

'Challenging case.'

Neither of them spoke for several moments, then eventually she said, 'Is there anything you want to share with me today?'

He hated the way she said it; he didn't like the way the onus was always on him. It didn't seem rigorous; in fact, seemed deeply lazy.

But he'd play along, like he always did. He might start with, 'Well, it seems that the prime minister is an old mate of my boss, so now we're secretly and illegally investigating the murder of an Argentine rentboy who'd been blowing off the foreign secretary, and, to be honest, the whole thing is getting heavy.' But instead he said, 'Nothing much — the usual, really.'

'Talk me through it. It doesn't matter if I've heard some of it before.'

He wanted to roll his eyes, but instead he sank back in the chair, opened his legs, and fixed eye contact. He allowed the impure thoughts to flip around in his mind, knowing that she knew what he was thinking and that it pleased her.

'Piocosta came and found me at the bar where I have breakfast. It looks like it's moved on from simple courtship to an all-out declaration of love.'

She snorted softly. 'What's on the table?'

'Two million.'

'One-off payment?'

'Yearly.'

She whistled quietly. 'Not bad.' Then: 'Why can't he let it go, do you think?'

He sighed, pulling a half-frown: 'I'm too useful, I guess, plus he's got some strange guilt-thing going on, some warped sense of duty to my father — he feels like he needs to offer me the kind of lifestyle the old man would have provided.' He looked away from her, taking his gaze to the window. 'Those old fuckers are strange — they live in their own tiny worlds.'

'You're romanticising it. You're a useful asset, that's all.'

She was tilting her head to one side now. He wanted to fuck her there and then — didn't care who might walk in.

'What did you tell him?'

He shook his head, tired. 'I told him I was very flattered, that it was good of him to think of me and all that, but I've set my course and I intend to keep to it.'

'Did he buy it?'

He sighed, rested his head against the back of the chair, and studied the ceiling once more. Hell, he wasn't even sure if *he* bought it. Was he using them, or was it the other way around? Should he and could he just cut them off, once and for all? And where would it leave him if he did?

'He just smiled at me like I was some hopeless kid. He said I'd change my mind soon enough, and that he'd be there when I did.'

'Could he be right?'

He returned his gaze to her. He wanted to punch her, kiss her, push her down onto her plush white rug. 'How the hell do I know? I can't see into the future.' Then, calming slightly, 'No, he's not right. Of course he's not right.'

She inclined her head the other way, looking at him oddly.

'What? What's the matter?' He threw up his hands. 'I thought the point of all this is that I'm honest.'

'Honest with yourself, Leo.'

He did roll his eyes this time. 'What's going into today's report then? Am I finally moving over to the dark side, proving all the naysayers right?' He pushed the air out of his cheeks. 'I can't win, can I?'

'Yes, you can.'

He ignored her. 'I'm doing good, really good. Everything's on track.' He stopped, and examined his shoes. They were a mess — scuffed and dirty, and a lace was hanging loose. He felt like an actor in a play, delivering lines that weren't his own. Lately, he'd been wondering whether he was living a life that wasn't his, wasn't what destiny had carved out for him: something in his DNA was out of kilter, made him feel like an imposter.

He looked up again, and saw that she was smiling at him now. 'I think you need to change breakfast bars,' she said.

He had planned to leave it ten minutes longer, get some of the useful talk out the way, but he could feel the heat rushing through him, up from his loins, along his gut, into his chest wall. He couldn't get a hold of it now — it was too late. He rose carefully from his chair, and she followed him with her gaze, eyes questioning. He came to a stop behind her chair, paused a moment, and then bent low to kiss her neck, the line of her hair, her shoulder blades, and then he slowly pushed his hand beneath her blouse. She moaned, eased her head back against his stomach, reached behind her, and dug her nails into his forearms. Their session would end as it always did — just somewhat earlier than normal.

12

He picks up the framed photo of Elisabetta, studies it, and inclines his head to one side.

'Your wife is very pretty.'

'Who said she's my wife?'

He frowns at him, disappointed, like he's hurt his feelings. 'Pino, my Pino. Why so defensive?'

He looks away, unable to keep eye contact anymore.

'Been married long?' A beat, then: 'I hear you have two daughters now.'

He can no longer bear to remain seated. He gets out from behind the desk, and stands behind the chair, using it as some kind of shield.

'What do you want?'

He grimaces at the coarseness of the question, and shakes his head a little. Then, after a while, he says, 'Just what you can give us, Pino — no more than that.'

THE FLAT WAS COLD and silent when Scamarcio walked in. He didn't like being there in the middle of the day: the light was too raw, showed up all the dust, made the place feel emptier. Once inside, he no longer knew where he wanted to be, where was right. He went into the bedroom and threw a few things into a bag, deciding that he might as well push north, grab a hotel, go visit Garramone's shamed officer, and be back in Rome by the evening. He knew now that he wanted rid of this case — wanted out as soon as possible. He told himself he'd get it done and dusted in a week, all sealed up for the chief and his famous friend, and then he'd take a rest and move onto something calmer. This whole thing was testing him, making him antsy and on edge. He didn't know where the lines were anymore, and he wanted out before they blurred any further.

After the session with his therapist, he slept most of the journey north, and was only awoken when the train screeched painfully as it slowed to enter the outer suburbs of Italy's second city. Milan: a spasming, wheezing monument to the true cost of the post-war economic miracle — row after row of soulless concrete blocks, their ugliness so profound that he wondered how bad it must have been for the millions of immigrants to abandon their beloved south for this. He knew the answer, of course — it was either the industrial cities of the north, or starvation. But when he looked around him, and registered the complete absence of any point of beauty, any connection with the past, he wondered whether he would have preferred to starve, would have preferred to eke out what little he could from the land, rather than have his soul crushed so completely and his spirit sucked away. He had never been able to comprehend how people could make a life here, could settle for this monochrome existence. He had travelled a bit, seen the world, and to his mind there were only two places worse than the suburbs of Milan: one was Bratislava, and the other was Glasgow's East End.

Giacomo Limoni's parents had an apartment in a salmon-pink block on Via Binda as it entered Barona — perhaps Milan's ugliest suburb, although the competition was fierce. It was done up in the usual suffocating style, untouched since the 1950s. Heavy wooden bookshelves crammed the walls, and garish, gilded pictures of the Baby Jesus filled the spaces in between. The stench of cooked cabbage hung in the air; ribollita for lunch. He didn't want to stay and eat, hoped they wouldn't ask.

Limoni was despondent, crushed into a beaten-leather

armchair, humbled in tracksuit trousers and a faded ITALIA sweatshirt. The shame and disappointment was tangible — so much hope, so much time and money invested in our boy, and look where it had ended? Scamarcio didn't want to talk here; didn't want the eyes of the squat mother and sickly father upon them. When he suggested they go for a coffee, Limoni shrugged, seemed resigned, and followed like a sheep. The mother said something about lunch, but neither of them responded.

'So, how's it going? Good to be back with the folks?'

Limoni stirred the bottom of his espresso, added another bag of sugar, and slouched in his chair. 'All this is so much shit. I shouldn't be here.'

He was 25, but could have passed for 18. He had a good face, the usual Mediterranean look: strong features and a respectable jaw. Scamarcio figured that he probably didn't have too much trouble finding girls.

'Why don't you tell me what happened?'

He could see Limoni surveying the street beyond the window: the cars backed up at the lights; the Chinese hurrying about their deliveries, tiny children in tow; a couple of Romanians leaning against a wall, undressing passing girls with their eyes. Limoni shook his head, obviously reliving a bad memory.

'It was Rossi. It was his idea from the start. I was never keen, tried to argue him out of it, but he wouldn't listen, didn't want to know ...' He tailed off, turned to face Scamarcio, threw open his palms. '... and now look what's happened.'

'Talk me through it from the beginning.'

Limoni downed his coffee, stretched out his long legs beneath the table, and took a breath. 'We were on the final stretch of our beat before returning to the station — Via Marche before it turns into Via Boncompagni. Suddenly, this guy comes up to us. He's wearing sunglasses, although by now it's nearly seven. He hands me this envelope and says, "I think you'd better take a look at this."

Then he turns and walks away, just like that, as if it was nothing.'

'Did you notice anything about him — hair colour, height?'

'No idea about the hair, cos he was wearing a baseball cap. But he was small, about Rossi's height, in a long, dark coat.'

'Then what?'

'We opened the envelope there and then — we wanted to see what was inside.' He shook his head again, as if wrestling with the memory. 'We couldn't believe it. We couldn't believe what we were seeing.'

'I know, I've seen the pictures.'

'I say to Rossi that we should show them to someone, maybe our chief, and get advice on what to do. He starts shouting, tells me I'm an idiot, and don't I realise we've just been presented with a once-in-a-lifetime opportunity. He says I'd have to be crazy to pass up a chance like this.'

'And what did you say?'

'At first I didn't get what he was on about, but then I twigged and I wasn't comfortable. I wasn't comfortable at all. But he was on a mission: he wouldn't let anything stand in his way. To be honest, he was starting to scare me. I had the feeling that if I went to the chief, he'd come after me.'

'So what happened next?'

'He comes up with a plan — tells me how we're going to get hold of Ganza and how we'll bleed him dry. In the end, he organised the whole thing, found a way to reach him, arranged a drop-off for the money.' He breathed out slowly, fiddling with the edge of the discarded sugar sachet. 'Then someone blew the whistle, and the next thing I know, I'm suspended.' He studied his reflection on the tabletop, his shoulders sagging a little.

'You tell all this to my chief?'

'Yeah.' He looked up. 'He called our boss at the precinct and gave him some cock-and-bull story, chose not to tell him what really went down — definitely better for me that way. It was real good of him; I'm forever in his debt for that.' He stopped. 'I don't know how Garramone found out. Do you?'

'No idea.'

'I don't understand what's going on — when I'm going back, if I'm going back.'

Scamarcio said nothing.

'Did Garramone say anything to you?'

Scamarcio chose not to answer.

The boy sighed. 'Why did he send you anyway?'

Scamarcio thought he read something like hope in the boys' eyes, and decided to milk it for what he could. 'He wanted to make sure he'd got it straight. I think he's weighing up the options, trying to decide how best to proceed.'

Limoni leaned forward and tried to meet his eye. 'Listen, we don't know each other, but if there's anything you can do to help, I'd really appreciate it. This job is everything to me, everything to my folks. I can't put them through this — not after everything they've done for me.'

Scamarcio gently patted his arm across the table. 'I understand,' he said. On a theoretical level, he did, but that was as far as it went, because his own father had never been someone he had wanted to impress. Lucio Scamarcio had been guided by a different compass, had traversed a darker, simpler world — a world of backhanders, intimidation, and torture, a world from which his son was still trying to break free.

He ran a tired hand through his hair, kneaded the knot in his neck once more. 'Listen, I'll try my best, because I can see you're a good kid. But, in return, I will need something from you.'

Limoni was still leaning forward, still locked in. 'Anything — you name it.'

'I need you to think back. I need you to remember every detail, every conversation. Are you sure of the way it went? Are you certain, for example, that you'd never seen that man before, or that Rossi had never seen him before?'

Limoni looked down, focussed on an unknown point between floor and wall. He was thinking hard, searching for any scrap to throw him. Scamarcio scanned the street: a Chinese man had pulled up at the kerb in a battered Fiat 500, and had started unloading boxes. From a child's seat in the back, a little girl with pink cheeks, laughing eyes, and hair scraped up in untidy bunches followed his every move.

'There is something.'

Scamarcio lifted his gaze from the road, considering the boy facing him.

'I don't know if it's anything — maybe just a hunch — but one night when we were on late and no one else was around, I heard Rossi in the locker room talking on his mobile, talking quietly like he didn't want anyone to hear. He was saying something about the photos, but I thought that it couldn't be Ganza he was talking to, because the conversation was too friendly, too light. And then I had this strange feeling that he was talking to the man, the man who had given us the pictures — that maybe it was all part of some bigger plan.'

He stopped and frowned. 'I don't know why I thought that, but I did. I asked him about it later, but he told me I was deluded, that he'd never seen that man before in his life. The way he was looking at me scared me, so I just left it. I never mentioned it again.'

13

It is the night of the victory party. They have hired out the top floor of
the Principe di Savoia, and ordered in twenty crates of Veuve. His closest
friends are there, and his mother has been brought from her home in
Lecco. He watches her, holding court in a corner, stroking her hair flat in
the same way she has always done: still refusing to admit she has aged,
that the best of life is behind her. His youngest daughter is asleep in her
lap, cheeks flushed, tiny arms outstretched. He sees his wife working the
room — a smile here, a laugh there, making sure everyone is comfortable.
This is meant to be the happiest night of his life, the pinnacle of all his
achievements. But then he sees him, standing alone in the doorway,
waving like an old friend just back from the war.

'We go back a long time, old friends from Gela', he hears him tell the
bodyguards. He freezes for a moment and feels the room freeze with him
before he collects himself and returns the wave, a heaviness in his heart,
a blackness in his soul. Then the visitor is inside the room, smiling at his
guests, helping himself to his champagne, heading towards him.

'Just wanted to pass on my congratulations, Pino.' He holds out a
hand, and he reluctantly takes it.

'Thank you.'

'I can't stay long — just passing through.'

'Of course.'

'So now you've really made it.' He laughs, raises his glass to him, and
downs the drink.

'Maybe.'

'You were always a modest guy: Prime Minister Pino. It doesn't get
much bigger than that.'

He takes another drink from a passing tray, and scans the room like a bird of prey. 'Those your daughters? How lovely.'

Pino feels an icy claw in his stomach.

'Like I say, I just wanted to pay my respects and let you know that we'll be following your success closely. There's nothing you can do that will escape our attention.' He drains his drink, hands him the glass, and then leaves.

THE SLOPES OF TUSCANY rolled away from him into the darkness. The sky was ripe with stars, and every so often they'd pass a cluster of houses, ghosts of smoke frozen in the air, illuminated crosses punching through the blackness. In two hours he'd be in Naples — back in the south, almost home, whatever that was.

Scamarcio slept. When he woke, the lights of the bay were coming into view, fragile and expectant, reaching out across the water. He couldn't decide whether to visit Rossi tonight or leave it until the morning. Somehow he wanted the answers now; he wanted to understand what he was dealing with. He headed for the taxi stand, running to beat the rush. The remnants of the day still clung to the air, dense and heavy: the heat had already arrived in Naples.

The driver edged the car out into a sea of traffic, but there was nowhere for them to go, no option of a left- or right-hand turn. Scamarcio tasted the pollution in the back of his throat, felt it hit his lungs. He wound up the window, watched the meter ticking over, saw the driver observing him in the mirror. He had switched on the radio: Juventus had just lost to Fiorentina. Again. He turned the problem over in his mind: if Rossi knew the man with the photos, why hadn't they done this in secret? Why pull in Limoni? What purpose did it serve?

The car lurched forward and a horn blared. The taxi driver cursed, wound down his window, and made the Cornuto — Scamarcio wasn't sure for whose benefit. They were moving now, edging along Via Cavour. Soon they would turn right for the dismal suburbs of Secondigliano. He watched as the liberty architecture of the centre gave way to the shabby palazzos of the Spanish Quarter.

Faded washing was strung across foetid alleyways, while kids with the faces of medieval urchins sucked on Luckies or tore up the neighbourhood on stolen motorbikes. Outside a Halal store, a couple of guys in Shalwar Kameez were drinking tea and playing backgammon. He caught a blast of Arabic music — sad and otherworldly, conjuring up the darkness of lost centuries.

The driver drew the car to a halt outside a brown block. It had that shiny bath-tile effect which made it look cleaner, less run-down than all the rest. There were well-kept flower boxes on the balconies, and decent-looking cars on the street — a couple of BMWs, and a Mercedes. A woman passed: tough face, lots of gold. He smelt Camorra; knew it when he saw it.

He paid the driver and scanned the entry panel, looking for Rossi. He found the name on the fifth floor. The front door was ajar, so he decided not to buzz the flat and alert them to his arrival. The elevator was gold panelled, with mirrors to the ceiling, marble on the floor, and none of the external doors to bother with. The journey to the fifth floor was cool and smooth, like in a luxury hotel. He stepped out, and nodded to an old couple who wanted to come in; they were smart, and well kept, and the gent tipped his hat in the old style. Number 54 was off to the right. There was an umbrella stand outside, and a tidy welcome mat. He rang the bell, and imagined the layout: a generous living room with a view onto the street, windows to the floor, flower boxes granting some privacy. He strained to hear better, but it seemed that nothing was stirring inside. He rang the bell again, stood back from the door, and scanned the corridor: still nothing. He knocked this time. 'It's Detective Scamarcio from Rome. I'm looking for Stefano Rossi.' Silence. Then he heard footsteps away to his right, and the scraping of a door. An old man blinked out at him from the neighbouring apartment, his tiny clam-like eyes exposed beneath bottle-end glasses.

'They've gone.'

'Gone?'

'Cleared out at four this morning. Made one hell of a racket.'

'Any idea where they were heading?'

'Well, they weren't off on holiday.'

They both fell quiet for a moment.

'You know them well?'

'Did my best to avoid them. '

'Why?'

The old man scanned the corridor furtively, looking like a weasel that wanted to scuttle back to his burrow. 'Who's asking?'

Scamarcio pulled out his badge. The old man wetted his lips, and pushed his glasses higher up his nose. 'Clan.' It was almost a whisper.

'You sure?'

'Fifty years in this city, and you know the signs.'

The old man scanned the corridor again, stepped back into his hallway, and slammed the door.

14

He opens the envelope. It is the last of today's pile. Early-morning sunlight spills onto the table, catching the cup of roses and the edges of an apple. He sees a still life.

He pulls out a photograph and turns it over. He feels the brioche he has just eaten force its way from his stomach and push back up along his throat.

It's a photo of a naked woman from a hard-core porn magazine, but they've done something with a computer — put the face of his teenage daughter above the neck.

'What is it, Pino? You look like you've seen a ghost,' says his wife.
He rises from his seat, almost kicking the chair away. 'It's nothing, sweetheart: just problems at work.' He kisses her and heads outside, where he knows his car and driver are waiting.

TERMINI WAS A SEETHING mass of people, stale and sweating in the early-summer heat. As Scamarcio picked his way through the crowd, soft currents of cigarette smoke stirred his deprived senses back to life. He spied a tobacconist at the end of the platform, and took it as some kind of portent — a sign that it was meant to be. He could try to give up the weed, deny himself an escape, but surely he could permit himself the pleasure of an uncomplicated smoke? He lined up his change, anticipating the buzz of the nicotine kick, and cast his eye over the towering pile of newspapers. Then he stopped, just stood there, frozen in time. Everything around him ground to a halt, and he felt the world cease to breathe.

The front page of *Il Giornale* showed a picture of Ganza with his wife and kids. The headline read:

FOREIGN SECRETARY IN RENTBOY SEX SHOCK

Graphic photos showing Foreign Secretary and father of three Giorgio Ganza in a drink and drug-fuelled orgy with two male prostitutes have come to light.

The photos, many of which are too shocking to print, show Ganza in various stages of undress as he frolics with the two prostitutes in a Tuscan villa. Ganza, who has always played up his family-man credentials for political gain, fled Rome several days ago. It is understood that he is hiding out at a secret retreat, near Florence. His wife and children have also left the capital and were unavailable for comment.

Scamarcio flipped through the paper, and found the least shocking of the photos on pages two, three, and four. He saw Arthur's young face in two of them, and scanned the article looking for any mention of his name and the killing at his apartment. There was none. How long, though, before they made that connection — before Filippi made the connection, and all hell broke loose? Filippi did not yet know what Arthur looked like, and the corpse was too damaged. But the desk sergeant would remember, and would waste no time in telling him. No doubt, a call would soon follow, asking Scamarcio to pay another visit to the precinct. If not Filippi, then Maria and the girls at Testaccio would hear soon enough, and would put two and two together. His mobile buzzed. It was starting already: all hell breaking loose around him.

It was Garramone. 'Seen the papers?'

'I'm looking at *Il Giornale* now. How did that happen?'

'The editors changed their minds — decided it was too good to sit on. Who can blame them?'

'But there's nothing about Arthur.'

'Not yet, but I'm not sure for how much longer.'

'What does your friend say?'

'He's furious. Says it's a breach of trust, that there'll be hell to pay.'

'What are we to do?'

'He thinks we should cool it for a while — keep our heads down while the storm blows over. Then see where it leaves us.'

'And you? What do you think?'

'It all depends on Filippi: if he makes the link to Arthur, the game is up. Then there are those hookers you spoke to down in Testaccio. Not to mention the friend upstairs in Trastevere — she's bound to speak to Filippi.'

'It's getting to be a long list.'

'Maybe you should pay the friend a visit, and cut her off before she can get to him.'

'Yeah, and what do I do about the desk sergeant at Trastevere? How do I persuade him to keep his mouth shut?' This thing was running away from them now; any possible control slipping through their fingers.

'Forget about the desk sergeant. Think about the friend.'

'That won't work. If Filippi decides to dig some more, which he will, he'll be back. And if I've been hanging around the friend, it won't look right.'

Garramone fell quiet. 'Our priority is to find the other guy in the photo. If someone is taking out these people for Ganza, he could be next.'

'But wouldn't that be a dangerous strategy, now that the story is out?'

'Whatever. We need to establish his identity.'

'And Ganza hasn't given your friend the prime minister anything?'

'For God's sake, Scamarcio, don't speak so loosely.'

They both fell silent a moment before the chief eventually said, 'Nothing. Ganza says he doesn't remember the guy. He says that photo was taken the first time they'd met, and he never saw him again.'

'None of the hookers down in Testaccio knew him either.'

'There must be others you could ask.'

'That means going back to Vice. I don't think that's wise — not with this all over the papers.'

He heard a radio in the background of wherever Garramone was calling from. An old song by Mina was playing. The chief exhaled like a man who knows his time is up. 'What happened up north? The boy give you anything?'

'He thinks Rossi might have known the man who handed them the photos — that they might have been in it together. But when I went down to Naples, his family had done a runner — at four in the morning, according to one of the neighbours. He has them for Camorra, by the way.'

'That right?' He could hear the chief sinking back in his chair. Scamarcio imagined him gazing into the middle distance, no longer sure where to take this thing. Eventually, Garramone said, 'See what you can get on the second guy in the picture. Then I think you need to leave town for a bit while we calm things down. I'll find you another case — move you off somewhere while it blows over.' He paused. 'If it blows over.'

15

THE NEXT CALL was from Aurelia D'Amato. 'Come to the morgue as soon as possible,' was all she said. Scamarcio sensed an uneasiness stirring in his chest, creeping out along his nerve endings.

She was sitting at a table out back, finishing some paperwork. He felt momentarily glad to see her like this, spared awhile from all the blood and body fluids. When she saw him walk in, she laid down her pen and scratched at the loose hair behind her neck. She was framed in a thin splinter of sunlight, and as he drew closer he saw a series of fine horizontal lines across her forehead, and the beginnings of crows' feet around her eyes. But she was still beautiful.

'Take a seat,' she said, as if he had come for a job interview. There was something in her eyes that he didn't like — a mixture of fear and something else.

He perched on a battered plastic chair, not sure that it would take his weight.

'So?'

From under her papers, she produced the morning newspaper and pushed it towards him across the desk. 'You seen this?'

'Yes,' he said, not bothering to pick it up.

'This have anything to do with Filippi's rentboy?'

His insides tightened slightly. 'Why do you think that?'

'Just a hunch.' She locked eye contact, uncompromising.

He stared back. 'A hunch?'

She looked away, seeming suddenly disgusted. 'I would have

expected you to show a little more remorse, to be honest.'

'Remorse? What have I got to be remorseful about?'

'You're a cold bastard, Scamarcio.' She was shaking her head now, her arms barred across her chest.

Slowly, he felt the hairs shift along his spine. He had no idea where this was going, but had a sense they were heading some place he didn't want to be. 'I don't understand what I've done, Aurelia. I just asked you for an opinion on a corpse. I know it was Filippi's case, but it's not the end of the world.'

'Maybe not for you, but it's hardly looking good for Filippi, is it?'

'What?'

She studied him. This time, it was her turn to be confused. 'Haven't you heard?'

'Heard what?'

'Filippi's been shot. Two .22s through the chest, drive-by on Via Pelliccia, 8.00am today.' She sighed. 'Right now, he's in a coma. You'll find him at the Borghese, if you can spare the time to visit.'

16

SLEEP ELUDED HIM. He had tried so many times to cross that boundary to a place where his thoughts no longer connected, to feel his body become heavy before floating away into weightlessness. Finally, he gave up, walked to the moonlight at the window, and stared out at the rooftops across the city, the tiny lights of a thousand apartments blinking in the distance. Far away, a horn sounded, and then, as if following some kind of hidden sequence, the rhythmic thud from a nearby bar ceased and young laugher spilled out across the alleyway.

He had told Garramone about Filippi — had told him that the detective had received the anonymous letter, and was now alerted to the case. And now Filippi was in a coma. What kind of mechanism was in play here? Why had the PM called Garramone? What did he want from him? If he was running a cover-up for his errant ministers, why get the police involved? And where did it leave him, Leone Scamarcio, already tainted by an inconvenient past, already less than clean?

He went to the kitchen, poured himself a whisky, returned to the lounge, and switched on the TV. He selected Sky News 24, hoping to lose himself in someone else's miseries, and reclaim some kind of perspective. It was a blonde newsreader, with the same look as all the rest: cheekbones too high, eyes too sharp. Why couldn't anyone look like themselves anymore? They were running pictures of Andrea Spezzi, as a teenager and a young man. Spezzi was the 34-year-old heir to the eponymous construction empire. He had never held down a proper job, had lived in New

York for a while, and had dabbled in the film business as a producer without ever attaching his name to anything of note. He'd hit the headlines a couple of years back when he'd been taken to hospital after overdosing on cocaine during a night spent with a male prostitute in Milan. *Another one*, thought Scamarcio. *It's all the rage now.* The tracker under the picture said, 'Attempted suicide.'

Scamarcio turned up the sound. Spezzi had been taken to Tiberina hospital after slashing his wrists, the reporter said. No one understood why: he had everything, no money worries, a new French girlfriend of six months, an apartment he had just bought in Paris, where he intended to settle. It was all a complete shock to the family, etc etc. *Money doesn't buy you everything*, thought Scamarcio. Well, his own mother had borne testimony to that.

He cradled the whisky, surveying the pelt of hair on his stomach, the dense muscles above his knees, and the toenails that needed a clipping. He was slowly aware of a thought forming, thick and troubling like the first smoke from a house fire: Spezzi had been into the rentboy scene — was known for it. Then the Ganza story breaks, and a few hours later he tries to kill himself. Could there be a connection between the two episodes, past and present? Or was Scamarcio finally losing his grip, seeing patterns where there were none?

17

Scamarcio walked up the ramp to the main entrance of the hospital on Isola Tiberina. There were a cluster of reporters milling around in the gardens; a young woman was delivering a piece to camera. He saw a unit of local police arrive, and unload a rope and poles from the back of their van — erecting a cordon, no doubt, to keep the press at bay.

He flashed his badge at the girl on the desk. 'I'm here for Spezzi.'

She looked around to check that no one was listening: 'Third floor, last room on the right as you leave the elevator.'

He thanked her and followed the signs to the lifts. Despite the press outside, it was strangely quiet in the corridors, as if all the action was to be found up on the third floor.

He entered the elevator, relieved to see there was no one else inside. He wondered what state he'd find him in, whether he'd be up to conversation.

After less than a minute, the doors opened and he caught an early glimpse of a knot of good-looking women in black hovering outside Spezzi's room. The nearest one had a BlackBerry clamped to her ear. She looked up as he approached and then raised a palm to stop him. He flashed his badge again. She cut short the call, and lowered the BlackBerry.

'He's not to have visitors.'

'Whose orders? Yours or the doctor's?'

'What do you want?'

'We were hoping he could help us with an inquiry.'

'What, right now? After what's just happened?'

'Especially after what's just happened.'

She sighed, stepped towards the door, and knocked tentatively, her ear against the wood so she could hear the great man's response. After a moment, she entered, slamming the door firmly behind her so he couldn't catch a glimpse inside. The remaining two assistants eyed him coldly. Spezzi had an impressive harem.

She was back after a few moments, her precarious heels clicking across the tiles. 'He doesn't want to see you,' she said with a note of triumph.

'He doesn't have a choice.'

She sighed again, rolled her eyes, and spun dramatically on her heels. He watched the muscles slide in her calves as she pushed the door open. A low murmur of voices came from inside, and then the door opened again: 'A few minutes only — he's very tired.'

The room was wide, carved up by sunlight. Dust motes danced above Spezzi's head like a thousand tiny angels come to claim him. Spezzi was low down in the bed, his head resting on a single pillow. He was deathly pale, his eyes red and swollen. His curly brown hair was standing up in tight tufts, making him look like an aged cherub. His gaze remained fixed on the window and its view of the Fabricio Bridge: pedestrians and cyclists, nuns and businessmen, gulls screeching as they dive-bombed for fish.

'Valentina, please give us a moment.'

She threw Scamarcio a look, tapping at her watch face with a finger. Spezzi remained motionless, keeping up his surveillance of the bridge.

'What do you want?' His voice was cracked and reedy, as though he needed water.

'I'm here about a young man called Arthur — got into a spot of bother with the foreign secretary.' He pulled the newspaper article from his jacket pocket, and placed it gently on the bed. Spezzi didn't move.

'Why now?' His hand was shaking where it rested on the blanket. He transferred it beneath the sheets, but Scamarcio could still see it moving.

'Seemed like a good time.'

For several minutes, neither man spoke. Eventually a siren cut through the silence as an ambulance pulled up at the gates below.

Spezzi's head turned slowly. His lips were parched and dry; the skin around his mouth, flaking. He closed his eyes for a moment and then opened them again. Scamarcio saw moisture there. He felt a fleeting pang of guilt. He shouldn't be bothering this troubled man on a whim. Suddenly, it felt like a bad idea.

The words came slowly and heavily, seeming to require a superhuman effort: 'You are young, like me. So leave it alone.' He was short of breath, like an asthmatic, or perhaps because he had lost a lot of blood. The last words were almost a whisper: 'Leave it alone, because it isn't worth it. Not in the end.' He sank deeper into the pillow, and his eyes closed again.

18

SPEZZI'S WORDS PLAYED in his mind over and over: they had suggested the presence of something bigger, bigger than the both of them. Was it big enough to make someone try to take his own life? Scamarcio felt the anxiety return, felt it twist and flip in his gut. He couldn't stay still — he needed to move, to press on. He clearly wasn't going to glean any more from Spezzi in his current state, so he decided to pay Filippi a visit up at the Borghese. It was to be a day of hospitals.

When he arrived, he found a couple of fellow officers outside Filippi's room, their faces sombre.

'Any change?' he asked.

'No, nothing. The doctors don't know when he'll wake up — if he'll wake up.'

'Can I go in?'

'Sure.'

Through the porthole of the door he caught a first glimpse of Filippi surrounded by complicated-looking machines and wires of every colour. His chest was moving up and down in strange, automatic movements, and his face was ashen. Scamarcio pushed the door and stepped inside. The room smelt of surgical cleansers, warm plastic, and human waste.

Scamarcio walked closer to the bed and looked down at his colleague. His chest was heavily bandaged, and there was strange bruising on his arms. Another spike of guilt: if he hadn't complained about Filippi to Garramone, the chances were that Filippi would be safe and well now, back home with his wife and kids. Had the PM had him taken out? And why? Or was there another, simpler explanation? Was there a small chance that this didn't have anything to do with the investigation into Arthur? That it was tied in to another of his cases? Filippi worked a difficult beat — that was well known. He dealt with drug dealers, Mafiosi, and pimps on a daily basis. The chances were good that this might be about another matter entirely, which didn't involve Scamarcio. This was something he needed to know if he was to have any peace with this case, if he wasn't going to be constantly watching his back.

He heard the door swing open behind him, and turned to see one of the officers enter the room. He stepped up to the bed, and stood at his shoulder.

'Any theories about this one?' asked Scamarcio.

The officer nodded slowly. 'Word is that it was the Calabroni boys. Trastevere has been working on an undercover op to sew them up for supplying heroin to dealers in Magliana and Testaccio. We've recently taken in a low-level operative who's started to squeal, so it looked like convictions were in the offing. Filippi was heading it all up: it was a big deal for him, a career-maker. We reckon this is our warning from the Calabroni to let it drop, to ignore the squealer.'

Scamarcio exhaled slowly, relief flooding in. This would make sense. It would also explain why Filippi had been so edgy these past few days. He prayed that this was the truth of it — that the Calabroni clan was more than a convenient cover.

'You guys ever hear of anyone called Geppo the bookie?'

The officer frowned, and shook his head. 'Doesn't ring a bell. Is he from Trastevere?'

'Not sure. He's dead — he was taken out recently, but I have no idea where he operated. Right now, I need to speak to his associates. It ties up with a case I'm on.'

The officer pulled a mobile from his pocket, and scrolled

through his contacts. Eventually, he found what he was looking for.

'Take a note,' he said, as he reeled off a telephone number. 'The name's Jacopo Brambilla in Gaming Enforcement. Tell him Marco Leto gave you his details. He should be able to help you — he runs all the grasses, so he'll get you to Geppo's guys.'

Scamarcio entered the number in his phone. 'Thanks — I appreciate it.'

'How do you know Oscar? I haven't seen you down in Trastevere.'

'No, I'm with the Squadra Mobile, but our paths have crossed a few times. He's a good bloke, and I just wanted to pay my respects, you know.'

The officer nodded. 'If you leave me your card, I'll be sure to let you know if there are any developments.'

Scamarcio patted his pockets. 'As it happens, I'm fresh out. But if he wakes up, tell him that Leone called to wish him well.'

The officer seemed surprised, but nodded again: 'Of course.'

19

SCAMARCIO EXITED THE BORGHESE and found a bench under a battered palm tree in the hospital gardens. He dialled the number for Brambilla.

'Brambilla — make it quick.' The man barked rather than spoke.

'Brambilla, Detective Scamarcio. I was given your details by Leone from Trastevere. I was hoping you might be able to help me with a case, but if you're busy I can call back.'

Brambillas's tone softened. 'No, don't worry. I thought you were the wife, that's all. Awful business that, down at Trastevere. How's the poor guy doing?'

'He's not looking great — still in a coma. They don't seem to know when he'll wake up.'

Brambilla whistled softly down the line. 'The Calabroni have no qualms now. These younger boys are worse than their fathers. Where's the respect?'

Scamarcio sighed. 'They're competing with Russia. I guess the game has got a whole lot dirtier.'

'You can say that again.' Brambilla paused for a moment. 'Scamarcio? Don't I know you from somewhere?' Then, after a beat, 'You're that Flying Squad guy who was in the papers last year!'

Scamarcio felt the familiar tightening in his temples. He had hoped that the whole thing was dead and buried, that people's interest had shifted elsewhere. Evidently not. However much time had passed, he was still the son of the Mafioso, the trafficker of traffickers who had pumped cocaine across Europe, had ordered the murders of state officials, and had met his own bloody end at the hands of a traitor from within his own *locale*. Yet again, the images spooled shakily through his mind like the frames of a deteriorated cine reel: that stifling summer day; the sweet, coppery stench of blood; the whites of his fathers' eyes looking up to the sky, as if preparing to finally meet his maker; his mother's sickening cries, her vomit sprayed across the step. He dragged himself back to the present in much the same way as he forced himself awake from the recurring nightmares.

'Guilty as charged.'

Brambilla laughed. 'Hey, man, don't feel bad. I think it's great you've made a go of things and got out from the shit, when thousands fail. You're a shining example of what this beautiful country might one day become!' Despite the eulogy, the man seemed genuine, and Scamarcio found himself warming to him.

'That's good to hear.' He paused for a beat so he could change tack. 'Brambilla, you ever hear of a guy goes by the name of Geppo the bookie?'

Brambilla laughed again. 'Ah, Geppo ... Hippo, we used to call him. They say he weighed in at 150 kilos. He didn't need to shoot his competitors — just sat on them.' Then, 'You know he's dead, got taken out a few weeks back?'

'I did know that, but wasn't sure who was behind it. A competitor?'

'Yeah, but not at the races. Geppo was an errand boy for the Sicilians, but wanted to move up in the world. He was dipping his fingers into some nasty pies.'

'Drugs?'

'Loan-sharking and contraband. There were two of them working Salaria. Geppo's direct rival, Magliotta, had links to the Calabroni. The two camps had been vying for months to get overall control. We think Hippo's death could trigger a full-out war between the Calabroni, or what's left of them, and the Cosa Nostra branch here — it could turn ugly pretty soon. To be honest, given all that, we were quite surprised they bothered to take out your friend in Trastevere. We would have thought they had bigger fish to fry right now.'

Scamarcio felt the uneasiness return. 'Where did Geppo hang out?'

'Bar Magenta on Via Cagliari. He was there most days — he had a rotary telephone on the wall for his personal business.'

'And the guy who took him out?'

'The Spaniard? He's on Via Nizza, has the bar at the end with the red awning. Bar Stella. He also has a phone on the wall for his personal business. Don't ask me — must be a Seventies nostalgia thing. That, or they enjoy feeding us dud steers.'

'He's Spanish?'

'Nah, born and raised in Latina. But has a Spanish grandma, hence the name.' Brambilla cleared his throat. 'What's your case anyway?'

'Geppo's name came up recently in a rape investigation. We were going to check it out, but now I'm wondering whether we'll bother. Seems like we're at a dead end. Literally.'

Brambilla sighed. 'You can't prosecute a dead man, Detective, however much of a hotshot you are.'

20

Via Nizza was growing busy with the lunchtime rush. Some workmen were digging up the road, there was dust everywhere, and disgruntled pedestrians were being forced off the pavement into the traffic. Horns blared and babies cried. Someone told someone else to go fuck their grandmother.

Scamarcio pushed his way through the crowd, coughing against the dust. He could see the red awning of Bar Stella up ahead on the left, sandwiched between a dry cleaner's and a Thai massage parlour. Everywhere you went in the city, there were massage parlours now. It was the new growth industry — they seemed to have replaced tanning salons after everyone started worrying about skin cancer.

The café's windows were tinted, so that only the top half allowed anyone to look inside. He saw the backs of several men's balding heads at the counter, and a group of punters playing cards off to their right. He pushed the door and entered. It was cool inside, and the scent of fresh coffee grounds reminded him that he had gone without breakfast. As he approached the bar, the men all turned in unison, making it clear that he wasn't welcome. He pushed on regardless, ordering a cappuccino, helping himself to a brioche from the cabinet, and studying the pink pages of *La Gazzetta dello Sport*. The men at the counter lost interest and slowly returned to their conversation.

Behind him, the card game was in full swing. Out of the corner of his eye he spied a handsome man, taller than all the rest. His dark hair was swept back in a style that reminded

Scamarcio of a photo he had seen of Rock Hudson as a young man. He was wearing a well-tailored, blue pinstriped shirt, a small cross visible against his chest. Beneath the table, his legs were crossed in perfectly pressed chinos, and on his feet were expensive suede loafers with no socks visible, as dictated by that season's fashionistas. No one looked 'Mafia' anymore, or maybe they just didn't look like the old Mafia of the south that he remembered. The style was now super-preppy — dressed-down banker or lawyer. The way most of them saw it, there was little difference between their professions, anyway; they just worked on different sides of the divide.

Scamarcio guessed that this had to be the Spaniard. As if in answer to his thoughts, an old 1970s phone trilled against the wall, and the elegant man gently laid down his cards and rose from the table. A waft of expensive cologne hit Scamarcio as he passed. He watched him lift the receiver, and hold it to his ear. After a minute or so had passed, he said 'OK', carefully replaced the receiver, and returned to the card table. As he took his seat, Scamarcio realised that the eyes of each of his fellow players were upon him — evidently, they'd been watching him watch the Spaniard. He briefly weighed it up: he knew when he was outnumbered, and this did not feel like the time or place for a chat with Magliotta. He'd take a rain check, save it for another day when maybe one or two henchmen were around, rather than eight. The eyes at the card table tracked him as he paid the barista, refolded the newspaper, and left.

He entered the dust cloud of the street, glad of the momentary camouflage, the anonymity. He reflected on Magliotta, on his clothes and natural elegance. How things had changed. His father had never cared about all that: he'd been too busy running a burgeoning business to bother with fripperies; besides, he would have called it 'poofterish'. A real man rolled up his shirtsleeves and got on with life — he didn't shop for the latest brogues.

He wondered what his dad would make of the new-found 'metrosexuality'. Did it in some strange way connect with the new violence, the new ruthlessness? Was it, in fact, a response — some kind of compensation?

The dustbowl heat was cloying and intense, and he decided to take a left into an alleyway that he felt sure had to connect with Via Velletri. He anticipated the cool of the shadows and the dampness of the stone, but instead the sweetish stench of fresh sewage hit him immediately. He decided to switch back to Via Nizza — the heat was preferable to the smell — but all at once he felt someone push up against his back, felt the sharp point of something metallic against his spine. It had been a foolish move going to Bar Stella: that much was immediately clear.

'Don't move.' It was a deep voice, but he sensed a younger man, someone who wasn't completely in control. A waft of rank breath hit Scamarcio. The blade pushed tighter against his spine.

'What do you want?' he said, deciding to play the innocent. 'I've just got a few notes — two twenties and a ten, I think. That's it. My credit cards are at home.'

'I don't want your money,' said the man.

Scamarcio felt the heat course along his spine to his neck. He wanted to get hold of his Beretta, swing back with his right arm and knock the man's blade arm away, as his training had taught. But what if the man was left-handed? There was no way of knowing from this angle.

'What do you want?' he repeated.

'To help you.'

Help him see the error of his ways, no doubt. Help him never to return to Bar Stella, or bother the Spaniard again.

'Help me with what?'

'Your investigation.'

Scamarcio felt the blade loosen slightly, and took a moment to deal with his surprise.

'Strange way of helping someone — holding a knife to their back in a dark alleyway.'

'Shut up and listen,' said the man. 'I have information, information that you need ...' He broke off. Scamarcio had a sense that he was looking behind him, watching out for someone.

'There's no time,' said the stranger, panicked, the words faster now. 'Elba, go to Elba, go now. It's happening there, that's the key. Go now and save a life.'

Scamarcio felt the blade release, and then heard the sound of footsteps running away. He swung around, but whoever it was had already left the alleyway. He rushed towards the sunlight of Via Nizza, scanned left and right, but saw no one in the crowd — no one who looked any different from the thousands of dusty office workers, eking out a life.

Part II

21

In the old town, the heat clung to the stone and made her nauseous. She squinted skywards and was dismayed to see no threads of white, no traces of grey. It would be an afternoon like all the others, smothering and unforgiving. She eased back against the bench, her dress moulding against her damp skin. She studied the villa, suffocating under dense webs of ivy: the roots were pulling at its brickwork, pressing down on its fragile diamonds of glass.

Someone laughed: a cluster of German holiday-makers had gathered at the doorway, and were passing round a flask of something, talking noisily, forcing others to turn and watch. She saw her husband hunched over a tattered map tacked to the wall, his wide shoulders stooped, his dark hair thinning. She wondered what had claimed him in these passing years. It was as if his soul had left his body, and a beaten, darker form had taken its place. She pushed away a damp strand of hair and breathed in the afternoon scent of honeysuckle. Why had they come? So many dusty kilometres for what? A new start, the sudden return of old feelings?

A bell chimed, and the Germans began to shuffle inside. Fabio turned and waved at her to follow. She pressed her lips into a thin smile and pulled herself up, the heat sapping her strength, pressing her to stay put under the meagre shade of the fly-bitten palms. She tried a brighter smile, but he had already gone. He never waited these days, barely acknowledged her silent presence.

As she entered the courtyard, her skin prickled against the sudden cool. The cluster of tourists had already moved on. She breathed in the earthy dampness of the stone, and imagined that this was her villa, her summer retreat far away from everything and everyone. A shard of laughter splintered out across the stonework, and she followed. The group had gathered around a statue, a young guide explaining its history in faltering English. Fabio caught her gaze and rolled his eyes. She turned away, unwilling to share the joke, tired of his arrogance. '17th century, present from a Tuscan duke, marble from Abruzzo', the guide stumbled on. Her mind was so full; everything was painful, circular, exhausting. She looked up, searching for an image to divert her. One of the Germans was staring at her, and she turned, instinctively seeking out her husband for protection. But she could no longer see him in the room. No doubt he'd wandered off, bored, believing he knew it all already. She scanned the far corners of the hallway to the chambers beyond, but she couldn't find him there. Perhaps he had stepped outside, needing some air. She headed back to the courtyard, her heels tapping on stone, shattering the sleepy silence of the afternoon. The wall of heat hit her as she stepped into the sunlight, almost forcing her back. She closed her eyes against the brightness. When she opened them, she expected to find him leaning against the wall, enjoying a cigarette, perhaps keen and exciting again like his twenty-something self. But the gardens were empty. What was he playing at? Now what was he trying to prove? She kicked several small stones, sending them scattering across the cracked earth, and headed back inside.

OFFICER PARODI THREW down his sandwich. He had been attempting to finish it for the last ten minutes, but the phone had been ringing nonstop. First it had been the xenophobic mayor of Porto Azzurro complaining about a gypsy festival that had run into the early hours, then it was a tourist from Bologna claiming that a 'tiny' boy had snatched her camera, and finally it was the Milanese woman for the fifth time asking if there was any news of her husband. It was obvious to anyone with half a brain that the guy had done a runner, although no one had the balls to break it to her. Needless to say, they wouldn't be wasting their precious resources trying to track him down. Like so many poor fellows these days, the man did not want to be found.

For the fourth time, Parodi edged the sandwich aside and attempted to swallow the remaining bites. 'Police,' he said.

He heard a ghost of a voice at the other end, fragile and scared. *Not the Milanese again*, he prayed.

'Can you help?' He could barely make out the words. 'Something awful …' She was speaking English, and he was struggling to understand. They had been given courses last year to help them deal with the summer tourists, but he had never taken to it and had found the weekly homework irksome.

'What problem?' His brain ached.

'Our daughter — she's, she's disappeared.'

'Where?'

'The beach at Fetovaia. She was playing in the sand and then …' The woman stopped. The words were getting harder to make out. 'I don't know — she, she vanished, she disappeared.' Sobs overcame her, and the last words were whispers: 'We've looked everywhere — we don't know what to do.'

Parodi struggled to remember the vocabulary they'd been taught. Now he wished he'd paid more attention instead of flirting with Rita from customs.

'How old?'

'Seven, seven years old.' The woman broke down again.

The sergeant sighed and pushed away the sandwich, defeated. This call spelt trouble. And God help them if Ignazio Calo had already sniffed out the story.

22

SCAMARCIO OPENED HIS EYES one at a time and assessed the level of sunlight in the room. He could barely make out the Fattori above the chest. He had no idea what time it was. He'd fallen asleep when he'd returned to his flat — maybe because of the stress of the encounter in the alleyway, or maybe the small shard of resin he'd found at the back of the kitchen cupboard. The low buzz of the telephone persisted, and he reached for it slowly, like an astronaut in a state of weightlessness, the dull cannabis ache deadening his temples.

'Scamarcio.'

'Sorry to wake you.' It was Garramone. He didn't sound sorry at all.

'I wasn't asleep.'

'Whatever. Listen, I've got a lead on the other guy in the photo. I need you to go to Florence.'

Scamarcio pulled himself up against the pillows. Now he was straight, he realised that it was a powerful headache starting at the base of his neck and reaching around both temples. He rubbed the thinning skin under his eyes.

'Florence?'

'Perfect opportunity to get you out of Rome for a bit. And the lead is solid — he'll be there.'

'What? Now?'

'He may not hang around. The lead just came in.'

Scamarcio sighed, and sank back into the pillows. 'Listen, boss, I've got a lead myself. I went down to Via Nizza to check out this

Geppo the bookie character, and some guy practically knifes me in an alleyway and tells me the answer to all this can be found on Elba — there's something going down on the island that's apparently connected.'

'On Elba? Nothing ever happens on Elba.'

'My thoughts exactly.'

Garramone fell silent a moment. 'Let me see what I can find out. I'll call you back.'

The phone rang again five minutes later. Scamarcio hadn't moved from his position on the pillow. He couldn't ever remember feeling more exhausted.

'An American child has gone missing from one of the beaches. The local cops are running around like headless chickens, and a media circus is on its way.'

Scamarcio felt a tightness in his chest. This investigation was getting too big for them, crossing boundaries it was better to avoid.

He knew the answer before he asked. 'So I check it out?'

Garramone sighed. 'Yeah, you check it out.'

Although it was just a little past 10.00am, the June heat already had the day in its stranglehold. Through the haze he could make out the island police waiting for him on the tarmac, their orange siren morphing lazily. Scamarcio braced himself for the usual friction, and watched as the door of the battered Fiat opened and a young lad stepped out, all arms and legs, a spider unfolding. As he made his way towards them, the young guy turned and spotted him.

'Welcome.'

'Detective Scamarcio, pleased to meet you.'

'Likewise.' The young guy led him back to the car, silent.

In the driver's seat was another officer, maybe a few years older. He nodded, also saying nothing. Scamarcio climbed in the back and they pulled away. A blur of dense palm trees and pastel cottages sped by, and in the distance he could make out the first traces of blue. He felt glad to be out of the city, away from the smog for a while.

'Talk me through it. It was the beach at Fetovaia, right?'

The younger officer was the first to respond: 'Yes. It's a popular spot, but it was pretty deserted on Tuesday; there were only three other families, and none of them seems to have seen anything.'

'What about the parents? What did they tell you?'

'The mother is hysterical, cries all the time — it's hard to get anything out of her. The father is very silent, doesn't say much, just broods. They have no idea how it happened, seem completely in the dark.'

'What do they do for a living?'

'The father's an engineer in Maine. The mother stays home, cares for the kid, used to be a lawyer, apparently.'

They were descending a steep hill, and the blinding azure of the sea came into view, framed by tumbling red-and-white bougainvillea. Scamarcio had been to Elba once before, many years ago with an old girlfriend. The fragments of a song came up to his mind — a song by an English band he used to listen to when he was a teenager, something about not loving someone as much as you used to.

He didn't remember a great deal about the trip, except that they had argued almost constantly and had split on their return. But it wasn't a split that he remembered feeling particularly cut up about.

'Here we are,' said the younger officer. 'The boss is waiting.'

As he got out of the car, Scamarcio spied a squat man, florid in the face, kneeling at the water's edge. He looked up, their eyes locked, and in that instant Scamarcio knew there would be trouble between them.

'Morning.' Chief Genovesi, head of the Elba squad, assessed him dispassionately for several moments before returning his gaze to the sea. 'I don't know why they sent you,' he said. 'We might be a small force, but we can handle this ourselves.'

Scamarcio tried a smile, but Genovesi didn't notice. 'They have every faith in you and your men. Perhaps it wasn't explained properly, but I'm here because it might tie in to another case I'm following down in Rome. Besides, you know what it's like when the press takes an interest. It's useful for us to be seen as pulling out all the stops.'

The chief tossed a broken shell into the water. 'You're all the stops, are you?'

'No. But you know what I mean.'

'No, Scamarcio, I don't. But I know you and your reputation, and I could have done without it. I don't want a circus.'

The detective shrugged. 'These days, it's hard to avoid. You know the press would have come whether I was here or not.'

Genovesi snorted. 'Whatever. I'm not running this for the media. It's the chief of police in Florence I work for. Anyway, what's your case in Rome? Another missing kid?'

'No. Right now, it looks like a child-porn inquiry.'

'Well, it is or it isn't, surely.'

'It's complicated.'

Scamarcio scanned the beach, his eyes settling on the line of blue police tape as it danced in the breeze. 'Was the scene secured straightaway?'

'What do you take us for — yokels?'

It was not unheard of for hours to pass before a scene was sealed off, particularly with the less-experienced rural forces. Many a murderer had escaped jail thanks to their shortcomings. Scamarcio said nothing, letting Genovesi defend himself.

'It was secured as soon as we arrived.'

'And you found nothing?'

'Nothing — as empty as a nun's you-know-what.'

Scamarcio felt a sudden desire to be back in Rome. 'Show me where they were sitting.'

Genovesi started towards the rocks at the far right of the bay, his portly frame wobbling across the sand. It was a smallish stretch of beach, no more than 250 metres long, flanked by wooded hills at either end. The sand was pristine, and he decided that the aquamarine waters were on a par with Cala Capreria — maybe better. As they approached the tape, Genovesi waved the two officers over. 'Zanini and Borghetti were the first on the scene,' he announced, panting slightly.

He gestured to a spot by the rocks where the sand was flat and smooth. 'The American family was sitting here. They had their towels spread out on the rocks to dry; the little girl was playing in the water with her bucket and spade, and had started to build a castle. The mother decided to sunbathe on her front for a few minutes. When she looked up, the girl was gone.'

'A few minutes?'

'Well, that's what she says. She could have lost track of time.'

'Or fallen asleep and been too ashamed to admit it. And what was the father doing?'

'He at least admits that he was sleeping. He'd been reading a book and had nodded off under the umbrella.'

'So that's possibly both parents out. They could have been asleep for ten, twenty minutes — who knows? And no cry from the little girl?'

'They say they heard nothing.'

'Whoever took her may have drugged her,' said Scamarcio. 'Any other families on the beach?'

'Just three. We've spoken to them all, and none of them saw anything useful.' Genovesi's tone implied that he was quite capable of assessing the intrinsic value — or lack of it — of any potential evidence.

'I'd like to talk to them after we're done with the parents.'

'You'd just be wasting your time.'

Scamarcio kicked some sand from his shoe. 'I'll be the judge of that,' he said.

23

THE AMERICANS WERE STAYING in a four-star hotel carved into the cliffs above the bay. It sprawled across the rock face, all pine and glass, its vast decked terrace looking out to the sea. The lobby was busy with the arrival of a party of Germans, tanned and athletic, all in their sixties or older. Scamarcio wondered if his police pension would stretch to such a comfortable retirement.

Genovesi opened his badge for the receptionist. 'We're here for the Bakers. Remind me what room.'

The receptionist darted a look at the Germans, and lowered his eyes. 'We've moved them. All the crying and screaming was upsetting the other guests.'

'Screaming?'

Scamarcio traded glances with Genovesi, and then noticed Zanini's attention shift. He followed his gaze to a blond man seated at the bar. Even though it was still early, he appeared to be nursing a scotch.

'Mr Baker,' explained the officer.

Baker was muscular with that handsome, generic all-American face that you saw on baseball players or fire-fighters. But with his golden tan and sun-streaked hair, he could also have passed for a surfing pro. Scamarcio realised that he had been expecting someone older and uglier.

'Bit early for the strong stuff,' observed Genovesi.

As they approached, Scamarcio saw that Baker's face was deeply lined. He'd put him at over forty now, older than his initial assessment. Sensing their approach, Baker looked up from his drink. His eyes were glazed over — maybe alcohol, maybe exhaustion, maybe tears, probably all of the above.

'What do you want?' He was slurring his words already.

'My name's Scamarcio. I'm with the police in Rome.'

Baker closed his eyes and rubbed at the lids, saying nothing.

Scamarcio leaned against the bar. 'How are you holding up?'

Baker said nothing for several moments, and then replied, 'My wife's making it all a lot worse.'

'I'm sure she's just very worried,' offered Genovesi.

Baker took a long drag on the scotch. 'We're all worried, but there's no need for hysteria. I think she needs a shrink.' He fell silent, studying the contents of his glass.

'Come now,' said Scamarcio. 'Any mother would struggle in a situation like this.'

'I need her to keep it together. I need a partner.' Scamarcio silently added ... *not a problem*, finishing the sentence for him. He'd said that himself to a girlfriend once. He let the silence breathe for a while, and then asked, 'Have you seen her like this before?'

'How do you mean?'

'Hysterical.'

Baker looked up from his drink, his eyes suddenly alert. 'That's a strange question.'

Scamarcio met his gaze but didn't respond.

'Are you suggesting that my wife might have something to do with Stacey's disappearance?'

Stacey. Scamarcio didn't like the name. It reminded him of his time in the States, and conjured up images of flabby girls and greasy diners.

'I'm not suggesting anything of the kind.' He wondered why Baker had jumped on that. It was an unusual reaction.

Baker stared into the middle distance, taking in the array of bottles. 'Stacey is her life, her everything.' He breathed deeply, studying the muddled reflections playing on the surface of the bar.

'She was a much-longed-for baby — we had been trying for years, but without success. So then we went through IVF, and Stacey was conceived. Jane was so relieved, so contented, and Stacey became her focus from then on in. After she was born, she decided to give up work and devote all her time to our daughter.' He paused. 'Whether that was the right thing to do, who knows?'

'What do you mean?'

'When I met Jane, she was a high-flying young lawyer — she would stop at nothing to get ahead, make partner. When Stacey was born, all that changed.' He took another sip of his drink, and asked for a refill. 'As the cliché goes, she was no longer the woman I'd married.'

Scamarcio helped himself to a handful of peanuts. Then he remembered that nuts at a bar were said to bear the traces of urine from five different men. He put them back in the bowl.

'So you felt a little left out? It happens.'

Baker sat straighter on the bar stool, and ran a hand through his hair, pulling it neater behind his neck. 'I love my little girl, more than anything.' He swished the ice around in his glass. 'What did you say your name was?'

'Scamarcio.'

Genovesi looked impatient, as though he wanted to shift the conversation onto more useful ground. Baker leaned his elbow on the bar and rested his forehead on his hand in a way that only a drunk would do. 'I slipped up. It started a few months before we came out here — a young intern at the firm.' He closed his eyes at the memory of it. 'Made your heart stop, just looking at her. In the end, I couldn't fight it. Sometimes it's just bigger than you.'

'It seems to me that none of us are hard-wired for fidelity,' said Scamarcio. He'd been grappling with this question for as long as he could remember. Genovesi nodded, and the two younger officers followed suit.

'Indeed,' sighed Baker.

'Did your wife find out?'

'A month before we came away. Sarah sent me a text, even though I'd told her never to contact me on that phone. Jane found it, and I had to confess the whole thing. At the time, I figured that denial would have been worse.'

'And she still agreed to come on holiday with you?'

'She was threatening divorce, kick-arse lawyers — the whole deal. I was panicked. But then, when she calmed down, we agreed that Stacey was still so young that we had to try to make it work. This holiday was our attempt to patch things up and move forward. Jane had always wanted to come to Tuscany, so it was kind of my "forgive me" gift.'

'So the "hysteria", as you call it, is about many things, not just your daughter.'

'I guess so, yes.' Baker rubbed his eyes again. Scamarcio saw moisture there. 'Maybe all this is my divine punishment.'

24

Fully aware of Genovesi's growing impatience, Scamarcio pulled out a seat next to Baker.

'Can you tell us what happened — everything you can remember? I know you've already been through it, but it's useful for me to hear again.'

The American hunched over his drink, refusing eye contact now. 'We got to the beach around two. We'd had lunch at that fish place in town — I forget the name, but the one with the green awning, on the piazza.'

'Da Claudio,' offered Genovesi.

'Da Claudio. We had lunch there, and then we decided to go to the bay for the afternoon. We'd been visiting the other beaches, but we wanted to be near the hotel, as Jane and I were tired, and thought we might go back inside for a siesta at some point.'

'Did you notice any of the other customers at the restaurant?'

Baker scratched his head. 'No, I can't say that I did.' He thought for a moment. 'I think there was a big group at one end maybe, quite loud: locals, not tourists.'

Scamarcio turned to Genovesi. 'Have the customers at Da Claudio been checked?'

'We've had our hands full.'

'We need to talk to the proprietor as soon as possible.' He turned to Zanini: 'Can you get on it — I want a full report, every detail that he can give. And we need to run a check on all the other places the family has visited since they first arrived on the island.' He tried to make eye contact with Baker. 'Had you visited anywhere more than once? Places where someone watching might have formed an idea of your routine?'

'We don't really have a routine; we're on holiday. We were trying different restaurants every night — and the same goes for the beaches. We never went to the same place twice.' He stopped, and looked up finally. 'Well, except the bay, actually — we went there the first afternoon we arrived.'

'And when you got to the beach, who else was there?'

'Just the three families. I believe you've already spoken to them.'

'Describe them.'

Baker sighed, turned his head to look at the three of them, and then turned back to the bar.

'There was the European family — mum and dad and two little boys, German or Scandinavian maybe. Then a young couple who I think might have been Italian, and then the retired English couple.'

'How do you know they were retired?'

'He was reading the international edition of the *Times*, and I asked him if I could borrow it.'

'Did you talk to him for long?'

'Maybe five minutes; maybe less. Just small talk — where they were from, where they had visited, where they were staying. He seemed like a nice-enough fellow.'

'And the wife?'

'I didn't really speak to her; she had her head in a book. We just said hello and goodbye.'

'Did you return the paper when you'd finished with it?'

Genovesi cast Scamarcio a look that said: 'It's confirmed, you *are* an idiot.'

Baker frowned. 'No, I don't think I did. When we realised that Stacey had gone, I didn't give it another thought. It must still be amongst our stuff, I guess.'

'I'd like to take a look.'

Genovesi was shaking his head now, seemingly no longer able to keep a lid on his frustration.

'And you didn't talk to anyone else on the beach?'

'No, not before Stacey was taken. After we realised she'd gone, we kept calling for her and shouting, and then they all came over to see if they could help.'

'All of them?'

'Well, I think all of them. It was chaos, we were in a panic — it's just a blur, really. I don't remember how things went.'

'And when you first arrived at the beach, you took that spot by the rocks? The same spot where you were sleeping when Stacey disappeared?'

He watched the guilt cloud his face. 'Yes, we didn't move from there.'

'And how much time passed between you arriving on the beach and your daughter disappearing?''

'I don't know. I guess about an hour — maybe more, maybe less.'

'But your wife called the station at three-thirty — that's an hour and a half if you arrived at two, as you told my colleagues.'

'Then it must have been an hour and a half. Like I say, I lost track of time.'

'And when you arrived on the beach, what did you do?'

'We left our things by the rocks, and then Stacey and I went for a swim. Jane wanted to stay on the beach to sunbathe.'

'How long were you in the sea?'

'It seemed like a while. The water was warm, and Stacey was having a wild time.' He smiled at the memory. 'Twenty minutes, I think — maybe more.'

'Is your daughter a strong swimmer?'

Baker swallowed slowly, trying to keep it together. 'She was doing really well at school with her swimming. They said they had high hopes for her with her sport. She takes after her dad — and her grandpa.' Fat tears were forming. Scamarcio watched them break surface tension, roll down one cheek, and drop from his chin. His shoulders were heaving now, and Genovesi turned away, embarrassed. Zanini rooted in his pocket for something, before finding a battered wad of paper tissues and handing them over.

Scamarcio pressed on. 'And when you came back to the shore, what did you do?'

Baker took the tissues, but wiped his face with his sleeve. 'I put up the umbrella and started with my book. Jane was still sunbathing.'

'On her back?'

'I think so, yes.'

'And where was Stacey?'

'She dried herself off, and then took her bucket and spade down to the water. I think she was trying to make a sandcastle.'

'Did she ask you for help?'

'No, she's quite determined, and likes to do things on her own.'

'How long was she down there?'

'I'm not sure — maybe twenty minutes, maybe more. Then she came back up because she wanted an ice-cream. She'd seen the man selling them, and asked me to buy her one.'

'There was a man selling ice-cream on the beach?'

'Yeah, I'm not sure where he'd come from. I kinda felt sorry for the guy that there were so few of us there that day. '

Scamarcio tried to keep his voice level, and turned to Genovesi: 'I didn't know about the ice-cream guy. You know about the ice-cream guy?'

The chief shrugged. 'First I've heard of it.'

Switching back into English, Scamarcio said: 'Did you tell my colleagues about the ice-cream man?'

Baker sniffed. 'I'm not sure — maybe not. I can't remember whether it came up when they interviewed me. Was that a crucial detail?' He breathed in deeply. 'Jesus, what's wrong with me — why didn't I think of it before?'

'Mr Baker, try to stay calm. It may prove to be important; it may not. Either way, we will look into it.'

Scamarcio had the sense that he was starting from zero — no thorough statements had been taken. Then another troubling thought struck him: 'I take it my colleagues brought the interpreter along when they interviewed you and your wife?' The fact that Genovesi showed little reaction to the last question only served to heighten his disquiet.

Baker shook his head. 'No, it was just these guys — the men with you now.'

Why the hell hadn't they found an interpreter? What was wrong with them? He wasn't certain, but he suspected that Genovesi's English fell far short of fluent and that his men were worse. He would put it to the test when they'd finished with Baker.

'This ice-cream seller — can you describe him?'

'He was African, tall. Wore a gown and a hat — he looked like he was from the Congo or somewhere like that. I was surprised that he would be here in Italy, actually.'

'A lot of Africans travel here looking for work. They come over on boats to Lampedusa, off Sicily. More and more of them are arriving each month.'

The American was nodding, but didn't seem to be listening.

'Did you see anyone else buy from him?'

'No, not that I remember.'

'After you got the ice-cream, what happened?'

'She sat down under the umbrella to eat, and polished it off pretty quickly. Jane gave her some tissues to clean her mouth with, and then she went back to the water again — back to her sandcastle.' He smiled. 'She seemed really happy: she was singing to herself.' A shadow crossed his face.

'And then?'

'And then I must have fallen asleep. The next thing I know, I'm being woken up by Jane shouting. Stacey had already gone.' He stopped and looked across the bar into nothing. 'That was the final time I saw her — down by the water singing.' His voice fell to a whisper. 'I hope to God that won't be my last memory of her.'

Scamarcio pushed on. 'And when you last saw your wife before falling asleep, she was still sunbathing on her front?'

'I think so, yes.' He thought for a moment. 'She'd got Stacey cleaned up after the ice-cream, and then I think she just lay down again, back to how she was before.'

'On her front?'

'I think so, yes.'

'But you're not sure?'

Baker rocked back on the stool. 'Fuck no, Detective, of course I'm not sure. I was tired; I'd had wine with my lunch. I don't know. I think that's what happened, but I could be wrong. She could have been on her back — it's possible. Why does it even matter?' He shook his head and took a drink.

'So you don't know whether your wife fell asleep or not after you?'

'No.'

'You don't remember seeing her sleeping before you dozed off?'

'No.' He stopped and looked towards Genovesi and the officers, canvassing support. 'Listen, if she says she wasn't sleeping, she wasn't. She wouldn't lie about that — she'd know it could be important.'

'Does your wife sleep a lot normally?'

Genovesi tried an eye-roll, but his officers didn't notice; they were following Scamarcio's interview with rapt attention.

'Normally, I'd say no. But in the weeks before we came away, she seemed to be sleeping more than usual — sleeping soundly. I

118

was surprised because I thought that, with all that had happened in our marriage, she would have had trouble switching off. I certainly did.'

Scamarcio made a mental note. He felt sure that he'd identified the first missing element. All he needed now was the evidence.

25

THEY LEFT BAKER at the bar, and took the elevator to the fourth floor. Despite the air conditioning, Genovesi was sweating, and the smell just added to Scamarcio's irritation.

'Who interviewed the Bakers?' he asked once they were alone in the lift.

'I did,' barked the little man. 'Got a problem with that?'

'Perhaps.'

He saw a vein swell up on Genovesi's neck. 'I've been a policeman for twenty-five years, and I will not be lectured to by the son of a Mafia whore.'

Scamarcio was taken aback by the intensity of his reaction, but he took time to separate his immediate emotions from his rational mind, as he had been taught. It was difficult — it took every ounce of self-control he could muster — and for several seconds he watched his own knuckles turn white. The two young officers studied the ground. The space was too small for a fight.

Eventually, he said: 'I don't understand how a detail like the ice-cream guy could get overlooked. You all know the first twenty-four hours are crucial.'

Genovesi was clasping and unclasping his fists, warming up now, thought Scamarcio. With his stubby arms, it made him seem even more primordial. He conjured up a cartoon image of the chief of the Elba squad, his huge red fists dragging along the ground behind his squat frame. That calmed him somewhat.

'Were we supposed to just guess that the ice-cream guy was there? The father didn't mention it.'

'First page of the textbook: the questions you ask.'

Genovesi threw open his arms in disgust. 'The textbook?? The fucking textbook? You don't learn policing from a textbook!' He gathered the tips of his fingers into a sharp point, and shook his right hand up and down. 'How dare they send me some wet-behind-the-ears son of a Mafia bitch to run my case, and then have him lecture me about bastard textbooks!'

Scamarcio felt the burn of anger along his spine, across his ribs, tearing at the pit of his stomach. He wrestled with it, trying to keep it down. He couldn't afford another fight.

Genovesi was in full flight: 'I did a bit of research when they told us you were coming, and I have to say that I really don't understand how you've managed to rise so high so fast, to climb that greasy pole down there in Rome. Tell me, Scamarcio, how did you get here, really? Did your father's old associates grease a few palms? Were they looking for an inside man?' He was panting now. His little outburst had robbed him of breath, and he was shaking with rage.

Scamarcio had faced these charges before, but wondered now with a sudden welcome detachment why Genovesi was quite so angry. He could understand that his nose might have been put out of joint by having a younger man sent over to assist with his case, but this reaction seemed disproportionate.

Quite calmly, in English, translating the familiar swearwords directly from the Italian, he said: 'No, you piece of piss whore's cuckold. I'm just extremely good at my job — unlike you, you shit from a bird that flies at arsehole height.' From his blank expression, it was clear that Genovesi hadn't understood a word. Theory confirmed.

Scamarcio sighed softly. He felt sorry for the young officers, who looked like they might expire from embarrassment. Or maybe it was the stench of Genovesi's sweat.

The elevator came to a stop, and they spilled out into the

hallway. The corridor was light and airy, and carpeted with that strange bamboo material that always smelt slightly stale.

'Here we go: number 423,' said Zanini breezily, attempting to restore normality. 'Polizia,' he shouted, but not too loudly.

After several moments, the door opened onto an empty room. A voice came from the bathroom: 'Come in. I'll just be a second.'

Scamarcio could smell scent; it felt expensive, with notes of junipers and roses, and something else. They filed inside and stood awkwardly around the beds — two big doubles and a small single in the corner. Both the doubles had been slept in; the little bed was untouched.

The waft of scent intensified as the woman entered the room. For a few moments, Scamarcio's brain struggled to make the connection, so very different was she from the picture he had ready in his mind. When he had been talking with her husband, he had imagined a once-good-looking woman who was now a little out of shape — flesh that sagged slightly, a few too many wrinkles across the brow, and one-too-many circles under the eyes. But now the phrase 'a racehorse of a woman' came to his mind.

'I'm sorry to have kept you waiting.' She moved with a swan-like grace, and with her lustrous, brown hair and long athletic limbs, she reminded him of the American supermodel Cindy Crawford.

'No problem,' said Genovesi, who was now dabbing at his forehead with a handkerchief, looking for a chair to collapse into.

'Would you like some water? It's so hot,' she said, hovering at the end of one of the double beds, her legs magnificent in denim. Scamarcio was trying to compute how Mr Baker could tire of such a woman, could prefer an unsophisticated intern to such class and elegance. His guess was that he must have felt very excluded and ignored to cheat on a wife like this. Maybe the affair was simply a warning shot to reclaim her attention. Or, returning to the perennial dilemma, maybe you just got bored with anyone in the end, however attractive they were. He wanted Mr Baker to come up from the bar so he could observe the two of them together, and try to figure it out.

They declined the water and pulled out some chairs from a small table under the window. It made for a slightly awkward situation: four men alone in a room with a stunning woman. They could have done with a female officer, but he wondered whether Elba even had one. If Genovesi was anything to go, by they were still living in the 1970s.

'Mrs Baker, can you talk me through what happened the afternoon that Stacey disappeared? I've been sent here by the Flying Squad in Rome, and I'm trying to make sure that we haven't missed anything crucial.'

She extracted a cigarette from a crumpled packet next to her on the bed. There was a lighter inside and she lit up, lifting her head and closing her eyes as she took the first drag.

'I didn't catch your name.' She opened her eyes again and surveyed him through the smoke.

Now she was closer, he noticed the swollen eyelids, and wondered whether she'd been crying when they'd arrived.

'I'm sorry. It's Scamarcio — Detective Scamarcio.'

'What does that mean in Italian?'

He paused. Genovesi smirked.

'It means something rotten,' he said. 'Our surnames can be strange.'

She smiled weakly and took the smoke down deep into her lungs. 'Where did you learn your English, Mr Scamarcio?' Her voice was tired and heavy, as if she was on autopilot. He noted a deadness in her eyes now, and a plasticity to her skin that he had seen on someone else, some years before.

'I spent five years in LA.'

'LA,' she said absently. 'Now you tell me, I can hear it in your accent.' She stopped, wrinkles carved her brow. 'Have we met before? I have a feeling that I've seen you somewhere.'

'No, I don't think so.' He hoped she hadn't. He had tried to consign those years to the past, although every now and again a photo came back to haunt him.

'Mrs Baker, can you talk me through the events of that afternoon? You'd been to Da Claudio, the fish place, for lunch, had you not?'

She sighed, cupping her chin with a hand. 'That's right.'

'Do you remember anything about the other diners?'

She shook her head. 'I really didn't notice them. I was in a bit of a haze that day — I hadn't slept well the night before.'

Why had the husband said she was sleeping soundly?

'Mr Baker mentioned seeing a big group there.'

'Yes, I think there was a party of locals, but I really didn't pay them much attention. You know what it's like when you have a little one — you spend all your mealtime making sure they eat.'

There was no energy in her words; no life behind them.

'And you don't remember any of the other customers?'

'No.' Then, as an afterthought: 'I'm sorry.'

'And when you got to the beach?'

She had finished the first cigarette, and was toying with the next. Scamarcio wanted to open a window; the heat and the smoke were getting to him.

She paused in thought, her unlit cigarette suspended in mid-air. 'There were three other families — the English couple Paul spoke to, the Scandinavians, and then the young Italian couple. They couldn't keep their hands off each other.' A bitterness caught her face, and for an instant she lost some of her beauty.

'And what did you do when you got to the beach?'

'We laid out our things by the rocks, and Paul and Stacey went down to the water to swim. I stretched out on my towel to sunbathe.'

'How long were they in the water?'

She thought about this for a while. 'You know, I'm really not sure. It seemed like a long time — maybe as much as half an hour.'

'And then?'

'And then they were back, and Stacey was asking for ice-cream.'

'She was asking for an ice-cream when she came out from the water?'

'Yes, I think so.'

'She didn't go down to the shore to play first?'

She sighed. 'God, I don't know — she might have done. How can I be expected to remember every tiny detail?'

'It's those details that will help us find your daughter.'

She said nothing.

'Your husband believes she went to build a sandcastle after she came out of the water, and that she did that for half an hour or so before asking for an ice-cream.'

'Well, if that's what he says, that's how it must have been. Like I say, I had my eyes closed. I was sunbathing.'

Most mothers would have opened their eyes from time to time to check on their children, thought Scamarcio. His theory seemed to be taking shape.

'And what about the ice-cream seller? Did you get a look at him?'

She sighed again. 'Not really.'

'Can you remember anything about him?'

'Well, I think he was black?' It was a question, as though she was waiting for him to provide the answer.

'You think?'

She threw down the lighter. It rolled off the bed, landing on the floor. 'For Christ's sake, how am I supposed to know? Paul took her to get the ice-cream, not me.'

'You were still sunbathing?'

'Yes.'

'With your eyes closed?'

'Do you know anyone who sunbathes with their eyes open?'

'Didn't you get hot? Maybe want to escape under the umbrella for a bit?'

'I have naturally dark skin — Cherokee great-grandparents.'

That explained the strong cheekbones and the deep-brown eyes.

'Where are you heading with this? Are you suggesting I'm an unfit mother?'

'Your words, not mine.'

'A mother is entitled to a rest once in a while, and Paul was looking after her.' She ran a shaky hand through her hair and raised her head to the ceiling, looking for help from someone up there.

Scamarcio rocked back in his chair and took a breath. There was a stillness in the room, and he registered Zanini watching him closely, rather like a lion cub waiting for its father to make a kill.

'Mrs Baker,' said Scamarcio, his expression neutral. 'Did you fall asleep that afternoon on the beach?'

Her eyes registered fury, then misery, and then finally defeat. Her perfect features collapsed into themselves, and she began to sob, her head in her hands.

Genovesi coughed and got up to open a window.

'There's nothing to be ashamed of.' Scamarcio felt that it would be inappropriate to lay a hand on her shoulder, although he wanted to. 'It could happen to anyone. You're on holiday — you have the chance to wind down. You can't be expected to watch your daughter constantly.'

Mrs Baker was still crying, not responding.

'All we need to know is how much of that time you think you were asleep for. That information could really help us.'

She sniffed and wiped her eyes and nose with her hand. The gesture jarred with the grace she had shown before. Her eyes were now red and shining.

'I honestly don't think I slept that much at all — maybe I just dozed for a few minutes, you know. I remember Stacey coming back with the ice-cream, and having to get her cleaned up. Then she went off with her bucket and spade. But she was where we could see her, at the shore, just a few metres away.'

'And then what did you do?'

'I just went back to sunbathing.'

'On your front or on your back?'

She hesitated for a moment. 'I think I may have turned onto my front.'

'How could you see your daughter if you were sunbathing on your front?'

He saw something like contempt in her eyes. 'I turned my neck so I could see what she was doing.'

'How often did you do that?'

'I don't know, I wasn't counting.'

'At a guess?'

She was rubbing at her temples, her eyes closed. 'Many times, probably every minute.' Her eyes remained closed, and he saw the perfect skin along her cheekbones flush slightly.

He coughed. 'Would you mind if I use your bathroom?'

She looked up, confused. 'Sure, go ahead.'

Genovesi was looking at him as if he had lost his mind, and so were the two young officers.

He stepped into the bathroom and locked the door. The room still smelt of her scent. He ran the cold tap and splashed some water onto his face. There was a small mirrored cabinet attached to the wall above the basin. He slid back the doors and looked through the bottles — bottles of all shapes and sizes, colours, and textures — but he couldn't find what he was looking for. He glanced down, and clocked a red-leather vanity case beneath the sink; it was one of those things you saw glamorous women carry onto aeroplanes.

He pulled down the toilet seat and sat, carefully placing the case on his lap. The lid opened easily. He reached for a catch on the side of the box, and two layers of make-up and creams sprung out. He saw that there was a third drawer beneath that had remained shut. He tried pulling at it, thinking it would be locked, but to his surprise it popped open immediately. Inside were two small, brown medicine bottles. He lifted them out one at a time, handling them carefully. On the label of the first bottle was written 'Diazepam: Valium 10mg — to be taken as directed'. The label on the other bottle said 'Fluoxetine: Prozac 20mg — to be taken twice a day'. He returned the bottles to the drawer and closed the upper layers. Then he shut the case and returned it to its original position beneath the sink.

He looked at himself in the mirror and frowned at the shadows beneath his eyes. He was right about what had happened: Mrs Baker had been out cold. The girl had been snatched while both her parents were sound asleep.

26

GENOVESI MIGHT HAVE had many faults, but he knew where to get a good lunch quickly. Scamarcio had chosen squid-ink spaghetti with clams, on Genovesi's reluctant recommendation, not knowing quite whether to trust him; but, as it turned out, it was a sound suggestion. It seemed that Genovesi was big enough to call a truce where the serious matter of food was concerned.

'So, the supermodel mother: what's the story there?' A creamy ribbon of tagliatelli hung from Genovesi's fork, and Scamarcio wondered whether he might find the space to try that, too.

'She's on Valium and Prozac — I found them in the bathroom. She would have been fast asleep when the girl was taken.'

The two Elba officers eyed him suspiciously. Genovesi's eyebrows bunched in confusion. Evidently, the women on Elba didn't resort to such measures, however humdrum the island life, however Neanderthal their husbands.

'You sure?'

'I found them in her cosmetics case. I think it likely that she was in a very deep sleep for much of that afternoon.'

Genovesi thought for a moment. 'So the child could have been taken at any point — the parents might have been out for quite some time?'

'Yes.'

'What a mess,' said the Elba chief as he piled more pasta onto his plate.

Scamarcio's mobile rang. It was Garramone, so Scamarcio stepped outside to take the call.

'How's it going?' said the chief.

'Slowly — the usual half-arsed approach. They've only just got around to taking proper statements.'

'Well, do what you can. Listen, you'll hear soon enough, but the Ganza thing has just gone off the scale.'

'What do you mean?'

'*Il Messaggero* have the Arthur death. They're running it on their front page tomorrow.'

'Shit.'

'The guys down at Trastevere are in for a shock.'

'You think they'll make a link with what happened to Filippi?'

'There is no connection.' The way he said it troubled him.

'Probably not, but to outside eyes it might look odd.'

Garramone fell quiet. 'Don't worry. Just try to concentrate on whatever Elba might give you.'

'OK, but what about Ganza? What will happen now?'

'The eyes of all of Italy are upon him, and tomorrow they'll be wondering if he killed that young man. The chief of police will probably appoint his own guys to run that investigation. The fact that you and I were there first shouldn't come to anyone's attention. Understood?'

'But is that it? You just want me to walk away from it? Like nothing happened? Is that what the PM wants?'

'Oh, Scamarcio, what choice does he have? What choice do I have?'

'So what now?'

'Just carry on with what you're doing, and I'll let you know.' He hung up without saying goodbye.

27

THEY HAD ARRANGED to meet the Italian couple at a café across from the restaurant. Once he'd calmed down properly, Genovesi made it clear that he wanted to regain control of the interviews, insisting that he be the one to make the introductions. Scamarcio hadn't the energy to fight, feeling too troubled by what was happening down in the Capital.

They were an interesting couple — intellectuals, artistic types, from Rome. The young man had shoulder-length dark hair and a strong nose and jaw, but his eyes were too small, almost rat-like.

The girlfriend was petite, blonde, and blue-eyed, with a delicate, round face. He worked for the press department of a political party that Scamarcio had recently lost patience with. She was finishing a PhD in global migration patterns. Scamarcio never ceased to wonder at the range of obscure subjects you could study these days. He considered whether, as a student in Palermo, he would have chosen differently had these choices been available to him then. He could be working for the UN, getting involved in international politics, changing history. It would have made more sense than chasing around after the dead. But he reminded himself that Stacey Baker might still be alive. Even though she wasn't the focus of his investigation, if they found her in time this would be one of those rare occasions when his job actually made a difference, when he could feel that he was on the right path. He didn't want to leave this inquiry just yet, and wondered how long it would be before the chief put pressure on him to return.

The girlfriend downed her espresso. Zanini was watching her, a venal absence in his eyes.

Scamarcio watched the boyfriend watch Zanini.

Genovesi cleared his throat, resting a hairy arm on the table.

'The American family told us that there was an ice-cream seller on the beach.'

'Yes, that's right,' said the boy matter-of-factly.

'Why didn't anyone mention this before?' the chief asked, averting his eyes from Scamarcio.

The couple exchanged glances. 'We didn't think of it,' said the girl. 'It was all such a rush when we spoke to you at the beach.'

Genovesi rubbed a hand across his balding pate. 'What did he look like, this man?'

'Black, tall,' said the boy.

'He was wearing African robes,' said the girl. 'With one of those hats. And he seemed dignified. He had a handsome face — strong bones.'

'What else?' Genovesi sounded bored, exasperated. He wanted them to know that they weren't giving him what he wanted.

'The Americans bought something from him, I think,' said the girl.

Genovesi had shifted his gaze, and was now watching the young barista serve drinks to a group of teenagers who were obviously underage. The girl seemed confused by the drift in his attention.

'Was there anything that struck you as unusual, out of place, that day?' asked Scamarcio from his standing position.

She threw a searching look at her boyfriend. He looked away for a moment.

'He was swimming with her in the water,' he said, finally meeting Scamarcio's eye.

'Who?'

'The ice-cream guy. I remember seeing them both in the water.'

'What? Together?'

'Yes.'

'You're telling me the ice-cream guy was with the little girl in the water?'

'Yes.'

'Didn't you find that odd? Where were the parents at that point?'

'I think they were asleep.'

The young man scratched at the base of his skull. 'And, yes, it was a bit strange, but then he kind of swam away from her, and I realised they weren't swimming together. He'd just been swimming near her.'

'And then what happened?'

'He just kept swimming away. And then she got out and went back to her parents.'

'You're sure about that?'

'Very sure, because I remember being relieved somehow to see her get out. I felt that I could continue with my book, that I didn't need to watch her anymore — if you know what I mean.' He looked into his lap awkwardly.

'But you didn't mention this before?'

He scratched again — his chin this time. 'When I first spoke to you guys on the beach, I did remember it, but because he swam away from her and she got out, I kind of thought that was that, that was the end to it, and it wasn't worth mentioning.' He paused. 'I guess I've been stupid.'

Genovesi tut-tutted, shaking his head now.

'No,' said Scamarcio. He could see Genovesi's shoulder blades tighten beneath his shirt.

'When the man swam away from her, what direction did he take?'

'He went around the rocks at the end of the beach.' He paused. 'To the left of where the family was sitting.'

'So he went out of sight?'

'Yes.'

'And did you see him again after that?'

'No, that was it. And not long after that, the mother started to scream.'

'How long after?'

'No more than half an hour, I'd say.'

28

ON THE BEACH at Fetovaia, a man was selling sarongs. They were all colours of the rainbow, and he had them laid out across a wooden rail that he carried over his left arm. Scamarcio imagined that it must be heavy, that it would bear down on his neck and shoulders after a while. The heat was intense, and he watched the man wipe his brow with a handkerchief that he kept in his pocket. He took it out every minute or so, then stuffed it away again while he hitched the rail higher up his arm. No one seemed to be buying from him, and after a while he walked to the back of the beach and rested the rail against the wall. From behind a stone he retrieved a battered bottle of water and sank down beneath a meagre scrap of shade thrown by several mangy palms.

Genovesi and his officers had returned to the station to follow up the remaining witnesses, leaving Scamarcio to track down the ice-cream seller. This was how he wanted it; he could work better alone. They'd got him a hire car, the latest Cinquecento, a boxy little thing that he'd parked above the bay. He was making the steep descent towards the beach by foot now, his jacket draped carefully over one arm. The sarong man noticed him walking towards him, looked to his right and then behind him to see whether Scamarcio might be heading for anyone else, realised he wasn't, and shifted uncomfortably, making as if to move. But it was too late — Scamarcio had him in his sights. No doubt he was working without a permit. They all worked without permits now; it was the only way to survive. Scamarcio drew up alongside him, taking a seat to his right beneath the shade.

'How are you doing?' he said, trying to make eye contact. On closer inspection, the man seemed more like a teenager. His skin was perfectly smooth, although his young eyes had a deadness behind them, as though he'd seen too much of life already.

'Are you going to arrest me?' said the man/boy.

'Arrest you? For what?'

He said nothing for a moment, and then: 'You're a cop, aren't you?'

'Might be.'

'What do you want?'

'Information.'

The boy's features relaxed slightly, and then the suspicion returned: 'What kind of information?'

'I'm looking for a guy who was selling ice-cream here on the beach yesterday. Tall guy, long robes.'

'Is he in trouble?'

'I don't know yet. I just need to speak to him.'

The boy gazed out across the sea. It seemed as though he was trying to find something out there.

'If I help you, what will you give me?'

Scamarcio could have come on all aggressive, blackmailing him with the permit, threatening to send him home. But he saw something in the boy's eyes that stopped him — made him feel that he didn't deserve the usual low-life treatment.

'I can help you with your permit, if that's what you need. Try to get things cleaned up for you.'

The boy nodded slowly, and studied the sand beneath his feet awhile. 'I think I know who you mean. That's Billy. He works this beach, and he would have been around yesterday.'

'Where's he from?'

'The Congo. Djibouti.'

'Where's he staying now?'

'Where we all stay — the flats behind the port.'

Scamarcio took his wallet from his pocket, pulled out a crisp 50-euro note, and handed it to the boy. He looked uneasy, unsure whether to touch it.

'If I give you this, will you take me to the flats, show me where he lives?'

The boy accepted the note gingerly, as if afraid the paper would disintegrate on contact with his skin. 'Deal.'

It was a grey concrete block, washed out and dilapidated. The windows were tiny slits, like the hollowed-out eyes on a corpse, thought Scamarcio. Washing was strung between the rusting balconies, and a group of barefoot children were playing out front on a burnt-out strip of grass. There was nothing to suggest that they were in walking distance of a prime tourist destination.

Scamarcio followed the boy inside. An overwhelming blend of smells hit him: cooking, dirty nappies, sweat, urine, and something else — something old and musty that he couldn't quite place, like the week-old odour of wet dog.

The boy didn't bother with the elevator and headed straight for the stairs, hoisting the rail onto his shoulder as he made the climb. When they reached the second floor he turned and told Scamarcio to wait while he unlocked a door to his left and carried the rail inside. Within seconds he was back, heading for the stairwell again. They climbed two more flights, the smell intensifying. The boy marched down the corridor before stopping in front of a door halfway down on his left.

'Here,' he whispered. 'But don't tell him I brought you. Let me leave first.'

Scamarcio nodded, and the boy ran back down the corridor, heading for the stairs again. Scamarcio leaned against the wall for a moment, the hum of cicadas rising up from the bushes below. He wondered again about the smell. How could people breathe this in, day after day? Maybe, after a while, you stopped noticing.

He went to knock, but before he did so the door moved back to reveal a tall, black man bending down, trying to shift a box of some kind out into the hallway. He spotted Scamarcio standing there, and looked up.

'What do you want?' The accent was thick and French.

'I'm looking for Billy.'

Scamarcio saw the brilliant whites of his eyes, saw fear — maybe smelt it, too. The man did not respond.

'I guess that would be you.'

The man straightened to his full height. He was well over 6ft 4, taller than Scamarcio. His skin was pure ebony, almost polished. His features were strong, with deep lines beneath the eyes and circling a full mouth. He was wearing a long blue-and-black robe with a matching kufi hat, and Scamarcio noticed tight rings of clear beads wound around his left wrist.

'Were you on the beach at Fetovaia yesterday?'

The man scratched his forehead and scanned the corridor in both directions, maybe looking for somewhere to run. He looked back at Scamarcio as if he was hoping he would just disappear.

'Is this about my permit?'

It was a clever response, but exactly what Scamarcio had expected. 'No, it's not.'

'You're a policeman though?'

He said nothing, hoping to draw him out with the silence. Eventually, the man said: 'I was there. Why does it matter?'

Scamarcio leaned back against the wall again, and yawned. It had been too early a start. 'A little girl went missing from Fetovaia yesterday afternoon: blonde, American, seven years old.'

The man seemed genuinely surprised, a dark cloud passing across his features, and then he just shook his head slowly, sadly. It was a solid performance, decently convincing, but Scamarcio had seen some great amateur dramatics in his time: he had observed widows hammering on the chests of their murdered husbands, crying and wailing in outpourings of grief so intense and protracted that they took your breath away, only to then watch the same widows give the finger to the judges when they were later sent down for poisoning. He'd also seen sons shaking, speechless and destroyed beside the battered corpses of their avenged fathers, only to find said sons' prints all over the murder weapon.

'You know the girl I'm talking about?'

The man waited a few moments before replying: 'I sold her an ice-cream. Then I saw her later, swimming on her own. Her parents were both asleep.'

'What time was this?'

'I don't know. I think around 3.30, or maybe 4.00pm.'

'Where was she swimming?'

'Near her parents, by the rocks.'

'And what were you doing?'

'I was swimming, too. It was hot and I hadn't had a break, so I just got in the water. I left my stuff on the beach for a second, and then I jumped in.'

'Is that what you normally do? Get in the water when you're working?'

The man was unperturbed. 'I don't usually, but yesterday was real hot — over 34 degrees. I couldn't stand it any longer. I needed to cool down if I was going to get through the rest of the afternoon.'

Fair enough, thought Scamarcio. 'But you chose to go in the water at the very moment the little girl was having a swim ...'

The man frowned, and shook his head at Scamarcio. 'But that little girl was in the water all afternoon. She was never *out* of the water — only when they came to buy an ice-cream.' Fair enough again.

The man sank down suddenly, his back sliding against the wall, his robes fanning out across the filthy floor. He rested his head in his hands.

'Am I going to be arrested? Are you going to send me to jail? I know what you Italians think of men like me: you hate us, suspect us, want us gone. Is that what's going to happen — you're going to send me to jail?' The man was breathing deeply now, breathing faster, altogether too fast.

Scamarcio felt a spike of compassion; he needed to calm him down.

'No one is sending you to jail. I'm just asking you if you saw anything that day — anything at all that could help us find this little girl?'

He didn't seem to have heard. 'I was a doctor in the Congo, studied hard for all my qualifications, tried my best to make it. But you know there are some places you will never make it. I had to leave my son and daughter behind, had to come here with nothing, had to live in this hole — just to sell ice-cream. Imagine if your best chance of making it in life was to sell ice-cream, Detective?'

That explained the flawless Italian. Scamarcio wasn't used to hearing word-perfect Italian spoken by immigrants from Africa. It wasn't common to hear them master the tenses, let alone the subjunctive — hell, there were millions of Italians who still hadn't managed that one.

The man was in full flow now. 'I feel sorry for those parents. I understand their pain. But I promise you I didn't touch their little girl, and I didn't see anything.' He paused a moment. 'All I saw was those two parents asleep — the whole time.'

'How long asleep?'

'All the time she was in the water after eating the ice-cream.'

Scamarcio crouched down so they were at eye level. 'So you just got out of the water and left the little girl swimming?'

'She wasn't my responsibility.' The man sighed. 'Yes, I got out of the water, got my stuff, and left. I'd done Fetovaia. I wanted to move to the next beach along.'

Scamarcio pulled out a card from his jacket pocket. 'If you remember anything, anything at all, could you give me a call?'

The man took the card, and turned it over. He seemed ashamed for a moment. 'I don't have a phone.'

'Find a pay phone and reverse the charges. We can run to that in the police department — just.'

The man finally looked up and met his eyes. He seemed to have aged since the beginning of their encounter. Quietly, he said: 'I'll tell you one thing. I wouldn't have left my little girl alone like that. I wouldn't have fallen asleep while she was in the water. It was as if they didn't care.'

29

SCAMARCIO STEPPED OUT BLINKING into the harsh sunlight. The children had gone from the strip of grass, and now he spied a couple of cats lounging by the bushes, lazily licking their paws. The air was less than fresh, but it was still a relief to be out of the apartment block.

The new mobile that Garramone had given him buzzed, and he pulled it reluctantly from his pocket. The caller ID was blocked. He sighed, held it to his ear, pressed 'answer', but said nothing.

'He's dead.'

'What?'

'He's dead.' It was Garramone.

'What are you talking about?'

'The other guy in the photo with Arthur, the one we traced to Florence. He's dead. He's been found hanging in an apartment.'

Scamarcio felt his insides flip over. 'Fuck.' Then: 'How did you find out?'

'A photo posted on the national system by Florence police. I was scanning the day's stiffs. I don't know why — call it a bad feeling. I rang them, and they said they weren't quite convinced it was suicide, but they didn't have an ID for him yet — they couldn't find any documents with the body or in the flat where he was found.'

'And they didn't make the connection with the pictures in the papers?'

'It seems not.'

They both fell silent for several moments. Eventually, Scamarcio said: 'What does your friend say?'

'He's not taking my calls. I can't reach him.'

'Jesus.'

'This Elba thing — maybe it's some wild goose chase. Maybe someone sent you up there to get you out of the way, to stop us from going to Florence.'

'That thought just crossed my mind.'

'And?'

'I'm not convinced. I want to run with this a while. Give me a few more days.'

Garramone sighed. 'What can I do anyway? The Florence police will investigate now. It's out of our hands.'

There was a gap in the conversation, but Scamarcio didn't try to fill it. His mind was too busy processing all the possibilities.

'Anyway, stay in touch. Let me know if anything turns up.'

Garramone sounded like a man who had just been handed a huge problem but denied the means to solve it. Scamarcio sensed anew that they were both on a one-way track to trouble. He took a seat on a dilapidated bench and closed his eyes for a moment. Just why had Garramone decided to sabotage his prospects like this? He had always felt that there was a reluctant empathy there, a quiet understanding. Now he wasn't so sure. He checked himself. Garramone probably had no idea where it would all end when he agreed to this 'favour for a friend'. They had both been duped. But somehow, now Scamarcio was inside this thing, whatever it was, he felt a growing need to get to the nub of it, to root out its rotten core.

He got up from the bench, his limbs heavy. He decided to head to the hotel where the English couple was staying, but when he got there he was informed that they'd left early that morning for a cruise around the islands. Had no one told them to stay put? He left his card at the desk for them so they might call him on their return. The Scandinavian family, it transpired, were at the end of their holiday and had flown home to Stockholm the evening before. The fact that neither Genovesi, nor his men, seemed to have been aware of their impending departure was yet another source of frustration for Scamarcio.

There was nothing for it but to head to the police station. Genovesi would no doubt find some broom cupboard for him to work out of. The headquarters of the Elba squad were next to the town hall, opposite the park in Portoferraio. It was an unprepossessing building made of cinderblock, with three floors of plain windows. Like so much recent Italian architecture, no attempt had been made to blend in with the older buildings circling the park; like so many Italian towns, the result was a faded hodgepodge of elaborate facades and soulless concrete.

He flashed his badge at the desk sergeant, who nodded and gestured to his right. 'In there,' he said.

Scamarcio was relieved to see no sign of Genovesi — only Zanini, hunched in a corner, thumbing through the telephone directory. The phone rang and he reached for it, spotting Scamarcio as he did so. He nodded a greeting.

It was a brief, one-sided phone conversation. Zanini just said 'yes' several times and scribbled in a notepad before replacing the receiver. Scamarcio drew up a chair opposite his desk.

'How's it going?'

'OK. I spoke to Claudio, the owner of, well … Da Claudio, and he tells me those locals the Bakers mentioned were from the estate agents down the road, just out for a working lunch. They come twice a week, apparently.'

'We should have a word with them.'

'I'm on it. I've arranged to go round there in an hour or so.'

'Good.'

He glanced at his notepad, and flicked through a few pages. 'As for the other places the family visited, I've contacted a few: they tell me that they don't remember anything unusual. They'd had a mixture of tourists and locals in, mainly families and couples.

They don't remember seeing any strange loners, or anyone like that.' He looked up quickly. 'Not that that means anything, of course — we know that these kidnappings are often carried out by couples.'

'Quite.'

'One problem I've got is that the Bakers are really sketchy about their dates. They're having trouble remembering which days they went where. It makes it hard to pin things down.'

'That's often the way when you're on holiday — one day blends into the next. I guess it's worse when you're out of it on prescription drugs.' Scamarcio glanced around the office. It was small and, apart from a narrow window facing the square, there was only one other window at the back, which looked straight onto a concrete wall. It was not exactly an inspiring working environment. 'Where's Genovesi?'

'They went to Lacona. A German woman rang in, saying she'd seen a blonde girl who fits Stacey's description being dragged from a supermarket by a "foreign-looking" man.'

' "Foreign-looking"?'

'She thought he was maybe from the East. Albania or Romania — one of those countries.'

'When was this?'

'She called it in half an hour ago, and they headed straight out.'

Scamarcio raised his eyebrows and frowned. They both knew this could mean everything or nothing. Zanini gave him a strange look, and then got up from his desk and headed towards the hallway. He poked his head into the corridor for a moment, glanced left and right, and then closed the door and returned to his seat.

'What you were saying earlier about securing the scene ...'

'What about it?'

'Well, it wasn't secured. Not until several hours after they reported her gone. The world and his wife trampled around there until Genovesi finally gave the word.'

Scamarcio shook his head and gritted his teeth. He wasn't even surprised. Why was it always the same story? Why could no one on this godforsaken peninsula ever do things right?

'OK,' he said. 'Thanks for the steer.'

Zanini looked down, flicking through the notepad again. 'You didn't hear it from me.'

The phone trilled, puncturing the awkward silence. Zanini picked up, said nothing for several moments, and just rolled his eyes. Then: 'We're not talking to the press. No. No comment. You'd need to ask Chief Genovesi — he's the one running this inquiry, but he's out and, like I say, we're not talking to the press.' The caller was evidently refusing to take no for an answer, so after a while Zanini sighed and put the phone down.

'It's started,' said Scamarcio.

'It was only a matter of time.'

'They're quick, though. I'll give them that.'

'Yeah, and it wasn't even the local guy — that was Rai Tuscany.'

'You men will need to set something up now. I take it you don't have a regular press guy down here?'

'No call for it.'

'If you like, I can try and get somebody sent up from Rome.'

'Sounds good, but obviously you'd have to clear it with Genovesi.'

The phone rang again, and they exchanged glances as Zanini picked up. It would probably go on like this all afternoon now. Scamarcio felt for the young officer. But instead of anger, Zanini was registering surprise at whatever the caller was telling him. After a moment, he said: 'Well, actually, he's right here, sitting opposite me. Would you like to speak to him?' He waited an instant, and then handed the phone across. Scamarcio mouthed 'Genovesi?', but Zanini shook his head.

He picked up. 'Scamarcio — can I help you?'

It was a man's voice, slow and deliberate. 'Detective Scamarcio, I'm glad to have found you. I work as a guard at Longone Prison here on the island. I have an inmate who is demanding to speak with you. He claims that he can help you with an inquiry.'

Scamarcio felt an iciness somewhere in his chest. 'What inquiry?'

'He didn't say, just that it was the inquiry you're working on right now — the inquiry here on Elba. I'm sorry to bother you with this. I was going to leave it, but then we wondered whether he might actually have something for you, and whether it would be best to call, after all.'

'Thank you. You did the right thing. Who is your inmate?'

The guard fell silent a moment, and then uttered two words that made Scamarcio's blood run cold: 'The Priest.'

30

THE PORTO AZZURRO PRISON was actually an old fortress carved into the cliff face on the island's eastern shore. The sun was dipping below the horizon when Scamarcio drove up, its eerie glow sculpting the rocks, defining them harsh and cold against the ebbing light of the sea. Seagulls screeched overhead, fighting for scraps in the crevices of the rock-face — their dusty wings pounding the air, their red claws livid against the stone.

Scamarcio pulled the car to a halt, and took a moment to compose himself and steady his climbing pulse. The entrance to the prison was barely visible; it could have passed as a break in the rock if you were far enough away. The walls were sheer and oily black, planed down by centuries of salt spray. There was no escape from here, no boulders to stagger your descent to the water, no path towards the shore: beyond the edge of the fortress lay nothing but the blackness of the sea and whatever treacherous rocks lay beneath. If you were foolish enough to try running past the entranceway, you'd still be left clinging to the cliff face, probably dodging fire, until your getaway craft showed.

Scamarcio felt a jitter in his right leg, and looked down so he could watch it move. But he saw nothing — it seemed still. Slowly, with detachment, he observed both knuckles turn white, and realised that he'd been repeatedly clenching and unclenching his fists, as if this was a tried-and-tested relaxation technique of his. But, as far as he could remember, it was something he had never done before. Like, as far as he could remember, he had never met a child killer before.

And those two words, 'child killer', as awful as they were, didn't adequately describe The Priest. Yes, he was a child killer — Italy's worst — but it was the manner in which he had sexually assaulted and tortured his 18 victims that had embedded itself forever in the memories of those unfortunate colleagues of Scamarcio's who had been set the task of capturing him. For the public it was a little easier, because the full nature of his crimes had never made it onto the news: these details would have haunted too many clean minds, would have proved impossible to rub out, unlike an earthquake in Haiti or an oil spill off Mexico. But the gist was bad enough, and when The Priest — Mario Pugno, 45, from Lecce, who, with his Catholic robes and rosary beads, had once fooled so many — was finally brought in, thousands lined the streets of Rome, thousands wept and spat and screamed as his blacked-out penitentiary van passed by, crushing their makeshift wreaths and sending smashed roses and lily stems scattering. Scamarcio had been 25 at the time, and had worries of his own, but even he had been touched by the anger that gripped the nation — the unbridled fury and disgust, the clamour for blood. Even Cosa Nostra, so they said, were revolted by The Priest. Even they had tried to seize him and bring him in as a gesture to the people, a gesture to the police. But even they had failed.

Scamarcio exhaled, reached for the door handle, and stepped out into the fading light. The salt spray hit his skin, pushing up against his nostrils. There was another smell lurking beneath: rotting seaweed or moss, or some kind of dead sea-life.

Waiting at the shore's edge were the boatmen who ferried visitors back and forth to the entranceway. A couple of them were dragging on cigarettes, chewing the fat. Scamarcio showed them his police badge, and they nodded their recognition of his status. One of them stubbed out his cigarette and gestured to his colleague that he'd take the detective. He pointed to a rickety boat to his left, and Scamarcio climbed in, taking a seat on the damp bench. The boatman said nothing, just took his place at the helm and manoeuvred the craft out into the darkening waters. The cries of the gulls above them — malignant custodians heralding their arrival — grew more intense as they neared the prison. Scamarcio could make out the little harbour in front of the entranceway and wondered how they ferried the food out here, whether a bigger boat came with supplies a few times a week. The boatman drew up alongside the wooden boardwalk and attached the rope before jumping onto the jetty, then once they were steady gave Scamarcio his hand and helped him out. The detective reached into his pocket to pay, but the boatman waved him away: no doubt it was standard policy here, as elsewhere, to stay on the good side of the force.

Scamarcio turned to face the broad, stone steps that led up to the prison gates. His pulse quickened once more, and he had the sense that he was heading towards a dark destiny, towards a new unsettling chapter in his life. The steps were covered with a thick, white coating of gull grime, but the tang of salt mist and damp stone was strangely invigorating. There was a halogen glow emanating from behind the studded wooden gates and he made towards it, wondering what would greet him on the other side. He spoke his name and rank into the intercom, and then a hatch slid open to the right.

The face of a prison officer came up to the window, and the intercom stuttered into life again: 'ID, please'.

Scamarcio held his card up to the window. The officer compared photo with features, and then scrutinised something below him.

'One moment, sir.'

After a few seconds, the gate swung open, and Scamarcio stepped into a warm entranceway with large stone slabs underfoot.

'This way, sir.'

The officer was gesturing to a room on the right behind a

wide glass window. Inside, two officers were monitoring CCTV, and a third was writing in a logbook. The officer from the gate approached him.

'Detective Scamarcio, from the Rome Flying Squad,' he announced to his colleague.

The man with the logbook didn't look up. 'ID, please.'

Scamarcio handed it over once again.

The man studied it in detail, placed it across a scanner, saw it appear on his computer screen, and then typed in a few numbers. He then entered various details into his book and pushed it towards Scamarcio to sign.

'You're here to see The Priest, right?'

His colleagues glanced up momentarily from their screens.

'That's right.'

'He's pretty subdued these days — seems like the fight has finally left him.'

'The fight?'

'When we first took him out of isolation, years back, he created bloodshed and mess wherever he went, so we were forced to put him back into the psych ward time and again. But in recent years he's completely calmed down, like he's had a personality transplant. Now all he does is read books, press flowers, and talk to the real priests who come visit.'

'Well, that's reassuring, I suppose.'

'Don't worry, we have your back. Gun, please.'

Scamarcio handed it over, and then the logbook man pressed a button and told someone to come and collect the detective. A few seconds later, a young blond officer walked in.

'D'Angelo will take you up.'

Scamarcio thanked him and followed the officer out into the hallway and along the long, stone corridor. There were no cells lining this floor — just facilities for the staff, it seemed. At the end of the floor an iron staircase led to the next level, and Scamarcio followed the officer up. They didn't stop on that floor, but continued to the one above. There, the officer turned to the right down the walkway, and Scamarcio saw a gallery of cells on either side, identified by small portholes in their steel doors. The officer came to a halt outside a cell in the middle of the left-hand row, and gestured to two officers at the opposite end of the walkway to come over.

When they were within earshot, he said: 'His visitor has arrived — the detective.'

One of the two officers, thickset and bald, extended his hand to Scamarcio.

'He was asking for you repeatedly, and said it was very important you spoke because he wanted to help you with something. It was me who called the station.'

'Thanks for that. I appreciate it.'

'Any idea what he might want?'

'None, I'm afraid — I'm as confused as you are.'

The officer shook his head and shrugged. 'Well, let's see what he's up to. We'll be right outside, if you need anything. The door will remain open behind you once you enter.'

Scamarcio nodded. The officer looked through the porthole and then punched a number into the keypad to the right of the door. After a few seconds the door sighed and released, and he stepped into the cell. Scamarcio felt his breathing become shallow, but pushed himself to follow. He couldn't make out who was inside because the officer's bulk was obscuring his view.

'Your visitor is here — the policeman you were asking for.'

'Thank you.' The voice was softly spoken, gentle: a priest's voice in the confessional.

The officer stepped aside and nodded towards Scamarcio before leaving. Scamarcio turned his gaze to the man sitting crumpled on the bed. He was small-boned and fragile. A thin crown of white hair circled his head, and his eyes were dark and unblinking behind bookish spectacles. He looked like an injured owl, and had aged considerably since the photos that had once been splashed across Italy's front pages.

'I won't get up to shake your hand, Detective Scamarcio, because it will cause our friends outside some alarm if I start moving around. But please accept my heartfelt thanks for making this visit. I am very glad you came.' The Priest gestured to a rickety-looking chair opposite him, and Scamarcio sat down.

'So what can I help you with?'

'Actually, it's more a case of the other way around.'

'Why do you want to help me?'

'That's not important now.'

Scamarcio chose to say nothing, letting him sweat it out.

'You're on the island investigating the disappearance of a child, I believe.'

'Why do you believe that?'

'Again, that's not important now. And let's not play games. As you yourself know, time is of the essence with these things.'

Scamarcio remained silent; just studied the man, then the walls of the tiny cell. Curled and browning A4 sheets of pressed flowers were dotted about — roses, pansies, and daisies mainly. The effect was bizarre and disquieting.

The Priest studied him back. 'I knew your father once.'

Scamarcio felt something twist inside him. He said nothing for a few moments, and then: 'I find that hard to believe.'

The Priest waved a hand away. 'Again, that's not for now.' He looked to the tiny window to his right at the top of the cell wall where a gull was pecking against the glass. With a sudden ferocity, he cried: 'These critters never leave me alone — all hours of the day they come.' The voice was no longer gentle; it belonged to a different person altogether. Scamarcio looked over his shoulder through the doorway and saw the reassuring forms of the officers waiting outside.

'OK, if time is of the essence, as you say, how can you help me?'

The Priest returned his gaze to the detective. His look cut through him, unblinking.

'It's all quite simple,' said The Priest. 'You need to talk to the Roma. They have the answers to this one.'

'Why the Roma?'

'It's not important?'

'How did you come to know they're involved?'

He waved a hand away. 'Again, not important.'

'What led you to believe that we're investigating the disappearance of a child?'

The Priest just shrugged.

'Why do you think I even need your help?'

The old man pulled himself up straighter. 'Because you know nothing, it's a complex case, and these island police are imbeciles. You need all the help you can get.'

Scamarcio fell silent a moment. 'So where do the Roma fit into this?'

'I've already told you that I'm not going into that now. Why should I do your job for you? Just come back and see me when you've made some progress.'

'But ...'

The ferocity returned. 'No, that's it. You'd better hurry — the clock is ticking.'

31

SCAMARCIO GOT INTO his car, his hand unsteady with the keys. The sun was now a dark orb hanging low over the sea, and within minutes the light would be gone. He pushed the car into gear and headed out along the coast road to Portoferraio, his thoughts quick and muddled. He'd tried to press The Priest further, but had got nothing. Why was he trying to help him? From what Scamarcio understood, he'd never bothered to offer the police any assistance in his own investigation, and to date had yet to confess to his crimes. And how did he know that Scamarcio was even on the island? How had he learned about the disappearance of Stacey Baker? More troubling still, what did he mean about knowing his father — what common ground would have brought those two together? What did a link to The Priest say about his dad? What final disappointment was coming, what further testament to evil? He wondered briefly whether to contact the old men to ask them, and the thought wouldn't quite go away. And with the Roma, wasn't The Priest just tapping into the latest wave of xenophobia? Recently, the papers had been full of the story of the brutal rape and murder of the wife of a naval captain outside a station in Rome's southern suburbs. The culprit had been found to be an unemployed Roma gypsy living rough in a sprawling camp of shacks nearby. The discovery had prompted countless TV debates, not to mention a string of bloody reprisals in various parts of the country. Might it be nothing more than this? Somehow, though, Scamarcio doubted it was so simple; The Priest probably wasn't one to bob on the tide of mass sentiment.

When he returned to the station, it was dark. The place was still empty, except for Zanini, still typing away.

'That supermarket lead came to nothing,' he said. 'Just a kid misbehaving with its parents.'

Scamarcio had forgotten all about the Lacona lead. He sat down at the desk opposite and studied the young officer for a moment. 'Genovesi is still out,' added Zanini. 'How did it go up there?'

Scamarcio put his feet up on the desk and pulled out a cigarette from the pack he had bought in Termini station. He lit up and inhaled, letting the relief flood his veins and soothe his tired synapses. Then he exhaled slowly, counting the seconds. 'He told me to talk to the gypsies — they have the answers we need, apparently.'

'The answers to the girl's disappearance?'

'Yes.'

'But how did he even know about it in the first place?'

'No idea. Maybe he heard the guards talking; maybe they'd got word.'

'I doubt it,' said Zanini, shaking his head. 'The gypsies — I wouldn't have thought to look there.'

'Where?'

'There's a small settlement on the island in the hills to the east, but they've never given us any trouble. They keep themselves to themselves.'

'Can you show me on the map?'

'Are you thinking of heading up there?'

'No time like the present.'

There were some impressive villas tucked into the cliffs that lined the way to the camp, their gate lamps blinking in the darkness, hinting at generous driveways and dense, tropical gardens beyond. These must be the holiday homes of rich Milanese and

Florentines, plush and sprawling, but only used a few months a year. It was crazy, he reflected, the number of houses that stood empty in Italy most of the time.

The engine of the little Fiat was breathless and rasping as it made its way up the hill, the wheels churning on the stones beneath. As they rounded the bend, Scamarcio could make out the lights of various shacks and caravans in a field to the right. The camp was surrounded by wooden fencing, with a gate in the middle. Zanini had told him that the farmer who owned the land lived in a stone house further up the hill and sometimes employed the Roma as fruit pickers. Scamarcio drew the car to a halt opposite the settlement, and stepped out into the darkness. He activated the central locking, taking no chances. As he approached the gate, low voices and the occasional flurry of laughter floated up towards him on the breeze.

Once through the gate, to his right he could make out the forms of several old wooden caravans that looked as if they had been off the road for a long time. They were decorated with flowers, bells, and other designs, but in many places the paint was cracking and the wood had rotted. He headed towards the first cluster of lights he could see. As he walked around the edge of the last caravan in the line, he saw a camp fire with several people standing around it, and behind them two women chopping something on boards. As he approached, a hush descended over the little group, and as he drew closer he felt many eyes upon him — not just those of the few people at the fire. He pulled his ID from his chest pocket, showing it to the men in front of him.

'Detective Scamarcio, Rome Flying Squad. Can I speak with you a moment?'

The men exchanged glances. By now, the two women had left their chopping boards and had come up alongside them, wiping their hands on aprons around their waists. One of the men, the taller of the two, stepped forward a little. 'What's the matter? We have permission from Signor Zilli to be here. It is all agreed.' The accent was thick, but the Italian wasn't bad.

'Don't worry, I know that. I was hoping you could help me with an inquiry — that's all.'

The group exchanged glances again.

'What inquiry?' said the man.

'A little girl has gone missing from the beach in Fetovaia.'

The women bunched their arms across their chests, and shook their heads.

'And, of course, you think it must be the gypsies! Fetovaia is miles away,' said the man, who seemed to be the leader of the group. 'Why are we always the first to get the blame?'

Scamarcio held up his palms to pacify them. 'There's no question of blame being apportioned right now. We're just asking everyone on the island, no matter who they are, whether they've seen or heard anything. We need to be thorough; we can't leave anyone off our list. I'm sure you can understand that, especially where a missing child is concerned.'

The group fell silent, and then started speaking softly in a language that Scamarcio couldn't understand. More people had come up to find out what was going on, and the disparate voices were growing louder now. Eventually, the leader said: 'We are sorry about the child, but we can't help you — nobody has seen or heard anything.'

Scamarcio reached in his pocket for his wallet and pulled out several cards, handing them around the group. 'If you do hear of anything, could you let me know? Reverse the charges if you don't want to pay for the call.'

They studied the cards for a moment, but said nothing. Eventually, the leader of the group just looked up and nodded gently, so Scamarcio took that as his cue to leave. As he headed back to the car, he felt their eyes upon him again, and heard their voices rise up on the wind. Here in the hills, the air was crisp and cold, but he could still taste the salt tang of the sea. As he walked, the breeze whispered through the branches of the pines, and he felt his unease stir along with them — a sense that things were running away again beyond his control. What did The Priest want with the Romany? Why did Scamarcio feel as though he was being played?

He got back in the car and fired up the engine, glad to be safe inside once more. He turned back onto the road and continued up the hill, looking for the stone house, trying to settle his thoughts. After a minute or so, he spotted the cottage on his left — thin tendrils of smoke rising from the chimney, well-kept stables, and a barn to the right. As he drew up outside, he heard dogs barking; three, maybe four, of them.

He stepped out into the chill air, his breath catching slightly. The stars were brighter than he'd ever seen them in the city, and he noticed one burning stronger than all the rest, very low to the land. What was that, he wondered? It didn't quite seem real.

He opened a rickety wooden gate and made his way up a stone pathway to the main house. The dogs were barking furiously now, but he still couldn't see them. He hoped he would make it safely to the front door before they caught up with him, wherever they were. As if in answer to his thoughts, a splinter of light hit the path and a tall, sinewy man peered out in the darkness. He seemed shocked to see him there, and on reflex stepped back into the house, reaching for something to his right — probably his gun.

'Sorry to startle you. I'm Detective Scamarcio from the Flying Squad down in Rome.' He quickly drew out his badge, although he knew the man would not be able to see anything in the darkness. The man put down whatever it was he'd just picked up and came back out onto the threshold to get a better look at him and his approaching ID. After he'd had time to examine the photo and make a quick appraisal of whether Scamarcio still constituted a threat, he said: 'Sorry about the dogs. I put some of them in the pen at night to keep the foxes away. But there are another two in here, so just hold on a second while I calm them down.'

The door swung shut in his face, and he could hear the farmer speaking softly to somebody inside before he was back again. He held open the door: 'Come in, Detective.'

The room was small and very warm. A roaring fire was alight in the grate, and the flames danced shakily across the bare, stone walls. In front of the fire were two Alsatians, sitting like sentinels instead of lying, soaking up the warmth — which Scamarcio guessed was what they were doing before he'd arrived. Zilli gestured him to an armchair opposite the fire, one of two placed there.

'Can I get you anything to drink? I'm enjoying a grappa myself.'

'Thank you, but no.'

'Of course, I forgot. You can't drink when you're working.' Zilli sank into his chair by the fire and took a sip of the grappa from a glass placed beside him on the hearth.

He was a handsome man with clean, even features and a strong jaw. Scamarcio noticed several photos of an equally handsome woman of about the same age lining the mantelpiece. Zilli spotted him looking. 'That was my wife. I lost her last year, to cancer.'

'I'm very sorry to hear that, 'said Scamarcio, slightly taken aback. After a beat, he said: 'I lost my mother to the same thing.'

'Ah, then you know,' said the farmer, and took another sip of his drink. 'So, Detective, how can I help you?'

Scamarcio talked him through the disappearance before he asked: 'The Romany on your land — have you ever had any problems with them?'

The farmer looked up from his glass. 'You think they have something to do with it?'

'We've not reached any conclusions yet, but we're exploring all the avenues, as we always must.'

Zilli was shaking his head. 'Well, Detective, I can honestly say that that's one place you don't need to look. I've never had any issues with them. They work for me as fruit pickers, and do a good job, and in return I let them stay on my land and I pay them a small wage. They've been here five years now, and there's never been any trouble. They have always treated me with respect and vice versa.' He paused a moment before going on: 'I know there was that terrible incident down in Rome recently, but I think it's just bad apples. The people here are peaceful and honest.'

Scamarcio nodded slowly. 'Well, thanks for setting me straight.' He reached for a card from his wallet again, and handed it over. 'If you hear anything, could you let me know?'

The farmer took it without studying it, instead eying Scamarcio quizzically. 'What's the Rome Flying Squad doing on Elba? Seems a bit far from home.'

'That, Mr Zilli, is a long story, I'm afraid.'

The farmer smiled and said: 'Are you quite sure about that grappa, Detective?'

32

HIS HEAD WAS SPINNING slightly as he descended back towards the sea: the lights of Porto Azzurro seemed to separate and dance in front of him before coalescing again and bleeding into one.

The phone rang on the seat beside him, and he knew it was Garramone. 'They're pushing for his resignation — no let-up,' he said by way of a hello.

'Ganza?'

'Who else?'

'My friend is very anxious. He's worried it could bring down his government — he's turning up the heat on me.'

'Well, he's a survivor, your friend. There aren't many people who could withstand forty votes of no confidence.'

'Scamarcio, you don't know him. He's a good man. I wouldn't be doing this otherwise.'

Scamarcio knew that wasn't strictly true. If you were the chief of the Flying Squad in Rome, and the PM asked for help with a personal inquiry, you were likely to say yes if you valued your career.

'Any news from Florence?'

'Not that I know of. I don't want to call them up asking.'

'Filippi?'

'Still out, thank God.'

Scamarcio grimaced slightly at the callousness.

'What about you? My friend, when he finally made contact, didn't seem best pleased to learn you were on Elba — thinks you're enjoying a holiday at the taxpayers' expense.''

Scamarcio couldn't give a shit what his friend thought. 'Remember The Priest?'

Garramone paused a moment, and then said: 'The child killer?'

'Yes, the child killer.'

'Actually, isn't he on Elba? At Porto Azzurro prison?'

'Correct. He called me at the station — well, one of his prison guards called me — saying he wanted to speak with me. When I went up to Porto Azzurro to see him, he told me that the answer to the girl's disappearance lies with the gypsies on the island.'

'What?'

Scamarcio brought him up to speed. After a while, Garamone said: 'But how did he know you were even here? How did he know what you were looking into?'

'Beats me.'

They both fell silent again before the chief said: 'Be careful. You may have a leak among the yokel squad, which would make me think you might actually be onto something. The Roma — have you spoken with them?'

Scamarcio filled him in on his visit to the camp. He could hear Garamone hitting something repeatedly, but couldn't tell whether it was his foot, or his hand, or a ball on a racket. 'Well, keep at it,' said the chief. 'We shall see where it all takes us. But get me something concrete soon. We need this to be the making of us, not the end.' Then he hung up.

Scamarcio pondered the words: the making of him or the end of him. If it was the end of him, he wasn't sure whether he would mind so much. A few days ago, even a few hours ago, he would have said no — the force was where he needed to be. Now he was no longer quite sure: the points of reference seemed to be shifting subtly around him. He felt overwhelmed by a string of conflicting thoughts and emotions — no longer sure where felt right, or where he fitted into it all.

33

BORGHETTI WAS COLLECTING coffee from the machine when he walked in the next morning.

'Sleep well, Detective? You want one?' He held up a plastic cup.

'No and yes: in that order.' Scamarcio flung his bag down onto the desk and yawned, not bothering to cover his mouth with his hand. 'That hotel is a rat hole. Couldn't you have got me a room in one of the tourist places?'

Borghetti frowned, seemingly put out. 'I'm sorry — we thought you'd want to be near the station.'

'I've got my stuff in the car. I'm going to move tonight, maybe to that nice place where the Bakers are staying.'

'You'll be lucky to get a room at this time of year.'

'Well, when one of you has a minute, can you try?'

Borghetti set the coffee down on his desk, along with a few sachets of sugar. 'No problem, I'll get somebody on it right away.' He disappeared out into the hall for a few moments, and Scamarcio sank back in his chair to enjoy his espresso. As he did so, he noticed some papers on the desk to his right: there was a missing person's form on top, and when he looked a bit closer he was surprised to see that it wasn't made out in the name of Stacey Baker, but for someone called Fabio Ella.

Borghetti came back into the room and sat down at the same desk, reaching for a pen, and drawing the missing person's sheet towards him. 'Sorry, Detective, I just need to finish this, and then I will be with you. The desk sergeant is seeing to your hotel.'

'You guys get a lot of missing persons on the island?' asked

Scamarcio as Borghetti painstakingly entered details on the form.

'Are you talking about this one?'

'Couldn't help spotting it.'

'As far as I know, it's our first — well, along with Stacey Baker, but this one came in earlier, I believe.'

Scamarcio sat up straighter in the chair, and tossed the used cup into the overflowing rubbish bin by his desk.

'You're telling me you've never had a missing person's report before, and now you have two?'

'Well, I guess so, yes. This one was called in a few days before Stacey Baker, I think.' He scanned the form again. 'Yes, four days before, but we're not taking it that seriously.'

'Why not?'

'It was some hysterical Milanese woman who kept calling, saying her husband had just vanished into thin air.' Borghetti gave him a knowing look. 'We all know what *that* means — it happens all the time. And then she told us she was heading back to Milan, so, you know, we thought we'd leave it to those guys. And, anyway, then the Baker case came in, and we had to put this one on the backburner.'

Scamarcio got up from the desk, walked behind Borghetti, and snatched up the sheet, scanning the details: 'Why wasn't I told about this?'

Genovesi bustled into the office. 'Told about what?'

'The disappearance of Fabio Ella.'

Genovesi waved the thought away. 'Why do you care about that?'

Scamarcio calmed himself by imagining Genovesi's fingers in a vice.

'Can we have a word in your office?'

Genovesi pulled a look of faux confusion: 'By all means.'

When they were safely out of earshot, Scamarcio said: 'Two disappearances in a matter of days, on an island that has never before seen one! Didn't this strike you as odd?'

Genovesi filled a small plastic jug with water from the dispenser in the corner of his room, and then proceeded to see to several dusty plants lining his filing cabinets.

'No, it didn't strike me as odd. And, anyway, it's not correct to say we've never had a disappearance on Elba. In 1974, a farmer vanished while herding his sheep.'

'What happened to him?'

'He was found several days later. Turned out he had a fancy woman in another town, but hadn't got around to telling his wife.'

Scamarcio sighed, he suddenly felt achingly tired.

'Look, I think we need to check out Fabio Ella — there may be a connection to Stacey Baker.'

Chief Genovesi turned around from his plants. Little drops of water were falling from the spout of the jug onto the cracked linoleum below, gently marking time in the momentary silence between the two men.

'Do as you wish, but we have limited resources, so I won't hesitate to complain to your bosses in Rome if it turns out you are time-wasting.'

'Don't worry, I'll see to this one myself.' He sprang out of the chair and slammed the door, leaving Genovesi standing there with his water jug.

Zanini and Borghetti were speaking in whispers when he got back to the desk. It was obvious that they had been trying to follow the conversation inside their boss's office.

Scamarcio ignored them and sat back down, reaching for the phone. He scrolled through the address book on his BlackBerry, looking for Cepparo's details in Milan. It was a contact he'd made at a police conference the year before, which might turn out to be useful now.

He dialled the number, and was about to give up when a breathless voice finally came on the line.

'Cepparo.' He'd been running in or out of somewhere.

'Cepparo, it's Leone Scamarcio. We met at that get-together in Naples last year.'

'Ah, Scamarcio, of course. You drank me under the table.'

Scamarcio smiled. 'Was it that bad? I don't really remember.'

'Well, of course you don't. How can I help you?'

'I'm on a case, and it's got some links to a disappearance on Elba — a guy from Milan called Fabio Ella.'

'He went missing from the island?'

'Yeah, a couple of days ago. He's a resident of Milan. I've got his fiscal code and address here. I was wondering whether there was any chance of you looking into him for me — seeing what you can find out?'

'What are you hoping to discover?'

'No idea, Cepparo. I just think it might be worth talking to the wife who reported him missing, and also worth searching the apartment if you can get permission without having to go through all the usual crap.'

'Leave it with me. I'm busy on something right now, but I can give it some time later today.'

'I owe you one.' Scamarcio read him the relevant details from the sheet before hanging up. The two officers had stopped what they were doing, making no attempt this time to disguise their interest.

'You really think there could be something in this Ella thing?' asked Zanini.

'It's worth a try,' said Scamarcio. 'It's always worth a try.'

He was about to talk them through the plan for the day when his desk phone rang. He didn't think he'd given anyone the number yet.

'Detective Scamarcio?' the voice was hesitant, male, and somehow familiar.

'Who's speaking?'

'It's Officer Erranti from Porto Azzurro prison. We met yesterday. I was the one who first called you about The Priest.'

'Ah, yes, of course.'

'The thing is, he wants to see you again.'

'Again?'

'He says he has something more for you. I don't know if he was any use to you yesterday, but I thought I should call, and let you know at least.'

Scamarcio felt confused, then irritated. He wasn't a puppet to be summoned at The Priest's beck and call.

'Thank you, officer. Any idea what he believes he has for me this time?'

'No, he wouldn't say.'

'I see.' Scamarcio sank back in the chair, cradling the phone in his chin. He could hear voices in the square down below, children shouting.

'There's one other thing.' Erranti was hesitant again. 'He wants you to come at midnight tonight — he says no other time will do. And you must come alone, apparently.'

Scamarcio yawned. He knew when he was being played. A night-time trek to the prison was the last thing he needed, but of course he had to go.

34

THE YOUNG OFFICER from the day before was waiting for him on the shore with a speedboat when he arrived. The normal boatmen must have gone home for the night.

'I was told to collect you,' he said. 'We didn't expect to see you back again so soon.'

'Neither did I,' said Scamarcio, tucking his coat around him as he took a seat in the boat. He saw that there were plastic-covered cushions this time, providing much more comfort than yesterday's ride.

As they pulled away from shore, the officer said: 'The Priest has mythical status among the sex offenders, you know — it's sick.'

'What about the other prisoners?'

'Oh, we don't mix them, of course. We keep the sex offenders together on the same floor for their own protection.'

'For their own protection.' Scamarcio considered the words. And what about the protection of the children? If it was up to him, he'd let the natural laws of the criminal jungle take their course, and leave The Priest and his like to the murderers, robbers, and wife beaters. This imperfect justice that was supposedly a marker of our civilised world — how bizarre it seemed to him sometimes.

The stars weren't visible tonight. A bank of cloud had pushed in from the east during the late afternoon, and now he could feel the first sharp spots of rain against his skin.

They travelled on in silence, the only sounds coming from the soft lapping of the waves against the hull or a melancholy gull cry echoing out across the water. Eventually, the officer killed the engine and they drew up alongside the tiny harbour, yellow splinters of light visible in the prison walls above them.

'We're a skeleton staff at night, but we'll be watching out for you, don't worry,' said the officer as they made their way to the gate. Scamarcio felt his pulse rise again; this time, though, the rush of blood in his ears felt more intense, more difficult to control.

Officer Erranti and another younger man he hadn't seen before were waiting for him outside The Priest's cell when they arrived.

'Erranti, we meet again,' said Scamarcio, nodding to the unknown officer. 'Thanks for the speedboat.'

'Not at all, Detective. We're glad to be of help. I just hope he's not wasting your time.'

A slightly strained silence descended before Erranti said: 'You ready?'

'As I'll ever be.' Scamarcio took a deep breath, and then they repeated the day before's procedure, with Erranti going in first.

The Priest was on the bed again, but dressed differently this time in a thick, knitted brown jumper and threadbare pyjama bottoms. He was no longer wearing eyeglasses. It was warm in the cell, so Scamarcio wondered why he needed the jumper.

'No funny business, Pugno, I'm warning you,' said the officer, pointing a finger before stepping back into the corridor. Scamarcio heard chairs being drawn up outside the door.

The Priest gestured to the rickety chair again, exactly as he had done the day before. For a moment, Scamarcio felt as if he were stuck in some kind of feverish dream or recurring nightmare.

'Again, Detective, thank you for coming. I realise you are busy.' The Priest sounded tired. Scamarcio saw dark, purplish rings beneath his eyes and a thin sheen of perspiration on his forehead. His hands were shaking slightly, and his knees seemed bony beneath the pyjama bottoms. They sat in silence for several moments, surveying each other; Scamarcio felt uncomfortable, and wanted to look away, but knew he couldn't. Then, in a sudden fluid movement that belied his age, The Priest was off the bed and kneeling at his feet. Scamarcio realised that he must have cried out in shock, because Erranti and the other officer were already running in from outside. 'Pugno, I told you, no funny business. Get back on the bed.' The little man did not respond; his eyes were shut as he rocked back and forth slowly on his heels, and his palms were drawn together, seemingly poised in prayer.

'Get back on the bed, I tell you!' But the man just kept rocking himself — forward, back, forward, back. The two officers looked at Scamarcio now, unsure what to do.

Scamarcio realised he'd actually stopped breathing for several seconds. He tried to pull himself together, steady his heart rate, and assess the situation. After a beat, he said: 'It's OK, I can handle it. I'll call you if there are any problems.'

The officers exchanged glances and seemed unconvinced, but left them to it, returning to their chairs by the door.

The Priest continued to rock back and forth silently. Scamarcio noticed that his hands were coarse and dry — the hands of a labourer.

'So, tell me what this is all about, Mr Pugno. You don't need to be on the floor to talk to me. Why don't you get back on the bed?' His voice came out shaky, slightly higher than normal.

The Priest started mumbling something to himself, but Scamarcio couldn't make out the words. Was the man having some kind of breakdown? It almost sounded as though he was speaking in tongues. Scamarcio felt a growing well of unease in his stomach. He just wanted to run from the cell, and get away from Longone as fast as the speedboat would take him.

Slowly, The Priest raised his head, and Scamarcio saw that his eyes were red-rimmed. The old man was crying: fat, bulbous tears running down his haggard jowls. Scamarcio was reminded of the one time he had seen his father cry, and of how uncomfortable it had made him feel, how he had just wanted to run away then, too

— which, in the end, was what he'd done.

'I need forgiveness.' The words came out as a sigh, like the last breath of a dying man.

Scamarcio felt his body go rigid. 'What?'

'Forgiveness.'

'Forgiveness for what?'

'You know what.'

'I don't.'

'For the innocents, those innocents.' The words were spoken so softly that Scamarcio could barely make them out. He felt nauseous, and forced himself to swallow down.

'For the children you killed?'

'Yes, the children,' whispered The Priest. 'The lost souls.'

Instinctively, Scamarcio shifted his chair away from the stricken figure on the floor.

'I can't be the one to give you that.'

'Yes. You're the only one who can.'

'What makes you think that? Perhaps you're confused? I'm a policeman, not a priest.' Scamarcio realised that he was speaking very fast now, the words running into each other. The Priest was shaking in front of him, sweating profusely.

'You're the only one — you know that. The only one.'

'Why do you say that? It makes no sense.'

'Don't deny it!' There was no anger in the words; just a tired insistence.

'No.'

'Yes!' He was shouting now, trying to get up from the floor.

'Listen, Pugno, I don't know what you're talking about. I think you're very mistaken about something.'

'It's you who's mistaken.'

Scamarcio shook his head, and took a breath. 'I have *work* to do. I will not allow you to waste any more of my time with your stupid games.'

'Games? You think this is just a game?' He looked up at him, incredulous, pleading.

'I'm a policeman, not a priest,' Scamarcio repeated, the words barely a whisper now.

The Priest just kept staring up at him, his eyes searching him out, trying to locate something deeper. Scamarcio fought the urge to look away. 'So just tell me: how else can you help this inquiry? What further information do you have?'

The Priest began shaking his head, frantic, as if he was having a seizure. 'No, no, no. That's not how it works. That's not how it works!' he hissed. The tiny cell was suddenly rank with sweat — the stench of fear. The Priest was rocking again now, his whole body quivering.

Scamarcio finally looked away. 'I decide how it works, Pugno. Not you.'

'You fool!' screeched The Priest. 'You stupid, deluded fool! You're in denial!' He stabbed a thin, bony finger at him; then, exhausted, his mouth fell open and a dribble of saliva ran to his chin.

Scamarcio could take it no more. He pushed his chair back, scratching hard against the stone, and fled the cell, ignoring the waiting officers outside.

He tried to light a second cigarette, but the wind was high and the air damp, and he needed several attempts. When he'd managed it, he shifted his weight against the wall of the prison and looked up at the moths circling the sodium lights above the gate. They were battering their tiny bodies against the plastic casing, seemingly on some kind of suicide mission.

He could still feel his heart in his chest and taste the bile in his mouth — the first cigarette did not seem to have had any effect. This would be the last he'd see of Longone. He wasn't coming back; wasn't going to waste his time pandering to the delusions of some sick freak.

'Detective Scamarcio.' The voice startled him. It was Officer Erranti, peering out into the darkness.

'I just came to check that you're all right.'

Scamarcio took a drag on the fag and then tossed it to the ground, grinding it in firmly with his shoe.

'Yeah, no worries. He just got to me a bit with the weird mind games in there.'

'We heard him confess,' said Erranti. 'After all these years, it's incredible. You must have some kind of power over him, Detective. I know it's none of my business, but I have to ask: why did he say what he did, about you being the only one?'

Scamarcio sighed, and felt the bile rising again. 'I have absolutely no idea, officer. No idea at all.'

35

Scamarcio was trying to drift into sleep. Now safely installed in the same four-star hotel as the Bakers, he could hear the waves lapping against the rocks below, and the new, comfortable surroundings brought a calm that had eluded him earlier. He wondered if he shouldn't have run. Maybe if he had stayed he could have learned more — perhaps given The Priest the opportunity to deliver information as a trade-off for forgiveness. Why had he reacted the way he had? He wasn't sure; but, reflecting on it now, it didn't seem wholly professional.

What game was Pugno playing with him? Was it a distraction maybe? Could he be involved somehow in the girl's disappearance, and have been tasked to keep him off the scent and occupy his thoughts? That seemed unlikely. He had wanted to meet at midnight, when the day's work was over, and the desire to confess had seemed genuine. What was it about Scamarcio that made The Priest think that only he could help him? What was it about his connection to Scamarcio's father? He turned once more in the bed, and knew that sleep would not come tonight. The remote control lay on his bedside table, and he reached for it, turning on the TV and searching for Sky News 24. The presenter was the same plastic blonde from the other night, along with her plastic Ken partner. Again, Spezzi was up in a picture in the top right-hand corner: odd, it was like travelling back in time watching this; again, he felt like he was stuck in some feverish dream. He turned up the sound: 'It is believed he threw himself from the window of his hospital room onto the concrete below. There were no witnesses. The Spezzi family is planning a small funeral at the chapel on their Piedmont estate next week. They have asked the media to respect their privacy at this very difficult time.'

Scamarcio sank back into the pillows. 'No way,' he whispered to himself. 'No way.' Instinct told him that the young man hadn't jumped — it couldn't have been that simple. The thought brought a heat to his skin, making him feel as though he really was getting a fever. Someone was at work here, someone with more power than he and Garramone — maybe with more power than Garramone's friend.

His BlackBerry buzzed beside him. It was an email from Cepparo, up in Milan: 'At Ella's office premises in the south of the city. Found something you might be interested in, will call you in five.'

Scamarcio decided to get dressed. It would be pointless lying here all night, trying to sleep. He was pulling on his jumper when the phone rang, but he was sure five minutes hadn't yet passed.

'Scamarcio?'

'Yeah, Cepparo. Your email sounded promising — what have you got?'

'We turned over the house. Nothing interesting there, and then the wife gave us permission to do his office, which is just two streets down. He repaired computers — he was born in Albania, by the way. So we search his PC and, after a while, find a hell of a lot of not-very-appetising stuff. It's got the officer I brought along with me pretty shaken up. He's young, wet behind the ears. He was the one who found it.'

'Found what?'

'Kiddie stuff, deeply unpleasant kiddie pics — you know the score.'

Scamarcio watched the building blocks of the case scatter and then slowly reassemble in his brain. He thought for a moment: 'The wife know?'

'Well, if she did, she certainly didn't let on. When we searched the office, she waited outside in the street, smoking. She doesn't know what we found yet.'

'OK, don't tell her.' He paused for a moment: 'Have you been through his emails?'

'We tried, but it looks as if they've all been wiped. I need to get a techie in to see if there's anything more we can do with that.'

'Sure.'

He fell silent again. After a while, Cepparo said: 'So what do you want me to do with this? Obviously, I got a case here myself now — can't let someone with a whole stack of kiddie porn on their computer go un-investigated.'

'No, of course not. Look, thanks for this. If in the course of your case you turn up anything else, let me know.'

'I should be thanking you, Scamarcio — these bastards need to be locked up for life, although, as we all know in this sorry excuse for a country, that currently means two-and-a-half years.'

'Albanian national, you say?'

'Yeah, born in Tirana, but moved to Italy 20 years ago, settled in Milan, and married the missus seven years back.'

'And you think she's clean?'

'Would seem so to me. That, or she's an excellent actress. She let us go through his office, no probs, and didn't seem to be hiding anything.'

'OK.' Scamarcio pushed the air out from his cheeks. 'So I guess this is your case now, Cepparo, I wish you luck and, like I say, if there's anything more, let me know.'

'Can you send me the missing person's report in full? Seems like I need that now.'

'Yeah, sure.'

'And, Scamarcio, what's your angle on this? Why are you interested in him?'

'If I told you, you'd never believe me, and anyway it won't help you with where you're at right now. But when it's all done and dusted, we'll go for a few more drinks and I'll talk you through it.'

'Sounds good. I shall hold you to that.'

They said their goodbyes, and he hung up. Scamarcio sank back on the bed. Now there was an obvious connection between Ella and the Baker girl, not to mention the images on Arthur's camera. Why had Ella gone missing, and where had he gone? Was he with the girl now? The thought was disquieting, to say the least, and he suddenly felt a strange kind of guilt, knowing that he possessed this new knowledge, but that her parents lay oblivious and possibly sleepless just a couple of floors above him.

He put on his coat and hurried out of the room, descending the stairs to the reception without waiting for the elevator. The lobby was cold, echoey, and quiet. There seemed to be no one manning reception. He headed out the front door towards the carpark. There were still no stars in the sky, and the air hung chill and heavy.

He didn't know where he wanted to go; he just knew he didn't want to be in the hotel anymore. He decided to head for the police station. He could make his calls from there.

It was deserted when he walked in, apart from the desk sergeant, a battered-looking old-timer he'd seen the day before, who was now nodding off over a crumpled copy of *La Nazione*. He startled into life again when the front doors slammed shut behind Scamarcio.

'Detective? Everything OK?' His voice was raspy from sleep.

'Yeah. Couldn't sleep, so I decided to catch up on some paperwork.'

'I admire your dedication. You'll go far,' he said, as if Scamarcio was a young recruit in training, and he an older, wiser chief of police.

Scamarcio headed through to the squad room and flicked the switch for the lights. The fluorescent beams stuttered slowly into action, clicking and humming a while before the light came through.

He walked over to his desk and switched on his computer. He could trigger a national alert for Fabio Ella from here by accessing the national police computer. It took him several minutes to get in, and then another few minutes to enter the relevant data. When it was done he left his contact details so he could be reached in the event of a sighting. He should probably have told Cepparo he was going to do this — he would call him later to explain. Suddenly, he felt a fog of tiredness overwhelm him, and he let his head rest on the desk.

After what seemed like only minutes, he awoke with a start, aware of a painful stiffness in his neck that was spreading up to his temples. Outside the window, he could see the first weaves of pink in the sky, and guessed it had been more than minutes he'd been asleep. A few birds were chirping lazily in monotone in the trees of the piazza. He walked to the coffee machine, pulled himself an espresso, drank it down with a swift turn of the wrist, and began to feed in the coins for another. But then he heard feet pounding along the corridor, and the desk officer came running in from outside. He seemed both stressed and excited, and there was fresh colour in his cheeks. He panted to a stop on the threshold, holding the swing doors with one hand.

'A call has just come in saying a body has been found on Barbarossa beach.'

Scamarcio's stomach flipped over. 'A little girl's body?'

'No — adult male. Found by a Dutch tourist out for an early-morning run.'

'Barbarossa — where's that?'

'To the south. You can get to it on the main road, turning left as you leave Portoferraio, heading for Azzurro. It will take you about fifteen minutes.'

'OK.' Scamarcio reached for his jacket and collected his phone before making for the door.

'Shall I tell the others to join you?'

'Yeah. And where's the kit? And who's the pathologist on the island?'

'Dr Barrabino, GP from down the road; I'll call him in one second.' The desk sergeant was reaching into a cupboard, pulling out several clear packs of overalls, shoe coverings, and gloves. Then he leaned in again and came out with two plastic cases: 'Crime-scene kit.' They looked like they had never been opened.

Scamarcio grabbed them and hurried down the corridor towards the car-park.

As he took the road to Porto Azzurro, the pink in the sky was becoming blue against the sea. The sea was calm and glassy, and the beaches were deserted. There was very little traffic on the road, save for a noisy truck behind him, which he presumed had just come in from the port with supplies. He left a message for Garramone as he drove, filling him in about Fabio Ella and the child porn on his computer. He decided not to mention the body for now. There was no point until he understood how it fitted in — if it fitted in.

When he reached the bay marked Barbarossa, he was surprised to see an Alfa Romeo Spider parked up by the gate to the beach. A tall man in his late forties with classic Mediterranean looks was fiddling with something in the boot. He was already dressed in the requirement overalls.

Scamarcio drew up alongside him, and the man turned. Scamarcio stepped out of the little Fiat and walked towards him, extending a hand. 'Dr Barrabino, I presume. How did you get here so quickly?'

Barrabino's mouth formed the outline of a smile. 'I probably had a head start on you — I live at the eastern edge of Azzurro.' Then he surveyed the boxy Cinquecento for a moment. 'And, not meaning to be rude, I imagine this goes slightly faster than your ride.'

He snapped shut a case, lifted it out, and then gently closed the boot as if not wanting to expose his precious car to any extra stress.

'The sergeant told me you're up here from Rome. Sounds like a lot has been happening since your arrival.' Something about the way he said this made it sound as though it was Scamarcio's fault.

'You could say that. A tourist called this one in, apparently.'

Scamarcio finished putting on his protective suit, and they headed towards the gate, which opened onto the beach.

'It's the first murder I can ever remember on the island.' Again, something about the way he said it made it sound as though Scamarcio bore some responsibility.

'You can't get much practice as a police pathologist, then?'

Barrabino turned to look at him a moment: 'Plenty of practice as a normal pathologist, and there have been several tourist deaths here among our elderly visitors that the police have had to sign off on.'

The man was conceited, and Scamarcio was not warming to him. Maybe it was the swept-back shoulder-length hair and the car. Maybe it was just his tone.

As they descended the last of the wooden steps to the beach, he saw a dangerously thin Nordic man in running gear pacing up and down, 20 feet-or-so away from a crumpled form at the water's edge. When he noticed the two of them approach, the man came jogging over, relief flooding his face.

'Are you the police?'

Scamarcio introduced himself and his new friend.

'I haven't touched anything. I've stayed away, but I know it's a body — no doubt about it. I called you from my mobile.' He held up the phone as if proof were needed.

'Thank you,' said Scamarcio. 'We appreciate that.'

'I'm just here on holiday — my wife's at the hotel. I go running every morning about this time.' He seemed to have already planned out a checklist of questions in his head that he thought

Scamarcio would require answers to. His English was clear and fluent, like so many Dutch people who had grown up with it as second language from an early age. The Italians should try a similar system, thought Scamarcio, but they were too proud.

'I hadn't been running long when I saw it. Our hotel is just back there.' He gestured around the bay to the left, and Scamarcio could see the outline of red roofs among the palms.

'It was about half an hour ago that I called you.' The man quickly looked down at his mobile and seemed to scroll through something. 'Actually, thirty-four minutes ago, to be precise.'

Scamarcio took a deep breath, and wished the man would do the same. 'Thank you, you have been very helpful. Why don't you just wait over there a moment by those trees while we take a look? My colleagues will be along in a moment, and will take a full statement from you.'

The man nodded and headed off towards a cluster of palms at the edge of the sand.

Scamarcio set off with Barrabino towards the crumpled heap, and as they drew near he was relieved to note that there was no smell and no flies. They stopped to attach their protective booties, and then walked the last few metres to the corpse.

It was the body of a man twisted into a foetal position. His face was round and pale, the eyes closed. His hair was dark and damp, pasted to the skull, and he was wearing brown trousers and a windcheater that was stained with blood. His left foot was bare, but a blue sock hung half on and half off his right foot. The sock was also stained with blood.

Barrabino knelt down by the body and undid the windcheater. After a brief examination of the eyes and mouth, he moved to the neck and arms, running his fingers along them gently, as if afraid to hurt him. After a while, he said: 'He's been stabbed. Repeatedly. It looks like there are just a very few blowfly eggs in the eyes and mouth so far, so I don't think he's been dead long — he was probably killed some time last night. There is rigor in the face and upper neck muscles, but not the larger ones yet, which tells me that he's been dead at least two hours. But that's all I can offer right now. When I get him on the table I will know more.'

'Was he moved afterwards, you think? Killed elsewhere?'

Barrabino stretched his legs after kneeling by the body on the cold sand. 'The lividity will tell me for sure, but for that I need him on the table. I don't want to compromise the scene by moving him around too much here.'

The doctor took a small digital camera out of his bag and began to take pictures of the corpse from various angles, before moving to wides, mid-shots, and close-ups.

When he had finished, Scamarcio reached down into the man's right-hand pocket, which was the only one available to him without moving the corpse. He fingers came upon a square, smooth surface, and he pulled out a brown plastic wallet and flipped it open. Inside was a driving licence in the name of Fabio Ella.

36

When Scamarcio called Cepparo, he told him that they hadn't found anything else on Ella's computer and that the lost emails were apparently irretrievable.

'Well, you can't prosecute a dead man.' Scamarcio had heard the same words just a few days before.

'If it is him. We have the wife coming down to do the ID. What are you going to do now, Cepparo?'

'We're going to carry on going through his web activity to see which sites he was visiting and whether we can draw in anyone else for this. We still have the wife as clean. But we do want to talk to her about his friends and associates, and I'd imagine that we'll be crossing your case with that.'

'So first she finds out her husband's dead, and then she discovers he's a paedophile. Maybe it'll help her handle her loss in some way.' They both fell silent to ponder that thought for a moment before Scamarcio said: 'You go ahead, Cepparo. I have no problem with that.'

'If we can't get a lead into anyone else, we'll tie it up — limited resources and all that.'

'Sure, I understand.'

'So then it's up to you if you want to investigate further.'

'Absolutely.'

'And, Scamarcio?'

'Yeah.'

'I'm really looking forward to that drink, cos your case seems kind of interesting.'

With Cepparo investigating Ella's friends and associates, and the local squad still at the beach, Scamarcio's thoughts turned to The Priest once more. Looking back on it now, it almost seemed as if the non-tip-off about the gypsies was a sort of precursor, a strange kind of gift that might pave the way for the later request for forgiveness. And that made him wonder if it wasn't such a non-tip-off after all. He decided that, with the others out, he might as well head back up to the camp and observe the families — unannounced this time. Casual surveillance had gleaned results for him in the past, yet there never seemed to have been enough time or money to repeat it on recent cases. It was strange he hadn't heard from Garramone, he reflected, following his message about Ella. Then there was the death of Spezzi hitting the news. Maybe that connection hadn't triggered yet in the chief's stressed-out mind?

The camp seemed shabbier in daylight. He smelt wood smoke on the breeze, and heard voices up ahead. Someone was shouting — maybe more than one person.

He decided to head west of the gate and follow the fence around to the left, in the hope of finding a point where he could look in unobserved. Eventually, he came across some bushes that allowed him to see into the clearing where he'd spoken with the small group the other day. He saw that the fire was still alight, and that several men and women were sitting around it, chatting. A short, busty young woman was standing to their right, yelling at a fat toddler who was trying to eat something he'd found on the ground.

The group around the fire talked on, oblivious to the woman with the child. After telling him off again, she scooped him from the ground and headed off in the direction of some shacks to the right, leaving Scamarcio with a glimpse of a teenage boy sitting morosely on the steps of a caravan straight ahead. Scamarcio shifted position in the bushes to get a better look. The boy kept glancing around him nervously while hugging his knees. Eventually, he pulled some smokes from his pocket and lit up, chugging the cigarette as if he were being paid to finish it as fast as possible. He was a strange-looking lad: dark hair gelled down in a side parting, eyes too close together, a small bony frame. He was wearing a tight T-shirt and denim jeans that were hugely wide at the bottom. Underneath, Scamarcio caught a glimpse of what looked like bright-yellow trainers. The boy looked around him a few more times, and then quickly got up from the steps and headed off to his right, checking that none of the people around the fire had seen him go. He then left the camp through the gate that Scamarcio had used the other day.

The boy's nervousness stirred the usual instincts in Scamarcio. He left his hiding place and headed back towards the gate. When he got there, he saw the embers of the boy's spent cigarette burning slowly through the long grass, and ground his foot on the stub to extinguish it. When Scamarcio looked up the road to the right, the boy was nowhere to be seen, so he got back in the Cinquecento and headed down the hill, the way he had come, driving slowly, figuring that the boy could not have gone far. Indeed, as he rounded the bend the boy came into view, ambling along on the left. Scamarcio drove straight past him, and then parked up at a vantage point on the right that offered a good view of Porto Azzurro and the aqua beyond. He pulled a map from the glove box, opened it, and, pretending to be a lost tourist, began to study it carefully. A quick glimpse in his side mirror told him that the boy was approaching. He returned to the map and let him pass. He waited a minute or two, and then drove on once more, passing the boy again. By his reckoning, the boy was heading for a village Scamarcio had seen at the bottom of the hill. He pulled the car into a service station behind some houses and waited for him to walk by. This time he saw him turn left at the service station and enter what looked like a bar on the other side of the street.

Scamarcio pulled the car over to the edge of the forecourt and parked, gesturing to the disgruntled attendant that he would be back in a short while. When he walked around the corner at the left of the service station, he saw that it wasn't a bar that the boy had stepped into, but a kind of internet café, of which he'd already seen quite a few on the island.

Scamarcio made a quick assessment, deciding it was unlikely the boy had seen his face in the car, and entered the café behind him, resolving to order himself a brioche and cappuccino, as he hadn't yet managed breakfast. The boy was already seated at a computer, one of several running along the right-hand wall. He seemed to be typing frantically, hunched over the screen like an old man. Scamarcio noticed that his right ear had three diamond studs in the lobe.

Scamarcio ordered from the waitress before picking up the day's *La Nazione* and finding a table from which he could keep the boy in sight. He was still typing frantically, unaware of the world around him. Scamarcio registered that *La Nazione* had the Ganza story on the front page as well as pages 2 and 3. They were now saying that the coalition was in crisis. They were even reporting talk of the PM's predilection for 17-year-old girls — a story that had been grinding the rumour mill in Rome for the past few months and had been triggered by the PM attending the 18th birthday party of a Romanian lap dancer he had recently befriended. If she played her cards right she could be looking at a cabinet post, along with all the ex-TV showgirls the PM preferred for the softer ministries, thought Scamarcio. How this country depressed him. He often wondered if he wouldn't have been better settling in the States. Maybe if he'd tried living somewhere like New York, instead of lonely and vacuous LA, the urge to come home wouldn't have been so strong. He returned his gaze to the boy. He had stopped typing, and was pushing back the chair and making for the bar. He handed over a coin and then headed for the door, seemingly in a hurry.

Scamarcio folded the newspaper and waved to the waitress to come over. When she reached his table, he pulled his badge from his pocket.

'Listen, I don't want to make a scene, but I'm from the Flying Squad, and I need to search that computer the boy's just used. It's important, and could save a child's life.'

The woman's eyes opened wide in amazement, and then she just nodded mutely. After a moment she seemed to gather herself together and said: 'The password is SATURN. Can I bring you anything else, Detective? On the house, of course.'

'Thank you. Another cappuccino would be good.'

She nodded and hurried away, and he headed for the computer the boy had been using. He sat down on the plastic seat, which was still warm — something he hated — and entered the password. He found the option for recent history, and saw that the boy had been on Yahoo Mail. He figured that he would have to call a techie in Rome to help him get into the boy's account, and was just debating who to contact when, after just one click, he realised that the boy hadn't even signed out of his mail box. That was not clever.

Scamarcio searched the 'Sent' list. The last email had been addressed to someone simply known as Mr Y. When Scamarcio studied the address in detail, it appeared as y12679 at gmail.com

The email the boy had written was short. Scamarcio scanned the English words: 'I'm stuck what now? I can't do this on my own.' He saw from the boy's address that he was called Dacian. He didn't know if it was a first or a second name.

He went back to the Sent box. There was another email, sent a few minutes earlier: 'I need instructions, this is all too much.'

He went to the inbox. Mr Y had written just one email to Dacian: 'Just keep cool and lie low, I will get word to you soon.'

It was the only email in the inbox; all the rest must have been deleted. He went back to the outbox again, and saw another, much longer email the boy had sent before the first two to Mr Y. It was addressed to an Irina Makala at gmail, but it was in a language he couldn't understand — Romany, he guessed. He pressed 'Forward' on the email and typed in Garramone's address, and then went back to the Sent file and deleted the forwarded mail. He then made a note of the boy's email address, and signed out of his account.

The waitress was back with his cappuccino, and he drank it down in one gulp before placing a five-euro bill under the saucer. The caffeine was racing in his blood now, and he knew he had no choice but to head straight back to the camp.

37

HE MADE A QUICK scan of the three narrow intersecting streets in the village to check that the boy wasn't hanging around, and then got back into the car, handing another tip to the angry-looking guy on the forecourt. Before starting the engine he typed a message to Garramone from his BlackBerry, asking him to find a translator for the email he had sent him from the boy. He also asked him to get a techie to see whether they could access emails received and sent in the last few months that now appeared to have been deleted from the boy's account. He gave him the boy's email address.

He turned the key in the ignition and backed out of the petrol station onto the main road, the two coffees giving him a much-needed energy hit that he hoped would last him a few hours yet. There was no sign of the boy on the drive going up, which worried him. Could he be that fast a walker? Maybe someone had given him a lift.

He arrived back at the camp, noticing the silence this time. As he walked in through the gate, he saw that the fire was still going but that the people around it had gone. He approached the nearest caravan and knocked on the flimsy door. A young woman with an old face came out. She was scrawny, her skin paper-thin and lined, but her eyes still pretty. Her brown hair hung lank and greasy, with faded orange highlights at the tips. He held up his card again.

She shook her head at him, stepped out of the caravan, and shouted something, again in a language he didn't understand. Quickly, a few more doors opened, and some of the men from the other day stepped out — including the spokesman, shirtless this time. He was wiping his hands down on his trousers, and didn't look pleased to see Scamarcio.

'Back again so soon? What is it now?' he said, striding towards him.

'You have a teenage boy here — I need to talk to him.'

'Why?'

'As part of the investigation, of course.'

'But our children haven't done anything wrong.'

'I'm sure they haven't, but I just need a quick word.'

The man paused a moment, seeming to weigh it up. Then he said: 'We have several boys here. Which do you mean?'

'If you bring them out, I'll tell you.'

The man shouted something, and another man turned back the way he had come.

While he was gone, Scamarcio and the spokesman just stared at one another uncompromisingly, neither willing to give any ground by being the first to look away.

After what seemed like a long time, the man was back, two reluctant teenage boys in tow. But neither of them was the boy he had seen in the café.

The leader placed a hand on the back of each and nudged them forward.

'No,' said Scamarcio. 'The boy I want has diamond studs in his ears, wide jeans, and bright-yellow trainers.'

'Dacian.'

Scamarcio feigned ignorance.

The spokesman turned to the small huddle that had formed around him. They were speaking their language again, but Scamarcio thought he could make out the word 'Dacian' several times. One man who was shorter than all the rest kept shrugging, and eventually held open his arms in defeat.

'His father doesn't know where he is — he says he hasn't seen him since the morning.'

'Can he take me to their trailer?'

The leader said something to the man, and he shrugged again before turning and heading back to the line of caravans. The leader nodded to Scamarcio, and they followed. After a while he said: 'My name is Pety.'

'Where did you learn your Italian?' asked Scamarcio.

'Night school — it was provided by the government for free when I was living in Milan.'

Milan, reflected Scamarcio. *Another connection to that place.* 'How long were you up there?'

'Just a year, when I first arrived in Italy. But I didn't like it; I couldn't wait to leave.'

Scamarcio could picture the scene. He had seen the camps lining the way in to the city towards Cadorna Station — a grim, filthy shambles of shacks against a backdrop of concrete decay and graffiti.

'Things better here?'

'No comparison.'

The other man had stopped beside a wooden caravan that seemed more dilapidated than the rest. Outside were a pile of dirty cooking utensils, rusty pots and pans, and a camping stove. Some partially cleaned plates were stacked in a rubber bowl; next to them were several empty liquor bottles. The man was shrugging his shoulders once again. Scamarcio noted that he had a drinker's nose.

'Can I have a look inside?' he asked.

Pety mumbled a few words to the man, and he pushed open the door, standing back to let Scamarcio go ahead. The caravan was more spacious than he had imagined from the outside. The room was divided by a curtain into two sleeping areas, with two single mattresses on the floor. Tacked to the wall above the mattress to the right were some ragged magazine photos of a good-looking woman whom Scamarcio didn't recognise. The air was musty and damp, and he thought he could smell some kind of fungus.

'Just the two of you live here?'

'Him and his son,' explained Pety.

'What happened to the mother?'

'She ran off with another man last year. The boy didn't take it too well.'

'How do you mean?'

'He's been drinking a bit too much. But that will pass. We all go through these phases as teenagers. I'm sure you did the same at some point?'

His eyes settled on Scamarcio, uncompromising again. There was something about the quiet dignity of this man that he liked.

'Oh, worse,' he said. 'Any chance the boy could be hiding out here in the camp?'

'I doubt it. As you can see, it's a small site. But take a look if you want.'

They headed back out of the caravan into the warmth, the promise of a stifling midday heat already heavy on the breeze.

'Has he done this before? Gone off like this?'

Pety smiled. 'He's a teenager, so of course he does his own thing sometimes, but we're sure he will be back sooner or later.'

They strode along a row of caravans, and Scamarcio stopped to take a peek inside and underneath them all, sometimes picking up on the same fungus smell again. They headed back towards the fire, and he checked the caravans around there as well. Finally, they strolled around the fence area, and he searched the bushes where he himself had hidden out earlier.

'Do you have a mobile?' asked Scamarcio.

'Yes, but I'm down on credit.'

Scamarcio pulled a 20-euro note from his pocket and handed it over. 'Can you let me know when Dacian gets back? It's important.'

Pety pocketed the money in an almost invisible gesture. 'So what do you think Dacian has done?'

'I don't know. I just want to talk to him, that's all. It's probably nothing.'

They headed back towards the gate, a group of men following a few paces behind them now. For the first time, Scamarcio felt slightly menaced by their presence.

'For nothing, you're putting in a lot of effort,' said Pety, turning back towards the men and leaving him alone at the gate.

38

BACK AT THE STATION, Zanini and Borghetti were changing out of their overalls. There was a hushed excitement in the air, and Scamarcio could tell that the experience of their first corpse had made a big impression on them.

'News?' he barked at neither one of them in particular.

'The doctor is with the body now,' said Zanini, cleaning something or other off his shoe. 'He called a bit earlier, saying he'd collected some trace evidence from under the nails that he thinks might be of interest. He wants to send it for analysis.'

'What kind of trace?'

'He didn't say — said he'd explain it all to you when he saw you.'

'Where is he doing the autopsy?'

'In his back room.'

'His what?'

'He has a surgery room in his house,' offered Borghetti helpfully. 'He is doing it there.'

'He must have a very understanding wife,' said Scamarcio.

The two officers exchanged glances. 'You should see her,' said Zanini. 'She's something else.' Scamarcio wasn't quite sure what that meant.

'Where's Genovesi?'

'With the English couple.'

'Ah, so they finally got back from their cruise?' Scamarcio would have preferred to have gone along for the interview. Genovesi couldn't be trusted to ask the right questions — that much was already clear.

One of the phones on the empty desks started ringing, and Zanini went to take it. 'He's just arrived,' he said, waving at Scamarcio. 'It's the doctor again.'

Barrabino sounded pleased with himself. 'Scamarcio, finally I reach you.' There was a hint of reproach in there as well.

'What have you got?'

The doctor paused for a moment, as if affected by his rudeness. 'Well, death from exsanguination, as was pretty obvious at the scene. There were five stab wounds in all, and one of them caused extensive damage to the heart and blood vessels. It was a short, thick blade, the kind you would find on a hunting knife. By my reckoning, he died sometime in the early hours of the morning. Those flies had only just started to lay eggs when we arrived. There's the beginning of an impression against the skin on his back — this slight indentation, surrounded by gravity-pulled blood, makes me think he was put on his back on a floor for a short time after death before being moved to the beach.'

'Anything else? The officers here mentioned some trace?'

'Yes, two interesting pieces: Skin samples under the nails — I imagine they must be from the assailant, collected in the struggle — and bite marks down his right arm.'

'Bite marks?'

'Yes, quite a few. And they look like they have been made by small teeth — infant teeth. You and your colleagues need to think about where he might have got those. And get me dental records, if you can.' Barrabino knew full well that a young girl had gone missing from the island, so why didn't he just come out and say it? And of course Scamarcio would get the dental records. He didn't need some local quack telling him how to do his job. 'Sure. And the skin samples, where do we process those? I can't imagine there's anyone on the island who can handle that.'

'Ah, you'd be surprised, Detective, but in this instance we

should probably send them to Florence for analysis. Obviously, it will take a few days.'

'We need to send them today.'

'It needs to be signed off by Chief Genovesi.'

'Right. I will make sure that happens asap.' Then: 'Thank you for the fast work.' He knew that by thanking him he could put him back in his place for a moment.

The bite marks were highly troubling, although it was impossible for Stacey Baker to have stabbed Ella to death. Scamarcio picked up the phone to Mr Baker, knowing that the request for dental records was going to set a thousand alarm bells ringing for them. He would head that off at the start by making it clear that they hadn't found a body. As it happened, Baker was much calmer than he expected — he sounded drugged out on lack of sleep — but promised to have the records faxed over as soon as possible.

The rest of the afternoon was taken up with calling Ella's widow in Milan and arranging for her to come down for the ID, processing the evidence from the corpse, and asking Genovesi for the relevant signatures. The chief seemed beleaguered when Scamarcio walked into his office; he was trying to persuade someone on the other end of the phone that he didn't need help with his investigation.

'No, we have it under control,' he was saying. 'Important leads have come in today that look likely to take us to the little girl.' He fell silent a few moments, listening to the response.

'Well, that is your decision, Sir, but I assure you it's not necessary.' There was another pause before eventually he said, 'Of course, Sir, I understand. I will let you know immediately.'

He replaced the phone in its cradle and let out a yawn before resting his head in his hands and running his fingers wearily through his thinning hair. He looked at Scamarcio as if he was an extra irritation he couldn't handle right now.

'I've got Florence on my back,' he said, by way of explanation. 'They're talking about sending in the big guns. They're worried about bad publicity.'

Scamarcio shrugged and took a seat opposite, uninvited. 'Well, it might be no bad thing to have some reinforcements.'

'You say that now, but they'll make my life and yours hell, I guarantee it. They'll have you off the case quicker than a rat's fart.'

'Well, I guess my boss in Rome would handle that.'

Genovesi sighed. 'Yeah, leave it to the big men — we're just the pawns in their power games, after all.'

Scamarcio smelt the years of stunted ambition and absent opportunity. 'I need to send those samples to Florence.' He pushed the paperwork across the desk.

'Great,' yawned Genovesi, pulling the forms towards him. 'This investigation is going to eat up most of our annual budget. Let's hope nothing else happens on Elba in the next six months.'

Just as he said it, Scamarcio's mobile rang, and he stepped out to take the call. It was Pety at the camp.

'Listen, Detective, Dacian has not come back all day. We're getting worried about him.'

Scamarcio glanced at his watch. It was 6.00pm. When he looked outside, he could see the light beginning to fade from the sky.

'So no one has seen him since I was there?'

'No one. It's not like him to go off for so long — an hour or two, yes, but not the entire day.'

'OK,' said Scamarcio, making a decision. 'Leave it with me. I will get back to you as soon as I have some news.'

Chief Genovesi's budget was about to take another hit.

39

After what he had witnessed in the café that morning, Scamarcio had calculated that it was best to let the boy Dacian return to the camp in the course of the day, rather than use precious resources tracking him down. But now that they were nearing the evening and there was still no sign of him, Scamarcio realised they would have to mobilise all the forces on the island to find him. It was possible he could lead them to the missing girl. Had it been Dacian who had stabbed Fabio Ella? Had they both been involved in the abduction of the American girl? Ella could no longer provide the answers, but Dacian could. Or was looking for the boy a complete wild-goose chase that had nothing to do with either of the cases that Scamarcio was investigating? For now, he resolved to keep his doubts to himself.

Genovesi had mustered officers from the other two small stations on the island, and they had organised a search of their towns, bars, and internet cafés. Scamarcio reckoned it was unlikely they would find Dacian on one of the tourist beaches. They had also put out alerts at Elba's two ports to make sure the boy couldn't leave the island undetected.

Scamarcio was at his desk, waiting for news and waiting for Stacey Baker's dental records to come in. If those bite marks belonged to her, he wasn't sure what he would tell the parents. Could he get away with not telling them? If they brought Dacian in tonight and put him under duress, maybe they could get to her in time. But who knew what had happened to her since she'd been taken? Even if she was alive, they might still be too late. He felt a pang of anxiety twist in his gut, and the last words of The Priest came back up to his mind like a haunting. He deserved to rot, the crazy freak. Scamarcio found himself hoping he'd be in Longone a good while yet, and that death wouldn't offer an easy way out anytime soon. Instinctively, though, he knew that Pugno's time was near. The red circles under the eyes and the sweating brow had attested to a serious illness of some kind. Scamarcio felt sure it was that which had prompted the midnight confession.

The fax bleeped three times, signalling the imminent arrival of a message. He went to the coffee machine and pulled an espresso, and then another. The bin was full to overflowing with the tiny plastic cups. Did no one ever clean this place?

Scamarcio added his two to the toppling pile and went over to the fax. The second page was indeed Stacey Baker's dental records from the States — the dentist had been efficient. Scamarcio would take them over to Barrabino himself.

The light had almost completely disappeared from the sky now; only a few fragile traces of red clung tentatively to the horizon. The air was still heavy with the heat of the day, and the breeze carried the warm scent of honeysuckle, mellowed by the sun. As he strolled past the little park, he noticed the pink-and-white proteas nodding gently, responding to the soft currents moving up from the sea down the road.

He realised that he had left his car keys in the office and turned around, heading back in to get them. As he did so, he noticed a small, elderly man hovering nervously by reception. The desk officer was nowhere in sight.

'Can I help you?' he asked the man.

'Thank you. I am looking for a Detective Scamarcio, from Rome.'

'I'm Detective Scamarcio.'

The old man seemed greatly relieved: 'Oh, good. Do you have five minutes, Detective?'

Scamarcio looked down at the dental records in his hand and knew he really didn't, but something about the old chap made him curious.

'I'm a bit pressed right now, but I can probably manage five minutes, yes. Do you want to come up to the office?'

The stranger nodded, and Scamarcio led the way. When the man was seated in Zanini's chair, Scamarcio offered him a coffee, but he waved a hand, dismissing the idea by saying: 'You're very kind, but no.'

Now they were under the halogen lights, Scamarcio noticed that the fellow had piercing blue eyes. They were the kind of eyes that had seen a lot and would not be lied to — the eyes of a real priest. And, in fact, when the man took off his shawl, Scamarcio immediately saw the dog collar and wondered what this was all about.

As if reading his thoughts, the stranger said: 'I will get straight to the point, Detective, because I can see you are a very busy man. I know that a little girl went missing from Elba a few days ago, and I can't begin to think of the hell her parents must be going through, so it's important you get back to that as soon as possible.'

Scamarcio was about to respond, but the old man pressed on. 'I am the priest at the prison of Longone. Last night I saw Mario Pugno in his cell, as I am wont to do several times a month. I'm not sure whether anyone has informed you, but Mr Pugno has cancer and may not survive the week. He has been asking to see you one final time — he says it's very important, and can help with the disappearance of this child.'

Scamarcio sighed and pushed back his chair. 'Has anyone told you about how much of my time he's wasted already? I've been there twice now, and he hasn't told me anything useful. The last time he seemed to think I was you, he was asking me to forgive him for his crimes.'

The blue eyes fixed on him, unblinking. The voice was soft

and measured. 'No, he was under no illusions, Mr Scamarcio. It was you he wanted forgiveness from. I am sorry if you feel he has wasted your time, but I do sense that he has something for you which could prove important. Maybe it's just that until now he has found it difficult to release the information; maybe he needed your forgiveness before he felt able to do so.'

'But why? What have I got to do with him and his crimes?'

'Only Mr Pugno can answer that.'

Scamarcio sighed again. Was this going to happen on a daily basis now? Was he going to be forever summoned to the prison at Longone to bear witness to the madness of this man?

'Why do you bother with him? As an emissary of God, how can you spend time with a creature so deeply evil?'

The blue eyes were unwavering: it still seemed as if he hadn't blinked. 'Evil is not an absolute, Detective. It is always tempered by some kind of goodness from within, some kind of light. It's the light that we work with, try to make stronger.'

Scamarcio shook his head. 'And you're honestly telling me that you believe there is some kind of light in him?'

'Oh, I am sure of it, Detective. Quite sure.'

40

Scamarcio told the priest that he would think about Pugno's request to see him one last time. Now, driving to Barrabino's, the same thoughts kept circling: just why did The Priest keep coming back to him? What was it he believed he had on him? Why the acquaintance with his father? The whole affair made him increasingly uneasy, and he felt the need to speak to someone familiar back in Rome. Why hadn't Garramone replied to his messages? What scheme did he have in play? Had something happened to him? His silence just fed Scamarcio's disquiet. And there was something else, too: the need for a friendly face, an easy chat. He thought about calling Aurelia, considered the implications, and then pushed the idea to the back of his mind. He surveyed the darkening sky as it sped past, and felt a new isolation from the world, stuck out here on this rocky outcrop, working alone, his presence known to just a few. Yet again, his instincts told him that it would not end well.

He had been told that Barrabino's house could not be missed. Apparently, it was the sprawling pastel-pink villa on the edge of town where the eastern-coast road began. And indeed he spotted it straight away: tall, iron gates offering a glimpse of a Mediterranean garden beyond, two lines of palms leading to an entranceway shrouded in wisteria, purple against pink creating an impressive effect. There was a hint of blue through the trees, and he guessed that there had to be a swimming pool off to the right somewhere. There was no way that a doctor's salary could have bought all this. Maybe the wife had money? Maybe Barrabino was dirty? Perhaps both.

He pressed the buzzer, and it crackled into life. 'Scamarcio here.' Then, as an afterthought, he said: 'For Dr Barrabino.'

There was no reply for a few moments, and then a woman's voice with a strange accent came on. 'Of course, please drive up to the main entrance.'

He couldn't quite place it — maybe Dutch or Swedish.

The gates rolled open slowly and he got back behind the wheel. The red in the sky was now pink, and what little light remained pooled dimly through the palms marking his approach to the villa. He pulled onto a gravel turning circle and realised that the house was even more extensive than he had first thought. He counted at least 12 vast windows on the upper floor: there were six huge bedrooms, from the looks of it.

As he stepped out of the car, the front door opened and a tall blonde stood there, smiling at him. She had the typical Scandinavian look: long, iron-straight hair, endless legs, exquisite blue eyes, and a strong mouth. He found himself hating Barrabino anew.

'He's in his studio,' she said, shaking his hand. 'I'll show you the way.'

He wondered at this. Barrabino wasn't an architect or an artist, so 'studio' seemed like an odd choice of word for a doctor and pathologist. But maybe it had just got lost in translation.

He followed her across a spacious lobby into a long living room with three immense floor-to-ceiling windows that displayed a spectacular view of the gardens. They passed though a dining room, where he noticed several impressive pieces of art, and into a conservatory that looked out onto the swimming pool. The woman he presumed was Mrs Barrabino unlocked a door into the gardens, and they took a small flight of steps that led to a path around the house to the back. There was a smaller bungalow off to the right in the same style as the main house.

'He's in there,' she said. 'Forgive me if I don't come any further, but there are certain aspects of my husband's work which I would really prefer to avoid.' She gave an ironic smile.

'I completely understand,' said Scamarcio, smiling back.

Their eyes locked for a moment before she headed back to the house.

He took the path to the bungalow and knocked on the door. There was no reply, but then he heard the sound of tapping against glass, and turned to see Barrabino's face at a window to the right. He was holding up gloved hands and signalling for him to let himself in.

Scamarcio pushed the door and entered a dark hallway. Off to the right, a door was open onto a large tiled area. Strip lighting ran along the length of the ceiling, and at the end of the room Scamarcio saw Barrabino stooped over a body, presumably that of Fabio Ella. He was finishing sewing shut an incision in the chest as Scamarcio approached. Another man in a suit was standing off to the right, observing the work with a mixture of horror and fascination.

'Good evening, Detective', said Barrabino, without looking up. 'Excuse me if I don't shake your hand. May I introduce my colleague, Dr Verdone? He is Porto Azzurro's best dentist, and I thought his expertise might prove helpful to us with regards to the bite marks.'

Scamarcio walked around the bottom of the table to shake Verdone's hand. He was a tall, thin man, his studious eyes magnified by thick glasses. Scamarcio took a position next to him as Barrabino continued his show. With a flourish, he finished the stitching in the chest, expertly doubling back on himself and extracting the needle in a single swift, fluid motion. Scamarcio had to admit to himself that he was impressed. For someone who did not get much practice, Barrabino seemed adept.

The doctor tossed his bloody gloves into a plastic bin behind him and put on a new pair from a box by the table. Then he reached for a large magnifying light overhead, positioning it over the left forearm of the corpse. 'Both of you come and look at this for a second.'

They shuffled over to the slab, like med-school students at a dissection. Verdone was the first to take a look through the lens. 'That's a very definite impression,' he said. 'Looks to me as if one of the upper-left teeth is missing — maybe number 3 or 4. If that matches the records, that gives us a pretty clear ID.' He turned to look at Scamarcio. 'Did you bring them?'

Scamarcio waved the envelope in his right hand. Verdone stepped away from the lens a moment and gestured for him to take a look. The impression from the bite shone purplish under the light, the teeth marks neat and tiny — clearly those of a child.

'Can you tell anything about the age from this?' he asked the dentist.

'I would say six, maybe seven — very young. But the records will tell us what we need to know.'

To the right of the table, Scamarcio saw a long desk running along the wall. 'May I?' he asked Barrabino.

'Be my guest.'

He carefully lifted the documents from the envelope, taking care to keep the photographs straight. Verdone had come up behind him and now stood at his shoulder. He scanned the photostats quickly, and then turned to the American dentist's written notes. After 30 seconds or so, he pointed to a paragraph of text: 'See this passage here?'

Scamarcio read it: 'Upper left 3 knocked out by a tennis ball at nursery. That must have been quite some hit.'

'Milk teeth are more fragile,' said Verdone.

Scamarcio sighed. 'So it's her, then?'

Verdone tut-tutted quietly to himself. 'I'm afraid it looks that way, Detective.'

'You are a glutton for punishment,' said the guard Erranti as they shook hands at the end of The Priest's corridor at Longone.

'I guess so.' It was cold in the prison tonight, and Scamarcio wished he had brought a warmer jacket along.

'He hasn't been himself since you were last here — much quieter than usual, and has barely touched his food.'

'I heard that he was ill.'

'Yes, cancer. Sorry if we didn't tell you before, but we weren't sure it was relevant — didn't feel like he needed any sympathy, if you know what I mean.'

'He wouldn't have got it from me.'

As soon as the words had left his lips, Scamarcio found himself wondering at that. After everything, Pugno was still a human being, so didn't he deserve some compassion? Scamarcio wasn't sure. He felt conflicted between his immediate impulse, which would have been to throw him to the lions of the prison, to show him no mercy, and something new, something less absolute. He wondered if this was his mother's character fighting his father's in him.

'He will probably be moved to the infirmary tomorrow,' said Erranti as they made their way to the cell. 'But for now, the same procedure as before.'

When the door was opened, he saw that Pugno was in bed this time, under the covers. He seemed surprised to see him.

He coughed as he tried to sit up straighter in the bed. Eventually, when he had got his breath back, he said: 'I didn't think you would come, Detective, not after last time.'

Scamarcio shrugged and pulled out the chair he had used before. 'You have a good priest.'

Pugno nodded sombrely. 'I am fortunate in that.'

Silence descended between them, and for a moment Scamarcio was unsure what to say. He ran a hand through his hair and leaned back in the chair.

'So your priest tells me you are still wanting my forgiveness?'

Pugno nodded.

'OK.'

'What?' the old man whispered.

'I said OK. You have it. You have my forgiveness.' Scamarcio tried to make it sound as sincere as possible, but was struggling to flesh out the words, to make them real.

Pugno nodded again, but would not meet his eye. Scamarcio noticed that his hands were trembling, and in that moment he couldn't stop himself from feeling a fleeting sympathy for the man. The silence returned, and Scamarcio wondered if that was it, whether his visit had been in vain.

But after many seconds had passed, and just as he was thinking about leaving, Pugno finally found his voice. It was weaker and raspier than last time, and Scamarcio had to lean forward to make out the words.

'I appreciate your decency in coming here,' whispered the old man, his words interrupted by another coughing attack. 'It took guts and great understanding, after everything that has happened to you.'

After everything that has happened to me? 'What are you talking about? Nothing has happened to me.'

The Priest sighed, a deep sadness contorting his features. 'Let's not dig up old pains; there is no point.'

Scamarcio tried to speak, but the old man held up a palm. 'In return for your kindness, I would like to give you some help. I just want you to know that instead of looking at who has been leaving the island, you should be watching who has been coming onto Elba in the last twenty-four hours.'

Again he tried to speak, but again The Priest barred him with his hand. 'There is no point asking me my sources. I will never reveal them.' The coughs came again in rapid fire, and it sounded now as if he was coughing up his soul itself. 'There's no point putting the pressure on — we both know I no longer have anything left to lose.'

With that, The Priest suddenly reached below his covers, and Scamarcio caught the glint of something metallic. Instinct told him it was a gun, and in the very next moment he felt a burning heat course through him. He sprang up from his chair, but it was too late. Pugno had placed the barrel against his own forehead, and before Scamarcio could get any words out he had fired.

41

THE COMMOTION AT THE jail had been as bad as he would have expected. There were all the predictable questions from the governor about how the gun had got there, whether Scamarcio had brought it in — *How could he have? They had signed him in as usual, and taken his firearm off him as the rules dictated* — who said what to whom, who did what to whom, did Scamarcio provoke him? Etc, etc. Then the bureaucratic machine had groaned into action, and because they were in Italy, and worse still not even on the mainland, this was just the start of a process that would be achingly slow and cumbersome, and would require him to sacrifice God knows how much of his time to endless interviews and statements. Barrabino had seemed both surprised to see him again so soon and also rather delighted that the circumstances appeared so troubling. He had managed to throw in a few of his — by now, signature — observations on how death seemed to follow on Scamarcio's tail, or, better still, how he appeared to invite it in. Scamarcio didn't know if his patience would hold out long enough to prevent him from punching the man in the face, so he had resolved to separate himself at the first opportunity. He couldn't have a Category-A prisoner kill himself in front of him only to then end up with a GBH charge against the police pathologist.

It was almost midnight when he made it back to his car. Dense clouds were passing across the moon, and the lamps along the harbour were no longer strong enough to mark a path to the Cinquecento. He used the central locking to locate it, again rueing his decision to go out in such light clothes. He climbed in and coaxed the struggling engine to life, swinging the car into reverse while tuning the radio to one of the island stations. It was the usual dire stuff: what they called 1980's 'classics' — cheap euro trash that had been unremittingly crap the first time around. Scamarcio reached in his top pocket for his smokes, but couldn't find them. This night couldn't get any worse.

His mobile buzzed on the seat beside him. 'Scamarcio,' panted Genovesi. It sounded like he was in the middle of a long climb. 'Listen up.'

'I'm listening'.

'Your boy Dacian — we've found him.'

'Really, where?'

'A farmer called it in, up in the hills above Capoliveri.'

'Called *it* in?'

'Yeah, doesn't look like he'll be doing much talking.'

Scamarcio's stomach turned over anew. 'Dead?'

'Very, by the looks of it.'

'I'll be right there.'

Genovesi rattled off some directions and then hung up.

Genovesi and two unknown officers he presumed were from another station were huddled around the body. It was in a storm drain not far from some picnic tables. As he'd passed, he noticed a man slumped at one of them. He appeared to be in a state of shock. The farmer, he guessed.

The boy's throat had been cut — a clean red necklace of blood was visible above his T-shirt. It looked to have been a swift and efficient slash, professional. The red was dramatic against the boy's white skin in the moonlight.

Genovesi gave him a nod. 'We're just waiting for Barrabino. Don't know what's keeping him.'

Scamarcio decided not to enlighten him. 'When was he found?'

'About forty minutes ago. The farmer, Mr Ronco, didn't have a mobile phone, so had to go home to make the call — that took him about ten minutes. We came after that.'

'No sign of the murder weapon?'

'None, but we need to get some more men out for the search.' Genovesi straightened. 'Any idea what's going on here?'

'The Priest tipped me to the camp on the island. I notice this young guy — he seems worked up about something. I follow him — his emails suggest he's got in above his head, is asking someone for help, doesn't know what to do next …'

'A hunch, then?'

'Yes, a hunch, but we know where hunches often lead. Besides, now he winds up dead, it's our second body in as many days, and the last corpse had some dodgy pictures on his computer — all this against the backdrop of a girl gone missing. There has to be something in it.'

Most of this Genovesi already knew. He pulled a cigarette from his pocket and lit up, without offering Scamarcio one.

'Can I have one?'

Reluctantly, Genovesi reopened the packet and handed him the lighter.

'Why do you think The Priest wants to help us?'

Scamarcio looked away for a second. 'I think he was trying to make amends, compensate for his past in whatever small way he could.'

'But how did he even know about the camp, the case? He seemed to have the low-down on Stacey Baker as soon as it happened.'

'It's a small island — people talk.'

Genovesi wasn't impressed. 'Elba is not that small, and I run a tight ship. My men know to be discreet.'

Scamarcio shrugged, unable to offer an explanation.

'I've a good mind to go up to Longone myself, get that bastard to explain himself.' Scamarcio figured that now was probably the right time to fill him in, but thankfully Genovesi's mobile began to ring.

Over the next few seconds he watched the colour gradually deepen along the man's neck until it reached his jaw, where he thought he saw a vein begin to twitch. 'Why am I only learning about this now?' There was a pause. 'Why would *he* have told me?' Then another: 'You what? You're kidding me.' He slammed the phone shut. His whole face was dangerously red now. *He has to get that blood pressure down*, thought Scamarcio, *or he won't make his pension.*

'Just what are you playing at, Scamarcio?'

'Sir?'

'Don't play the dumb ass with me. Why didn't you tell me about Pugno?'

'I was just getting to that when your phone rang.'

'Bullshit!' Genovesi jabbed a finger at him. 'I'm sick of Rome trampling all over this investigation. This is a Tuscan case on Tuscan soil, so why the hell are you here? I've had it up to here with your attitude and your methods, Scamarcio. I'll be calling your boss tomorrow to get you moved off.' With that, he hurried off in the direction of the picnic tables, the unknown officers looking on nervously.

42

GARRAMONE HAD FINALLY phoned from Rome mid-morning, offering no explanation for his recent silence. Instead he said that Genovesi had been tranquilised and that Scamarcio was to proceed as before. When he'd asked how this had been achieved, Garramone had not been forthcoming; he'd said it was just a question of the usual political manoeuvring. *A promotion promised, a favour granted*, figured Scamarcio.

Back in the squad room, Genovesi had shut himself in his office and pulled the blinds down, which was a relief. Zanini and Borghetti both looked up as Scamarcio walked in.

'Barrabino called,' said Zanini. 'He has a time of death on the boy, but wanted to talk to you first.'

'I'll call him in a moment.' Scamarcio had not hung around for another noisome ribbing from the doctor last night; he had figured that whatever he had to say could be left to the morning. Besides, Genovesi had given him his marching orders, which provided him with a useful cue to leave the fat man to deal with the aftermath. Scamarcio had, however, stopped for a chat with the farmer on his way out, who did not have anything useful to add.

Scamarcio pulled out the chair from the desk he had been using and laid down his papers. 'We've got a lot of work to get through today.'

The two officers nodded in unison like those ridiculous dogs he'd seen stuck to the back windscreens of the cars of stupid people.

'I want you to contact all the ferry operators servicing the island. We are interested in who has been coming onto Elba in the days before Stacey Baker's appearance, as well as who has been leaving. I want you to get the operators' manifests, and run their names through the national and international criminal databases.'

'All the names?' said Borghetti. 'We're probably talking about thousands of people here.'

Scamarcio slammed his hand down on the desk to silence him. 'I don't give a shit. This is a little girl's life.'

Borghetti hung his head in shame. Scamarcio didn't care if he'd upset the boy, but he softened his tone slightly, nevertheless, remembering his management training. 'It's a big job, and we'll work through the night if we have to. You need to get on the phone to the ports straight away, and get those records.'

'How many days back are we talking about?' asked Zanini.

'Right now, I'd aim for five days before the girl disappeared. I don't reckon they would have been on the island much longer than that, but we can take the search back further if we need to. And bring it right up to yesterday, when the boy Dacian was murdered. I've a feeling someone came to the island to meet with him before killing him.'

'But what about Fabio Ella? He was killed earlier,' said Zanini.

'You're right, but we're not sure yet that the two are connected. Just bring it up to yesterday to be on the safe side.'

Zanini nodded and pushed back his chair.

'Where are you going?'

'Down to the ports — it'll be too slow trying to get them to do what we want over the phone. It doesn't work like that here.'

Scamarcio nodded.

Borghetti got up to join his colleague, still refusing to meet Scamarcio's eye.

'Good luck to the both of you — I know you're capable officers, so I'm sure we will come up with something.' He tried a smile, which seemed to ease the tension slightly. The two men nodded and went on their way.

Scamarcio sighed and slid back down in his chair. Zanini was right: it was a huge if not impossible task, but they had to try. The Priest seemed to have been on to something with Dacian, so the chances were that his final tip-off would also hold weight.

He eyed the telephone, dreading the call he would have to make to Barrabino.

He picked up the receiver and dialled the number that Borghetti had written neatly on his note. Barrabino answered on the first ring, allowing him no time to formulate a counter-attack. However, his tone was surprisingly neutral. 'Ah, Detective, good. I think I've got a few pointers for you.'

Barrabino spoke quickly. He seemed caught up in his work now, too enthused by it to make jokes: maybe this many murders were finally giving him the experience he craved. 'Time of death was 8.00pm, so two hours before he was found. His throat was cut with a hunting knife, expertly done. I would hazard a guess that the attacker was medically trained.'

'Surgeon?'

'Could be, or a veterinarian.'

That could prove a useful piece of information in narrowing down the trawl of the manifests.

'Any joy in locating the weapon, Scamarcio?'

Given that the two officers hadn't mentioned it, Scamarcio presumed not. 'Not that I'm aware of.'

'Right, well let me know — it seems similar to the one used on Ella.' Barrabino rattled on: 'Death by exsanguination, obviously. Other than that, he was pretty fit — all the organs were in good nick.'

'Had he put up much of a struggle?'

'Didn't look like it: seems like his attacker took him by surprise from behind, and placed one arm across the neck while the other made the slash. But he was a bit of a weedy boy, not much muscle on him, so the assailant wouldn't necessarily have needed to be that strong.'

'Did he die there?'

'I think not. It looks to me like he spent some time on a tiled surface before being moved — maybe a bathroom or a kitchen floor.'

'Thanks, fast work.'

'Want to drive down, see the body?'

'No time, I'm afraid.'

He was still half-waiting for a pop about last night, but none came. 'OK, you'll have my report within the hour.' The doctor hung up.

As soon as Scamarcio had put the phone down, it rang again.

'Can I speak to Detective Scamarcio?' It was a female voice, husky, slow. There was something affected about the way she hesitated before she said the name, something insinuating. His guard went up.

'Who is calling?'

'Fabiana Morello, crime desk *la Repubblica*.'

He knew the name. She'd written a grim profile piece on him when the news about his father had first come out. The young detective Scamarcio as a living metaphor for the country — could the goodness of youth triumph over the evil of old? Vomit-inducing stuff. He'd resolved never to speak to her again.

'He's out right now. Can I take a message?'

An affected laugh tinkled down the line. 'Come, come. I'd know that Calabrian accent anywhere.'

'Listen, I'll tell him you called.' He hung up. Childish, he knew, but he really didn't have the time. Then a thought struck him: if Morello knew he was there, the chances were that the rest of them were also now on to it. He got up from the desk and headed to the window. As if on cue, down in the square several TV crews were setting up, their satellite vans parked up to the right. A huddle of some of the national print guys he recognised were comparing notes on the front steps. Morello was down there with them, dressed like a southern tart, as usual, the legs decent but the face battered by years of sun and nicotine abuse. He sighed, reaching for the fags in his pocket that he'd restocked that morning. It hadn't taken them long — the circus was in town, just as Genovesi had predicted. Indeed, Genovesi seemed to have responded to some kind of telepathic message and was now standing in the doorway of his office, watching him watch the reporters. He joined him at the window, and after a quick glance muttered: 'Fucking brilliant. That's all we need.'

He shuffled back into his office and slammed the door.

Scamarcio took a long drag on his fag, savouring the moment, and then made for the espresso machine. *It would be good if they offered one with a whisky kick*, he mused. *It would take the edge off the day.*

He had decided to head back to the camp, pay his respects, and ask some more questions. But it had been a wasted trip. The boy's father had been inconsolable, grief-stricken anew, and nobody claimed to know what Dacian had been involved in. But to Scamarcio, not all the pleas of ignorance rang true. Surprisingly, there was something in the eyes of Pety that troubled him — a slight move to the left that betrayed him, that showed he was using the part of his brain responsible for invention, for lies. But Zanini had called, saying they were back with the records, and he'd decided it would have to wait.

Now back at the station, they'd been slumped over the database for the past two hours with nothing to show for it, save a conviction for petty theft that Scamarcio had deemed irrelevant. Even with all the children and teenagers eliminated, the manifests still amounted to several thousand names. They had decided to start simultaneously on passengers from the day before as well as those from five days back, so as to tackle the problem from both ends.

Zanini yawned, and stretched his shoulders.

'The reward is in the hard graft,' said Scamarcio, sounding like his father. It was a strange comment, he'd always thought, coming from someone who had never done a day's honest work in his life.

They laboured on in silence, interrupted by the phones every five minutes or so. They'd scheduled a press conference for the next day to get the journalists off their backs for a few hours — the calls coming in to the squad room had been relentless, and it seemed the only way to win some peace. Florence was dispatching a media-relations unit, but they wouldn't be with them until the day after tomorrow, which Scamarcio deemed ridiculously late. He turned from his monitor to the window, and watched a milky light descend outside. He sensed the heat of the day ebbing away, and regretted that he'd been unable to feel the sun on his skin for a few minutes, to taste the early summer. The days on Elba just seemed to be disappearing into night almost before he was aware of them.

Borghetti shifted in his seat. 'I think this might be something.'

Scamarcio got up from his desk and headed over to the young officer, now hunched over his terminal.

'Ernst Ratsel, a German national, entered the island yesterday, the day of the boy's murder. He's 53 years old, has two convictions for GBH and sexual assault on a minor, and was released from Preungesheim prison in Frankfurt five years ago.'

'Any other background?' asked Scamarcio.

'It says here that he was a practising surgeon for ten years at the city's Krankenhaus Nordwest until he was arrested for the sexual assaults.'

'That could be him,' said Scamarcio. He placed a hand on Borghetti's shoulder. 'Good work.'

He returned to his chair, stretching his legs up on the desk. 'Now we need to ring around the island, and find out where he's staying, if he's still here — Borghetti, that's your job. Zanini, go through today's departures, and see if he's already hot-footed it out.' He paused for a moment. 'Could he have got on a boat last night after the murder, presuming the boy was killed around 8.00pm?'

They both shook their heads. 'Last boat is at seven,' said Zanini.

Scamarcio felt uncomfortable about the closeness of the timings, but decided to take it no further for the time being. 'OK, get to it. Borghetti, I'll help you with the hotels.'

Borghetti told him there were more than 150 hotels on the island, but that he could narrow it down by choosing the ones near the beaches. Wasn't it possible that Ratsel might try to combine business with pleasure? Scamarcio agreed, and they hit the phones. After around 30 tries, Borghetti got lucky again. He scribbled something on a piece of paper before saying: 'What room?' Then he hung up before he could be put through.

'OK, he's at the Hotel Valle at La Guardia — a decent place, four stars.'

Scamarcio gathered up his things, and Zanini ended the call he was on.

'Let's go. No time like the present.'

43

The Hotel Valle had an infinity pool that melted away into the sea. Gentle music was playing by the bar, and a series of green, blue, and yellow lights were pulsing under the waters, throwing an ever-changing light on the palm fronds above. It was a nice effect, and Scamarcio decided if he ever made it out of Rome, he might try it in his own place one day. The loungers were all empty at this hour, the guests no doubt showering before coming down for dinner. If Ratsel was still there, they would be lucky.

They walked into the lobby at a brisk pace, not wanting to run in case the German spotted them and tried to escape. Scamarcio kept his voice low. 'Can you tell me what room Ernst Ratsel is in, please?' The boy on reception eyed Borghetti's uniform worriedly before muttering '55. Is everything OK?'

'We might have a situation,' said Scamarcio. 'Could you or a colleague accompany us up there?' If Ratsel tried to do a runner, it would be useful to have someone with them who knew the layout. The boy's eyes danced briefly with excitement before he said: 'Just one moment.' He went out back and then returned almost immediately with a pretty brunette who took his place at reception.

'Have you got the master key behind there somewhere?' asked Scamarcio.

'Sure.' The boy took it from a drawer beneath the desk and showed them the way to the lifts.

'You think he won't open up for you?'

'It's a possibility. What floor is 55?'

'Fifth.'

'Could he jump out of the window from there if he wanted to get away from us?'

At that moment the lift arrived to reveal a group of buxom, middle-aged German women laughing raucously. They stepped aside to let them out before entering. 'Not without a broken leg or neck,' answered the boy.

'Good.'

They made their way slowly to the fifth, Scamarcio feeling frustrated by the lumbering elevator and the dire muzak. When the doors finally opened, a thin man in a Hawaiian shirt was standing there nervously, huge sweat stains under his arms. His thinning hair was pasted to his forehead, and his eyes seemed filmed over. In his left hand he carried an overnight bag. The receptionist confirmed Scamarcio's instincts and said: 'Ah, Mr Ratsel.' Ratsel gave Borghetti's uniform the quickest of glances before turning on his heel and speeding down the corridor behind him. But Borghetti was quick, and after just a few seconds had wrestled him to the ground.

Scamarcio ran up, towering over the pair of them. 'Mr Ratsel, as it appears you have already worked out for yourself, we'd like to ask you some questions about a murder that happened here on the island yesterday.'

The man's English was faltering. 'I know nothing about it. I want, er, I want my lawyer.'

'All well and good,' said Scamarcio. 'Can we go into your room for a moment and discuss this there? It's all a bit too public out here in the corridor.'

Borghetti pulled Ratsel up from the ground while the receptionist opened the door to Room 55 with his key card. Borghetti followed behind, pushing Ratsel in before him.

The room was in almost perfect order, and Scamarcio had the sinking feeling that if there was any evidence to be found, Ratsel had scrubbed it away by now.

'So, Mr Ratsel, tell me what brings you to Elba?'

Scamarcio took a seat at one of the tables by the window. Ratsel slumped down onto the huge double bed.

'I'm a tourist like everyone else — isn't it obvious?'

'No, not really.'

'I'm not saying anything else without my lawyer.'

'Why do you need a lawyer if you're just an ordinary tourist?'

Ratsel looked away in disgust, saying nothing.

'Borghetti, can you call Barrabino? I want this place checked for prints, blood, what-have-you. I need him asap.'

Borghetti nodded and left the room to make the call.

'What do you think I might find?' asked Scamarcio.

'Nothing is what you'll find.'

'We'll see about that.'

The two men sat in silence for what seemed like several minutes until Scamarcio said: 'You know how these things work. According to your records, you've been around the block a fair bit. Sexual assault on a minor is pretty bad — makes you the lowest of the low, really. Were you on the nonces' wing at Preungesgheim? Or did you have to sweat it out with the other prisoners? Give you a hard time, did they?'

Ratsel's eye burned with rage. 'Fuck you, you Italian piece of shit. Fuck you.' He barred his arms across his chest, looked away into the wall. Scamarcio figured that he wouldn't turn violent; the man realised it was too late for that.

'So, tell me, what do you know about the boy Dacian?'

Ratsel shook his head slowly, as if Scamarcio were talking nonsense. 'No idea who you're talking about.'

'Yes you do — the boy who was helping you with whatever disgusting scheme you had conjured up after being released from prison.'

'Bullshit.'

'Do you have the American girl? Where is she? Is she here?'
Scamarcio jumped up and took a quick look in the bathroom, and
then opened the wardrobes, without expecting to find anything.

Ratsel was shaking his head faster back and forth now, his chin
jutting out as if he were grinding his teeth. 'You are wasting my
time with this *bullshit.*' He shouted the word.

'Somehow I don't think so, and, as I'm sure you're well aware,
if you co-operate now it will be that much easier for you later
down the line. The game's the same here as it is back home in
Germany.'

Ratsel sighed, leaned back against the wall, and closed his eyes
for a moment. But when he opened them, all he said was: 'I want
my lawyer.'

44

SCAMARCIO SLEPT WELL that night; he put it down to pure exhaustion rather than any sense of calm from the inquiry, which seemed to be complicating itself further by the day. They had thrown Ratsel in the slammer for the evening, but would have nothing to hold him with past the morning — not unless the tiny traces of blood in his hotel bathroom that Barrabino had found came back as a match on Stacey Baker or the boy Dacian. Genovesi, for once, hadn't needed a lot of persuading that it would be worth the extra cost of rushing the blood through processing. He knew that if it led them to the girl in the next twenty-four hours, it would be a huge feather in his cap with the chief in Florence.

As Scamarcio was driving to the station, Garramone called from Rome: 'I had that email translated — the one you sent me from the boy.'

'Anything interesting?'

'Well, it's a bit cryptic, but basically he seems to be telling her that the job opportunity that had come up for him has got complicated; he was told to do something, which he did, but now the boss has gone quiet on him and he doesn't understand why. He's worried that the whole thing could go wrong, that they might get found out.'

'And he never says what this thing is?'

'No. He just keeps repeating that he's worried, but that if it does all come off OK, he and Irina — that's the girl he's writing to — can start a new life somewhere. He's desperate to leave that camp and his father, apparently.'

Garramone was already up to speed on the boy's death. After a pause, the chief asked: 'How long after this was sent did he die?'

'About nine hours.'

'And you believe this is connected to Stacey Baker's disappearance?'

'That's my hunch, yes.'

Garramone didn't question his use of the word; he knew how important hunches often turned out to be. 'I spoke to my contact up in Florence. The other guy in the photo with Arthur and the foreign minister goes by the name of Simon. He used to work as a rentboy in the area, and then went quiet. He was strangled, apparently, before he was attached to the light fitting to hang.'

'So they're mellowing? It seems a bit kinder than stabbing someone to death.'

'If they're one and the same …'

'What? You think they're not?'

'We can't be sure yet, but my contact tells me he was involved with some local drug dealers, so it's not clear whether his death was directly connected to Arthur's.'

'Seems odd, though, that the story breaks, and then both guys in the incriminating photo are murdered.'

'Well, yes, so it does, but you know the score. We've got to explore the other avenues, too.'

Both fell silent for a moment before Scamarcio said: 'You hear about Spezzi killing himself?'

'Yeah, strange. But what's that got to do with anything?'

'He was involved in that scandal with the rentboy a couple of years back, remember?'

Scamarcio heard him push the air out from his cheeks, and shift in his chair. 'Ah, come on, Scamarcio. Now you really are clutching at straws.'

'Am I, though? The Ganza story breaks, Arthur is killed, then this guy Simon, and now the heir to the Spezzi empire — who

226

supposedly had everything going for him — suddenly decides to end it all, and there's this nasty dirty secret in his past that we never really got the full story on.'

'Yeah, but coincidences happen. I don't see why the Ganza thing would affect him.'

Scamarcio paused a moment before saying: 'I went to see him.'

'Who — Ganza?'

'No — Spezzi, the day before he died, when they'd just taken him into hospital.'

'Why? And why didn't you tell me sooner?'

'I guess I never got around to it. But listen, he made me think that my hunch wasn't so far out. He told me: "Leave it alone, because it isn't worth it." He made me think that "it" was something significant.'

'Yeah, but if he'd just tried to top himself, maybe he wasn't all there.'

'Maybe,' said Scamarcio, but he wasn't convinced.

Garramone said he had to rush off and would call him if he had any more news. Scamarcio had the sense once again that he wasn't being entirely open with him, that he was keeping certain things to himself. But for now he pushed the thought to the back of his mind — he didn't want to deal with it. He hurried into the station, and when he entered the squad room, a man and a woman wearing suits were waiting for him. He noticed that Zanini and Borghetti seemed quite uncomfortable in their presence. There was no sign of Genovesi.

The woman rose from her seat and held out a hand: 'Detective Scamarcio, I presume?'

He shook her hand, and reached out to grasp the man's. 'Yes, and you are …?'

'Silvia Morandi, and my colleague here is Gianluca Ferrera. We work for the press department of the Tuscan police.'

'Ah.' Scamarcio felt relieved to have them here so soon. 'You're earlier than I was led to believe.' He held up his hands. 'But I'm not complaining.'

'Good.' Morandi sat back down again. She was an attractive woman — long, brown hair, tanned, even features, toned calves — all in all, a very presentable package, which Scamarcio guessed was pretty essential these days if you had to face the media. She crossed her legs, seeming to have picked up on his appraisal. 'We decided to expedite things. The American networks have started to run the story, and we're anticipating a big media presence here on the island from now on. It seemed sensible to get down here as quickly as we could.'

Ferrera coughed, covering his mouth with his hand. He leaned back in his chair slightly. He was less good-looking than his colleague, but very presentable in his grey Armani suit with a royal blue tie. Scamarcio had a feeling he was about to say something difficult.

'Listen, Scamarcio, we just need to clear something up with you.' The tone was confident and strong; there was no sense of hesitancy about what was to come.

'Sure.'

'Obviously, your name is known to the Italians — the whole story about you and your father was everywhere last year.'

'And?'

'Well, we're figuring it's only a matter of time before our Italian hacks fill in the Americans on your colourful past, and when that breaks we think there's going to be some diplomatic fallout. I mean, look at it their way: they already see us as a country of Mafiosi incompetents who can't run a government, let alone an economy, and now we have a detective involved in a crucial inquiry whose father was one of the leading figures in the 'Ndrangheta. Whichever way you cut it, it looks bad.'

Scamarcio was about to take a seat, but decided to remain standing. 'My father's past has nothing to do with me. How long do I have to keep repeating myself on that? It should be clear by now that I chose a different life. And, when all is said and done, I'm probably far less corruptible than anyone else — I've been there, rejected it. My department in Rome will attest to the fact that I'm clean. I'm regularly vetted, and have been since day one. I'm probably more vetted than any other figure in the department.'

'I hear you, Scamarcio. Your colleagues all obviously believe in you and rate you, otherwise the Flying Squad in Rome would never have taken you on, but that's not the issue here, and you know it. The point is that television and television news — especially American television news — can't handle such nuances. It's black and white for them. They'll never spend any time talking about you being clean, or looking at your past successes. For them, all that counts is that your dad was a gangster: plain and simple. The Americans would never countenance that in *their* police system.'

Scamarcio tried to speak, but Ferrera was in full flow. It sounded like he'd been preparing this little speech on his way over from the mainland. 'The chief in Florence and, I believe, several political figures, are up to speed on your involvement in the Stacey Baker case, and it's causing them concern. Firstly, for the reasons I've outlined and, secondly — and this is perplexing all of us, because we're wondering just why you're crossing onto Tuscan jurisdiction — how does this girl's disappearance concern Rome?'

'Look, Ferrera, my chief has already briefed your chief on my case, I believe.' Scamarcio knew full well that there was no way Garramone would have given him the real story. 'All I can tell you is that Stacey Baker's disappearance ties into a murder I'm investigating, but I can't go around divulging the details — it's sensitive right now. If the chief in Florence and the politicos are still worried, they just need to speak directly to Garramone, my boss. They all know the score and, to be honest, I imagine they've already consulted and that it's been sorted between themselves. It's just you who has a problem with me being here, because you're worried it's going to create extra work for you.'

Ferrera was shaking his head, but his tone remained measured and reasonable. 'That's not the case, Scamarcio. I just think it would be a lot easier if you were out of this. Genovesi and the chief in Florence, who will be arriving here soon, should take the lead. I want the focus on them, and none of the tittle-tattle of last year.'

Scamarcio understood where he was coming from, but could not let himself get pushed out just when he sensed he was finally getting somewhere. 'Listen, we both know that you don't have the power to lift me off this case: that has to come from our respective bosses. But I do appreciate your predicament, and I've got no desire to hog the media spotlight. OK, let Genovesi and your boss in Florence take the limelight, but please just let me stay under the radar doing my job. The sooner I get the answers I need, the sooner I'm out of your hair.'

Ferrera sighed. 'I know you're a genuine guy, Scamarcio, but this is already beyond your control. It's too late for you to just pop back under the radar.' He bent down and pulled a neatly folded newspaper from his briefcase, handing it to Scamarcio. He saw that it was that day's *la Repubblica*.

'Turn to page three.'

Scamarcio did as instructed. The article was at the top, and took up more than half the page. Its headline read: 'Flying Squad maverick to investigate American disappearance.' The by-line was Morello's.

The opening paragraph contained the usual claptrap to be expected from that woman: *The Flying Squad's enigmatic black sheep … dark past … witness to his father's murder … well-documented temper outbursts, but renowned for his frequent maverick brilliance.* He couldn't read any more, and tossed the paper onto the desk.

Why was he a maverick, he wondered. He had always done his job, and delivered results — there was nothing of the maverick about that. Why did his past have to make him an enigma? Would he be justifying himself and his chosen role in life until the day he died?

'See what I mean?' asked Ferrera. But there was nothing carping about the tone; he simply sounded regretful, if not a little apologetic.

'Yeah, I get it.' Scamarcio sighed. 'All I can do is lie low as much as possible, but please just let me finish my investigation here unhindered.'

Ferrera exchanged glances with his colleague. Zanini shuffled some papers distractedly. Scamarcio wished they hadn't had to have this discussion in front of the two officers.

'As you say, it's not for us to decide. But we wanted to flag it up, because right now it's being discussed by the upper echelons and we thought you should know.'

'Sure,' said Scamarcio.

Fererra looked down to the floor for a second before saying. 'I'm sure I speak for all of us here when I say I have great admiration for the distance you've come, Scamarcio, and the work you do. Please don't take my words amiss.' He rose from his seat and gathered his bag, motioning for Morandi to do the same. 'Anyway, we've got a press conference to organise, so we must get on. Hopefully, things will work themselves out in the coming days.'

He turned to Zanini: 'You said you had a room we could use?'

'Sure, I'll show you the way.' The officer headed for the doors, making sure he held them open for Morandi. Borghetti got up and made for the coffee machine. 'You want one, Scamarcio?'

'No, thanks. I'm going to take a walk.'

The anger was burning a hole in the pit of his stomach, so he decided to drive out to the nearest stretch of sea to calm his nerves and get some perspective. Everything Ferrera had said made sense. It was just that he couldn't help taking it as a personal insult. He hated the fact that he was forever tied up with the misdeeds of his father, as if they were one and the same. Why did he seem so tainted to everyone? He'd worked hard to clear the slate and to establish a separate identity for himself, but it still always came back to the same thing. Sometimes he wondered if he hadn't actually made an expensive mistake — whether it would have been an easier life on the other side. And who was he kidding anyway? Maybe they were right. Once tainted, always tainted? Evil was in the genes, after all. Shouldn't he have accepted his paternal heritage, gone into the family business, and opted for a simpler life — a life that at the end of the day would have been more honest than the one he was trying to live now, labouring so hard all the time to carve out this fresh identity for himself, an identity that maybe, when all was said and done, wasn't really his to own? He needed a talk with Dr Salvai — well, more than a talk — but right now she was hundreds of kilometres away.

He pulled the battered fag packet from his pocket and lit up shakily; thankfully, there was very little breeze on this stretch of beach, and he was able to take a long drag, drawing the nicotine down deep into his lungs. He exhaled slowly, counted to ten, and took in the scene: through the haze of smoke he watched a trio of gulls dive-bombing a patch of foam a couple of metres away, expertly focussed on the task in hand. To the right, a young family was setting up for the morning, the father fixing the umbrella, the mother tending to their two little girls. Maybe it was time for him to change his life. Maybe finally settling down would help quell all these questions. For the second time, he felt like calling Aurelia; for the second time, he pushed the impulse away.

He took a few more drags until the cigarette was spent, and then he got up, still holding the butt — not wanting to leave it in the sand. He dusted himself down and headed back to the car, thinking through the tasks for the day. He wanted Ratsel cleared up one way or the other. If he wasn't their man, they needed to know about it quickly.

45

'I HAVE AN UNDERSTANDING of Italian law, and I know that if you don't find something concrete soon you will have no choice but to release my client.'

Scamarcio pushed his chair back against the wall and took another drag on the fag, surveying the pair of them. Ratsel looked even more battered than when they'd first found him at the hotel. He'd had to share a cell with a man called Quattrocchi, who, according to Borghetti, was the worst of the town drunks and had a passion for the songs of Adriano Celentano, which he would recite word — if not tone — perfectly during his frequent brushes with the bottle. It looked like Ratsel had had to bear the worst of it. According to the desk sergeant, Quattrocchi had not burnt himself out until around 5.00am — late for him. Maybe having an audience had given him newfound confidence.

Ratsel's lawyer appeared to be in his mid-30s, with close-cropped blond hair, constantly blinking brown eyes, and wire-framed glasses. There was nothing to suggest that he had had to be up in the early hours to reach the island by lunchtime. His was a hard-vowelled, brusque efficiency.

'So then, Detective, I'm asking you: what do you have?'

Right now, if truth be told, Scamarcio had absolutely zero. Barrabino had failed to turn up anything other than the blood, and they were still waiting on the results from Florence. Scamarcio had asked them to do a comparison with Dacian's DNA, but his confidence was low that they'd be able to get it to him in time. So Scamarcio decided to ignore the question. 'Last night I asked your client what he was doing here on the island, and he was not forthcoming. I think it's in his best interests if he co-operates with us.'

The lawyer gave Ratsel a curt nod. They had obviously planned what he was and was not going to say beforehand.

Ratsel shifted in his seat, uwilling to make eye contact with Scamarcio. 'Like I told you, the usual tourist stuff.'

'Could you elaborate?'

Ratsel rolled his eyes, and sank back in his chair with his legs apart. 'I just wanted a short break in the sun. I couldn't get the time off for a full week, so just decided to take a long weekend.'

'So you were planning to stay until Sunday?'

'That's right.'

'Why come alone? Wouldn't it be more fun with ...' Scamarcio was about to say 'a girlfriend', but wasn't sure in which direction Ratsel's tastes ran, or if he was even interested in adult relationships, '... a partner?'

'Prison is not conducive to long-term relationships, Detective. And now I'm on the outside, it's not been that easy to meet people.'

Scamarcio nodded, resolving to move on. It was never useful to damage a man's pride at this stage. 'So you decided to take a short break. What was the plan? To hit the beaches, see the sights?'

'Yeah, basically. But mainly the beach — I just wanted to go home with a tan. Good way to start the summer.'

'You working back in Germany?'

Ratsel shuffled in his seat again. 'I've had a few short-term contracts. Obviously, I couldn't go back to medicine.'

'So what are you doing now?'

'I've been employed by a pharmaceutical company as a consultant.'

'They know about your past?'

'I wasn't required to declare it.'

'They don't ask you if you have a criminal record there?'

The lawyer placed a hand on Ratsel's arm, and turned to Scamarcio. 'Detective, how is this relevant?'

'Never mind,' said Scamarcio. 'So you just spent the last couple of days at the beach?'

'Yes.'

'Which one?'

'The one right by the hotel. I didn't feel like going far.'

'Can anyone account for your presence there?'

Ratsel pushed up his lip in a childlike way, shaking his head slightly. 'Well, I don't know. I suppose it depends on whether they remember me. I'm not sure my face is that remarkable.'

'Well, we'll try anyway. Did you leave the beach at any time?'

'Only to go back to my hotel room to use the bathroom.'

'You ever go to the beach at Fetovaia?'

'No.'

'Sure?'

Ratsel scowled. 'Quite sure. Why?'

'No matter.'

Ratsel's lawyer placed his hand on his client's arm again. 'Where are you going with this, Detective? We've both seen the papers. You can't pin that on him — he wasn't even on the island.'

Before Scamarcio could respond, there was a knock on the door. Zanini was clutching a sheaf of documents. 'Sorry to interrupt, Sir, but I thought you'd want to see these.' He walked around the desk and handed them to Scamarcio without looking at Ratsel or his lawyer. 'I'll be outside if you need anything.'

To his great surprise, Scamarcio saw that they were the blood results from Florence. The fact they were in already was some kind of miracle. Maybe somebody high up had pushed the green button to look good in front of the Americans. He skimmed through the first paragraphs to the conclusion on the front page: the blood in Ratsel's apartment was that of the boy

Dacian. He flipped through the pages to see the confirmation for himself in the columns of figures and symbols comparing the two analyses — the one from the body, and the other from the sample in Ratsel's room. His head was light with excitement. Finally, a breakthrough. His hunch about the boy had been right.

He leaned back in his chair, savouring the moment. 'You'd better be praying that old Quattrocchi doesn't get too much liquor in him tonight.'

Ratsel looked confused.

'Quattrocchi, your cellmate from last night,' Scamarcio spoke slowly, as if Ratsel was an imbecile. 'You're in for another evening's entertainment — quite a few evenings, probably — and, believe me, that will seem a paradise compared to where you'll be heading afterwards.'

Scamarcio watched the realisation slowly dawn. Ratsel shifted violently in his seat, looking at his lawyer pleadingly. All at once, the small interview room was rank with the man's sweat.

'Are you going to enlighten us, Detective?' asked the lawyer calmly. 'Or are you just resorting to idle threats now?'

'No idle threat, Mr Himmel. The blood results confirm that the blood found in your client's hotel bathroom is that of Dacian Baboescu, the boy murdered on the island two days ago.'

'Mr Scamarcio …' Scamarcio knew that the lawyer was about to argue that the blood could have been left by the previous guest before Ratsel, could have been left anytime; indeed, on such a small sample, that argument might hold its weight in court. But it was a strategic mistake because, instead of concentrating on Scamarcio, the lawyer should have been keeping his client under control, making sure he kept quiet before it was too late. Instead, Ratsel was rocking in his chair, breathing rapidly now. The words tumbled out of him, like coins stolen from a till: 'He just said it was a small job — a free holiday for me if I helped him sort out a problem. I didn't know it would end up like this. I had no idea.'

The lawyer barked something at Ratsel in German, but he didn't seem to notice. 'He said this boy working for him had turned traitor — killed an associate and stolen some merchandise. He wanted me to sort it out by talking to the boy, finding out what he'd done with the goods.'

'Talking to him?'

'Just interrogating him, threatening him — there was no mention of murder or anything like that.'

'And these goods, what were they?'

'He never said. He just called it "the merchandise".'

'So if you were just supposed to talk to the boy, why was his blood in your bathroom?'

The lawyer had risen from his chair and was practically screaming at his client. Ratsel gave out an exhausted sigh and used his last strength to gesture at him to sit down again. He looked like a man defeated.

'He came at me with a knife. I had no choice but to defend myself.' He had his head in his hands now. 'What a bloody mess. All I wanted was a free holiday.'

46

THE LAWYER HAD ASKED for a five-minute break. But Scamarcio, while desperate for a coffee, didn't want to leave him alone with his client. He needed to keep Ratsel in full flow.

'So, this merchandise — you never discovered what it was?'

'He said I'd find out once I was on the island, but I never got the chance to talk to the boy. He attacked me from the off.' He paused a moment. 'I think he was scared — someone or something had got to him.'

'And who is this "he" you keep talking about? Who was it who sent you here?'

'I met him online.' He began to falter. 'In a chatroom.'

The lawyer was gripping his client's arm for dear life now. Scamarcio's German was basic, but he thought he understood *Don't go there.*

'What kind of chatroom?'

Ratsel just shook his head. 'He went by the name of Mr Yellow; that's all I can tell you. He wired me a lot of money for this trip — much more than it would actually cost.'

Mr Yellow, Mr Y, thought Scamarcio. 'Payment for the job?'

'Payment for the job.'

'And how did you communicate? By phone, email?'

'No, it was always in the chatroom. He insisted on that.'

'And you don't have a phone number, an email address, any way to contact him?'

'No. We'd just arrange what times to talk in the chatroom. I was to let him know when I'd spoken to the boy.'

'How did he know where to wire the money?'

'I gave him my details online.'

'Any sense of where the money had come from?'

'I think it was a bank in the Netherlands, but I'd need to check my statement.'

'And what made him think you were right for this particular job?'

'No idea.' He was shaking his head tightly, and Scamarcio knew that this wasn't the half of it — there was a reason, but he wasn't going to hear it now. Ratsel was clamming up on him; he'd had his moment.

'So you have no idea who this guy is?'

'Like I say, we'd never met. It was all done in the chatroom.'

'If you tell me the name of that chatroom, you will do a lot to reduce your sentence.'

The lawyer had grabbed him by the arm now, and was repeating 'Nein, nein, nein', and this time Ratsel appeared to listen. 'I'm saying no more, Detective. That's it.' Then his strength seemed to desert him and he appeared to crumple in on himself, collapsing into the chair. He started sobbing softly, and Scamarcio decided it was finally time for that coffee.

When he re-entered the room, the stench of stale sweat was overwhelming.

'So,' he said. 'Stacey Baker.'

'He wasn't even on the island,' repeated the lawyer.

'I'd like to hear it from him,' countered Scamarcio.

Ratsel sighed, sinking even lower in the plastic chair. 'Honestly, as God is my witness, I know nothing about that girl.'

'Bullshit!' Scamarcio slammed his fist into the desk. The men on the other side of the table shrank back. So he did it again. 'Bull. Shit!'

Ratsel looked down and then up, as if invoking the Lord. His voice dropped to a whisper. 'I swear to you, I know nothing about it — only what I read in the paper. I absolutely swear that's the truth.'

'You can improve your sentence.'

'I know, but I don't have anything for you. If I did, I'd tell you. You've got to believe me.' The words were shrill, pleading.

'Why should I believe anything you tell me?'

Ratsel looked pitiful. He'd never seen a man more desperate. 'You have no reason to trust me, I know. I'm just telling you that I wasn't involved. Please, I don't know anything about it. Really, I don't.' He threw out his hands.

Depressingly, Scamarcio knew he was telling the truth this time.

47

RATSEL MIGHT NOT KNOW anything about Stacey Baker, but Scamarcio's hunch that Mr Y's 'merchandise' might refer to the American girl was growing stronger by the minute. He tapped on Genovesi's door.

'Come in.' It was an exhausted sigh rather than the usual bark.

The Elba chief looked tired. Scamarcio sensed he'd had the world and his wife on the phone from Florence, lamenting the slow progress of this case.

'Scamarcio, what fresh misery do you have for me?'

'Ratsel confessed to killing the boy Dacian. In self-defence, apparently.'

'All well and good, but how does that help us with Stacey Baker?'

Scamarcio filled him in on the rest. When he was done, Genovesi said: 'But how can we be sure that Ratsel's merchandise and Stacey Baker are one and the same?'

'We can't, but for now we need to proceed as if they are. I want to do two things: trace this Mr Y online, and see what we can find out about him and, two, organise a thorough search of the camp and surrounding woods asap.'

Genovesi leaned back in his leather seat, drumming his fingers against his chin. 'That's going to send out a very bad message to the media: again, the gypsies are to blame.'

Scamarcio was surprised that he was actually sensitive to this stuff. 'Genovesi, there's no time for this bullshit political correctness right now. We've got to get results, be seen to be moving.' He knew this would chime with him.

Genovesi looked down at his desk for a moment and then nodded slowly. 'At this point we need to pull men in from Piombino. If we're going to do a fingertip search, that is.'

'I don't think we have a choice, Sir. Dacian Baboescu is implicated — he's supposedly made off with Mr Y's merchandise, and if he's hidden it anywhere it's going to be in or around that camp, where he could keep an eye on it.'

The reinforcements had come in from Piombino on the 3.00pm boat, accompanied by the police chief from Florence. Genovesi was there to meet them at the port. Scamarcio had stayed well out of it, knowing there would be a big media presence filming their arrival.

At the camp, Pety was pacing up and down. 'You know what this will do to us? To our life on this island?'

Scamarcio knew all too well, but couldn't stop it. That train was already in motion.

'We've worked so hard to keep our noses clean, lead an honest life. That has not been easy, I assure you. People were not happy when we showed up.'

Scamarcio pulled out a cigarette, and offered him one. Pety took it, and waved it in the air unlit. 'They will push us off here in days, I guarantee it. That bastard mayor of Porto Azzurro has had us in his sights for years.'

'Listen, Pety, calm down. We search; if we find nothing, we move on. Then we search somewhere else, and the attention moves there. It will all be forgotten about in a few days.'

'You know that's not true. No smoke without fire, is what they'll say. Our lives on this island will become a hell.'

Scamarcio lit up for him. He watched him take a long drag, grateful for the momentary silence.

'Pety, just what are you so afraid of?'

'I've just told you.'

Scamarcio sat down on a log. 'I'm not sure it's so simple.'

Off to their right, silent columns of police were turning over the camp. Women were shouting, toddlers crying, dogs yelping. The search team had been at it for nearly three hours now. The light was draining from the sky, and they'd soon have to call it a day.

He was about to press Pety further when there was a shout from one of the rows of police working to the left of the camp, where it met the woods. The shout was repeated several times. It was the call to say they'd found something. Scamarcio stubbed out his cigarette and headed over, with Pety in close pursuit.

There was very little daylight left in the woods, but Scamarcio could make out a cluster of policemen huddled over a pile of something whitish and glistening. His stomach turned over, and he hoped against hope that it wasn't a girl's clothing. But when he drew closer he saw that it was actually something more troubling, if that were at all possible: stacked tightly inside a hole in the ground were what looked like tens, maybe hundreds, of kilo bags of white powder. Genovesi, who had panted up alongside him, immediately knelt down and tore open one of the bags, sweeping his finger through the powder and bringing it to his lips. He tasted it on his tongue for several seconds before confirming to the hushed crowd: 'It's coke, no doubt about it.'

Then he turned to Scamarcio, his eyes alive with bitterness. 'There's your merchandise, Scamarcio. Happy now?'

48

Scamarcio sensed a hundred eyes upon him, including those of the chief of police from Florence, a man he'd heard very little about previously but who was now making his presence very much felt.

'Do you have any idea how much it has cost to pull these men out of Piombino today?'

'Yes, sir.'

'The world's media are watching our every move — we simply can't afford these kinds of mistakes. It's all very nice to have a drugs bust, but Chief Genovesi convinced me that this would take us to the girl. It seems that you have been pursuing the wrong path right from the start.'

Scamarcio didn't know what to say, but there was no need, as the Tuscan chief was in full flow, addressing both Scamarcio and Genovesi now. 'It's clear to me that you haven't got the faintest idea where this little girl is. We have the eyes of the world upon us, and we don't have a clue. I'm going to send you some of my best men from Florence, the crème de la crème. There must be no more mistakes now. No more time wasted.'

With that, he turned on his heel and barked something at one of his Piombino officers. Genovesi hurried after him — no doubt to lament the fact that Scamarcio had been thrust upon him against his will, and that he'd never really gone along with this whole theory.

Scamarcio felt a crushing tiredness overwhelm him. He had indeed fucked up; there was no doubt about that. It was a dud hunch, and he'd probably have to take the hit career-wise. Case-wise, once the Tuscan chief got onto Garramone down in Rome, he'd probably be pulled off. Stacey Baker's disappearance was becoming political, and when the Americans got onto the PM, he'd be feeling the heat on that, too, and would want to get things done right. Scamarcio's time on Elba would soon be over.

He trudged back to the Cinquecento, his limbs heavy and his head pounding. Yet, despite the tiredness, one thought kept circling, coming back at him like a hungry shark: Ratsel said Dacian had killed an associate, and that associate could well have been Ella — would have to have been Ella, surely? Indeed, if the stab wounds on Ella matched the stab wounds on Dacian, he'd tried to use the same knife to kill Ratsel as well. Hadn't Barrabino said the knives were similar? He needed to ask Ratsel about the knife. Was it his or Dacian's? And returning to the nub of it all: Ella had child porn on his computer and Stacey Baker's bite-marks on his arm. Those drugs were an unintentional red herring — they had to be. Or was Mr Y simply running two parallel operations? It wasn't unheard of. His own father had had his finger in so many different pies. But how to prove that Mr Y was linked to Stacey Baker? How to pin down this elusive online presence — for now, nothing more than an avatar? After today, persuading Genovesi and the chiefs that there was more to it than the drugs seemed impossible. It felt like his chance with them had gone forever.

His mobile buzzed in his pocket, and he was surprised to see it was Cepparo from Milan calling. He couldn't think what he'd have to say to him, now that Ella was dead and the Milan case was closed.

'Scamarcio, is now a good time?'

'You're a welcome distraction from my troubles, Cepparo.'

'Sounds bad. Listen, I'm not sure it's of interest, but we've got some sad cases up here in our tech department. So much so that they have nothing better to do in their spare time than take their work home with them, regardless of whether the case is open or shut, it seems. Tragic, really.'

Scamarcio felt a quickening in his chest. 'Go on ...'

'They were so challenged by that guy Ella's computer that they took a bet on it. The first one to crack those emails gets a new piece of software or some such sad shit.'

'And?'

'Well, they got in. I've got those emails, if you still need them.'

'You're kidding me. Anything interesting?'

'I haven't taken a look, to be honest.'

'Cepparo, this could not have come at a better time. I could kiss your guy up in Milan.'

'I wouldn't do that, Scamarcio. He's butt-ugly.'

Cepparo said he'd forward the emails to Scamarcio's address, and now he lounged on the bed in his hotel room, scanning the inbox on his laptop. Cepparo's colleague had managed to get around 1,000 emails dating back one year, but they all seemed to be from Ella's inbox rather than his outbox. There was one contact, a Leka Ymeri, who piqued Scamarcio's interest — if only for the simple reason that he was the only person whose surname started with a Y. As far as he could see, there were around ten emails sent between him and Fabio Ella, their correspondence beginning six months before.

In the first, Mr Ymeri wrote: 'My clients are discerning, they are prepared to pay above the odds for a second-to-none service. If you wished to get involved in our supply chain I can guarantee rich rewards both of a financial and personal nature.'

The second email from Ymeri, sent a few days later, was even more cryptic. Scamarcio could not find Ella's response to the first, although he later saw it was contained in the body of Ymeri's reply. Ymeri wrote: 'I don't think you should concern yourself too much with the risks. This operation is well under the radar and has been for a very long time. Remember that these clients are highly influential so it is unlikely that we would ever be subject to "outside interference".'

Ella's original reply beneath read: 'I can confirm that I am very interested. I only wish to check with you that this operation is watertight. I am a family man with a business in Milan and cannot afford complications.'

Another email from Ymeri came in two days later: 'I am pleased to have you on board. I will be in touch soon with some more detailed information.' Ella's original email below had said that, on reflection, he was now up for the job in hand.

Then there seemed to be a month's hiatus in their communications, until Ymeri wrote: 'We have been asked to procure a specific set of goods and I'm wondering whether this might be the right order for you to cut your teeth on. Stand by for further details.'

Two days later, Ymeri brought him up to speed: 'You will be required to travel to some of your popular tourist beaches when the summer months arrive. I will leave it to you to choose the resort, I only ask that it not be too far from Rome ...' For the first time, Scamarcio sensed that this might possibly be about something other than drugs, and his pulse quickened. Ymeri pressed on: 'The preference this season is for blonde and blue eyes, female, no more than nine, minimum fuss, minimum hassle. Our clients do not want street riff-raff or runaways, they want premium. Clear?'

Scamarcio felt his stomach turn over: a mixture of queasiness, disgust, and excitement that he might finally be on to something. In the next email, Ella had written underneath that he understood and Ymeri had replied that he would be wiring him his agreed fee in advance. There was no mention of the sum.

One month later, Ymeri wrote: 'Our clients are ever more demanding, any chance you could get down there earlier?'

Scamarcio had the sense that other emails may have been exchanged that for some reason had not been retrieved. The next email from Ymeri contained Ella's reply: 'I need to wait for the good weather otherwise the tourists won't be there.'

That seemed to shut Ymeri up for a few days, until he wrote. 'When this is all over you should come to Trastevere for a drink. Stand by for delivery instructions.'

Trastevere! Scamarcio felt vindicated. They had a location for Mr Y and, better still, it tied him to Arthur. He could be sure now that he had not been mistaken in his initial hunch. All he needed was information on where they were planning to send the child whom Ella found. But when he scanned the remaining emails, he could find no mention of this — the talk was just of money transfers and whether they had been received or not, and then a final note wishing Ella luck in his 'endeavour'. The use of the word brought bile to Scamarcio's throat.

He slammed shut the laptop in frustration. Why was there no talk of the delivery? Was Ella supposed to hand the child to Dacian, who would then pass it on — was that how it was going to work? He couldn't understand why there was no email explaining this, and then he wondered whether this part had been organised by telephone. They were taking a huge risk even using email in the first place.

He dialled Garramone in Rome, and brought him up to speed.

'Good work, Scamarcio,' he said when he'd finished. 'I can tell that cock in Florence where to stuff it now.'

'Which cock in Florence?'

'The one you infuriated today. I've had him bending my ear for the last forty minutes.'

'We need to find Ymeri in Trastevere. I doubt he's in the book. Maybe the station down there has heard of him, or maybe we could get a PI onto it? When we find him, we need to put a tap on him.'

'You think he'd be stupid enough to use a landline to run this kind of thing?'

'I doubt it. We'd need to organise a break-in, and put a bug on his mobile.'

'I'm onto it,' said Garramone. 'We'll find him.' Then he sighed and said: 'I still don't know how this takes us back to Ganza and Arthur.'

'I'm not clear on it either yet, but if that guy who accosted me in the alleyway is to be believed, they *are* linked, and now we have Ymeri living in Trastevere, along with the photos on Arthur's camera. These elements are connected somehow.' Scamarcio paused a moment. 'What are you going to tell your friend?'

'Nothing, for the moment. He's busy. I haven't heard from him in a while, and I'd prefer to leave it like that.'

'What about Trastevere? How much are they sniffing around now?'

'Minimal — they've got their hands full with their upcoming drugs bust.'

'Right.' Scamarcio couldn't help thinking that this all felt rather convenient. What strings had Garramone pulled? Or the PM, for that matter?

'And, Scamarcio, it seems to me that you could get off Elba for the time being, and bring this back to Rome. It will keep some of the stuffed shirts happy, too.'

'I was thinking the same thing.'

49

SCAMARCIO FELT LIKE one of those country yokels in American films who find themselves overwhelmed by their first sight of Times Square. After the lazy cicada rhythms and mellow Mediterranean scents of Elba, the car horns and fumes of Rome felt like another country. He had decided to take the metro to Trastevere, unable to face the prospect of another hour in traffic.

Garramone had tracked down Mr Ymeri, thanks to the unwitting help of the Trastevere squad, who knew of a pusher who claimed to know an Albanian living above one of Rome's most famous restaurants in Via del Vascello. Albanian, because Garramone had quickly established from Google that Ymeri was an Albanian name. The lead from the Trastevere squad was one of ten on various 'high-profile' Albanians living in the quarter that had slowly been whittled down. In passing, Scamarcio had asked about the health of Filippi, and had been told he was off the critical list. He felt both guilty and relieved at the news — guilty because, if truth be told, he had barely given Filippi a thought in the last few days.

He headed to the address that Garramone had given him, where they had set up shop above a bakery opposite the restaurant. After a successful break-in, which at one point had threatened to be anything but, they had spent almost a day listening to Ymeri's phone conversations: these ranged from him placating various offended girlfriends to calling his sick mother in Tirana, but didn't include anything of interest until he mentioned a name that set someone's bells ringing. The team assembled by Garramone had scrambled to call the chief, who had decided to attend himself and was now waiting for Scamarcio to show.

Scamarcio looked up and down Via del Vascello, and then rang the bell. The door buzzed open immediately, and he headed up to the first floor. In what looked like somebody's living room were Garramone and two men he had never seen before, both seated before a blacked-out window, wearing headphones. One was fiddling with some recording equipment on a desk in front of him. To their right, Garramone sat on a rickety directors' chair that was threatening not to support his weight for much longer. He was sipping coffee from a foam cup, and next to him was a man of medium height, muscular, and olive-skinned, with a head shaved smooth like a bullet. He was leaning against the wall, sucking hungrily on a cigarette.

Garramone and cigarette man looked up as he came in, but the other two remained absorbed in their work. Garramone rose carefully from the chair.

'Scamarcio, I want you to meet Davide Nepi — Anti-Mafia Squad.' Scamarcio felt his internal trip wires activated.

Nepi clenched his cigarette between his teeth and took Scamarcio's hand with both of his. 'Very pleased to meet you — heard a lot about you.'

'Likewise,' said Scamarcio.

'I've brought Davide in,' said Garramone, 'because we could do with some advice. A name has come up that is definitely of interest to his team.'

'Go on,' said Scamarcio.

'First, I want you to listen to this.' Garramone clicked on an audio file on his laptop, handing a small pair of headphones to Scamarcio and pushing out his chair so he could sit.

There was some interference on the line, and then he heard a man say: 'I can't move without the brothers' say-so. They're waiting on instructions their end.' The Italian was heavily accented. He wasn't sure whether this was Ymeri or someone else speaking.

'So what do we do in the meantime? We can't just leave the goods unattended.' The Italian was flawless, the accent Milanese. The other man had to be Ymeri.

'No, I've sent someone down there to keep an eye on things until we get moving.'

'Can you trust them? Is it going to be another fuck-up?'

'Just stay calm. There's nothing to worry about.'

The other man sighed. 'You know what it is, it's the Moltisanti — they're loose cannons. I'm not sure we chose well. I'm not sure we'll see the cash.'

'We'll see our money,' said the man who Scamarcio presumed was Ymeri. 'I'll make sure of that.'

Then the line went dead.

Scamarcio removed the headphones. 'I'm not clear on what I was listening to.'

'The guy with the accent was Ymeri,' said Garramone.

Nepi stubbed out his fag in an already-overburdened ashtray. 'There are two points of interest in that conversation. One is the mention of the "brothers"; the other is the name "Moltisanti". The Moltisanti brothers are long-time Cosa Nostra who have recently fallen foul of the main leadership — they've put too many noses out of joint. They're now perceived as lone wolves, and the dons have been watching out for their next move. We'd been anticipating turf wars over drug and contraband, but now Garramone tells me you're possibly looking into child trafficking with this guy Mr Ymeri. So that's obviously of great interest to us.'

'We did find coke on Elba,' said Scamarcio.

'Yes — Garramone filled me in.'

'Obviously, we don't know here whether they are talking about drugs or the snatched girl. If it's the snatched girl, that makes me think she's still on Elba. They're keeping her there until they know what to do with her,' said Garramone.

'That would be my assessment, too,' said Scamarcio. 'What do we do? Advise the reinforcements on the island to keep searching in the vicinity of the camp, near where the drugs were found?'

'I'd say so,' said Garramone. 'The other question now is whether we put the thumbscrews on Ymeri.'

Nepi was shaking his head violently. 'No. He has to lead us to the brothers, and for him to do that he needs to be a free man — free of any suspicion he's being watched.'

'You have no idea where they're based?'

'Well, no doubt they're in Sicily, but they're in hiding like the rest of them, changing locations every twenty-four hours. They're not stupid enough to go on Facebook with their dongles, like some of the younger generation, so we're up against it there.' He pulled a fag packet from his shirt pocket and offered them around. Scamarcio took one gratefully. Nepi lit up for the both of them. 'But the priority is not their location right now. We first need them to incriminate themselves on the telephone to Ymeri, and incriminate themselves to a level sufficient for conviction.' Nepi spoke fast, his words coming like machine-gun fire. 'It's great we now have this new conduit to them. But, for the moment, we just need to sit tight and listen, and hope that they'll come on the line and say something they shouldn't. Only then do we go in.'

'I probably don't need to remind you that there's a girl's life at stake here,' said Scamarcio, trying to keep his tone even.

'I know, but you've got to keep your eye on the endgame, the bigger picture. If they're involved in a child-trafficking ring, and it's not just drugs, we're talking about many more children — not just the one — and to put a stop to that we have to put them away, and that takes time and patience.' He took a furtive suck on the cigarette. 'Anyway, it sounds like the Moltisanti may not know where she is for now; it seems that that's more in the hands of your Mr Ymeri. And like your chief says, all you can do is keep searching that island and hoping you come up trumps. Although if you don't, it's better for the investigation. Obviously.'

'What?'

Nepi gave a tired smile. 'Oh, don't worry. I'm not for a minute saying I don't want you to find the girl. It's just that, obviously, the calmer they are, the more confident they are, the more likely they are to incriminate themselves.'

Scamarcio wasn't quite sure he bought the justification. 'When you say *incriminate themselves,* just what are you looking for? It's probably all going to stay cryptic.'

'Not necessarily, and it depends on whether we can tie their words into any developments on the ground. It's all a matter of interpretation, contingent on the evidence that comes along.'

'OK,' said Scamarcio, taking a deep breath. 'So where now?'

Garramone turned to Nepi: 'Would you mind if my detective and I just stepped outside for a second?'

'No problem,' said Nepi, sucking on his cigarette as if his life depended on it. Scamarcio wondered if the man was on coke.

Once they were in the corridor, Garramone said: 'I'm going to leave these guys to listen here, and then I'll alert our friends back on Elba. You'll have the time now to tie up some of your loose ends, Scamarcio. And I've got a good place for you to start.'

'Tell me.'

'Ganza's wife is back in Rome. She'll see you this afternoon — at Café Milano on Via dei Gracchi, at 2.00pm.'

'Why is she talking?'

'Pressure from on high, would be my guess. God knows if she'll give us anything, but a woman scorned and all that ... After you're done with her, any thoughts on your next move?'

Scamarcio fell silent for several moments before answering. 'I'm thinking that I'd like to go back down to Naples and nail that second officer, Rossi, who was present when the photos of Ganza were first handed over. As I told you, his colleague seemed to think he knew the man who gave them the pictures. I want to talk to him, and hear what he has to say.'

'Yes, track him down. He needs to give me an explanation for why he's gone AWOL,' said Garramone. 'But if that family's Camorra, like the neighbour suggested, you need to tread carefully — very carefully.'

50

VIA DEI GRACCHI was quiet. Everyone, it seemed, had scuttled back to their offices for the afternoon, and the tourists were headed elsewhere. Café Milano was the typical high-end affair: buffed gold and polished mahogany, wide mirrors and elaborate icing, pretty young waitresses gliding up and down in starched white. He spotted her in the far corner on the right, recognising her immediately from the society pages and her recent photos in the press. It was the usual perfect package for a woman such as this: her posture was ram-rod straight; her hair, a long, lustrous brown; her features, delicately sculpted — the nose gently upturned, the cheekbones high and strong, framing deep-brown eyes with thick lashes and brows. She was dressed in a buttoned-over grey cashmere cardigan with long sleeves that almost covered her hands entirely. He wondered momentarily at the choice, given the weather, and then realised that the air inside the café was much cooler. She was no doubt a regular, and knew to come prepared. She was looking out onto the street, absent-mindedly tracking the passers-by.

He approached the table. 'Mrs Ganza? Leone Scamarcio. Thanks for seeing me.'

She seemed surprised, as if she hadn't been expecting him, and then quickly composed herself and held out a hand. They shook, and he took a seat. There were fine lines around her eyes and mouth, but the rest of her skin was smooth and even: for a woman in her mid-forties, she was in impressive shape. He guessed she'd had help with that.

'Would you like a coffee, Detective?' Before he'd answered, she'd waved over the waitress in that way that people who had always had money felt comfortable doing. She was the daughter of an oilman, he seemed to remember; she was much richer than Ganza himself.

'Caffè latte, thanks.'

She placed their orders and then looked down at the table, delaying the moment when they would have to make eye contact.

After a few seconds, she lifted her gaze to him and said: 'I'm sorry, but I fear I'm not going to be of much help to you, Detective.'

There was a deadness behind her eyes, and he wondered if it was exhaustion, both emotional and physical.

'I just need to ask you a few basic questions — we're crossing the t's and dotting the i's, really.'

She nodded, seeming to steel herself.

'How long did you know about your husband's relationship with Arthur?'

She shook her head gently, and cast her eyes down again. Her voice was low and tired. The words came slowly. 'It was a complete surprise. I had no idea.'

'So he never said anything?'

'Well, would *you*?'

The comment threw him slightly, and he was momentarily lost for words. Thankfully, the waitress was back with their coffees. He pulled the caffè latte towards him and took a sip, and then asked: 'So all seemed well in the marriage?'

'We had been married for 17 years, Detective. A marriage like that takes a lot of work. There were the usual ups and downs.'

'But nothing that led you to suspect he could be having an affair?'

She carefully replaced her cup on the saucer, turned it around so the handle was pointing to her right, and then looked up, fixing him squarely in the eye. 'Detective, it was not an affair. He was a whore. He used him for sex.'

Scamarcio decided not to push it for now. 'So when those photos appeared in the press, it was the first you had heard of it?'

She sighed, exasperated. 'No, my husband had warned me the night before that they were about to come out. He'd told me we all needed to get out of Rome for a while.'

'Did he explain what had gone on between him and Arthur?'

She laughed — a defeated, bitter little laugh. 'It's funny how you keep calling him that.'

'Why?'

'Well, I'm sure that's not his name.'

'Why do you say that?'

'What Argentine calls their child Arthur?'

He smiled, playing along. 'So did your husband explain the nature of their relationship?'

'He just told me what I've told you. He was a whore, and he paid him for sex.' She paused a moment. 'Why the gay stuff? Well, he didn't go into that and, frankly, I wasn't in the mood for asking.'

'Did he have any idea who had killed him?'

She shook her head. 'No, none at all.'

'Do *you* have any ideas?'

She exhaled, leaning back against the wall. 'Why would I know? I didn't even know of this … this person's existence until a few days ago.'

Scamarcio nodded and then said: 'How did your husband seem? When he heard about Arthur's death, I mean?'

She fell silent for a moment and then said: 'He's scared.' She paused. 'He's not saying, but I can tell.' There was something strangely triumphant in her tone.

'Why do you think he's scared?'

'I guess because he's worried that you lot will think he's responsible.'

'Do *you* think he's responsible?'

She went to bar her arms across her chest, and then seemingly thought better of it and placed her hands on her lap under the table.

'My husband is a selfish, deluded fool, Detective, but he's not a murderer. Seventeen years with someone, and there are certain things you know about them.'

'You didn't know he'd been having sex with men.'

She flashed him a look of anger. 'That's very different.'

Scamarcio decided to change tack. 'Do you think he'd be capable of hiring someone to commit murder on his behalf?'

She didn't hesitate this time. 'Certainly not. In his mind, it would amount to the same thing, whether he did it himself or not. He has a logical mind — he's always been a highly rational thinker.'

To Scarmacio, there was nothing very rational about setting up a rentboy and his friend in two apartments in Trastevere; nothing very rational about attending the kind of parties that Ganza did. Maybe that's what happened to exceptionally rational people, Scamarcio reflected — they were inevitably prone to moments of breathtaking irrationality. Base nature would always triumph over intellect.

'Do you think your husband has any idea who might have done it?'

She sighed, exasperated again. 'You would need to ask him yourself. He's never said anything to me. But I guess Arthur, as you call him, inhabited a dirty little world where dirty little people do dirty little things.' It was clear that this was a world that, for Mrs Ganza, was as distant as Venus.

'I'd very much like to talk to your husband, but it seems quite difficult to reach him right now.'

She smiled bitterly again, fixing him with a hard stare. 'I'm sure that when he leaves the retreat, you'll be the first person he calls, Detective.'

51

HE FILLED IN GARRAMONE about the fruitless meeting with Mrs Ganza. Reflecting on it, as he headed down to Naples the next morning, he wondered about the deadness in the eyes, considered anew if, like Mrs Baker, she was also on some kind of medication to ease her pain. Now he thought back, when she turned her head a certain way, the light revealed a plasticity to the skin. But that could be the botox, rather than any anti-depressant drug. He thought about the Moltisanti, wondering about their connection to Ganza and his world.

Although it took just an hour and a half by car to get from Rome to Naples, the heat in the city was far more cloying than in the capital. There was a rank intensity to it that made Scamarcio desperate to leave the place almost as soon as he had arrived. The foetid miasma of two weeks' worth of garbage hung over Rossi's street, and as he entered the building he saw the ribbed red tail of something feral disappear between some broken bin bags. A resident held the front door open for him, and he took the lift to the fifth floor, figuring that the family had to be home, that they couldn't hide out forever. He left the elevator and stepped out into the corridor. This time there were no neighbours around. He found the door, pushing the square buzzer on the wall to the right. He waited, but once again there was no sound of footsteps from inside, no TV murmur, no chatter. He tried the buzzer once more, but he was greeted by the same silence. He was about to turn away when, from nowhere, a tattooed arm reached over his left shoulder and placed a large, hairy hand on the door in front of him.

'Who wants them?'

Scamarcio turned to see a tall, muscle-bound man with close-cropped hair, over-tanned skin, bulldog features, and a gold stud in each ear standing directly in front of him, barring his way to the elevator.

'And you are?'

The man pushed him in his chest, throwing him against the door. It caught the back of his head.

'I ask the questions, arsehole.'

Scamarcio rubbed at his skull and tried to straighten up. The meathead barred his huge arms across his chest, setting his feet apart. The message was clear: Scamarcio wasn't going anywhere for the time being.

'I'm looking for Officer Rossi. I'm a colleague of his from Rome.'

The man shook his head. 'As far as he tells it, his colleagues sold him down the Swanee.'

'It's not that simple.'

'What do you want with him?'

'Just to talk.'

'Well, he's not here.'

'When is he coming back?'

'That's none of your business.'

'Now listen, Mr …?'

'Again, none of your business.'

Scamarcio decided he'd had enough. He looked to his right a moment, as if he'd seen something alarming approaching down the corridor, and when the idiot turned to follow his gaze, he rushed forward and kneed him in the groin, spinning him around to the left so that, from behind, he could push his arm across his neck and Adam's apple, holding it hard under his chin. He tightened the vice and pulled the man down towards the floor while, with the other hand, he twisted his balls.

'It's time to be polite.'

The man began whimpering like a baby.

'It's actually very simple. I want you to tell me where Rossi is, and I want the truth, otherwise you'll be looking at losing a testicle — maybe two.' He twisted harder, and the man screamed.

'Could you manage without them, do you think?'

The man screamed again.

'Spit it out.'

Scamarcio's heart was pounding, and he wasn't sure how much longer he could resist the push of the man's huge thigh muscles against his arm.

'He's in their summer house ... in Scala.' The meathead gasped, and Scamarcio pulled harder. 'The hills above Amalfi,' he spluttered. In one movement, Scamarcio prised his arm free from between the man's legs, and swung it around to his left-hand jeans pocket, where he grabbed his cuffs from their usual place. He then opened them with his teeth, and attached one to his left wrist and the other to the man's right, where he was trying to prise Scamarcio's arm from his neck. Scamarcio then quickly swung the right half of his body free. The lout was too slow to follow what he was doing and react.

'You're going to take me there,' said Scamarcio.

As he was bundling him into the elevator, the numbskull spat in his face.

'Didn't you hear what I said?' asked Scamarcio. 'I have a new set of knives that I'm dying to try out.'

The colour seemed to drain from the man's face, and they rode down to the lobby in silence.

Once outside, he pushed the man into the passenger seat of his car, detaching the cuff from his right wrist and transferring it to the door handle on the passenger side. He swung the door shut on the blockhead and walked around to the driver's side. He got in and pushed the car into gear, scrabbling for his fags in the tray under the radio. He found his lighter in his shirt pocket, and lit up.

'Sorry, I should have asked you if you wanted one.'

The man just looked away in contempt.

They left the garbage-strewn suburbs, and headed off in silence along the A3 towards Salerno. Scamarcio only asked the man for directions as they neared the city. He grunted a few rights and lefts until they were ascending a steep hill with the Amalfi coast spread out beneath them. Scamarcio thought he could spot the spires of Positano cathedral glinting in the sun, silver fishing boats dancing in the harbour below. Eventually, the road became dust and, above it, low stone walls appeared, studded with cacti and bougainvillea. Small farms branched off to either side, their red shutters baking in the sun.

'Next left,' spat the man.

Scamarcio turned onto a long track. Fields ran alongside it, and at the end of the drive stood a large white villa; terracotta pots lining the paved entranceway to the porch, and pink bougainvillea framing the front door. A couple of black Labradors yapped as they ran up and down the gravel.

There was only one car parked in front of the garage — a black Suzuki jeep. Scamarcio took that as a good sign. It might mean that there weren't too many of them home.

'Give me your mobile,' he said to the man.

'It's in my right-hand pocket.' He rattled his wrist in the cuff to show he couldn't get to it.

Scamarcio reached over. 'Sit up a second.'

The man did so, and Scamarcio managed to pull it from his pocket and place it in his own. He opened the car windows slightly and killed the engine before stepping out into the afternoon heat. He clicked the central locking: Meathead could stay where he was for now.

Scamarcio patted the Beretta in its holster inside his jacket and walked up to the house. The Labradors ran up to him, barking, but he ignored them and made straight for the door, pressing the buzzer.

Almost immediately, he heard footsteps inside and several latches being pulled. The door opened slowly, and he saw a young man standing there, probably no more than 23 years old.

'Gianfilippo Rossi?'

'Who wants to know?'

Scamarcio flashed him his badge. 'I'm a colleague of yours from Rome. Your pal Limoni may have told you about me.'

Rossi's reaction was reflex: he swung around and started running through what appeared to be a huge, tiled lobby. Scamarcio ran after him, slamming the front door behind him to stop the dogs from following. The boy was heading for some patio doors that opened onto a back garden with fields beyond. Before he could reach the sliding doors, Scamarcio leapt onto his back, bringing him crashing to the floor. He rolled him over and sat on his chest, pinning his arms behind him against the tiles, palms up. There was no sound of footsteps running to find them, and no shouts, so he presumed the boy was alone in the house.

'Not so fast, Rossi,' he gasped.

The boy was only about 5ft 8 and thin, so he was no match for Scamarcio's 6 ft 3 bulk. He gave Rossi a hard slap across the side of his face, and then pulled his gun from its holster.

'How would you feel about having that pretty face of yours cut up a bit?'

There were tears in the boy's brown eyes, and he saw one of them break and roll slowly down his right cheek.

Scamarcio sighed, suddenly tired from the day, tired of the whole thing. 'Now listen, Rossi, let's just keep this simple. I'm a busy man — places to go, people to mutilate.'

The boy wouldn't meet his eye, and was blinking away the tears.

'That guy who handed you and Limoni the photos of Foreign

Secretary Ganza — did you know him?'

The boy shook his head, so Scamarcio smashed the gun into the side of his face. The boy was shaking now, and blood was mixing with the tears.

Scamarcio kept his tone even. 'I will ask you again: did you know him?'

The boy nodded feebly, turning his head to the wall so he wouldn't have to look at Scamarcio.

'*How* did you know him?'

When it came, Rossi's voice was high and shaky. 'He knew an uncle of mine, my dad's brother.'

'How did he know him?'

'Just a business associate, I think.'

'Name?'

'My uncle?'

'No, the man.'

'Zaccardo — Paolo Zaccardo.'

'How did he get the photos?'

'I don't know.'

Scamarcio smashed the left side of his face with the gun, as he had often seen his father do. The boy howled. He was panting now. 'I promise that's the truth. I don't know how he got them. I was just told that I had to take them from him, that I could make some money from them if I wanted, and that I'd have to share the money with him.'

Scamarcio looked towards the patio doors and then behind him, checking for unannounced visitors. He returned his attention to the boy.

'Where is he now?'

The boy said nothing, so Scamarcio raised the gun. The boy started shaking again. 'I'm not sure. But there's a place he might be — Pogerola. It's not far from here — fifteen minutes or so. I can show you how to get there.'

'Good idea.'

Scamarcio dragged the boy to his feet and then stabbed the gun into his back, pushing him to lead the way. When they reached the car, the boy was wide-eyed at the sight of Meathead, handcuffed to the passenger door. They exchanged furious glances, but neither of them said a word.

Scamarcio pushed the boy into the back of the car behind the driver's seat, and pulled out a spare set of cuffs from the glove pocket. He attached the boy to the door handle and then slammed the door shut, locking him inside.

He hopped in front and started the engine, slamming the car into gear and taking the drive as fast as possible. He didn't want to encounter any relatives back from the shops or a Camorra killing spree.

'Quite the family outing,' he said as they approached the main road.

Neither of the men responded.

'Right or left here?'

'Right,' muttered the boy behind him.

It was past midday, and the air conditioning in his Toyota was not up to the job. He could smell the sweat of the two strangers, and opened his window wide. As the sea came into view, the tourist villages of the Amalfi coast blinked back at them, the small sailboats still bobbing in their harbours, the surf rolling gently towards the hills. The boy was murmuring oaths to himself, entreating all the saints, calling God a pig. Eventually, the meathead shouted at him not to take the Lord's name in vain, and he finally fell silent.

Pogerola was more a hamlet than anything else, a scattering of ten-or-so houses with a tiny chapel at the end of the road. The boy grunted at him to make a right-hand turn, and he pulled up outside a stone cottage set slightly back from the drive, its wooden fence circling a sloping patch of lawn that ran downhill with the gravel lane. The windows were in the old style with yellow wooden shutters, and painted on the stone slabs of the ground floor was a kind of nautical design. There was a large tiled area before the front door, where two black-and-white cats were sunning themselves lazily. The place was well kept: the grass was freshly mown, and two blue pots full of primroses marked the entrance to the house. Scamarcio wondered at the English lawn — getting that to work this far south was quite an achievement.

He turned in his seat to face the boy. 'Give me your mobile.'

'I don't have it.'

Scamarcio got out from the driver's seat and unlocked the boy's door. He patted him down, but could find no sign of a phone. 'Right, stay here while I have a chat with your friend Zaccardo.'

Once again, he felt for his Beretta in its holster and took the path to the house. He was tired, but somehow he liked days like this — it felt like he was cleaning up, tidying away, so they could all move forward. He knocked on the wooden front door, noticing the antique knocker and sliding bolt. A horseshoe hung over the porch above him. Maybe it would turn out to be his lucky day.

He heard footsteps, and the old door creaked open. If this was Zaccardo, he was not what Scamarcio was expecting. He had anticipated Meathead Mark II, not the small wiry man standing before him now. His hair was curly, his face tanned and taut, his narrow eyes a gimlet blue.

'Yes?' The accent was undiluted Neapolitan.

'Paolo Zaccardo?'

The man surveyed him for a few moments, as if weighing up their relative physiques and his chances of winning in a fight. Although the man was small, he was well muscled; nevertheless, Scamarcio reckoned he could take him without too much fuss.

'Who's asking?'

Scamarcio showed him his badge. 'Detective Leone Scamarcio, Rome Flying Squad.'

Scamarcio saw the cogs whir, and figured the man was assessing anew whether it was worth the effort. In the end, he surprised him completely by opening the door wider and saying: 'You'd better come in.'

The ceilings in the house were low. Downstairs seemed to be all open plan, exposed stone walls, and terracotta floors, creating a French farmhouse effect. Zaccardo gestured to a leather armchair by the fireplace. 'Take a seat, Detective. Can I offer you something?'

Scamarcio wondered if he was playing for time, giving whoever was upstairs the chance to arm up and come down. But he couldn't hear anyone else in the house.

'No, thank you. I'm fine.'

Zaccardo took a seat on the sofa opposite. 'I think I can guess why you're here.'

'You can?'

Several seconds of silence followed, in which all Scamarcio could hear was the lazy hum of the cicadas outside.

Eventually, Zaccardo said: 'Arthur dies, and now, from what I hear, Simon up in Florence. Another acquaintance of mine, Geppo, has also been killed.' He sighed. 'The fact is, they're all linked to the same thing.'

'Geppo the bookie, you mean?'

'You knew him?'

'I knew of him. But not when he was alive. He was connected to Arthur and the other guy?'

'In a manner of speaking.'

Scamarcio stopped a moment, deciding it was best to take things one step at a time.

'I've been told you were the one who handed the photos of Ganza to my two colleagues in Rome?'

Zaccardo sank back into the sofa, crossed his legs, and sighed again. 'I was just trying to make a bit of extra money.'

'What was the deal between you and officer Rossi?'

'He'd share any proceeds with me.'

'Proceeds from blackmail?'

'Correct.'

'Why are you being so open with me?'

Zaccardo got up from the sofa and went to a low shelf cut into the stone to his right. On it stood various bottles of whisky. He selected a Jamesons, and poured himself a generous measure. 'You sure I can't offer you anything, Detective?'

'Quite sure.'

Zaccardo sat back down, said nothing, and just sipped tentatively at the whisky. Scamarcio didn't take him for an afternoon drinker. 'Blackmail comes with a hefty sentence, so I'm wondering why you're willing to own up so readily. I'd expected much more of a fight, to be honest. It's not usually this easy.'

Zaccardo put down his glass. 'Actually, Detective, I've been thinking about all this for some time now — well, since the deaths started, really. I'd been weighing up whether to approach the police myself, asking them to cut me some sort of deal. Now you're here, you've made up my mind for me. I definitely want a deal.'

'A deal?'

'I want to go into witness protection.'

'You what?'

'You heard me.'

Neither man said a word for several moments. Somewhere down the corridor, an antique grandfather clock was marking out another fifteen minutes of Scamarcio's life, gone forever.

After a while, Zaccardo said: 'To put it simply, I'm scared. Too many people I know, too many associates, are losing their lives, and I've got a hunch that I'm going to be next.'

'Associates to what?'

'This is where the deal comes in. If I tell you what I know, I want you to guarantee that you'll provide me with protection.

The same deal as you make with the penitents. I want a new house, a new identity, a brand-new life — the works. Somewhere up north, preferably.'

Scamarcio took a breath. 'But those kinds of deals are cut on huge cases — cases where many others are going to be brought into the frame. I don't think this one quite ranks in the same league. It's hardly going to result in a maxi trial.'

Zaccardo shook his head. 'Then you don't understand this case at all.'

His words silenced Scamarcio, bringing bitterness to his mouth. He thought for several moments and then said: 'Look, I'd like to hear what you know. Tell me what I need to do right now to speed that along.'

'Do you or do you not have the authority to cut me a deal?'

Scamarcio sighed. 'Not without talking to my boss first.'

'Then call him, and tell him what I've said. Then we can talk. While you make the call, I'll be in the kitchen.'

Zaccardo got up and left him alone in the room.

Scamarcio dialled Garramone and filled him in. When he was done, the chief surprised him by saying: 'Just give him what he's asking for. We'll sort it all out later.'

'If he wants a paper contract?'

'Just sign it.'

As Scamarcio hung up, he saw that Zaccardo was back in the room. He must have been listening to the end of the conversation.

'Yes, I want it all down on paper.'

'OK, so draw it up.'

Zaccardo reached for a pad and pen in a cupboard next to the dining-room table, and pulled out a seat to jot down a few lines. When he brought it over, Scamarcio saw that it was crude stuff — just one paragraph, replete with spelling and grammatical errors, asking for protection and a new identity as they'd discussed. It reminded him of the letter sent to Filippi. Scamarcio signed beneath the text, knowing that, if push came to shove, Garramone could invoke a whole set of laws to deem it invalid.

Zaccardo took the paper, folded it, and put it in his shirt pocket. He sat back down on the sofa and crossed his legs again. Scamarcio took out his phone and pressed the recording device. Zaccardo saw him do it and nodded.

'OK, Detective. Where do you want to start?'

'So how did you get the photos in the first place?'

'I took them myself.'

'Where were they taken?'

'At a villa, outside Radda in Chianti.'

'How did you know that Ganza was going to be there?'

'Due to my work, I knew where a whole lot of important people were going to be on certain dates at certain times, and what they'd be doing when they got there.'

'Go on.'

Zaccardo looked up to the ceiling for a moment, and his shoulders seemed to sag. Scamarcio thought he read guilt on the man's face. When they finally came, there was a tiredness and resignation in the words: 'I suppose you could call it a kind of exclusive club, although they did their best not to pin it down, or give it any kind of definition or identity. That would make it real, you see.'

Scamarcio decided not to say anything; he didn't want to get in the way for now.

'They'd organise get-togethers every few weeks. Only a select few were invited: figures from the world of high politics and big business.' He paused for a moment. 'Actually, Andrea Spezzi was one of them until he conveniently killed himself.'

That chimed with Scamarcio's initial instincts.

Zaccardo sighed again. It seemed as if the burden of this knowledge was weighing him down, was getting harder to carry by the second. Sharing it with someone else didn't appear to make it any easier. 'These get-togethers, well …' He took a deep breath. 'Imagine the sickest sexual perversion you can find online, and then imagine it catered for to the very last detail, with no expense spared. And I'm not just talking adults, if you get my drift. All tastes were catered for there.'

Scamarcio nodded gently, anxiety churning in his stomach.

Zaccardo continued: 'The locations were luxurious; the drink and drugs on tap. Preparing for an event took two weeks of around-the-clock organisation. Sometimes it looked like they were creating a film set.' He paused a moment, reflecting. 'In fact, in some cases I do believe they were.'

Scamarcio leaned forward. 'And where did you come into all of this?'

'I supplied the drugs, Detective. I had the contacts, I got them the best, and they paid me … well, they paid me …' He shrugged. 'I guess "decently" would be the word I'd choose. But, just that — nothing more. In the end, it wasn't enough. When I heard what they were charging the clients to attend, and I compared it with the cut they gave me, I decided to try and make a bit more profit with those photos.'

For Zaccardo to confess so readily to several major crimes, he had indeed to be extremely scared of something, figured Scamarcio. 'What were they charging the clients?'

'Twenty grand a night, with 100 grand paid up-front just to be a member. You couldn't attend the get-togethers unless you were a member, and members were extremely highly vetted. Quite a few famous names were rejected.'

'What were they vetting for?'

'It wasn't just status, it was discretion. They didn't want people who would talk, brag around too much. Membership was on recommendation from other members. If someone recommended you, and you passed the vetting, then you'd be invited.'

'Was anyone invited who didn't accept? Wouldn't that have

potentially exposed what they were up to?'

'As far as I know, that never happened. They made quite sure they chose people who would jump at their invitation.'

'So how did Arthur and his friend in Florence fit in?'

'They were good-looking boys, well ripped, everything just right, and there were quite a few clients who were into that — Ganza among them — so they were there to cater for that particular preference.'

'You met Arthur at these get-togethers?'

'A few times, but usually only at the start of the night, and then I'd head straight off. They didn't like me hanging around, and I didn't want to, anyway.' He paused a moment. 'One time, quite close to the end — I mean to when Arthur died — we had a particular conversation which has stuck with me, given everything that's happened since.' As if as an afterthought, he added: 'I sometimes used to have a drink at one of the bar areas; they let me have free beers, and that's where we got talking.'

Scamarcio nodded at him to continue. 'Arthur had noticed something that upset him. Despite his line of work, in some ways he was quite naïve about the world, and it seemed like he hadn't really developed a thick skin for certain things. Well, to cut a long story short, one time at one of the villas he'd seen two little girls — I mean, when I say little, probably just around seven or eight — being led into a room. And when he saw that, it clicked for him, just what they were up to in there. I think until then he'd just reckoned it was adult stuff for adults only. But that freaked him out, and from that point on he wanted out of this thing, and that night he told me as much. I think he'd had a couple of drinks — they'd loosened his tongue.'

'And how did you respond when he said he wanted out?'

'I said I knew where he was coming from.'

'Did you want out, too?'

Zaccardo weighed this up for several moments. 'I think, in

some ways, maybe I did. I mean, I knew bad stuff went on, and I lived with that, but what was beginning to get to me was their arrogance — the fact that cos they had all this money, they knew they could do whatever the hell they wanted, to whoever they wanted. They could get away with murder.' He looked directly at Scamarcio as he said the word. 'And when I say murder, I mean murder. Don't think for a second that the whole snuff thing wasn't catered for. That was one of their bestsellers.'

Scamarcio swallowed. He felt bile in his throat. 'They killed people?'

'Quite a few people.'

'How many?'

'I don't know precisely, but I heard at least ten.'

'Yeah, but surely those people had been reported missing?'

Zaccardo laughed, but it sounded more like a sigh. 'Detective, they chose carefully — people who wouldn't be missed.'

A new thought struck Scamarcio, and settled like a blade of ice in his gut. 'Children?'

'Sometimes.'

Scamarcio let that sink in for several moments. He took a breath: 'So, looking back, you think Arthur wanted to let the world know what they were doing to kids there?' He decided not to mention the images they'd found on the camera for now.

'I'm not sure I'd go that far, but he had doubts and wanted out, and I guess they got wind of it and thought they couldn't trust him. Whether that happened before or after I released the photos, I don't know. But surely once they were out there, their suspicions were confirmed.'

'But if you knew Arthur had these doubts and wanted out, why did you take those photos of him? Didn't you see what might happen?'

Zaccardo was shaking his head again. 'I didn't think they'd kill him. I really didn't. He was one of their most popular guys. I didn't think it would end like that.'

'But they were killing people for snuff movies! Why would they care about some Argentine rentboy?'

'No, it doesn't work like that. He was a valuable commodity, in demand. I didn't think they'd kill *him*.'

He had his head in his hands now, and Scamarcio understood that the guilt was for Arthur, not the children, and this both disturbed and confused him. 'But didn't you think you'd get him into trouble?'

'No, he wasn't to know I was in the wardrobe taking photos and, anyway, I thought maybe this could be his way out, you know?'

'But you just said he was a valuable commodity. It doesn't sound like they'd let him go easily.'

'No, but if he felt like his identity had been compromised, they might see his point of view, and it could get all get settled amicably. They might have offered him a painless exit.'

In that moment, Scamarcio got it. 'You were in love with him, weren't you?'

Zaccardo took a sip of the small slither of whisky still left in his glass. 'Love is a big word, Detective.'

'So why the other guy, too? And why Spezzi?'

'The other guy was in the picture with Arthur. I guess they figured they shared the same doubts, I don't know — they were close, always together, those two.' He sighed. 'Spezzi, well, there's an interesting one. When it came out on the grapevine that Arthur had died, Spezzi was gutted, cos he'd been one of his most loyal clients and still was, even though he was about to marry that French girl. He got really scared that it was all about to come out again. From what I heard, he actually *was* suicidal, but I think they gave him a helpful push because they worried about his state of mind — worried that if he got into a confessional mood, he might spill all to the girlfriend before she could read it in the papers.'

'And the bookie, Geppo?'

'Poor old Geppo had a problem, and of late it was getting a lot worse. He supplied fags and booze to the parties, and was touting for more trade; but, unlike me, he was getting high on his own supply. If you ask me, long before the Ganza thing came out, they were thinking of letting him go; they were concerned about him being indiscreet. It just so happened that that coincided with a whole lot of other shit hitting the fan.' He paused a moment. 'But I know that he got on with Arthur. They seemed to be friendly, so that could have worried them, too.'

'For a group of people who want to keep their activities under the radar, they seem a bit heavy-handed to me.'

Zaccardo nodded. 'They never were in the past, before the brothers, but they certainly are now, and *that* is going to be their downfall, Detective. It's just a matter of time. When the brothers got into this, they took it down a road that, if you ask me, it would have been better to avoid.'

For the past few minutes, Scamarcio had had the sense that all this was building to the one dreadful, inevitable conclusion, and now he felt sure that his instinct was about to be confirmed. He was struggling to process the concept that these parties were where Stacey Baker might have been headed — that this was where she would finish up. He prayed to an inner god he didn't quite believe in that he'd soon be proved wrong.

'You're talking about the Moltisanti?' He almost crossed his fingers when he posed the question, desperate for Zaccardo to utter the one word, 'No.'

Zaccardo paled slightly, and then just nodded. Scamarcio felt like properly throwing up now. Eventually, he said: 'Too many of their heavies running around sorting out cock-ups?'

Zaccardo nodded again.

'So it's just the brothers?'

'There's another guy who had the initial idea, but I don't know much about him. Lately it's just the brothers I hear mentioned — I chat with the private drivers they use for the parties, as well as a few of the staff. I know there's been trouble of late because they farmed out some of the operation to a group of Albanians, but they haven't been up to scratch. It's causing friction and, if the gossip is to be believed, they're about to ditch them.'

Scamarcio nodded. 'And the great and the good who attend these get-togethers, can you give me any names?'

Zaccardo looked him squarely in the eye, but his voice was shaky now. 'Can we leave the names for later? What I will say is that you're looking at another cabinet minister, a couple of regional police and intelligence chiefs, and a few of our heavy hitters in industry, a la Spezzi. There's a mayor in there, too, of a big northern town.'

Scamarcio exhaled. 'Are there many of them?'

'No, it's very exclusive.'

'All men?'

'Yes.'

'Does the PM know, you think?'

Zaccardo exhaled, and shook his head sharply. 'He's never been invited because his tastes are plain vanilla. Plus he's renowned for getting over-excited: he likes nothing more than to brag about his achievements, as we all know. They figured it would be best to leave him to his little harems at home with his geriatric buddies.' He paused a moment. 'Besides, I heard that there's some bad blood between him and the brothers.'

'That so?'

Zaccardo shrugged. 'I don't have the details.'

'So why are *you* so worried, Zaccardo? Why would they kill *you*? You're just their dealer.'

'Look at it from my point of view: they seemed to know that Arthur had doubts, so they had him done in, along with Simon and Spezzi. Geppo is also now out of the picture. I was often seen chatting to Arthur — they knew we were friendly. The way I see it is that they seem to be cleaning up after themselves, clearing the slate of problem people, and I guess I could fit into that. They'll just want some new guy to take my place who doesn't know about any of this past stuff. Someone uncompromised — someone cheaper, probably.'

'And if you're wrong, and they're perfectly happy with you?'

Zaccardo's gaze was unflinching. 'Then I've just made the biggest mistake of my life talking to you, Detective.'

52

Scamarcio pulled his fag packet from his pocket. 'You mind if I smoke in here?'

'Actually, I'd prefer it if you went outside. I'm kind of house proud.'

Scamarcio thought that none of this would matter now if Zaccardo was about to be spirited to a new life up north. Or bumped off. But instead he said: 'Yeah, nice place you've got here. I'll be a couple of minutes.'

Zaccardo showed him to the front door, and he stepped out onto the patio where the two cats were still sunning themselves. His captives remained where he'd left them, except they now seemed to be engaged in an animated conversation which, from where he was standing, sounded more like an argument. Zaccardo squinted into the sunlight behind him. 'Is that Rossi in the car there? What's going on?'

Scamarcio waved the question away. 'Don't concern yourself with that. We've got bigger things to worry about just now.' He held up the cigarette. 'I'll just be two minutes finishing this.'

Zaccardo got the message and stepped back into the house, leaving the door ajar. Scamarcio took a long drag on the fag. He wasn't entirely surprised by what Zaccardo had told him — disgusted, yes, but not completely surprised. Since the case of the Monster of Florence, still unsolved after more than forty years, the idea that high-ranking figures could be involved in the murders of young couples for sexual gratification had been in the public consciousness. That the great and the good were above the law was not just public perception, but a deeply entrenched reality — corruption slowly crushing the state in its stranglehold, a swelling octopus with its tentacles in every area of public life. A Carabinieri officer from Tuscany had once confided to him that they knew full well who had been behind the sixteen Monster of Florence slayings, but that the perpetrators were high-ranking masons and they'd been advised by their Caribinieri bosses that they were untouchable.

To Scamarcio, this felt like a similar deal; maybe some of the same people were even involved. He had the sense that securing prosecutions was going to be extremely challenging, if not impossible. And would the PM even have the will? Especially if he had once locked horns with the Moltisanti? He stubbed out the cigarette onto the patio, and then, remembering Zaccardo's sensibilities, picked it up again and popped it into a handkerchief in his pocket — best to keep on the good side of their one useful witness for now.

He stepped back into the cool of the house. Zaccardo was seated on the sofa again.

'Listen, Zaccardo, there's something I need to ask you.'

'Knock yourself out.' Zaccardo sounded down now, exhausted from it all.

Scamarcio perched on the edge of the armchair, and leaned forward: 'Did you hear anything about the kidnap of an American girl from Elba — a kidnap on order for these guys who would be delivered to their next party?'

Zaccardo shook his head. 'No. Are you talking about the little girl who has been all over the news?'

'Yeah, that girl. So you didn't hear it mentioned?'

He shook his head again. 'No, nothing. I'm sorry.'

Scamarcio chose to believe him. 'Did you ever find out how they got the children?'

He shook his head again. 'No, nobody spoke to me about that. That was never discussed.' He paused. 'But, um, I'm guessing that maybe the Albanian side would have come into play there. They have a history of child-trafficking, don't they?'

He was right, but it was just supposition and wouldn't hold up in a court of law. They needed watertight evidence, and for that they'd have to rely on the Ymeri wiretaps.

'They've been involved in that in the past, yes.' Scamarcio exhaled, scratching the back of his neck. 'The thing is, it would be really useful if you could go on the record on that side of things, too.'

Zaccardo shrugged. 'Yeah, I imagine it would be but, as I say, I'm in the dark — maybe more in the dark than you are.'

It seemed to be a question, but Scamarcio chose not to answer it. He thought for a second. 'You know anyone, any of the staff there, who might be up to speed?'

Zaccardo inclined his head to one side, and then barred his arms across his chest: 'Come on, I can't ask them that. That would be suicide — for all of us.'

Scamarcio took his point. He was about to concede it when there was a commotion outside. He heard several pairs of heavy boots pounding up the path, and then knuckles rapping on the door.

Zaccardo looked petrified. 'What the hell is that?' Then: 'You got a gun?'

Scamarcio nodded. Zaccardo ran over to the cupboard by the dining table and knelt to pull out a box from the bottom shelf. He placed it on the table and flipped open the lid. He took what looked like a Beretta 92 from inside and quickly loaded the chamber, his hands shaking. Then he gestured to Scamarcio to follow him to the door. Once Scamarcio was positioned the other side of the doorframe, he nodded at Zaccardo to open up. He did so slowly, and then just shrugged his shoulders and sighed, stowing his weapon away in his pocket. 'What the fuck are you lot playing at?'

A trio of meatheads bundled into the house. The tallest and fattest of the three said: 'Rossi called us — said he'd been kidnapped and that you were in danger.'

The little bastard had managed to conceal his mobile on him, realised Scamarcio.

Zaccardo was now covered in perspiration and his hands were shaking, but he just tut-tutted like a bored headmaster, trying to disguise his fear: 'Oh, for God's sake, there's nothing to worry about. I was talking to this man here on business.' He waved a hand in dismissal. 'I'll explain it all later.'

The fat meathead said: 'Yeah, but Rossi's handcuffed in the car!'

Zaccardo raised his eyebrows at Scamarcio, who kept his expression neutral, then said: 'It's a long story. Everything is under control.'

Scamarcio decided to take the interruption as his cue to leave. He turned to Zaccardo and extended his hand: 'Many thanks for your help. I'll be in touch.' Zaccardo's palms were wet.

'Is that it? Can't you offer me anything now? Just to make sure I'm all right until I see you guys next?'

Scamarcio knew he was talking about a police presence in the house.

'It seems to me your three friends here are quite capable of looking after you. But I'll be in touch very soon.' He gave him a backhanded wave and left the house. The last thing he saw was Zaccardo's horrified expression. How the little man was going to square all this with his Camorra colleagues, he had no idea.

He'd thrown Rossi and the meathead outside Zaccardo's, and now the car stank of their sweat. The azure of Amalfi glinted below, and he suddenly wanted a swim and a cold beer. But he knew that was impossible for now, so he dialled Garramone. All he could say when Scamarcio had finished filling him in was, 'Holy Christ.'

'You think they're untouchable?'

'I don't know. I need to run it past my friend.'

Scamarcio felt the rage rising up from his lungs, into his chest. It was rising much faster than he could control, and it took him by surprise. 'Ah, right then, and if he says it's too uncomfortable, we just drop it, I guess?'

'Don't take that tone with me, Scamarcio.'

'I'm asking you, Garramone. You got me into this: are we going to pursue these men to the end, or are we just going to let it lie like the faithful dogs we are?'

'Now listen here!'

'No, you listen to me. I've barely slept in the last few days. I'm exhausted, fed up, worried for my future, but most of all I'm sickened by what I'm hearing. I will not let this one go. I will not let it drop, you understand? People are dead. Children are ruined. A little girl's life is at stake. There's a limit!' He slammed down the phone, surprised anew by this fresh outburst of anger.

Part III

53

He gently places the mobile on his desk, and then sinks back against the leather of the swivel chair. The birds are singing in the courtyard — a melancholy melody that makes him think of dusk long before it's due.

What was it they had said to him the last time they'd met? Something about taxis? 'We're not just a taxi where you pay the fare and then leave. Once you're in, you're in for life.'

And he'd adjusted. He'd been so desperate to throw them off, start anew, but he'd slowly grown to accept their presence. When he thought about it, it was more a haunting than a presence, an occasional manifestation to remind him that he wasn't safe, and would have to carry them with him to his grave. He'd tried to do good, and knew that for all the good he was doing they would make him do bad. But at least sometimes it felt right, uncompromised.

But now, where did this leave him? How was it that it had come back around to them? How he wished he'd just let it be! But was that even true? Despite what the papers said, he had a conscience and a heart. He was a human being, with children and grandchildren of his own — a human being who loved and protected others. In the eyes of God, where should he stand? What was required of him now?

He pulls the golden cross his mother gave him on his communion from beneath his shirt and turns it in his palm. Its edges catch the sunlight.

How could any man be expected to sacrifice his daughters on the altar of the greater good? How could he be condemned for protecting them, for making sure they came to no harm? Of course, his old friend was right: these men should see trial; the lid should be lifted on their twilight world. In abstract, that was all correct and proper. But in reality, his reality, *that could only mean the end, for all of them. If they'd stop just with him, that would be all right. But they wouldn't, and that's how he had become their prisoner. No man could live with that.*

SCAMARCIO FELT EMBARRASSED: he didn't know what to say to Garramone. They were sitting in a café on Via Nazionale, just down from the flat where the chief had first shown him the photos of Ganza, and had first brought him into this mess. Garramone had foam from his cappuccino on his upper lip. He was looking even more liverish than the last time Scamarcio had seen him. No doubt the case was getting to him as much as it was to Scamarcio. It couldn't be easy having the PM on your back, knowing that your career hung in the balance.

'Listen, Chief Garramone, about yesterday …'

Garramone waved the thought away. 'You'd just heard a whole lot of awful shit, and that would get to anyone. I just ask that you don't repeat the performance. I've got enough stress from other quarters.'

Scamarcio nodded. 'So, what's the news from Elba?'

'Nothing. They've searched all around that camp with a fine-tooth comb, but they haven't found a thing.'

'How are the parents holding up?'

'Both in a complete state, as far as Genovesi tells it. You've seen the non-stop coverage?'

'Haven't had a chance.'

'It looks bad for us. The Tuscan chief is in line for a demotion if they don't sort this. The PM says he's getting five calls a day from the US secretary of state.

'So what did the PM say — does he want Zaccardo's story swept under the carpet?'

'Contrary to your preconceptions of me, Scamarcio, I argued quite heavily for a trial and for Ganza to take the stand. I told him we have a good witness in Zaccardo.'

'And?'

'And he said he needed to think about it.'

Scamarcio shook his head. 'There's nothing to think about.' Then, after a beat: 'There's no way he's going to play ball.'

'We'll see. He's a better man than you think.'

'I'll take your word for it.'

Garramone took a bite out of an apricot brioche. 'Ymeri's been jabbering like a canary, been getting stressed.'

'Oh yeah?'

'Nepi is delighted. We've got him on the line to the brothers — twice.'

'What did they say?'

Garramone pushed a few buttons on his iPhone and then slid it across the table to Scamarcio. He pulled a small set of earphones from his pocket and slid them across, too. 'Hear for yourself.'

Scamarcio put in the earphones and pressed 'Play'.

'So when are you going to deliver?' someone with a Sicilian accent was saying.

'There's a problem,' said the voice that Scamarcio recognised as Ymeri.

'What kind of problem?'

'Pigs got there first.'

'For fuck's sake,' barked the Sicilian. 'Can't you get anything right? I'm about to lose my usual supplier. If you don't get me those goods, I … am … without … a … supplier.' He enunciated the last words deliberately, slowly, as if Ymeri were a simpleton. 'You understand that? You understand what that means? No supplier means no clients and no business.'

'Listen, Luca, we're sorting it. Stay calm.'

'Don't you dare tell me to stay calm, you son of a bitch!'

Ymeri exhaled. It came out as a low whistle down the line.

'And the girl?' asked the Sicilian after a few moments. 'Tell me that's bloody happening.'

'We're seeing to it, yes.'

'She has to be on the mainland in two days' time. Two days, you hear me? You call me tomorrow, and I'll give you an address.'

'OK.'

'And, Ymeri, if you fuck this up, that's it. I'll let loose my little brother Marco on you. You've heard of him, his *reputation*?'

Scamarcio heard Ymeri swallow down hard. 'It will all be sorted, trust me.'

The conversation ended there. Scamarcio pulled out the headphones. 'So she's still on Elba?'

'Sounds like it, yes.'

'Have the police been talking to Dacian's friends and family again?'

'Yeah, they've been putting the pressure on, but nobody's giving up anything.'

'I had the sense that one of them, goes by the name of Pety, knew a bit more than he was letting on. He seemed to be the spokesman for them all. It might be worth them putting the heat on him.'

'I think they've been turning the heat up under all of them, but I'll pass that on. In the meantime, listen to this other recording.'

Scamarcio saw that Garramone had lined up a second file on the iPhone. He pressed 'Play' again.

It was the same angry Sicilian, who he now presumed was Luca Moltisanti. 'Don't write this down. You're going to Monticiano, south-south-west of Siena. As you head into the village, take a left at the first roundabout. Follow that road along for five minutes. Eventually on the right you'll see a sign for the Tre Santi vineyard. Go up that track, and then turn left. At the end of that road you'll find a villa. They'll be waiting for you — 7.00pm.'

'Got it,' said Ymeri.

'We'll have your money ready. You take it, and then you leave immediately. Understood?'

'Understood.'

'And, Ymeri, you'd better get this right — otherwise there won't be a next time.'

'OK.'

'You don't sound confident, Ymeri.'

'It will work out, I assure you.'

The Sicilian just hung up.

Scamarcio pulled out the headphones. 'Are we going to raid the villa?'

'It's in discussion.'

'What does Nepi think? Have they said enough for the magistrates there?'

'He's happy enough with the evidence so far, but less happy about the raid — he wants to give Ymeri more rope to hang the brothers with so we can get a fix on their location. He doesn't expect to find the brothers at the villa — just a few minions and, obviously, Ymeri when he shows up with the girl. He still doesn't reckon the Moltisanti would have left Sicily. They're in hiding like all the rest, and run their operations from the different basements they move to every twenty-four hours.'

'What put them in hiding? What does he have on them so far?'

'I'm not sure he does — nothing concrete, anyway. They're naughty boys, in hiding more from their masters than from the squad. Nepi wants them to open up about their former employers. I guess he's on a fishing expedition for a few names and burial sites. He needs something to reel them in with, that he can use to cut a deal.'

'And that's where the parties come in?'

'I guess so.'

Scamarcio nodded. 'So what now?'

'We wait. Like they say, Ymeri is supposed to be bringing the girl tomorrow.'

'And the Moltisanti?'

'Nepi is working hard through his contacts to fix a location for them — he thinks somewhere in central Sicily, but he still needs to narrow it down.'

'What about Gela?'

'Why do you say that?'

'You mentioned before that you'd known the PM from there.'

'So?'

'It's just an idea — the place just popped into my head.'

'The Moltisanti are Gela boys.'

'Really?'

The chief just nodded.

'Did you know them, too?'

He shook his head, but Scamarcio wasn't quite sure he believed him.

'They are Gela boys, Scamarcio — it would be too obvious for them to be there.'

'Sometimes obvious is best.'

Garramone leaned back in his seat. 'I actually put that one to Nepi, but he says not in this case.'

'But it could be days, if not weeks, before he gets a location on them. I presume Nepi had been trying for a long time before we came along.'

'Maybe. Maybe not. Not if he didn't have anything concrete on them. He keeps his cards close — I'm not in the loop.'

'We need that raid. We need to get to the girl.'

'We'll get it. Don't worry about Nepi.'

Scamarcio thought for a moment. They needed to make it easier for Nepi to let the raid go ahead.

'Listen, boss, I've got a call to make. Mind if I step outside for a moment?'

'Take the time you need.'

Scamarcio pulled a cigarette from his jacket pocket and lit up, leaving the jacket hanging over his chair. He stepped out into the dusty chaos of Via Nazionale. It was forecast to reach 34 degrees today: it was turning into one of those tropical Junes, hot and dry with the odd afternoon monsoon. Usually, they heralded a disappointing August.

He didn't have the number on speed-dial, and didn't have it written down anywhere. That had been drummed into him from an early age. The old guy had said to call when he felt the need. He knew he shouldn't be doing this, but desperate times and all that. Principles were all well and good, but they only worked on paper. Reality often called for something different, didn't it?

'Yes,' croaked the old man. Scamarcio pictured him sitting up at the bar, his blue beret tilted to the right, the eyes black and beady behind thick lenses, scanning every hapless visitor that came in.

'It's Leo.'

There was a pause down the line. Then: 'Ah, Leo, my boy. What a nice surprise.'

'Listen, I need a favour.'

'A favour? Well, you know there's nothing I wouldn't do for you. I promised your father that much.'

Scamarcio took a breath. 'Can we meet?'

It was just as he'd pictured it when they'd spoken on the phone. He was sitting at the bar when Scamarcio came in, his blue beret inclined to the right. The old man hugged and kissed him on both cheeks, and then ushered him out back.

A huge table was laid out with spaghetti and ragù, prosciutto and cheeses, bruschetta — the works.

'You hungry?' The old man didn't wait for an answer. He just started loading food on a paper plate and set it down in front of him.

Two of his lieutenants were eating at the end of the table, giving Scamarcio a nod as he sat down.

'It's Lucio's boy,' explained the old man. The two lieutenants nodded again, placing their fists on their hearts, as was the way.

'Eat, eat — you don't look like you get enough to eat.'

Scamarcio started on the ragù. It was one of the best he'd tasted. The old man pulled out a seat next to him, and leaned in. 'Good, huh? You can't fault Chiara — she's the best.' Scamarcio remembered that Chiara was his sister, and murmured in agreement.

'So, Leo, what is this favour you need from us?'

'You know the Moltisanti brothers?'

'Sicilians?'

'Yes.'

The old man exchanged glances with his two lieutenants. They all seem surprised by the question. 'I know of them, yes, but have never had the pleasure.' The sarcasm was acidic.

'What do you know of them?'

'I heard they fell out with their commanders, have become loose cannons, got a few backs up — that kind of thing.'

'Would you know where to find them?'

The old man clapped his hands together and laughed. His lieutenants laughed with him. 'Would *I* know where to find them? Ah, Leo!'

Scamarcio said nothing, and just stared him out. Eventually, the old man said: 'We're Calabrians, Leo, not Sicilians.'

'Come on, I wasn't born yesterday,' said Scamarcio. 'You know people who know people. I need this, Piero, and I need it fast.'

Piero Piocosta nodded slowly, as if weighing it up.

'And?'

'And you know I'd make it worth your while.'

54

HE DECIDED TO TAKE a walk along the Tiber. He felt sick. It wasn't the quantity of food he'd eaten, but the thought of what he'd just done. In terms of his personal development, he'd probably set himself back five years. He couldn't tell Doctor Salvai about this — he mustn't allow it to come tumbling out when he next had a confessional moment. And what would they want in return? He kicked an old shoe lying by the wall, and then kicked it again. Oh, who gave a shit? It was a girl's life at stake, and they needed that raid to go ahead — it mustn't be headed off by Nepi and his squad. This was how it worked, how their damaged little world turned. He couldn't beat himself up if he strayed to the dark to get back to the light. Could he? Once again, he felt the need for someone or something to ground him, to help him make sense of it all.

His mobile was ringing. He flipped it open, but for some reason decided not to say anything.

'Scamarcio, is that you?' It was Garramone. He sounded beaten.

'What's up?'

'Still no progress on Elba, and I'm having trouble getting the green light on that raid.' He could tell that Garramone just needed to let off steam to someone, and that Scamarcio was the only person he could talk to right now.

'Great.'

Scamarcio kicked the wall. Some slimy moss attached to his shoe. Were they just going to stand back and allow Stacey Baker to be ruined? Were they so calculating that they were willing to sacrifice a child? And there might be other children being delivered to tomorrow's get-together. If the raid went ahead, there was also a chance of reaching them.

'Scamarcio, you've gone quiet.'

'I can't believe that it's actually come to this: that the squad is just going to turn a blind eye to a little girl getting led to the slaughter. Is their greater good so fucking important? We need that raid, Garramone.'

The chief sighed down the line. 'The Anti-Mafia guys are the gods, you know that. If there's a major conviction in the offing, the chiefs will back a delaying strategy. They'll just put it on the slate for next time.'

'But next time will be too late.'

'My hands are tied — I can't see a way around it, as hard as I try.'

The call-waiting signal kicked in on Scamarcio's phone. 'Listen, I'm going to have to call you back.'

He switched to the new caller. 'Scamarcio.'

'It's Ms Santa, Arthur's friend from upstairs. Do you remember me?'

'Yes, of course.' He took a deep breath. 'How can I help?'

'You said to call any time, so I thought I should let you know that Arthur's father and brother have arrived here from Argentina. I think you should speak to them — it might be useful for your investigation.'

Something about the way she said it had him turning right immediately over the Ponte Garibaldi towards Trastevere.

Along Arthur's staircase a slight tang of iron still tainted the air, but the police ribbons had gone, and there was nothing to suggest that just a few days before this had been a murder scene. He knocked on the door to Arthur's apartment, and Ms Santa opened up. She seemed battered and drawn, and wasn't wearing any make-up. 'Good afternoon, Detective,' she said, keeping her voice low, and gesturing to two men standing looking lost to the right of the trashed living room. They were both lean and tall: the older one was slightly stooped, with greying hair, clutching a white handkerchief; the other, maybe thirty years younger, was resting a hand on his back. 'They wanted to see her place,' she explained. 'I'm not sure it was such a good idea.' Scamarcio said nothing. He just smiled gently and raised an eyebrow.

'Anyway, I shall leave you to it, Detective. I will be upstairs if you need anything.'

He thanked her and took a few steps into the room. The men turned as he did so, so he gave them a nod and pulled out his card. He quickly showed it to each of them, and then shook hands with them both.

In English, he said: 'Detective Scamarcio, Rome police. I'm deeply sorry for your loss.'

The younger man nodded. 'Thank you. My father speaks no English, and mine is not so good, so do you mind if we go slowly?'

'Not a problem,' said Scamarcio. 'Would you like to stay here, or would you prefer somewhere ...' he looked around him, '... more comfortable?'

The younger man, who he put in his early forties, shook his head. 'My father prefers to stay here. He wants to be close to José. You understand?'

For a moment, Scamarcio was confused, and then remembered that Arthur had started life as José. He was glad the man had mentioned the name — it cleared up the diplomatic issue of how to refer to him. 'You and José were brothers?'

'Yes. José was my younger brother. We are, we were, four boys, and he was the youngest, the baby.' He looked to his father for a moment. 'My parents are very, very sad about this — destroyed. I worry for them. It was such a bad way to die.'

'How old was José?'

'He just turned 18. One month ago.'

Scamarcio swallowed, feeling suddenly down. 'When did you last see your brother?'

The man shook his head. 'A long time ago, I don't know the years — maybe two, maybe three — José left La Quiaca. He had always imagined a better life for himself. After that, we didn't see him so much.'

'You stayed in La Quiaca?'

'I was different from José. For me, the simple life was OK. It was enough.'

Scamarcio surveyed the old man standing next to them. His eyes were red-rimmed with tears, and he was clasping and unclasping his hands. On closer inspection, Scamarcio saw that it wasn't a handkerchief he was clutching, but a note of some kind.

'You sure your father doesn't want to sit down somewhere? It would be easier for him.'

The son shook his head again. 'No, really, it's OK. He's a strong man. He wants to be here now.'

'What's that he's holding there?' asked Scamarcio.

'It's the last letter José wrote us. When we got it, we were so worried that we spent our savings to come here to Italy.'

'Nobody told you about his death?'

'It's not their fault. They didn't know how to contact us. The kind neighbour, the one here just now, she said José never told her where we were — she didn't know how to tell us.'

Something was troubling Scamarcio. 'What was it about the letter that worried you so much?'

The man reached over and took the note gently from his father. Scamarcio saw the old man's hands tremble as he gave it up.

'You speak Spanish?'

'I'm afraid not.'

The man opened out the paper. Scamarcio saw several lines of neat handwriting in fountain pen.

'I try to translate it for you.'

'OK.'

'I should explain you something first. José had written before — a few weeks before. He had asked to come back to La Quiaca to live at home with my mother and father. It was a big surprise. But my father had never forgiven José for what he had become. You know what he had become?'

'I know he was homosexual. I know the work he did.'

The brother gave a sharp nod of confirmation, keen to press on. 'For my dad, all that was a big shock. He found it disgusting. It was a big embarrassment for the family. La Quiaca is a traditional town, you know?'

Scamarcio nodded.

'So when José wrote to us after all those years, my dad said, *No, don't come back. You have brought too much shame on this family. We don't want you here.*'

'Did you agree?'

The man sighed. 'I'm not sure. You know he was still my brother. It's not easy to explain.'

'I understand,' said Scamarcio. 'So, this letter here?'

'After my father said no to José, he wrote to us again — this letter.' He waved it in the air.

'What did José say in the letter this time?'

'I translate it now.' The man scanned the lines for a few seconds and then raised his head, looking into the middle distance. The sunlight caught his profile, and Scamarcio saw that he was good looking, his even features reminding him of the photos of Arthur he'd seen.

The man returned his attention to the note in front of him and started to read. 'This world, this earth, it is full of, um … *mal*. Um, how do you say?'

'*Mal* — *male* in Italian. In English, evil?'

'Yes, *male*: evil. José always like the drama.' He coughed softly and read on: 'I have no more choices now. The only good thing left for me to do, the only useful thing, is to leave this life, so I say goodbye and God bless to you.' He folded the note in two again and passed it back to his father, who took it absently. 'We tried to contact José, but we couldn't reach him on the number he'd given. That's why we got the plane. We thought he was going to kill himself. We worried that we would be too late, and we were.'

55

Scamarcio felt disorientated. He stepped out into the harsh sunlight of Arthur's street, narrowly avoiding a group of American tourists and their guide. His throat was dry, and there was a burning behind his eyes and a humming in his ears. He felt the most tired he had done in days, and the thought that everything about this case now had to be turned on its head almost pressed him to the ground. It was too exhausting to process.

The fact remained that Arthur had been knifed repeatedly. He couldn't have done that to himself, could he? And why choose frenzied stabbing as a mode of suicide? It was one of the worst ways to go — there were easier, far less painful options. He thought of Buddhist monks and their acts of self-immolation as a form of political protest. Was Arthur protesting something? Was his death meant as a statement? And what about the morphine in his system? Had he really administered himself a painkiller before stabbing himself to death?

He took the blue line in the vague direction of Salaria, and then walked the rest of the way. The guy on reception looked more rested than the last time he'd seen him.

'Things calmed down, then?'

'There's been a slight lull, but we don't want to talk about it in case it tempts fate. We can't have another two weeks like the last — it'll kill us. 'Scuse the pun.'

'How's Aurelia?'

'Just about getting through the backlog now. Down the hall, if you want her.'

Scamarcio nodded. Along with his growing anxiety, he felt a small flutter of excitement at the thought of seeing her again. But he tried to tamp it down for now, push it away.

When he came in, she was stacking files on a desk. He noticed a sheaf of paperwork in a neat pile ready to be sent off to various parties.

'How's it going?'

She spun around and seemed a bit flustered to see him there, pushing some stray hair back into a clip, and pulling some more behind her ears. She looked younger than last time — her skin was smoother and had more colour. 'Ah, can't complain. Nobody's decided to shoot, strangle, or drown anyone for twenty-four hours now.'

'Glad to hear it.'

'Filippi's on the mend.'

'So I hear. Great news.'

She threw him a quizzical look, and then walked around the desk and took up her usual seat. She gestured him to the chair opposite. 'Is this business or pleasure?'

'It's always a pleasure, Aurelia.' He hadn't meant it to sound so lame.

She rolled her eyes, and a slightly awkward silence followed. Scamarcio wanted to cut it off, so leaned forward across the desk. 'Listen, remember that dead rentboy, badly cut up?'

'Yeah, just about,' she sighed.

'Could it have been a suicide?'

Aurelia rested her elbows on the arms of her chair, cupping her chin with her hands in thought. 'A suicide? Well, that would be way out there; it would demonstrate a serious degree of self-loathing. I'd need to check the wounds again, measure the reach, and the entry and exit angles. Come to think of it, I don't remember there having been much of a struggle. And if memory serves, it was a short, thin blade — they require less pressure. So

302

in theory, yeah, it's possible. But it's a very unusual way to go. I've never seen a suicide with knifework like that; usually they opt for a simple cut, just one wound. Or most of the time far-less awful ways, like an overdose or drowning. Besides, with repeated stabbings, at a certain point your strength would leave you. That many punctures takes a lot of effort.'

'And the morphine?'

'Hmm, the morphine ... I guess he could have dosed up and then set upon himself with the knife. But he'd have to move quickly, because that quantity would have knocked him out fast. If he really wanted to make sure he wasn't coming back, he'd have had to work very efficiently.'

'He couldn't have started the stabbing and then taken the morphine?'

'But why endure all that pain? Besides, that's riskier, because he could have passed out before he had a chance to finish with the knife. That would have been the scarier of the two options for him. I'd put my money on the first one.'

Scamarcio nodded, thinking about the camera. He felt sure it had been thrown on the floor and smashed in the general trashing, so exactly when had Arthur put it back on the shelf? Before he took the drugs, and before he picked up the knife? But did it really matter? The more important question was why it was positioned like that. Maybe if the camera had been left on the floor, it would have been interpreted the wrong way. Yeah, that was it, he decided — the interpretation. It *had* been a kind of protest. Arthur had wanted someone in the police to notice those photos, and the best way to get them noticed was to stage a dramatic death. As his brother said, José was dramatic. And there was something else he'd said. What was it now? He spun back through the conversation in his head. Yes, that was it, those last words of the letter. He'd said that the only *good* thing, the only *useful* thing he could do, was to take his own life. In Arthur's mind, this was a good act, a useful act, an act that would bring attention to these crimes against children. Scamarcio believed he had a grasp on it now. It finally made sense to him.

Aurelia was eyeing him strangely. 'You all right, Scamarcio?'

He looked up, remembering where he was. 'Yeah, sorry.'

'Thought I'd lost you there for a moment.'

He got up. 'Actually, I need to go. Sorry.'

She frowned at him. 'Stop saying sorry. You're always saying sorry.'

56

He picks up the telephone, his hand shaking slightly. How long would it be before they tipped them off? How much time did he have to collect his family and bring them in? Madalena, his youngest, answers after a few rings. She is laughing at someone's joke, telling them to shush.

'What is it, pappy?' She sounds happy with life, unburdened by worries. He wonders if he was ever like that. He thinks not.

'I need you home now. I've sent a car for you. He'll be there within the hour …'

'But pappy …'

'But nothing. There is no argument. I need you home.' He replaces the receiver, and dials again.

'Dad, can I call you back? I'm right in the middle of something.'

'No. I've sent a car. You and my grandson must return to Rome immediately — there's to be no discussion.'

'But …'

'Just do as I say. I'll explain later.'

He hangs up and rests his head against the leather back of the chair. There are dark motes floating in front of his eyes, but he doesn't think they're dust particles. The sun is bright outside, the leaves in the courtyard aflame, moving slowly, so slowly, in the breeze. He calls Stefano, the head minder, into his study.

'Sir?'

'I want to take a stroll around Villa Borghese.'

He watches Stefano as he tries to conceal his surprise and alarm, tries to remain polite. 'Now?'

'Yes, right now.'

Stefano looks at the door that leads to the corridor and his colleagues outside, silently entreating their help. 'But, Sir, the area hasn't been cleared — it's exposed. We need notice to prepare.'

He holds up a palm to stop him. 'Forget all that. I don't care. I have to go now. I will hear no arguments.'

Stefano shuffles, transferring his weight from one foot to the other. 'Sir, I can't allow it.'

'You can and you will. Get your coat — we're going.'

They turn into Viale Pietro Canonica. He loves the shade of this park, the dappled light pooling around the trunks, the scents of fresh grass cuttings and honeysuckle. He sees two lovers locked in an embrace beneath an ancient pine; a young mother in jogging gear running as she pushes a baby buggy; two old men feeding the birds, one drinking from a flask. How good it feels to be outside in the fresh air, away from the stench of power.

They pull up outside the entrance to the villa. Stefano steps out of the front passenger seat, scans the area, consults with his colleagues, and then finally opens the door.

'I need to be alone for several minutes. Just wait for me here.'

'But Sir …'

Again he raises a hand to silence him, and then turns and heads towards the back of the villa.

The gravel path is longer than he had expected, but then he sees him, waiting on the bench as they'd arranged. He is unrecognisable in his beret and dark shades. Wordlessly, he takes a seat beside him. There is no embrace, no kiss, no handshake even. A note is passed between them — two ghosts from a different world, a different time.

'Be there at 6.00am,' says the man, and then he gets up from the bench and silently walks away. There is no look back, no wave. He is a dead man returning to his grave.

57

SCAMARCIO SAT UP in bed. He'd only meant to take a catnap, but beyond the window the sky had bled purple. The metallic haze over the rooftops had finally melted away, leaving washing lines and roof gardens burned gold.

The mobile that Garramone had given him trilled beside him, but somehow he knew it wasn't the chief this time.

The caller didn't bother to introduce himself. The accent was thick, Calabrian, as Scamarcio would have expected: 'There's a nature reserve above Gela, slightly to the right: the Niscemi Reserve. On the southern edge is an abandoned gamekeeper's hut. Until 6.00am tomorrow you'll find them, but after that they'll move on.' The caller hung up, and the phone clicked.

Scamarcio placed his mobile on the table beside him and sank back into the pillows. He'd been right — they hadn't strayed far from home at all.

'There'll be ten of us,' said Davide Nepi later. 'You coming along for the ride, Scamarcio?'

'Why not?'

They were back in the flat opposite Ymeri's place, the two surveillance guys still glued to their cans. Someone had rigged up a small TV in the corner, and he saw that Sky was running non-stop coverage on the Stacey Baker disappearance. Holiday snaps of her at the beach kept flashing up. Scamarcio wondered if they'd been taken in the days leading up to her disappearance — the age seemed about right. Her parents had been filmed leaving the police station in Portoferraio, flashbulbs exploding all around them. Mrs Baker was hiding behind huge sunglasses, and seemed to have lost several kilos since Scamarcio had last seen her.

Garramone turned away from the TV to face Nepi: 'So if this goes down OK, we can proceed with the raid?'

'We shall see,' answered Nepi. 'It depends on whether things develop as we want them to.'

Scamarcio resisted the urge to punch him. He wondered what 'as we want them to' meant — the brothers alive, no doubt, and ready to talk.

Nepi took a slurp of his coffee. 'So, Scamarcio, you planning on telling me how you came upon this little gem of info, and so quickly, too?'

Scamarcio sighed, took a drag on his fag. 'Nepi, you're with the Anti-Mafia Squad. You're probably the very last person I'd tell.'

Nepi laughed, nearly choking on his coffee. 'It's right what they say about you, then?'

Scamarcio eyed him tiredly. 'Nothing's ever as simple as they make out in the papers. You should know that by now.'

The knock comes on the bathroom window of the guestroom, as he is expecting. He opens the window and clambers up onto the basin. One of them is waiting for him outside. He is dressed entirely in black, complete with balaclava and electronic mouthpiece. He hoists him out and onto the ladder. He can hear the crackle of communications on the walkie-talkie strapped to the man's belt. The freelancer whispers into his mouthpiece: 'Target A collected, descending now.'

He helps him down the ladder, taking each step before him, there to catch him if he falls. They descend silently, rapidly. Waiting for them on the ground are two others. Wordlessly, they usher him to an Audi, also black, humming, poised to leave. They glide away, the engine nothing more than a purr. The streets around the centre are quiet now. Only a few taxis wind their way along Via del Quirinale, but on Via 20 Settembre he

sees no one. The motorway will be a clean sweep to the field, where they
will take off. No record will be made of this flight; no trace.

He winds down the window, tasting the air. There's a salt tang on
the breeze as they head towards Pomezia. He imagines the rusty musk of
rotting hulls, ships long forgotten, abandoned to the tides.

Scamarcio felt newly awake, alert to all that was to come. In a
building off the runway, the Antimafia guys were running through
a final inventory of their weapons, checking ammunition and
comms. Nepi was heading up the operation, having shown them
satellite photos of the nature reserve, and explained the road
leading to the abandoned gamekeeper's cabin, and its entrances
and exits. His team seemed young and keen, fired with the zeal
of rooting out the nation's cancer, cell by cell, regardless of the
personal risk. Scamarcio was dislocated by their presence — a
combination of admiration, insecurity, inferiority, and something
that felt like resentment. Somehow they represented a new
challenge, a further questioning of where he quite fitted in to this
life.

Nepi consulted his wristwatch and then gave the sign.
Scamarcio followed the team out onto the tarmac — red, green,
and yellow cats' eyes blinking up ahead of them, the control
tower spinning in the distance. The plane was waiting for them,
its turbines whirring. He saw two military pilots in the cockpit,
consulting their clipboards. He wondered at how much the
operation would be costing, aware that sentiment in Rome was
subtly shifting against the anti-corruption crusaders — certain
statesmen within the state feared that they were taking their work
too far.

He took a seat behind Nepi, surveying the darkness outside. If
all went well, in less than two hours the Moltisanti brothers would
be taken into custody. Another head would be taken off the hydra
— another head that would quickly grow back. Was there a point

to all this? Were they really making a difference? To a few, but that was all. That was all the squad could do for now — basement by basement, branch by branch. Mussolini was the only one who had ever managed to slay the beast, who hadn't baulked at torture, or taking women and children hostage, to get there. What Italy needed was a benign dictator, reflected Scamarcio. That was the only solution for a country such as theirs.

The engines roared beside him, and they began to move up the runway, gaining speed, faster and faster until the lights from fishing boats flashed beneath them and the sea was a dark emptiness swallowing everything around it. He felt a nervousness in the pit of his stomach now — a new sense that things might not go to plan, that he and Garramone had created trouble for themselves or that it had found them, a sense that Stacey Baker might not come out of this alive.

58

So many years have passed since he last set foot here. The outskirts have retained their brutal ugliness, their stench of battered hopelessness. If you grew up in Gela, all you ever thought about was the day you would get out. They leave the city limits behind, heading up into the darkness of the hills. The stars are sharp in the sky tonight, reminding him of winter evenings spent with the brothers when he should have been at home, when his mother was frantically calling for him up and down the street.

He winds down the window and hears the gentle movement of goat bells in the distance, feels the breeze as it moves through the olive groves, catches the citrus scent that stirs memories and then emotions.

He closes the window and sinks back against the comfortable leather. Soon it will all be over. One way or the other, it will finally be over.

He loses himself in the past for many minutes, somehow administering them their last rites, collecting and assembling the important scenes from their lives. Then there's a tap on the glass partition, and they tell him they've arrived. He looks out at a dilapidated stone cottage, shutters hanging loose from the hinges, moss clinging to broken roof tiles. The men — his men, expensive men — have already surrounded the house and are going in. He can hear the back and forth of communication running through the headset of the one sitting up front, the man who will guard him until it's over. Then a strange silence, then two shouts, and then the rapid pop-pop-pop of fire — three, maybe four shots. Then someone knocks on the front window, and his temporary guardian rolls it down.

'It's done,' says the man. His colleague up front nods, and then his door is opened and he's helped out. His legs feel weak, and he struggles to

*stand. Two arms support him on either side. He follows the men inside
the cottage. It's dark, and the air is damp and musty and laced with the
sulphur taint of gunpowder. He sees them then — two corpses crumpled
in the corner, legs splayed, hands grasping for their guns, blood-splatter
on their clothes. He draws closer, the metallic sweetness of fresh bloodspill
catching the back of his throat. He bends down and checks for a pulse —
first the one, then the other. Nothing. He feels his legs give way, but the
arms are reaching for him again.*

Scamarcio wished he could wind down his window so he could
catch a taste of the island. Too many years had passed since his
last visit. He would have preferred to have seen it by day, knowing
that the citrus aromas would have stirred the same sorrowful
excitement in him they always did when he ventured south. It
was a clear, cool night, and his initial anxiety was gradually being
replaced by adrenalin — the sense that he was about to be a part
of something significant.

'Almost there,' said Nepi from the front seat of the van.
'Everyone ready?'

One by one, over their headsets, his team gave the affirmative.

'Approaching n ...' Nepi stopped in mid-sentence, and
Scamarcio felt his spine tighten and his initial nerves return. The
team stiffened beside him.

'What on earth ...?' whispered Nepi.

Scamarcio leaned forward so he could see through the middle
of the van between Nepi and the driver. Standing there, seemingly
caught in their headlights, was a group of men in balaclavas with a
short man in a long overcoat at their centre — a man who looked
exactly like the prime minister. Scamarcio leaned forward some
more. The similarity was remarkable. He blinked out into the
night, closed his eyes, and then opened them again. It *was* the
Prime Minister; the resemblance was too close.

'What the ...?' repeated Nepi.

'I'm getting out,' said Scamarcio, not waiting for permission. He stepped out into the darkness and walked around the van so he was facing the prime minister and the frozen group of men. He sensed Nepi come up alongside him, and felt his heart in his throat.

One of the men with the prime minister stepped forward, his hand tightly on his gun. 'Who are you? What do you want?'

Nepi pulled his badge from his pocket and handed it to the man, who then handed it to the PM. The PM scanned it briefly, and then handed it back to Nepi. The PM gave him a curt nod, and then repeated the gesture for Scamarcio. With that, he simply turned and got back into his waiting car, his men quickly following, climbing into a van parked behind. The engines buzzed and then choked into life, and within seconds they had sped off into the night, the smoke from their exhausts trailing in the darkness. Scamarcio had never felt such silence. And as he turned to Nepi, he finally caught the scent of citrus on the breeze.

59

Garramone's voice was raspy from sleep. When Scamarcio finished his account of the events of that morning, the chief said flatly: 'Yes, that would make sense.'

'How in any way does what I've just told you make sense?' asked Scamarcio.

'They knew each other as children. Rumours were that they'd been a thorn in his side since he'd come to power.'

'So he just decided to off them in the middle of the night? Risky strategy, don't you think?'

'Maybe he felt he had no choice.'

'But why?'

Garramone sighed. He heard him shift position and adjust something on his night table. 'He knew we were looking into them in connection with Ganza.'

'And?'

'Maybe he thought that if we went for them, they'd go for him. As I say, maybe he felt he had no choice.'

'But now half the Anti-Mafia Squad have seen him at the scene of a Mafia slaying!'

'My guess is that it won't go anywhere. It will stop with what you saw tonight.'

'He might be powerful, but he's not *that* powerful!'

'I'm not so sure.'

Garramone hung up before he had a chance to reply.

Scamarcio threw down the phone on the taxi seat beside him. Ymeri was more important than ever now, and Ganza would need to give evidence. With the Moltisanti dead, Nepi would not want the raid. With the Moltisanti dead, it would remain unclear who else was involved in the child-trafficking operations beyond the few men they already had in their sights. Depending on the deal they offered him, Zaccardo might cough up a few more names, but the tangible evidence still lay with Ymeri. He asked the taxi driver to drop him at Via Ludovisi so he could walk the last few streets to his flat. He wanted to lose himself in the morning scrum, enjoy some fleeting sense of freedom.

He paid and started to walk towards Via Boncompagni, where there was a bar he could get a coffee. People were in a hurry on their way to work, laughing and cursing, whispering sweet nothings or barking instructions into their mobiles, all blissfully unaware that their PM had just slaughtered two Mafia players in the middle of the night. Scamarcio sensed Stacey Baker slipping away from him, spiralling into some foreign place, a place he never wanted to know. He felt a hollowness in his chest, a persistent nausea rising up from the acid in his gut. He realised that when this was over he would need to get out of Rome for a while, out of Italy, and take some time to reflect on whether he was where he wanted to be. The bar was coming up ahead and he was about to turn away, already disheartened by the queue, when he felt his mobile buzz in his pocket.

Garramone was on the line again, sounding even more exhausted than before: 'I have good news for you.'

'Somehow I doubt it.'

Garramone ignored him, pressing on. 'Nepi has seen the light — he's going to let us have the raid. He figures that Ymeri and a few cronies might be better than nothing; he doesn't reckon that there's any bigger fish left to net. He's depressed, and is seeing the whole thing as game over.' Garramone paused for breath. 'I couldn't do his job.'

Scamarcio didn't see the difference. 'Are you drafting the unit?

Is the case on the books at HQ then?'

Garramone sighed. 'Sometimes, Scamarcio, you remind me of my wife. In a vague kind of way it's on the books, but you're the only one who knows the background; the rest of them just think this raid is about the American girl. Be at the station by midday so you can go along for the ride. We don't know if the minions have got wind of the fate of the Moltisanti yet, but surveillance says there's been activity — it does still look like something might be happening at the villa tonight.'

Scamarcio sighed. 'We have to find her in time.'

'We will.'

'Any news on your friend? Anyone questioning him yet about his involvement in a Mafia ...'

The line went dead.

60

GARRAMONE HAD HAD YMERI tailed from Rome. At 5.30pm, at
a service station on the Autostrade del Sole, he met up with an
associate in a people carrier. It was their suspicion that Stacey
Baker was in the back. How she had been spirited across from
the island was as yet unclear, but they suspected a vegetable truck
or some such method. The forces on Elba did not possess the
manpower to search every car, despite the new reinforcements.

Ymeri and his associate then proceeded south towards Siena
in the people carrier, never clocking less than 120 kph. A series
of different unmarked cars took over the tail so as not to arouse
their suspicions, although Scamarcio formed the impression from
their erratic driving that they were both nervous and hapless, and
wouldn't have noticed anyway. Once they arrived at Monticiano, the
people carrier turned left at the first roundabout, as instructed, and
stayed on the road for five minutes before indicating left again at
the sign for the vineyard. At this point, Scamarcio and the other five
members of the unit passed the entranceway and transferred to a
chauffeur-driven limo that had approached from the other direction
and was now drawn up on the kerbside 100 metres down the road.
They switched cars in seconds, as they had been briefed, and were
now approaching the entrance to the vineyard from the right.

As they made their way up the tarmac drive and its twin
columns of cypress trees, Scamarcio spied a man in a dark suit,
talking into a walkie-talkie. He cut short his conversation and held
up a hand to stop their driver as they approached. The chauffeur,
who was actually a fellow Flying Squad detective, informed the

man that he was bringing representatives of the Moltisanti. The gatekeeper seemed momentarily confused and peered into the car to get a better view of its passengers, but was unable to see anything due to the blacked-out windows. He hesitated a moment, and then seemed to think better of it and waved them through. They swung into a large gravel turning circle with an elaborate fountain at its centre. To their right was a sprawling villa in caramel Tuscan stone. Along its walls, small fires were burning in gold torches, and the wide stone steps leading to its entranceway were decked with a long, red carpet, immaculately clean. Scamarcio noticed a couple of other limos pulled up ahead of them to the left of the circle. Parked right in front of them now, just a few metres away, was the people carrier.

Scamarcio knew that the moment had finally come, and he and the team commander beside him exchanged a curt nod. The commander then gave the one-word instruction and, along with the unit, Scamarcio leapt from the car, keeping well back and low to the ground, letting the marksmen ahead of him do their jobs. These were Garramone's best men, Flying Squad guys, but in every way just as capable as Nepi's crack commandoes — if not a little less arrogant.

Ymeri and his associate, who were in the process of opening the boot, swung around at the commotion on the gravel behind them.

'Freeze, Flying Squad — you are under arrest,' barked the unit commander. 'Lay down your weapons.'

But it was immediately clear that Ymeri's associate had other ideas. He was reaching for his gun, but the sniper to Scamarcio's right had already spotted it and fired. The man fell to the ground, shaking and convulsing. Ymeri, fat and sweaty, looked desperately around him, shocked and confused, trying to run, scanning for the exits. Suddenly, a group of men in the same black suits as the gatekeeper with the walkie-talkie were running from the house, shouting, their rifles at the ready, poised in mid-air. Scamarcio didn't have time to take them all in, but he thought there were at least five of them and that they were wielding Franchi SPAS 12S — futuristic and frightening semi-automatics with a hefty price tag. Then, all about him, the air exploded in a barrage of gunfire, and he could do nothing but press himself to the ground, deep into the gravel, reaching for his Beretta 92 inside his jacket holster. Almost in slow motion, he watched the shoulders of the marksmen in front of him readying and recoiling, readying and recoiling, over and over again. It was as if time had become stuck in a loop, sucking them all into a wormhole. Then, all at once, it was still, utterly silent: the birdsong had ceased, the cicadas had abandoned their evening rhythms, the traffic on the mainroad had died away to a nothing. It was as if all life had ended here in this one place, at this one precise moment.

'Headcount,' barked the commander, shattering the dead air around him.

The snipers all answered in the affirmative: no one was down. Scamarcio raised himself off the gravel onto his elbows, peering through the gunsmoke towards the people carrier. Ymeri was rolling around on the ground, clutching his leg. Good: he'd still be able to talk; they'd been told to avoid a fatality there. The boot of the car seemed undamaged; again, the snipers had been briefed to steer clear.

Scamarcio stumbled slowly to his feet, and saw a mass of black-suited corpses lining the entranceway to the villa, like a mound of diseased crows, waiting for the sun and the flies to claim them. He hobbled towards the people carrier, his muscles stiff and cold, the acrid taint of gunpowder coating his tongue. He heard the boots of the team behind him running up the steps, ordering whoever was inside the house to freeze. He reached out a shaky hand towards the lock, steadying his fingers to press it, the catch sliding under his sweat. He tried again, and then again.

Finally, the boot of the car sprang open, causing him to take an involuntary step back. Inside was a little girl curled into the foetal position, trembling but alive, her fine, blonde hair plastered to her head. Scamarcio took a breath, stepped forward, and lifted her gently from the car. Stacey Baker just whimpered in his arms, and wouldn't open her eyes. 'It's OK,' he whispered in English. 'I'm a policeman, and I'm going to take you to your mum and dad now.'

la Repubblica, 9 June

MISSING AMERICAN GIRL FOUND ALIVE!

The international search for the missing American child Stacey Baker reached a dramatic conclusion last night when armed police raided a villa outside Monticiano, Tuscany following an anonymous tip-off. The swat team located the seven-year-old alive and well in the grounds of the house and immediately rushed her to Rome, where she was reunited with her desperate parents.

According to police insiders, the handover was deeply moving and brought tears to the eyes of even the most hardened of the crack commandos. The success in tracking down the missing child is being heralded as a major achievement for the new Rome Police chief, Gianfilippo Mancino, who scrambled his specialist anti-kidnap squad in a matter of minutes following the tip-off. Just why she had been brought to the villa is as yet unclear.

Stacey Baker's father Paul told reporters: 'My heartfelt thanks goes to the Italian police force, whose efficiency and dogged determination we will never forget. I cannot thank them enough for all they've done. They have literally saved our lives.' It is believed that the family, from Maine, will return to the States tonight. They have no plans to visit Italy again.

Theories about the Baker abduction abound. It is possible that she could have fallen victim to an Albanian child-trafficking gang working across Italy. Such operations have mushroomed in recent years and are causing the police mounting concern. It is equally likely that she could have been snatched by an individual, acting alone. The Rome police department has not yet commented on the motive behind the crime but it is believed further details will emerge in the coming days.

The Elba tourist office, as well as other resorts the length and breadth of the peninsula, have reported a surge in cancellations following the little girl's disappearance while, in many communities across the country, children are no longer being allowed to play in the streets unsupervised. 'It is a sad testimony to our changing times,' commented Marco Sordi, the mayor of Porto Azzurro.

61

Frantic birdsong echoed along Via Boncompagni as Scamarcio searched for his key in his pocket. Yes, they'd got Stacey Baker, but there was a hard knot of frustration in his chest — a burning disbelief that they'd failed to find any clients inside the villa last night. Maybe the news of the Moltisanti deaths had them running scared; maybe someone in the know had tipped them to the Flying Squad's involvement? And two further questions still vexed him: Who was it who had grabbed him in the alleyway that time, and told him to go to Elba? What was their agenda, and what were they hoping to achieve? One possibility troubled him, kept circling: was it his father's old lieutenants trying to push yet another favour his way, to pull him closer into the fold and drag him back in? Or were they attempting to oust their rivals — jeopardise a competitive operation? But that didn't feel right to him. Yes, they were criminals and gangsters, but they had never touched children. They were old-style, the old guard: extortion and contraband; killing when required, but sparingly. They would never touch children — never in a million years. His father would never have countenanced that. He stopped, and this was the second question: What had The Priest been getting at when he alluded to his connection to his dad? Why did he seem to think that Scamarcio was the only one who could offer him forgiveness? The memory of the events at Longone chilled him anew. He resolved to speak with Piocosta one last time, and to finally get an answer. And, of course, *they* still expected a favour in return for the Gela tip. But he had no scraps to throw them right now.

His phone shuddered in his pocket. Aurelia didn't bother with 'Hello', as if she were somehow a reluctant caller: 'That knifework — just got round to it. The reach is OK, and the entry and exit angles don't show much variation. Could have been him. But I worry about the strength he would have needed to finish it off — too many punctures to complete. Yet no obvious defence wounds either, and no trace under the nails.' She paused. 'It's not clear. Perhaps I need a bit more time with it.' She'd gone before he had a chance to respond.

He sighed, struggling for the key some more. Tiredness was preventing him from functioning. Tiredness was playing tricks with his mind, making him imagine that someone was touching his arm. But it was no illusion, he now realised: a tall, thin man in dark glasses was standing in front of him on the pavement. Scamarcio was too exhausted to feel afraid.

'Detective Scamarcio?'

The voice was somehow familiar, but he couldn't place it.

'Who wants to know?'

'Could you come with me a moment?'

'No.' He was done, had had enough. 'It's 7.00am, and I've been working all night.'

The man raised his glasses quickly so Scamarcio could see his eyes. It was Giorgio Ganza, the foreign secretary.

'Would you mind sparing me half an hour? If you accompany me to my home in Prati, I'd like to give you some information.'

Scamarcio sighed and then nodded. Sleep would have to wait.

It was a sumptuous apartment, probably 200 metres square. Fitted out in the liberty style, the cornices were perfect, the windows high, the oak floors polished to perfection. The study where they were sitting was painted a duck-egg blue, and mahogany shelving ran the length of the walls, bearing leather-bound books arranged by height and colour. It was one of the most immaculate offices Scamarcio had seen. On the oak desk in front of Ganza were several family photos in silver frames, and behind him on the wall was a portrait in oils of what could have been a father or a grandfather. Scamarcio seemed to remember that the older generations had also been in politics. Something about the partisans came up to his mind, but he couldn't quite home in on it.

'I'm sorry to drag you off the street like that,' said Ganza. 'But I couldn't think how else to do it. Can I offer you anything — a coffee, perhaps? Have you had breakfast?'

'I was planning on that when we met.'

'In that case I will get you some brioche also.' He rang a small bell on his desk, and a Filipina in full maid's outfit came into the room. Scamarcio didn't know people still had maids at home, or still made them dress up like this. He felt as though he had stepped back into the oil painting with Ganza's grandpa, or whoever he was.

Ganza placed the order with his maid, and she hurried off. He grew thoughtful for a moment and spent some time studying the empty desk in front of him, as if looking for an answer there. Scamarcio decided to break the silence, to try to make the atmosphere more comfortable. 'So you said you had some information for me?'

The maid came back in with the coffee and pastries, and set them down beside him on a side table. She placed an espresso on the desk in front of Ganza.

'Thank you, Aurora.'

The woman smiled and left. Scamarcio had the sense that Ganza treated his staff well, and was in some respects a decent guy — if that could ever be said of someone who attended the kind of parties he did. He also had the sense that his wife was not as kind.

'Sorry, you were saying?'

'I was asking why you wanted to see me — what it was you wanted to tell me?'

Ganza leaned forward in his chair and then leaned back again, as if unsure of quite what to do with himself. He rubbed a forefinger under his nose and stared back down at the desk, searching for the answers there again. Eventually, he looked up and met Scamarcio's eye.

'I could have gone to your boss, but I wanted to deal directly with you. I thought it would be cleaner somehow.'

Scamarcio was intrigued by the choice of phrase, but didn't want to distract him. 'Go on.'

'There's no easy way to say this, so I'll just come straight out with it. I killed him, you see — trashed his apartment, too.'

Scamarcio felt time stand still. He no longer heard the ticking of the carriage clock on Ganza's desk that he had noticed when he'd first sat down.

'Are you talking about Arthur?'

'Yes. You've seen the pictures, I presume?' The tone remained strangely businesslike.

'Of the two of you at the party? Yes.'

Ganza nodded. 'I should have told you sooner — I realise that. I just needed some time to get my thoughts together.' Although the delivery was neutral, his hands were trembling slightly.

Scamarcio tried to keep the shock out of his voice: 'Why did you kill him, Mr Ganza?'

Ganza sank back into his chair, and slid down in it slightly. 'The shame, I guess. I panicked. I didn't want to lose everything I had, didn't want him to talk, didn't want to see him on some evening chat-show dishing the dirt.' The words made sense, but the tone didn't. Despite the water collecting in the corner of his eyes, Ganza now sounded like he was reciting lines in a play — the emotion was absent.

'So you just went to his place and stabbed him to death?'

'Yes.'

'Why all the chaos?'

'I wanted it to look like a burglary.'

'Where was he when you entered the flat?'

'On the bed.'

'Awake or asleep?'

'Asleep.'

'And you gave him the morphine, too?'

Scamarcio registered an unmistakeable flicker of surprise. Ganza didn't know about the morphine.

He pretended to ignore it and pushed on: 'So you gave him the morphine?'

'Yes.'

Scamarcio knew now that he was lying, both about the morphine *and* the murder. But he was at a loss to understand why. If his father and brother were to be believed, Arthur had apparently committed suicide, had finally had enough. So why should Ganza now be trying to take the blame for his death? Was he scared? Was it fear now pushing him towards a prison cell? Were years behind bars preferable to what was waiting for him on the outside? Was he afraid of the same thing as Zaccardo? He sighed quietly, patting his jacket pocket for his cuffs, but realised they were in his car.

'So I guess I'm going to have to arrest you.' He felt like the other actor in Ganza's little play.

'I guess so.'

'I don't have any cuffs with me.'

'I'll accompany you willingly to the station. We can take my car.'

'Right you are.'

Scamarcio drained the dregs of his coffee and stood up. They headed back out through the vast polished living room towards the front door.

Ganza stopped in front of him. 'Can you give me a second? I need to use the bathroom.'

Scamarcio nodded for him to go ahead. He walked on into the lobby area towards the front door, and took in the chandelier, the oil paintings, and the large, lavish black-and-white floor tiles. As he was admiring the decor, he noticed a door ajar to his right. There was a light coming from within, so he stepped a little closer, curious to catch a glimpse inside another of the rooms. But as he drew nearer he realised that Mrs Ganza was standing just beyond the threshold — getting dressed, it seemed. In this light, her profile was even more elegant, her cheekbones higher, her nose more delicate; even if he hadn't known it, he would have been able to tell just by looking at her that she had once been a society girl. He was about to step away, not wanting to be taken for a Peeping Tom, when he noticed something else about her: her left wrist was bandaged, and there was something wrong with the colouring on her right forearm. He drew a little closer, and saw that it was badly bruised — blue and raw-looking. And at that exact moment, she looked up, and their eyes locked. And it was then that he knew it was she who had killed Arthur.

62

AT THE STATION, Mrs Ganza remained composed and dignified while her husband, left alone for several minutes in an interview room, was racked by sobs, shaking and heaving back and forth — a humiliating spectacle that Scamarcio felt embarrassed to be observing on the monitor. He thought that Ganza should at least be allowed some element of privacy.

Mrs Ganza had told them that she didn't want to wait for her brief and would prefer to push on with the interview until he arrived. Garramone had nodded his assent, so Scamarcio turned the recording device on, duly noting the date and time, and the names of the three individuals present.

'So, Mrs Ganza, your husband has told us that he's responsible for the death of Arthur Maraquez, also known as José, at his apartment in Trastevere last week ...' He was about to ask her what she thought of this, but she was ready with her response.

'He isn't.'

'What makes you say that?'

There was silence for several moments before she replied: 'Because I killed him myself.' The words were flat and cold. There was an icy bitterness in her stare, too — an expression that intimated *What of it? Wouldn't you have done the same in my position?*

For a moment, the air seemed to desert the little room.

'That is not the account you gave me the other day,' said Scamarcio finally.

'I wasn't ready the other day.' She paused. 'I had things I needed to get prepared first.'

Scamarcio gave a slight nod. 'Could you explain what happened — talk us both through it?'

'He was about to ruin my husband's career, and destroy my family, my reputation, everything we'd worked so hard for.'

'He wasn't the one who published the photos.'

'No, but he was in them, and he was the one who had been manipulating him, extorting him, all these years.'

'Extorting him?'

'Giorgio had been paying him a small fortune. I saw the money leave his account every month.'

So she *had* known. She'd lied well at their first meeting, thought Scamarcio — very well. Instead, he said: 'I think you may be confused there, Mrs Ganza. Your husband was being blackmailed for the photos by the man who had taken them.'

She shook her head, looked away for a moment, and bit down on her lip. 'I'm not confused at all, Detective. I'm not talking about the last few months, but the last few *years*. He's been paying that whore … that creature, that boy, for years. He bought him that flat in Trastevere. You know that? He paid for his flat.'

She barred her arms across her chest, staring him straight in the eye, uncompromising, unflinching, challenging him this time. There was none of the slow tiredness of their previous meeting.

'So you wanted to put an end to it?'

'It *had* to end. The photos were the final straw: I wanted Arthur out of our lives. I wanted an end to his games — the exaggerated vulnerability, the false portrait of the perfect companion. I know the score: I know why he went to him — I'm not stupid. So I made a plan to go to his place. But when I got there, he seemed drugged, completely out of it. And it threw me. He was so smashed I even told him what I was about to do to him, and you know how he reacted? He just laughed weirdly and said, "OK, then, do what you must." Then he did something odd. He staggered over to his camera, smashed it against the wall, and then put it back on the shelf. After that, he just lay back on the bed and waited for me to get on with it.'

She was shaking her head again, uncomprehending. 'It infuriated me. I had wanted him to suffer, to pay for what he'd done, and the family he'd destroyed, but in the end I don't think he suffered at all. He just made me think I was doing him a favour.'

'That camera — didn't you want to take it with you?'

She nodded slowly. 'Yes, because I wondered what was on it and whether it would incriminate my husband.' She paused for a moment, sighing softly. 'But I made a mistake: I was angry at him, just lying there like that, waiting for me to kill him, so I only thought about the implications of that camera after I'd heard the sirens. I didn't know if they were coming for me, but I couldn't risk it. Maybe a neighbour had heard something, and called the police? I was actually going to go get the camera, but the sirens were getting closer, and I panicked. I felt I had no choice but to get out of there. There was no time to retrieve that camera.' She stopped for a second, searching both their faces. 'Why, what was on there? Was it important?'

Scamarcio looked away from her, momentarily disgusted.

It was Garramone's turn to speak. He leaned forward slightly, trying to keep his tone neutral. 'Mrs Ganza, just why are you telling us all this? Why not let your husband take the blame? He's confessed, after all.'

She leaned back in her seat and shifted to the side slightly, her lips stiffening into a bitter smile, contorting her beauty for a moment. 'Two things: one, his career's already ruined — it's beyond help, and there's nothing I can do about that now; two, I've achieved my secondary objective, which was to make him suffer.'

Garramone frowned. 'So you wanted to punish him for what he'd done?'

She paused and nodded slowly, not speaking for a moment. Then, almost as an afterthought, she said: 'I wanted to hurt him like he'd hurt me. He was in love with him, you see, and for me that's a kind of death. Prison makes no difference to me now.'

63

GANZA HAD PLEADED with them, had said his wife was a manic-depressive who hadn't been taking her lithium — he could produce a doctor's note to prove it. She couldn't go to prison, he insisted; she wouldn't cope. His relentless entreaties made Scamarcio wonder whether Mrs Ganza had in fact underestimated her husband's feelings for her; made him wonder whether it wasn't as simple as him being 'in love' with Arthur. Ganza claimed to know nothing about 'last night's party' or why the guests hadn't shown, and insisted that if he did he would have given it up freely — anything that might help lessen the charges facing his wife. But when it came to the wider question of the parties themselves and their regulars, he remained tight-lipped. This was his limit, figured Scamarcio. Fear would stop him from going any further.

Scamarcio left Garramone at the station, wanting to head over to Aurelia at the morgue to run the new scenario past her. But he was aware that it wasn't just her professional opinion he courted. The events in Sicily and Tuscany had left him wrung out, in need of some kind of emotional connection: again that sensation returned, building for several days now, that he needed someone in his life who counted, who he had to be there for and vice versa. Instinctively, he sensed that that person might be Aurelia. If he were honest with himself, he'd been quietly wondering about this for a while now.

When he walked into her office, she was resting her head on her desk, with her arms crossed above her. Somehow it disturbed him. She looked as if she might have been shot.

'Are you all right?'

She jumped. 'Oh, Scamarcio! I was just tired, that's all. You caught me napping.' She held up a finger. 'Whatever you do, don't say you're sorry.'

He raised both palms. 'Understood. May I sit down?'

'Help yourself.'

He pulled out a dilapidated plastic chair, and took a deep breath: 'Any chance we could be dealing with both a murder and a suicide?'

'Your dead rentboy again?'

He nodded, and talked her through the events of that morning. When he was done, she stood up and walked towards the window, and looked out. Her hair was good in the sunlight, glossy, like something out of one of those TV ads, thought Scamarcio.

'It's certainly possible that he injected the morphine and then used his last moments of lucidity to position the camera before he was set upon.'

'Would morphine do that to you? Make you so acquiescent in the face of death, would you just lie there like that and let someone stab you?'

'Depends on the amount you'd taken, but, given his now supposedly suicidal state, I'd say, yes, it could. And there were no clear defence wounds, as I said.'

'If Mrs Ganza hadn't come along, what would he have done with that camera, I wonder? Just left it beside his bed to be discovered along with his body?'

'Seems like it, yes. Was it left running when it was put on the shelf?'

'The CSIs seem to think so, yes. It looks as if he wanted it to be seen straight away when the body was found. Maybe he hoped an inquiry would start from there.' He checked himself; he'd said too much.

'Why did he want it to be seen? What was on it?'

Scamarcio remembered that he'd kept the contents of the camera to himself, and had chosen not to divulge them to Aurelia. He wanted to share it with her now, but knew that it would have to keep: he had to wait until all the loose ends were tied up. 'If you can hold on a couple of days, I'll tell you then. Let me take you for that drink, and I'll fill you in.'

She raised her eyebrows at him: 'Whatever you say, Scamarcio.'

He wasn't certain if that was a yes or a no, or whether she'd forgiven him for last time, but he smiled anyway. 'I'll give you a call.'

'Sure.'

He didn't know what to do next, so he just pushed back the chair, turned, and left the room.

As he headed home, the exhaustion felt bone deep. Now, nearly forty-eight hours after they'd first left for Gela, the sun was low in the sky once more, and he resolved to turn in as soon as he got home, to try to get some sleep and recover from this, the strangest of days.

As he reflected on it now, he saw that Arthur had probably intended those photos to be seen immediately in the hope that an inquiry would start from there. Although he hadn't considered stabbing as a suicide method, ultimately it had served his purpose in rendering his death more dramatic and triggering a police investigation. Ironically, Mrs Ganza had simply aided him in his final aim and made it more likely that her husband would face trial for his involvement with this depraved club. If she had in some ways been attempting to protect his professional reputation and financial security while dealing him a huge personal blow, she had only succeeded in the latter.

His mobile buzzed in his jacket. Garramone was on the line: the tone was flat, neutral now, from exhaustion perhaps: 'The lawyer claims that there's a clear case for diminished responsibility with Mrs Ganza. Doctors' records show that she's been in and out of private mental facilities for years. And, of course, they're not best pleased we talked to her without a brief being present. They're saying that, given her illness, they'll strike her statement before it gets to court.'

'Could they?'

'Possibly, but we'll just get her to say it all again with the lawyer there. She doesn't seem to have any problem talking right now.'

'They'll sedate her and shut her up.'

'No, Scamarcio, they won't. Don't worry, it will come good.'

'Any news on your friend? Anyone grilling him yet about his involvement in a Mafia …'

The empty line echoed back at him.

64

SCAMARCIO OPENED THE DOOR to his apartment, half-expecting to find it turned over — for what precise reason he didn't know, but there were surely several stacking up by now. But everything was as it should be. He went into the kitchen, opened the cupboard where he kept the spirits, and poured himself a large measure of Glenfiddich.

He took a seat at the small table and took several gulps. Then he picked up his mobile and dialled Pinnetta.

'Long time no hear,' said his trusty dealer.

'Been trying the straight and narrow.'

'I'm impressed.'

'You shouldn't be. It's bad for business.'

Pinnetta snorted like the fattened pig he was. 'So what will it be? You calling to offer me a severance package?'

'Maybe next time. For now, I'd like the usual, and as soon as you can manage it.'

'Sounds like it's been tough going, the straight and narrow.'

'You could say that.'

He slumped back into the sofa, surveying the darkening sky outside. He had a fresh glass of Glenfiddich in one hand and a joint of Pinnetta's best in the other. Finally, the world around him seemed to level out, find its balance. It had been too long. He thought about Aurelia and where he'd take her for that drink. There was a fun place in Trastevere he liked — laid-back atmosphere, not too pushy.

He took another toke. Pinnetta had excelled himself. He was the master. Maybe if he'd had a crappier dealer it would have been easier to give up. He needed to find a crappier dealer.

He pushed himself up from the sofa and eased himself into the window seat so he could get a better view of the street below and the ebbs and flows of a Friday night. In the distance, beads of car lights wound their way across the seven hills, along the river, through the parks. Behind the tiny slats of light of the apartments he imagined children watching TV, spinsters cooking their brodo, couples fighting. This beautiful hodgepodge of a city: could he really live anywhere else?

He returned his gaze to the street. A group of teenagers, all dressed in black, were heading out for the night, smoking and shouting. They used to call them Goths, but now they were known as Emos, he believed. Their faces were so pale, as though the blood had been drained out of them, and they walked as if they had the weight of the world on their shoulders. Across from them on the other side of the street, the old lady from the apartment upstairs was pushing her shopping along in a little red cart, her tiny Chihuahua by her side, fretting at her heels. But something was bothering him now; he couldn't quite identify the source of it, but just felt that something in the picture wasn't right. Then he realised what it was: a short man in a baseball cap was on the corner, looking up, apparently directly at him, from the end of his street where it joined Via Piave. The man just kept on looking, bold as brass — he was still staring now. Scamarcio felt a surge of paranoia course through him. He sprang from the window seat and ran to the cupboard in his bedroom where he kept the Beretta 92 FS Inox his father had given him for his 16th birthday. He loaded it quickly and returned to the window. The man was still watching him, gazing in, undaunted. Scamarcio gripped the gun tighter, and brought it closer to him so he could feel the cold steel on his skin. But then, as if in response, the figure just doffed his cap, waved, and headed back into the darkness of Via Piave.

Scamarcio ran from the window, grabbing his keys from the apartment door before slamming it shut behind him. He sprinted down the two flights to the lobby, pushing open the heavy glass doors onto the street. He headed right, and ran across the road in the direction of Via Piave, dodging a braking car. He kept running, the drugs making his heart beat faster and his head pound. Cars and Vespas were everywhere on the street, taxis sounding their horns, bikers flipping the finger, and then he caught a glimpse of him between some parked bicycles at the end of the road, about to make the turn. He pushed himself on, could taste blood in his chest, faster, faster, faster until he could almost reach out and touch the man's back and his heaving shoulders. He stretched out his right arm, grabbed him, and brought him crashing to the ground, hard.

'Who the hell are you? What do you want?' he gasped.

The man was fighting and kicking in the dirt beneath him. 'Get off me. Get off me.' The voice was younger than he'd expected, scared.

'Why were you looking at me? How do you know where I live?'

The figure kicked again beneath him. 'Get off me. Get off.' He sounded petrified.

He pulled the stranger to his feet. The cap was on the ground now, and when he spun him around he saw that the man was probably no more than 25 years old. He had blue eyes, blond hair, a good-looking face. He was shaking under his grip. Scamarcio no longer felt afraid.

'Listen, calm down, OK? Calm down. Just tell me what you're up to, that's all. I've had a difficult week. I'm tense, and I don't like strangers staring up at me when I'm trying to relax at home in my flat.'

The young man nodded, took a gulp of air, and bent over his knees to get his breath back. After ten seconds or so, he straightened himself up and met Scamarcio's eye. 'I'm sorry,' he said, still panting. 'I didn't mean to scare you. I just came to say, "Thank you."'

'"Thank you"?' Scamarcio's head was spinning. 'Why? Who are you?'

The boy had bent down again, still gasping for air. 'I can't tell you that.'

'What are you thanking me for then?'

'For your hard work,' he panted. 'I had hoped to lead you in the right direction, and I did.'

65

SCAMARCIO BROUGHT TWO GLASSES of Nero d'Avola over to the table. The young man had regained his composure and was leaning back against the wall, surveying the other drinkers. They were in a place that Scamarcio liked to come to when he needed to get out of the flat but didn't want to go far. It was done up like a wine cellar with oak barrels as tables, low stone walls, and rustic lighting. The reds were good and the prices acceptable.

Scamarcio set the wine down in front of the stranger, who nodded his thanks. Scamarcio drew out a chair and sat, feeling crushed with exhaustion now that Pinnetta's special blend was wearing off. 'So was it you who sent me to Elba?'

The young man took a sip of his wine and nodded again.

'Why?'

He sank back against the wall, ran a hand through his hair, and watched a group of girls who had just come in. 'I thought it would help — help you to understand what was going on.'

'But how did you know what was going on? Where do you fit in?' Scamarcio took several large gulps of his wine.

'It's not that easy to explain,' said the young man. He shifted in his seat and studied the floor awhile, seeming to be searching for some kind of strength. Finally, he returned his gaze to Scamarcio: 'I was brought there, as a young boy. What I mean is, I was brought to the kind of place where they were taking that girl — brought for the same people.'

Scamarcio froze, unable to find any words. The man in front of him looked to be in his mid-twenties. How long had these parties been going on? 'How old are you?' he asked finally.

'Twenty-one.'

He seemed older than his years, and had no doubt seen the worst of life already. 'What age were you when you were brought there?'

'Eight. It was a month before my ninth birthday, the first time they took me.'

'So these parties have been going on for well over ten years?'

The young man took another sip of his wine. 'They've become something of a tradition, a time-honoured club, you might say.' Then, seemingly as an afterthought: 'A bit like the Freemasons.'

It seemed a strange comment. Scamarcio sensed he was being thrown a hint. 'I'd been wondering about that — wondering whether they were involved.'

'There's a crossover, but only with some members.'

'How many times were you taken there?'

'Five. After that, I was left alone.'

'Why was that, do you think?'

'No idea. Maybe I'd served a purpose.'

Scamarcio shifted his attention to his drink, unsure where to look. 'How did they find you in the first place? Were you kidnapped, taken from your parents?'

'No. I was in care. When I was fostered out, I was sent to live with a family outside Rome, near Monterotondo. The men from the parties collected me from there, and returned me at the end of the evening.' He exhaled, and paused a moment. 'The foster family must have been in on it — they just handed me over at the door, like I was going on an outing.'

'The name of that family?'

'The foster parents are both dead; the last one, the mother, died five years ago.'

Scamarcio wanted to press him on what happened at the villas, but it seemed too soon. Right now, he didn't want to cause him any more stress than was necessary. 'So after the fifth time, they just stopped showing up?'

'Yeah, I never saw them again. I was moved from the foster family, and adopted by a wealthy surgeon and his wife with an apartment on Via Licia. After that, life got a whole lot better, and it's not been bad since.'

'So how come you knew about Elba and the girl?'

The boy sighed, and shifted his weight back against the wall. 'Do you have a cigarette?'

Scamarcio reached for the fags in his pocket and opened the packet for the boy. He took one, and Scamarcio lit up for him. The young man drew the nicotine deep into his lungs, blowing the smoke away to his left, clear of the table. 'I never told my adopted parents what had happened to me. It seemed shameful, and I didn't want them to see me as … as in some way tainted.' He took another drag. 'So I kept it to myself. But there was a part of me that felt guilty about not speaking out. I worried that other children were suffering and that I'd had the power to do something about it, but hadn't.'

'So what *did* you do?' Scamarcio realised that his voice had dropped to almost a whisper.

'I set about finding out all I could about them, these people, if you can call them that: where the parties were held and when, who organised them …'

'How did you manage it?'

'There were certain things I remembered about being brought there — things that my mind hadn't managed to block out. One was that I was always collected by a man with a Tuscan accent, and that we took the motorway north to Siena, after which point he put a sack over my head and made me lie down on the floor of the back seat. When we arrived, I heard other Tuscan accents.'

He paused for a moment, exhaled deeply, and downed the rest of his wine.

'You want another?' asked Scamarcio.

'Yes.'

He went to the bar, and was back within a minute. He'd brought a second glass for himself as well. 'Take all the time you need.'

'No, I want to get this over with.' The young man took another couple of sips and then seemed to locate some kind of inner resolve. 'The other things I remembered, well, they actually only became a memory later on — crystallised, as it were — when I had worked them out.'

Scamarcio was puzzled, but tried not to show it; he just wanted the man to press on uninterrupted. 'They formed a memory when I saw them on TV.' He stopped a moment. 'I'm probably not making any sense: what I mean is, when I saw their faces on TV, I recognised who they were.'

'Saw whose faces?'

The young man looked down, searching for the words. Scamarcio felt stupid. 'Sorry, carry on.'

'One was a high-ranking cabinet minister at the time — he's dead now; the other was the mayor of a major city — he's now retired, I understand.'

'Both these men were at the parties?'

He nodded. 'When I recognised them, I realised that if I went to the authorities they'd never believe me, and, even if they did, these men would stop them from taking it further. You know how it is.'

Scamarcio nodded, saying nothing.

'So I thought the only thing I could do was investigate it myself, and collect as much evidence as possible. Maybe one day the time would be right and I could present that evidence and see it through.'

'And how did you go about doing this?'

'I have a girlfriend whose father is a politician, a good guy for once. He had heard rumours — a few names had been mentioned. I bought some bugging equipment online, got myself a job as a cleaner or dressed myself up as a repairman, and got into the places where I knew these men worked. I bugged their landlines, and, when I could, their mobiles. For a year or so I got absolutely nothing, and then finally one day it happened: I listened in to a conversation where they mentioned the parties for the first time and talked about where one was being held. So I went up there, watched the place for a couple of days before the scheduled event, and identified who the organisers were. Then I got inside and placed a tap on one of their mobiles. There were three of them planning everything — bringing in the drugs, the children, the other horrendous stuff — but I only managed to bug one of them. It was a stroke of luck I'd managed to get in there in the first place: pest control, that time. But, as it turned out, that one person's phone was enough.' He paused, and took another mouthful of wine. 'From him, I went on to find out where the other parties would be held and when. I tried to collect some video evidence as children were brought in, and guests arrived — but I was always filming in the bushes, and it was always dark, so I don't think any of it has come out.'

A second team had been recording in the bushes at the villa the night before, but if the prosecution could prove that these parties had been going on for many years, the boy's video would bolster their case, thought Scamarcio. 'Actually, they can touch that stuff up now — do quite a lot with it,' he said. 'You might have something useful there, even if you don't realise it.'

The young man exhaled. 'Well, that would be something.' He pushed on: 'Everything I'm telling you happened within the last year; until then I'd drawn a blank, as I said before. Then, just a week or so ago, I overheard the man I'd been bugging talking about a premium child. By that, they mean blonde and blue-eyed — the same category I think I'd fallen into. This child had been identified on Elba. She was going to be brought in by a group of Albanians who'd started working for the organisers, but they didn't quite trust them; they were worried they were going to screw up. Then the next day, I think it was, my guy, the organiser, was in a right state about that boy Arthur who has been in all the papers with Ganza. He was worried because he'd been a regular at their parties, and they thought it was going to open a can of worms for them. They were extremely worked up; they were considering cancelling the parties for a while. Then, when it came out he'd been killed, they really freaked — they thought the police would be sniffing all around his death, although one of their clients had apparently promised to keep a lid on it for them. Anyway, that's when I knew the time had finally come to push the police in the right direction and hand over what I had.'

'How did you know to come to me?'

'I hung outside Arthur's flat for a while, and saw a few people come and go. I saw you come by a second time, and thought you seemed to be taking it pretty seriously, so I followed you and I heard you answer your mobile and say, 'Scamarcio'. That rang some bells for me, so I googled you and realised you were the Flying Squad guy who everyone was talking about last year because of your father. That's how I knew to come to you.'

Scamarcio was impressed. 'You ever considered a career in the police?'

'Actually, I'm training to be a doctor. I've had enough listening in and spying to last me a lifetime. I'll be glad to lay this thing to rest once and for all — I just want to move on now.'

Scamarcio smiled. 'Well, let me know if you ever change your mind.' He paused, and took another long sip of wine. 'It sounds like you might have some interesting evidence there, but are you prepared to testify? It would help the prosecution case significantly.' Scamarcio knew what he was asking, but decided to just come right out with it.

The young man shook his head slowly, a different kind of sadness in his eyes now. 'I can't, Scamarcio. I can't do that to my parents. I can't face these men in court. I just want to get on with my life — be normal, successful, have a family of my own.'

Scamarcio nodded. 'We could give you anonymity.'

The young man sighed. 'You know that's never enough. They'd find me in the end. Make me pay, one way or the other. They'd know people — judges, police, court officials — and word would get back. You know how it is.'

Scamarcio fell silent. He saw the case splintering apart in front of him, the illustrious clients still smug in their top jobs, snug in their immunity.

'I can give you all the evidence I collected — the recordings of the phone conversations I made. It's all very well filed and documented,' insisted the boy.

'That's very helpful, but to date we only have one decent witness, and his account alone may not be enough to seal the prosecution case. There's Giorgio Ganza, but I'm not sure he can be compelled to testify. We've taken another, one of the Albanians, into custody, but it's unclear yet whether he'll talk.'

'I'm sorry, Scamarcio. I can't.'

Scamarcio nodded slowly, and took a long breath. He felt like smashing his glass in frustration, but just said: 'Thank you for all your hard work.' Then he added, 'I suppose you know we raided the party last night?'

The boy nodded. 'I saw the news coverage, and put two and two together. They didn't say anything about the parties, though — just mentioned you'd found her at a villa.'

'No, they wouldn't; probably they never will,' said Scamarcio, stubbing his cigarette into the ashtray as if he wanted to eliminate it from the face of the earth.

'Did you get Enzo? That was my man, the guy I've been following. I don't know the surname, but he's Tuscan, like I said. I have all that evidence against him.'

Scamarcio sighed, finally giving up on the butt. 'He went down in a firefight. He'll be no good to us now. None of the big fish showed up — someone must have warned them off.'

Neither man spoke for a while. Scamarcio couldn't rid himself of the fact that here was their golden witness, a child who had actually been brought to these parties, and seen what went on. A witness like this would seal the deal; he'd nail the prosecution case. They could offer him top-level protection, the works. But, somehow, he knew the boy was right. It wouldn't be fair or proper, it would never be justice, for someone who had already spent so much of their childhood in a different kind of prison, who just wanted a fresh start and a settled adulthood. How could Scamarcio do that to him, especially after he'd already shown such courage?

The boy nodded slowly, resigning himself to the reality in which they both lived. 'I can offer you one thing, Scamarcio: I can talk to the papers, tell my story to them — if you find me a journalist you trust, who you know won't betray my identity.'

Scamarcio pondered this for a moment. It might make a difference, in the court of public opinion at least — which, when all was said and done, did still occasionally exert some sway over judicial proceedings.

'I'll find you someone. Leave it with me.' He downed his glass and then said: 'You've got a girlfriend, you say?'

The young man smiled in the affirmative.

'You happy now? Things good?'

He nodded. 'I'm getting there. I've got a feeling things are going to turn out OK in the end.'

Scamarcio nodded, and smiled back. 'I'm sure they will. The past is another country, as they say. All that matters is your present and your future, and you're going to do just great. I can tell.'

66

SCAMARCIO STRETCHED OUT in bed, and opened the newspaper across his lap so he could read the double-page spread inside. Carfagna had done a good job, and Scamarcio knew he had made a sound choice: the journalist was one of the few decent guys around, a solid reporter with a strong moral compass and a genuine sense of outrage when it counted. The subeditors had pulled out several key pieces of text from the article and put them up in bold. One of them read: 'They call themselves The Few.'

'Arrogant,' thought Scamarcio.

His mobile buzzed and he reached for it, annoyed that it was interrupting his reading.

'What the fuck???' screamed Garramone down the line. Scamarcio held the phone at arm's length for a moment before returning it to his ear.

'What the hell are you playing at, Scamarcio?'

'Sorry, Sir, but I have no idea what you're talking about.'

'The double-page spread in *la Repubblica* is what I'm talking about. That had to come from you. I know you're the only one tight with Carfagna. And where the hell did this mystery witness suddenly spring from?'

Scamarcio took a deep breath. 'He came to me last night, I put him onto Carfagna, and they did the piece straightaway — held the presses and rushed it out for this morning.'

'Wouldn't it have been better to save it for court?' Garramone sounded like he was about to have a heart attack. 'Or maybe run it past me first?'

'He won't go to court, because he's scared. He doesn't trust the judges to keep his identity secret, and thinks the perverts will come for him in the end, which they probably will.'

'Oh, for God's sake, Scamarcio! The PM will finish me for this. There are references to the death of Arthur and Ganza all over the bloody piece!'

'Well, that's the truth, isn't it?'

'Right now, who gives a fuck about the truth? You've cost me my job, Scamarcio, and this will definitely cost you yours!'

'Well, screw you and screw my job! The PM was witnessed at the scene of a Mafia killing by half the bloody Anti-Mafia Squad. Can you grasp that? Do you even *get* what that means? He has serious questions to answer!'

'He'll never face those questions. You don't understand the realities of the situation.'

'The *realities of the situation*? You know what, Garramone, you're not going to just shut me up and sweep all this shit away, just to save your fat arse. As soon as I put down the phone to you, I'm going to call Carfagna and tell him just who it was who first asked us to look into the death of Arthur, to conduct our own secret little investigation. It will move his story on beautifully to the next level.' He hung up and threw the phone down, punched the wall beside him, and then punched it again. 'Fuck it, fuck it,' he shouted. 'Fuck every last one of you.'

He'd probably just blown his career, blown it all — all those years of hard work — for good. He sank back into the pillows, took a few long breaths, sighed, and then sighed again. But he had had no choice. He couldn't just stand by and let this cover-up happen. He couldn't be like all the rest of them. Otherwise, what was the point? He might as well have stayed put with Piocosta and his boys, enjoying Chiara's ragù every day.

He went into the kitchen and made himself a coffee, lit a cigarette, padded into the living room, switched on the TV, thought about Pinnetta's special blend, and then resolved to wait a bit, maybe half an hour if he could manage that. On Sky, the PM — the disgusting, two-faced, hypocritical fucker — was giving a press conference. Bulbs were flashing, and journalists were firing question after question. The ticker along the bottom of the screen said: 'The prime minister steps down, will be leaving politics for health reasons, with immediate effect. Basile to step in.' Scamarcio leaned forward, and turned the sound up. The prime minister looked tired, older, and more bowed than usual. Almost humble for once. He was addressing the journalists: 'After my many years in power, my health and my family have to take priority now. I will be leaving politics *and* Italy for retirement abroad.'

'Why? What's wrong with you?' the journalists were screaming. 'Where are you going?' 'Why now?'

The PM had always held onto power so tenaciously, despite all the court cases and public slurs against him. But now, after all these years of struggle, he was finally bowing out, doing a Craxi. Scamarcio sighed and took a long drag on his fag. Of course, it was always going to end like this; there could be no other way. His mobile rang, and he knew it would be Garramone again.

'Have you seen the news?' He sounded disorientated, as if someone had hit him over the head with a hammer.

'Watching it now.'

'Turn it off and come to the station. No buts.'

67

'So, Scamarcio, your new witness, what did he give you?' asked Garramone, trying but failing to keep his tone level.

Scamarcio talked him through the things that had not already come out in Carfagna's piece. He reiterated the young man's unwillingness to stand trial. When he'd finished, Garramone said: 'Why didn't you tell me all this before?'

'I thought it could wait. I knew you had your hands full with the raid and the Ganzas.'

Garramone sighed, and shifted his bulk under his desk. Neither man said a word for almost a minute.

'So let's do the maths. We've got three guys from the raid — no guests, just staff and minor players who seem to know next to nothing about where they were working. For some reason, the guests didn't show: it seems like someone on the inside tipped them off. So, right now, none of the men we took are saying anything. Ymeri has buttoned up, too, and Ganza's way too scared to be of use.'

Scamarcio had sensed this would be the outcome. He wondered briefly if Garramone had been the insider, had alerted the clients to the raid. But his instincts told him otherwise.

'About our phone call this morning,' said Garramone. 'Obviously, things have changed a bit in light of my friend's decision.'

'You spoke to him?'

'I didn't tell him you'd seen him at Gela. *He* didn't mention the article in *la Repubblica*. But we talked about a trial.'

'What were his thoughts?'

'He didn't fancy our chances. But he told me, in his words, *to do what you've got to do.*'

'Will you? Do what you've got to do?'

Garramone leaned back in his chair, barring his arms across his wide chest. 'You don't think much of me, do you, Scamarcio?'

'Does it matter?'

'It depends on whether you remain working under me or not.'

'I rather got the impression from our phone call this morning that that was no longer an option.'

'It depends — on you, Scamarcio. You're a good detective, one of my best, but I will not indulge you in these outbursts of temper. You simply cannot speak to your superiors like that. And I won't accept you going behind my back. That's not the way this works, and it can't keep on happening. Either you play by my rules, or you get out.'

Scamarcio nodded.

'So what's it to be?'

Scamarcio studied his shoes for a moment, not wanting to meet Garramone's stare. Eventually, he said: 'Honestly, Sir, I don't know right now. I need some time to think.'

Garramone eyed him, puzzled. 'Is this to do with the children? Or is it that we wouldn't let you play the hero with Stacey Baker, and take the limelight on TV?'

Scamarcio sighed, exasperated. Did the chief still understand so very little about his character? 'You know I don't give a shit about that stuff,' he said.

'So it's the case?'

'Yes. And no.'

The chief leaned forward, resting his elbows on his desk. 'Well, take a bit of time — let the dust settle. It's been an intense few days.'

Scamarcio nodded.

'In the meantime, how about joining me for a chat with our friendly penitent, Zaccardo? He, at least, has been singing like the proverbial.'

Scamarcio smiled for the first time that day. 'I'd like nothing better.'

Zaccardo was looking even wirier than the last time he'd seen him. His face was gaunt, and he'd lost some of his tan.

'So,' said Garramone, pulling out a seat and throwing down a huge stack of papers. 'Where were we, Mr Zaccardo? Ah, that's right, you were about to give me the names of the great and the good who attended these secret soirées. The Few, as I believe they liked to call themselves.'

Zaccardo shifted in his seat, and twitched his shoulders. There was something simian about the man, thought Scamarcio.

'My deal, is it sorted? You got everything in place?'

'The wheels are in motion,' said Garramone calmly. 'We've found you a nice house up north, not too far from Switzerland. We're working on a new identity now for you. That will take slightly longer, so you will need to bear with me.'

Zaccardo nodded, seeming reassured.

'So, those names? Care to enlighten us?'

Zaccardo nodded again, quickly, feral like a rat. 'I can only give you the ones I'm certain on. There could be others, of course.'

'Of course — just what you know for sure. Hearsay will not hold up in court.'

Zaccardo nodded and slowly began counting them off on his fingers. With each name, Scamarcio made a shaky note on a yellow Post-it. When Zaccardo had finished, neither Garramone nor Scamarcio said a word. The interview room must have been silent for a full minute; the only sound came from the seconds hand of the cracked plastic wall clock and the scratching of Zaccardo's anxious feet, back and forth beneath the desk.

Eventually, he laughed nervously and said: 'You see now why I wanted witness protection?'

The chief prosecutor was not greatly optimistic. The only one they had talking was Zaccardo, and it was still unclear whether they could compel Ganza to testify about the parties, as there was little they could offer him in return — giving him his wife's freedom was not an option, and anyway they doubted this would be enough to outweigh his fear. The prosecutor annoyed Scamarcio by telling him what he knew already: namely, that the young man would be their star witness, if only he could be persuaded. As for his video and audio evidence, it would need to be reviewed before they could make a judgement on its value. He said he was worried about the powerful figures implicated — worried that they were untouchables, and that any attempt to go after them would result in dire professional, if not personal, consequences for all involved in the prosecution. Garramone shifted in his seat nervously at this point, unwilling to meet Scamarcio's eye.

Scamarcio kept his composure, and bade farewell politely to the pair of them when their meeting was over. He decided to head down towards the Tiber; it was a beautiful, bright afternoon, and he wanted to watch the ducks on the water. He made the call to Piocosta as he walked. 'Can you meet me at the café by Ponte Garibaldi, the Trastevere side? Ten minutes?'

He cut the call, and watched the sunlight etch its way across the yellow stonework of the liberty buildings up ahead. How he loved and hated this city in equal measure. But if he ever left, he knew he'd always be thinking about coming back. He made the turn down to the riverbank, and saw that quite a few people were out and about, enjoying the summer heat. Tourists were taking photos on the bridge; handsome couples were smiling as they walked arm in arm. He headed out along the river, crushing stone and moss underfoot. The balcony of the café was full — waiters hurrying back and forth, children darting around, trailing chaos in their wake. Eventually, he felt a hand on his back, and knew it was the old man.

They both turned to face the water. A mother duck was leading three infants: two were keeping in line, but the last one was speeding off in all directions.

'So, did you get what you needed in Gela?'

Scamarcio smiled. 'I'm sure by now you know I did. But thanks — for the trouble.'

'No trouble.' Piocosta fell silent for a moment. Scamarcio knew what was coming. 'You thought some more about my offer?' asked the old man.

Scamarcio sighed. 'I'm a bit confused right now. About everything.'

'You young people today are always confused. Nothing like a war to shake that out of you.'

He sounded just like his father. Scamarcio pulled the paper from his pocket, holding it for a moment so it was buffeted by the wind, but making sure not to let it go.

'You ever heard of a man called The Priest? That paedophile, who killed all those kids years back?'

Piocosta spat on the ground, and straightened. 'Disgusting story. He was a beast, not a man. He wasn't human.'

'He ever know my pa?'

He felt Piocosta catch his breath beside him and, for a moment, all he could hear was the lapping of the water and the dull roll of bicycle tyres across the bridge. Eventually, the old man said: 'I never heard that, no. Why would he know your pa?'

Scamarcio didn't answer for a while, and then said: 'You ever hear bad stuff about my pa?'

'What kind of bad stuff? He wasn't exactly Mother Teresa, Leo.'

'The kind of bad stuff The Priest was into. You know, little kids?'

This time he felt Piocosta's whole body freeze. It seemed like minutes passed before he finally said: 'Leo, why are you asking me these terrible questions? Coming at me with such awful thoughts? Lucio would never have been into anything like that — I swear it on the Madonna and the Baby Jesus. Never, never, never.' Then, as an afterthought: 'And, anyway, I would have known.'

Scamarcio nodded. 'That's what I thought.'

They stood in silence for several minutes, the shouts and laughter from the café dying away on the breeze. A couple of colourful male ducks glided past them, their eyes fixed ahead — miniature sentinels on a secret mission of their own. Eventually, Scamarcio passed the piece of paper to Piocosta.

'You'll know these names. They're no different from The Priest, but, unlike him, they're untouchable.'

Piocosta took the yellow Post-it note and nodded. Then the two men went their separate ways.